The Raiders Attack!

Gale stood aghast, with his rifle clutched tightly. He could not divine the intention of the raider, but he suspected something strikingly brutal. The horse answered to that cruel guiding hand, yet he swerved and bucked. He reared aloft, pawing the air, wildly snorting, then he plunged down upon the prostrate Indian. Even in the act, the intelligent animal tried to keep from striking the body with his hoofs. But that was not possible.

Gale could bear no more. He took a quick shot at the rider. He missed the moving figure, but hit the horse. There was a bound, a horrid scream, a mighty plunge; then the horse went down, giving the Mexican a stunning fall. Both beast and man lay still.

Gale rushed from his cover to intercept the other raiders before they could reach the house and their weapons. One fellow yelled and ran wildly in the opposite direction; the other stood stricken in his tracks. Gale ran in close, and picked up the gun that had dropped from the raider leader's hand....

Shower of Gold

Zane Grey®

LEISURE BOOKS NEW YORK CITY

A LEISURE BOOK®

December 2007

Published by special arrangement with Golden West Literary Agency.

Dorchester Publishing Co., Inc.
200 Madison Avenue
New York, NY 10016

ISBN 10: 0-8439-6016-7
ISBN 13: 978-0-8439-6016-7

Visit us on the web at www.dorchesterpub.com.

Shower of Gold

FOREWORD
JON TUSKA

Ripley Hitchcock was Zane Grey's editor at Harper & Bros. He was an editor who inflicted his personal agenda on authors. Prior to working for Harper & Bros., he had been an editor at D. Appleton. It was Hitchcock who had rejected Stephen Crane's novel of a woman of the streets, *Maggie*, and it was Hitchcock who would completely transform Crane's *The Red Badge of Courage* into the opposite of what the author had written. Hershel Parker, in an essay titled "Getting Used to the 'Original Form' of *The Red Badge of Courage*" (1986), has detailed just how Hitchcock worked. "It was at this time," Professor Parker wrote, "after the big cuts were made, after the manuscript was quite superseded, that Hitchcock prevailed upon Crane to compose a new and upbeat final paragraph: 'Over the river a golden ray of sun came through the hosts of leaden rain clouds.' As John T. Winterich said in 1951, this sentence 'bears the unmistakable spoor of the editor' and 'sounds like a concession to the send-the-audience-home-feeling-good school.' With these last changes—maybe the little decisively placed addition was the last of all—Hitchcock had engineered disproportionately great changes in the apparent meaning of crucial passages. In the first stage of expurgation, he had purged the book of the passages likely to prove most objectionable, those where Henry Fleming indulged in vaingloriously adolescent ontological heroics; in the second, the mopping-up stage, he had purged it of those where Fleming displayed a heartlessly triumphant egotism. Hitchcock got what he wanted. . . ."

Hitchcock, later at Harper & Bros., had Zane Grey substantially rewrite *The Heritage of the Desert*, Grey's first Western romance, according to Hitchcock's specifications. Hitchcock rejected the manuscript for *Riders of the Purple Sage* as unpublishable. Even after Grey was able to convince the executive vice president of the firm to publish that novel, it was only with the provision that Grey would have to accept the editorial changes that would be imposed on the text. In their way these changes were as dramatic as those Hitchcock had imposed on *The Red Badge of Courage* that turned an anti-hero into a hero and an anti-war story into one supporting the Spanish-American War.

Grey titled his third Western novel *The Ranger of Forlorn River* on the holographic manuscript that was kindly furnished for the preparation of this restored edition by the Special Collections of Brigham Young University Library. Hitchcock objected to this title and in the end Grey went along with the title Hitchcock favored: *Desert Gold*. Loren Grey, the author's younger son, did not think the original title should be restored, in large measure because Zane Grey subsequently wrote a novel titled *Forlorn River* (1927) and the similarity in titles might prove confusing to readers. Zane Grey's proposed alternative title for the book was *Lluvia d'Oro—Shower of Gold*. So this is the title that has been used for the restored edition.

Beginning with the manuscript of *Riders of the Purple Sage*, Ripley Hitchcock dispensed with having Grey himself do any rewriting. He felt perfectly capable himself of changing the text according to his personal view of what was and was not acceptable in a Western story. Perhaps the most dramatic example of Hitchcock's mania for rewriting Zane Grey came with his version of what he called *The Lone Star Ranger*. For the first half of the book, he followed Zane Grey's manuscript of *Last of the Duanes*, but then dropped the second half entirely. To complete the novel, he substituted the second half of a magazine serial Grey had published titled "The Lone Star Rangers", in the rewrite changing a first-person narrative to one narrated in the third person. When it came to what Hitchcock titled *Desert Gold*, he had no such daunting task as that of changing an anti-war novel into one supporting war, but all sexuality became muted. The violence with which the Yaqui cuts loose Rojas's grip on a precipice, limb by limb, vanished. The climactic fight at the end was deleted altogether. No character now cursed, and dialogue was frequently recast so that characters spoke the way Ripley Hitchcock wanted them to speak. These changes are sometimes subtle, sometimes blatant, but in combination the story Zane Grey wanted to tell was totally altered into something that quite definitely was not what he had intended. As was the case with *Riders of the Purple Sage*, the book publisher controlled serial rights, so the text of the six-part serial that appeared in Street & Smith's *The Popular Magazine* (2/8/13–4/19/13) was not Zane Grey's but Ripley Hitchcock's expurgated version. *Desert Gold* was published in book form by Harper & Bros. in April, 1913. There was in it one concession to Zane Grey. Douglas Duer's oil painting depicting Nell Burton and the white horse, Blanco Sol, titled *Lluvia d'Oro*—"Shower of Gold" served as the frontispiece as well as the jacket illustration. However, Zane Grey's text had to wait ninety-three years before it would be published as he wrote it.

PROLOGUE

A face haunted Cardashan—a woman's face. It was there in the white heart of the dying campfire; it hung in the shadows that hovered over the flickering light; it drifted in the darkness beyond.

This hour, when the day had closed and the lonely desert night set in with its dead silence, was one in which Cardashan's mind thronged with memories of a time long past—of a home back in Peoria, of a woman he had wronged and lost, and loved too late. He was a prospector for gold, a hunter of solitude, a lover of the drear rock-ribbed infinitude because he wanted to be alone to remember.

A sound disturbed Cardashan's reflections. He bent his head, listening. A soft wind fanned the paling embers, blew sparks and white ashes and thin smoke away into the enshrouding circle of blackness. His burro did not appear to be moving about. The quiet split to the cry of a coyote. It rose strange, wild, mournful—not the howl of a prowling upland beast baying the campfire, or barking at a lonely prospector, but the mourn of a wolf, full-voiced, crying out the meaning of the desert and the night. Hunger throbbed in it—hunger for a mate, for offspring, for life. When it ceased, the terrible desert silence smote Cardashan, and the cry echoed in his soul. He and that wandering wolf were brothers.

Then a sharp *clink* of metal on stone and soft *pads* of

hoofs in sand prompted Cardashan to reach for his gun and to move out of the light of waning campfire. He was somewhere along the wild borderline between Sonora and Arizona, and the prospector who dared the heat and barrenness of that region risked other dangers sometimes as menacing.

Figures, darker than the gloom, approached and took shape, and in the light turned out to be those of a white man and a heavily packed burro.

"Hello there!" the man called as he came to a halt and gazed about him. "I saw your fire. May I make camp here?"

Cardashan came forth out of the shadow and greeted his visitor, who he took for a prospector like himself. Cardashan resented the breaking of his lonely campfire vigil, but respected the law of the desert.

The stranger thanked him, and then slipped the pack from his burro.

It was always necessary for a prospector to be careful of his beast of burden, and this man was, also, gentle and kind. He brushed the tired burro, strained the water he gave him, and then led him away into the darkness, evidently to find a little patch of grass. When he returned, he carried a bundle of mesquite and greasewood sticks. These he broke into short pieces, some of which he laid carefully upon the fire. Then he rolled out his pack and began preparation for a meal. His movements were slow and methodical.

Cardashan watched him, still with resentment, yet with a curious and growing interest. The campfire burst into a bright blaze, and by its light Cardashan saw a man whose gray hair, somehow, did not seem to make him old, and whose stoop-shoulders did not detract from an impression of rugged strength.

"Find any mineral?" asked Cardashan presently.

His visitor looked up quickly as if startled by the sound of a human voice. He replied, and then the two men talked a little. But the stranger evidently preferred silence. Cardashan understood that. He laughed grimly and bent a keener gaze upon the furrowed, shadowy face. Another of those strange desert prospectors in whom there was some relentless driving power besides the lust for gold. Cardashan felt that between this man and himself there was a subtle affinity, vague and undefined, perhaps born of the divination that here was a desert wanderer like himself, perhaps born of a deeper, an unintelligible relation having its roots back in the past. A long forgotten sensation stirred in Cardashan's breast, one so long forgotten that he could not recognize it. But it was akin to pain.

When he awakened, he found, to his surprise, that his companion had departed. A trail in the sand led off to the north. There was no water in that direction. Cardashan shrugged his shoulders; it was not his affair; he had his own problems. And straightway he forgot his strange visitor.

Cardashan began his day, grateful for the solitude that was now unbroken, for the cañon-furrowed and cactus-spired scene that now showed no sign of life. He traveled southwest, never straying far from the dry streambed, and in a desultory way, without eagerness, he hunted for signs of gold.

The work was toilsome, yet the periods of rest in which he indulged were not taken because of fatigue. He rested to look, to listen, to feel. What the vast silent world meant to him had always been a mystical thing, sensed in all its incalculable power, but never understood.

That day, while it was yet light and he was digging in a moist white-bordered wash for water, he was brought up sharply by hearing the *crack* of hard hoofs on stone. There down the cañon came a man and a burro. Cardashan recognized them.

"Hello, friend!" called the man, halting. "Our trails crossed again. That's good."

"Hello," replied Cardashan slowly. "Any mineral sign today?"

"No."

They made camp together, ate their frugal meal, smoked a pipe, and rolled in their blankets without exchanging many words. In the morning the same reticence, the same aloofness characterized the manner of both. But Cardashan's companion, when he had packed his burro and was ready to start, faced about and said: "We might stay together, if it's all right with you."

"I never take a partner," replied Cardashan.

"You're alone . . . I'm alone," said the other mildly. "It's a big place. If we find gold, there'll be enough for two."

"I don't go down into the desert for gold alone," rejoined Cardashan with a chill note in his swift reply.

His companion's deep-set luminous eyes emitted a singular flash. It moved Cardashan to say that in the years of his wandering he had met no man who could endure equally with him the blasting heat, the blinding dust storms, the wilderness of sand and rock and lava and cactus, the terrible silence and desolation of the desert. Cardashan waved a hand toward the wide, shimmering, shadowy descent of plain and range. "I may strike through the Sonora Desert. I may head for Pinacate or north for the Colorado Basin. You are an old man."

"I don't know the country, but to me one place is the same as another," replied his companion. For moments he seemed to forget himself, and swept his far-reaching gaze out over the colored gulf of stone and sand. Then with gentle slaps he drove his burro in behind Cardashan's. "Yes, I'm old. I'm lonely, too. It's come to me just lately. But, friend, I can still travel and for a few days my company won't hurt you."

"Have it your way," said Cardashan.

They began a slow march down into the desert. At sunset they camped under the lea of a low mesa. Cardashan was glad his comrade had the Indian habit of silence. Another day's travel found the prospectors deep in the wilderness. Then there came a breaking of reserve, noticeable in the elder man, almost imperceptibly gradual in Cardashan. Beside the meager mesquite campfire this gray-faced thoughtful old prospector would remove his black pipe from his mouth to talk a little, and Cardashan would listen and sometimes unlock his lips to speak a word. And so, as Cardashan began to respond to the influence of a desert less lonely than habitual, he began to take keener note of his comrade, and found him different from any other he had ever encountered in the wilderness. This man never grumbled at the heat, the glare, the driving sand, the sour water, the scant fare. During the daylight hours he was seldom idle. At night he sat dreaming before the fire or paced to and fro in the gloom. He slept but little and that long after Cardashan had gone to his own rest. He was tireless, patient, brooding.

Cardashan's awakened interest brought home to him the realization that for years he had shunned companionship. In those years only three men had wandered into the desert with him, and these had left their bones to bleach in the shifting sands. Cardashan had not cared to know their secrets. But the more he studied this latest comrade the more he began to suspect that he might have missed something in the others. In his own driving passion to take his secret into the limitless abode of silence and desolation where he could be alone with it, he had forgotten that life dealt shocks to other men. Somehow this silent comrade reminded him.

One afternoon late, after they had toiled up a white winding wash of sand and gravel, they came upon a dry water hole. Cardashan dug deeply into the sand, but without avail. He was turning to retrace weary steps back to the last water when his comrade asked him to wait. Cardashan watched him search in his pack and bring forth what appeared to be a small forked branch of a peach tree. He grasped the prongs of the fork and held them before him with the end standing straight out, and then he began to walk along the streambed. Cardashan, at first amused, then amazed, then pitying, and at last curious, kept pace with the prospector. He saw a strong tension of his comrade's wrists, as if he was holding hard against a considerable force. The end of the peach branch began to quiver and turn. Cardashan reached out a hand to touch it, and was astonished at feeling a powerful vibrant force pulling the branch downward. He felt it as a magnetic shock. The branch kept turning and at length pointed to the ground.

"Dig here," said the prospector.

"What?" ejaculated Cardashan. Had the man lost his mind?

Then Cardashan stood by while his comrade dug in the sand. Three feet he dug—four—five, and the sand grew dark, then moist. At six feet water began to seep through.

"Get the little basket in my pack," he said.

Cardashan complied, and saw his comrade drop the basket into the deep hole, where it kept the sides from caving in and allowed the water to seep through. While Cardashan watched, the basket filled. Of all the strange incidents of his desert career this was the strangest. Curiously he picked up the peach branch and held it as he had seen it held. The thing, however, was dead in his hands.

"I see you haven't got it," remarked his comrade. "Few men have."

"Got what?" demanded Cardashan.

"A power to find water that way. Back in Illinois an old German used to do that to locate wells. He showed me I had the same power. I can't explain. But you needn't look so dumbfounded. There's nothing supernatural about it."

"You mean it's a simple fact . . . that some men have a magnetism, a force or power to find water as you did?"

"Yes. It's not unusual on the farms back in Illinois, Ohio, Pennsylvania. The old German I spoke of made money traveling round with his peach fork."

"What a gift for a man in the desert!"

Cardashan's comrade smiled, the second time in all those days.

They entered a region where mineral abounded, and their march became slower. Generally they took the course of a wash, one on each side, and let the burros travel leisurely along, nipping at the bleached blades of scant grass or at sage or cactus, while they searched in the cañons and under the ledges for signs of gold. When they found any rock that hinted of gold, they picked off a piece and gave it a chemical test. The search was fascinating. They interspersed the work with long restful moments when they looked afar, down the vast reaches and smoky shingles to the line of dim mountains. Some impelling desire, not all the lure of gold, took them to the top of mesas and escarpments, and here, when they had dug and picked, they rested and gazed out at the wide prospect. Then, as the sun lost its heat and sank lowering to dent its red disc behind far distant spurs, they halted in a shady cañon or likely spot in a dry wash and tried for water. When they found it, they unpacked, gave drink to the tired burros, and turned them loose. Dead mesquite served for the campfire. While the strange twilight deepened into weird night, they sat propped against stones, with eyes on the dying embers of the fire, and soon they lay on the sand with the light of white stars on their dark faces.

Each succeeding day and night Cardashan felt himself more and more drawn to this strange man. He found that after hours of burning toil he had insensibly grown nearer to his comrade. He reflected that after a few weeks in the desert he always became a different man. In civilization, in the rough mining camps, he had been a prey to unrest and gloom. But once down on the great heave and bulge and sweep of this lonely world, he could look into the disquiet of his soul without bitterness. Did not the desert magnify men? Cardashan believed that wild men in wild places, fighting cold, heat, starvation, thirst, barrenness, facing the elements in all their ferocity, usually retrograded, descended to the savage, lost all heart and soul and became mere brutes. Likewise he believed that men, wandering or lost in the wilderness, often reversed that brutal order of life and became noble—wonderful—superhuman. He had the proof in the serene wisdom of his soul when for a time the desert had been his teacher. So now he did not marvel at a slow stir, stealing warmer along his veins, and at the premonition that perhaps he and this man, alone on the desert, driven there by life's mysterious and remorseless motive, were to see each other through God's eyes.

His companion was one who thought of himself last. It humiliated Cardashan that in spite of growing keenness he could not hinder him from doing more than an equal share of the day's work. The man was mild, gentle, quiet, mostly silent, yet under all his softness he seemed to be made of the fiber of steel. Cardashan could not thwart him. Moreover, he appeared to want to find gold for Cardashan, not for himself. Cardashan's hands always trembled at the turning of rock that promised gold; he had enough of the prospector's passion for fortune to thrill at the chance of a strike. But the other never showed the least trace of excitement.

One night they were encamped at the head of a cañon. The day had been exceedingly hot, and long after sundown the radiation of heat from the rocks persisted. A desert bird whistled a wild melancholy note from a dark cliff and a distant coyote wailed mournfully. The stars shone white until the huge moon rose to burn out all their comrades, and yielded to interest he had not heretofore voiced.

"Pardner, what drives you into the desert?"

"Do I seem to be a driven man?"

"No. But I feel it. Do you come to forget?"

"Yes."

"Ah!" softly exclaimed Cardashan. Always he seemed to have known that. He said no more. He watched the old man rise and begin his nightly pace to and fro, up and down. With slow, soft tread, forward and back, tirelessly and ceaselessly, he paced that beat. He did not look up at the stars or follow the radiant track of the moon along the cañon ramparts. He hung his head. He was lost in another world. It was a world that the lonely desert made real. He looked a dark, sad, plodding figure, and somehow impressed Cardashan with the helplessness of men.

Cardashan grew acutely conscious of the pang in his own breast, of the fire in his heart, the strife and torment of his own passion-driven soul. He had come into the desert to remember a woman. She appeared to him then as she had looked when first she entered his life—a golden-haired girl, blue-eyed, white-skinned, red-lipped, tall and slender and beautiful. He had ruined her. He had never forgotten, and an old sickening remorse knocked at his heart. He rose and climbed out of the cañon and to the top of a mesa where he paced to and fro and looked down into the weird and mystic shadows, like the darkness of his passion, and farther on down the moon track and the glittering stretches that vanished in the cold blue horizon. The moon soared, radiant and calm; the white stars shone serenely. The vault of heaven seemed illimitable and divine. The desert surrounded him, silver-streaked and black-mantled, a chaos of rock and sand, silent, austere, ancient, always waiting, it spoke to Cardashan. It was a naked corpse, but it had a soul. In that wild solitude the white stars looked down upon him pitilessly and pityingly. They had shone upon a desert that had once been alive and was now dead, and would again throb to life, only to die. It was a terrible ordeal for him to stand there alone and realize that he was only a man facing eternity. But that was what gave him strength to endure. Somehow he was a part of it all, some atom in that vastness, somehow necessary to an inscrutable purpose, something indestructible in that desolate world of ruin and death and decay, something perishable and changeable and growing under all the fixity of heaven. In that endless silent hell of desert there was a spirit, and Cardashan felt hovering near him what he imagined to be phantoms of peace.

He returned to camp and sought his comrade.

"I reckon we're two of a kind," he said. "It was a woman who drove me into the desert. But I come to remember. The desert's the only place I can do that."

"Was she your wife?" asked the elder man.

"No."

A long silence ensued. A cool wind blew up the cañon, sifting the sand through the dry sage, driving away the last of the lingering heat. The campfire wore down to a ruddy ashen heap.

"I had a daughter," said Cardashan's comrade. "She lost her mother at birth. And I . . . I didn't know how to bring up a girl. She was pretty and gay. It was the . . . the old story."

His words were peculiarly significant to Cardashan. They distressed him. He had been wrapped up in his remorse. If ever in the past he had thought of anyone connected with the girl he had wronged, he had long forgotten. But the consequences of such wrong were far-reaching. They struck at the roots of a home. Here in the desert he was confronted by the spectacle of a splendid man—a father—wasting his life because he could not forget—because there was nothing left to live for. Cardashan understood better now why his comrade was drawn by the desert.

"Well, tell me more," suggested Cardashan earnestly.

"It was the old, old story. My girl was pretty and free. The young bucks ran after her. I guess she did not run from them. And I was away a good deal . . . working in another town. She was in love with a wild fellow. I knew nothing of it till too late. He was engaged to marry her. But he didn't come back. And when the disgrace became plain to all, my girl left home. She went West. After a while I heard from her. She was well . . . working . . . living for her baby. A long time passed. I had no ties. I drifted West. A few years ago I got a letter that had followed me from place to place. It was from my girl. She had married. She had kept her secret. But her life was torture because she feared the dishonor would ferret her out and fall upon her daughter. Always it had followed her from one town to another. At the time of writing she was still safe. But it would find her. And she begged me to get a license . . . a certificate . . . anything from her old lover . . . a paper with names and dates so that when little Nell grew up to hear things, to ask questions, she could not be ruined by evil tongues. I went back to Illinois. Her lover had gone West. In those days everybody went West. I trailed him, intending to force a certificate from him . . . or kill him. But I lost his trail. Neither could I find any trace of her. She had moved or been driven no doubt by the hound of her past. . . . Since then I have taken to the wilds, hunting gold on the desert."

Cardashan slowly rose to his feet.

"Yes, it's the old, old story, only sadder, I think," he said, and his voice was strained and unnatural. "Pardner, what Illinois town was it you hailed from?"

"Peoria."

"And your . . . your name?" went on Cardashan huskily.

"Warren . . . Jonas Warren."

That name might as well have been a bullet. Cardashan stood erect, motionless, as men sometimes stand momentarily when shot straight through the heart. In an instant, when thoughts resurged like blinding flashes of lightning through his mind, he was a swaying, quivering, terror-stricken man. He mumbled something hoarsely and backed into the shadow. But he need not have feared discovery, however surely his agitation might have betrayed him. Warren sat brooding over the campfire—oblivious of his comrade—absorbed in the past.

Cardashan swiftly walked away in the gloom, with the blood thrumming thickly in his ears, saying to himself over and over: *Christ, Nell was* his *daughter*.

As thought and feeling multiplied, Cardashan was overwhelmed. Beyond belief indeed was it that out of the millions of men in the world two who had never seen each other could have been driven into the desert by memory of the same woman. It brought the past so close. It showed Cardashan how inevitably all his spiritual life was governed by what had happened long ago. That which made life significant to him was a wandering in silent places where no eye could see him with his secret.

Some fateful chance had thrown him with the father of the girl he had wrecked. It was incomprehensible; it was terrible. It was the one thing of all possible happenings in the world of chance that both father and lover would have found unendurable

Cardashan's pain reached to despair when he felt this relation between Warren and himself. Something within him cried out to him to reveal his identity. Warren would kill him, but it was not fear of death that put Cardashan on the rack. He had faced death too often to be afraid. It was the thought of adding torture to this long-suffering man. All at once Cardashan swore that he would not augment Warren's trouble, or let him stain his hands with blood. He would reveal himself, and tell the truth of Nell's sad story and his own, and make what amends he could.

Then Cardashan's thought shifted from father to daughter. She was somewhere beyond the dim horizon line. In those past lonely hours by the campfire his fancy had tortured him with pictures of Nell. But his remorseful and cruel fancy had lied to him. Nell had struggled upward out of menacing depths. She had reconstructed a broken life. And now she was fighting for the name and happiness of her child. Little Nell! Cardashan experienced a shuddering ripple in all his being—the physical racking of an emotion born of a new and strange consciousness.

As Cardashan gazed out over the blood-red darkening desert, suddenly the strife in his soul ceased. The moment after was one of realization of incalculable change, in which his eyes seemed to pierce the vastness of cloud and range, and mystery of gloom and shadow—to see with strong vision the illimitable space before him. He felt the grandeur of the desert, its simplicity, its truth. He had learned at last the lesson it taught. No longer strange was his meeting and wandering with Warren. Each had marched in the steps of destiny, and, as the lines of their fates had been inextricably tangled in the years that were gone, so now their steps had crossed and turned them toward one common goal. For years they had been two men marching alone, answering to an inward driving search, and the desert had brought them together. For years they had wandered alone in silence and solitude, where the sun burned white all day and the stars burned white all night, blindly following the whisper of a spirit. But now Cardashan knew that he was no longer blind, and in this flush of revelation he felt that it had been given to him to help Warren with his burden.

He returned to camp, trying to evolve a plan. As always at that long hour when the afterglow of sunset lingered in the west, Warren plodded to and fro in the gloom. All night Cardashan lay awake, thinking.

In the morning when Warren brought the burros to camp and began preparations for the usual packing, Cardashan broke silence.

"Pardner, your story last night made me think. I want to tell you something about myself. It's hard enough to be driven by sorrow for someone you've loved, as you've been driven, but to suffer sleepless and eternal remorse for the *ruin* of one you've loved, as I have suffered . . . that is hell . . . . Listen. In my younger days . . . it seems long now, yet it's not so many years . . . I was wild. I wronged the sweetest and loveliest girl I ever knew. I went away, not dreaming that any disgrace might come to her. Along about that time I fell into terrible moods . . . I changed . . . I learned I really loved that girl. Then came a letter I should have gotten months before. It told of her trouble . . . importuned me to hurry to save her. Half frantic with shame and fear I got a marriage certificate and rushed back to her town. She was gone . . . had been gone for weeks, and her disgrace was known. Friends warned me to keep out of reach of her father. I was young, cowardly. I did not go to him. I honestly tried to find her and failed. I honestly tried to make up for my wrong. But too late!"

Warren leaned forward a little and looked into Cardashan's eyes, as if searching there for the repentance that might make him less deserving of a man's scorn.

Cardashan met the gaze unflinchingly and again began

to speak: "You know, of course, how men out here some-how lose old names, old identities. It won't surprise you much to learn my name really isn't Cardashan, as I once told you."

Warren stiffened upright. It seemed that there might have been a blank, a suspension, between his grave inter-est and some strange mood to come.

Cardashan felt his heart bulge and contract in his breast; all his body grew cold, and it took tremendous ef-fort for him to make his lips form words.

"Warren, I'm the man you're hunting. I am Burton. I was Nell's lover."

The old man rose and towered over Cardashan, and then plunged down upon him, and clutched at his throat with terrible, stifling hands. The harsh contact, the pain awakened Cardashan to his peril before it was too late. Desperate fighting saved him from being hurled to the ground and stamped and crushed. Warren seemed a maddened giant. There was a reeling, swaying, wrestling struggle before the elder man began to weaken. Then Cardashan, buffeted, bloody, half stunned, panted for speech.

"Warren . . . kill me . . . if you want. But hold on . . . give me a minute. Give me . . . a chance. I'll save the child . . . little Nell . . . her happiness."

Cardashan felt the shock that vibrated through Warren. He repeated the words again and again. As if compelled by some resistless power, Warren released Cardashan and, staggering back, stood with uplifted, shaking hands. In his face was a horrible darkness.

"Warren! Wait . . . listen!" panted Cardashan. "I've got that marriage certificate . . . had it . . . by me . . . all these years. I kept it . . . to prove to myself . . . I meant right. Let me fill in dates and names. . . . It'll be false . . . but what. . . . the hell . . . does that matter? Old Lee, the preacher I meant to have . . . he's dead. And the old court-house, with its records, burned down. Let me fill in the dates and names. Then you get out of the desert. Go day and night till you find Nell. Give her the certificate. Maybe when the child grows to a woman . . . it'll save her happiness . . . surely her name. Think it over, Warren. I'll leave you alone a little. Then, when I come back . . . let's do it . . . for Nell's sake."

The old man uttered a broken cry.

Cardashan stole off among the rocks. How long he absented himself or what he did, he had no idea. When he returned, Warren was sitting before the campfire and once more he appeared composed. He spoke, and his voice had a deeper note, but otherwise he seemed as usual.

In the pack outfit Cardashan had a little tin box in which he kept a notebook, a few letters, papers, and mementoes of the past, and in this was the marriage certificate. As he took it out, his hands shook. It was badly soiled on the folded edges. He spread it and smoothed it upon a flat rock.

Then, actuated by one compelling thought, the two men began to deliberate. Warren had a pen, but the ink in it had long been dry. They scraped out the ink, ground it into a powder, and dissolved it in a few drops of water. Cardashan practiced writing names and dates in his notebook . . . wrote them again and again in different styles of handwriting. Then with somber passionate care he filled out the blanks on the certificate, and gave it to Warren.

"Now go . . . get out of the desert," he said.

"Come," was Warren's reply.

They packed the burros and faced the north together.

Cardashan experienced a singular exaltation in the effect of his forgery. He had lightened his comrade's burden. Wonderfully it came to him that he had also lightened his own. From that hour it was not torment to think of Nell. Subtly and unconsciously the falsehood became truth to him. Walking with his comrade through the silent places, lying beside him under the serene luminous light of the stars, Cardashan began to feel the haunting presence of invisible things that were real to him— phantoms whispering peace. In the moan of the cool

wind, in the silken seep of sifting sand, in the distant
rumble of a slipping ledge, in the faint rush of a shooting
star he heard these phantoms of peace coming with whispers of the long pain of men at the last made endurable.
Even in the white noonday, under the burning sun, these
phantoms came to be real to him. In the dead silence of
the midnight hours he heard them breathing nearer on
the desert wind—Nature's voices of motherhood—
whispers of God—peace in the solitude.

There came a morning when the sun shone angry and red
through a dull smoky haze.

"We're in for sandstorms," said Cardashan.

They had scarcely covered a mile when a desert-wide,
moaning, yellow wall of flying sand swooped down upon
them. Seeking shelter in the lea of a rock, they waited,
hoping the storm was only a squall, such as frequently
whipped across the open places. The moan increased to a
roar, and the dull red slowly dimmed, to disappear in the
yellow pall, and the air grew thick and dark. Warren
slipped the packs from the burros. Cardashan feared the
sandstorms had arrived some weeks ahead of their usual
season.

The men covered their heads and patiently waited. The
long hours dragged, and the storm increased in fury. Cardashan and Warren wet scarves with water from the canteens, and bound them around their faces, and then
covered their heads. The steady hollow bellow of flying
sand went on. It flew so thickly that enough sifted down
under the shelving rock to weight the blankets and almost
bury the men. They were frequently compelled to shake
off the sand to keep from being borne to the ground. And
it was necessary to keep digging out the packs. The floor
of their shelter gradually rose higher and higher. They
tried to eat and seemed to be grinding only sand between
their teeth. They lost the count of time. They dared not
sleep for that would have meant being buried alive. They
could only crouch close to the leaning rock, shake off the

sand, blindly dig out their packs, and every moment gasp
and cough and choke to fight suffocation.

The storm finally blew itself out. It left the prospectors
heavy and stupid for want of sleep. Their burros had
wandered away or had been buried in the sand. Far as eye
could reach, the desert had marvelously changed; it was
now a rippling sea of sand dunes. Away to the north rose
the peak that was their only guiding mark. They headed
toward it, carrying a shovel and part of their packs.

At noon the peak vanished in the shimmering glare of
the desert. The prospectors pushed on, guided by the sun.
In every wash they tried for water. With the forked peach
branch in his hands Warren always succeeded in locating
water. They dug but it lay too deep. At length, spent and
sore, they fell and slept through that night and part of the
next day. Then they succeeded in getting water, and
quenched their thirst, and filled the canteens, and cooked
a meal.

Here, abandoning all the outfit except the shovel and
scant food and the canteens, they set out, both silent and
grim in the understanding of what lay before them. They
traveled by the sun, and after dark by the stars. Hours
were wasted in vain search for water. Warren located it,
but it lay too deep.

And that night, deceived by a hazy sky, they toiled on
to find at dawn that they had doubled back on their trail.
Again the lonely desert peak beckoned to them, and
again they wearily faced toward it, only to lose it in the
white glare of the noonday heat.

The burning day found them in an interminably wide
plain where there was no shelter from the fierce sun. The
men were exceedingly careful with their water, although
there was absolute necessity of drinking a little every
hour. Late in the afternoon they came to a cañon that they
believed was the lower end of the one in which they had
last found water. For hours they traveled toward its head,
and, long after night had set, found what they sought.
Yielding to exhaustion, they slept, and next day were

loath to leave the water hole. Cool night spurred them on with canteens full and renewed strength.

Morning told Cardashan that they had turned back miles into the desert, and it was desert new to him. The red sun, the increasing heat, and especially the variety and large size of the cactus plants warned Cardashan that he had descended to a lower level. Mountain peaks loomed on all sides, some near, others distant, and one, a blue spur, splitting the glaring sky far to the north, Cardashan thought he recognized as a landmark. The ascent toward it was heartbreaking, not in steepness, but in its league and league-long monotonous rise. Cardashan knew there was only one hope—to make the water hold out and never stop to rest. Warren began to weaken. Often he had to halt. The burning white day passed, and likewise the night with its white stars shining so pitilessly cold and bright.

Cardashan measured the water in his canteen by its weight; evaporation by heat consumed as much as he drank. During one of the rests, when he had wetted his parched throat, he found opportunity to pour a little water from his canteen into Warren's.

Another dawn showed the bare blue peak glistening in the sunlight. Its bare ribs stood out and its dark lines of cañons. It seemed so close. But in that wonderfully clear atmosphere, before the dust and sand began to blow, Cardashan could not be deceived as to distance. The peak was 100 miles away.

Muttering low, Cardashan shook his head and again found opportunity to pour a little water from his canteen into Warren's.

The rising heat waved up like black steam. It burned through the men's boots, driving them to seek relief in every bit of shade, and here a drowsiness made Warren sleep standing. Cardashan ever kept watch over his comrade. Their marches from place to place became shorter. Cactus blocked their passage. The spears and spikes, like poisoned iron fangs, tore grimly at them.

At infrequent intervals, when chance afforded, Cardashan continued to pour a little water from his canteen into Warren's.

At first Cardashan had curbed his restless activity to accommodate the pace of his elder comrade. But now he felt that he was losing something of his instinctive and passionate zeal to get out of the desert. The thought of water came to occupy his mind. Mirages appeared on all sides. After a while he was seeing beautiful clear springs and hearing the murmur and *tinkle* of running water. He looked for water in every hole and crack and cañon. But all were glaring red and white, hot and dry—as dry as if there had been no moisture on that desert since the origin of the world. The white coalescing sun, like the surface of a pot of boiling iron, poured down its terrific heat. The men tottered into corners of shade, and rose to move blindly on.

It had become habitual with Cardashan to judge his quantity of water by its weight and the faint *splash* it made as his canteen rocked on his shoulder. He began to imagine that his last little store of water did not appreciably diminish. He knew he was not quite right in his mind regarding water, nevertheless he felt this to be more of fact than fancy, and he began to ponder.

When next they rested, he pretended to be in a kind of stupor, but he covertly watched Warren. The man appeared far gone, yet he had cunning. He cautiously took up Cardashan's canteen and poured water into it from his own.

This troubled Cardashan. The old irritation at not being able to thwart Warren returned to him. Cardashan reflected and concluded that he had been unwise not to expect this very thing. Then, as his comrade dropped into weary rest, he lifted both canteens. If there were any water in Warren's, it was only very little. Both men had been enduring the terrible desert thirst, concealing it, each giving his water to the other, and the sacrifice had been useless. Instead of ministering to the parched throats of one or both, the water had evaporated. When Cardashan made sure of this, he took one more drink, the last, and poured the little water left into Warren's canteen.

Soon afterward Warren discovered the loss.

"Where's your canteen?' he asked.

"The heat was getting my water so I drank what was left."

"My son!" said Warren.

The day opened for them in a red and green hell of rock and cactus. Like a flame the sun scorched and peeled their faces. Warren went blind from the glare and Cardashan had to lead him. At last Warren plunged down exhausted in the shade of a ledge.

Cardashan rested and waited, hopeless, with hot, weary eyes gazing down from the height where he sat. The ledge was the top step of a ragged gigantic stairway. Below stretched a sad, austere, and lonely valley. A dim wide streak, lighter than the bordering gray, wound down the valley floor. Once a river had flowed there, leaving only a forlorn trace down the winding floor of this forlorn valley.

Movement on the part of Warren attracted Cardashan's attention. Evidently the old prospector had recovered his sight and some of his strength. For he had arisen, and now began to walk along the arroyo bed with his forked peach branch held before him. He had clung to that precious bit of wood. Cardashan considered the prospect for water hopeless because he saw that the arroyo had once been a cañon and had been filled with sand by desert winds. Warren, however, stepped in a deep pit, and, cutting his canteen in half, began to use one side of it as a scoop. He scooped out a wide hollow, so wide that Cardashan was sure he had gone crazy. Cardashan gently urged him to stop, and then forcibly tried to make him. But these efforts were futile. Warren worked with slow, ceaseless, methodical movement. He toiled for what seemed hours. Cardashan, seeing the darkening, dampening sand, realized a wonderful possibility of water, and he plunged into the pit with the other half of the canteen.

Then both men toiled, around and around the wide hole, down deeper and deeper. The sand grew moist, then wet. At the bottom of the deep pit the sand coarsened, gave place to gravel. Finally water welled in, a stronger volume than Cardashan ever remembered finding on the desert. It would soon fill the hole and run over. He marveled at the circumstance. The time was near the end of the dry season. Perhaps an underground stream flowed from the range behind down to the valley floor, and at this point came near to the surface. Cardashan had heard of such miracles.

The finding of water revived Cardashan's flagging hopes. But they were short-lived. Warren had spent himself utterly. He had only strength to force upon Cardashan the little tin box that contained the marriage certificate.

"I'm done. Don't linger," he whispered. "My son, go . . . go."

Then he fell. Cardashan dragged him out of the sand pit to a sheltered place under the ledge. While sitting beside the failing man, Cardashan discovered painted images on the wall. Often in the desert he found these evidences of a prehistoric people. Then from long habit he picked up a piece of rock and examined it. Its weight made him closely scrutinize it. The color was a peculiar black. He scraped through the black rust to find he held a piece of gold. Around him lay scattered heaps of black pebbles and bits of black, weathered rock and pieces of broken ledge, all of which contained gold.

"Warren! Look! See it! Feel it! Gold!"

But Warren had never cared and now he seemed too blind to see.

"Go . . . go," he whispered.

Cardashan gazed down the gray reaches of that forlorn valley, and something within him that was neither intelligence nor emotion—something inscrutably strange impelled him to promise.

Then Cardashan built up stone monuments to mark his

gold strike. That done, he tarried beside the unconscious Warren. Moments passed—grew into hours. Cardashan still had strength left to make an effort to get out of the desert. But that same inscrutable something that had ordered his strange involuntary promise to Warren held him beside his fallen comrade. He watched the white sun burn to gold, and then to red and sink behind mountains in the west. Twilight stole into the arroyo. It lingered, slowly turning to gloom. The vault of blue-black lightened to the blinking of stars. Then fell the serene, silent, luminous desert night.

Cardashan kept his vigil. As the long hours wore on, he felt creep over him the comforting sense that he need not forever fight sleep. A wan glow flared behind the dark uneven horizon, and a melancholy misshapen moon rose to make the white night one of shadows. Absolute silence claimed the desert. It was mute. Then that inscrutable something breathed to him—telling him when he was alone. He need not have looked at the dark, still face beside him.

Another face haunted Cardashan—a woman's face. It was there in the white moonlit shadows; it drifted in the darkness beyond; it softened, changed to that of a young girl, sweet, with the same dark haunting eyes of her mother. Cardashan prayed to that nameless thing within him, the spirit of something deep and mystical as life—he prayed to that nameless thing outside, of which the rocks and the sand, the spiked cactus and the ragged lava, the endless waste with its vast star-fired mantle were but atoms. He prayed for mercy to a woman—for happiness to her child. Both mother and daughter were close to him then. Time and distance were annihilated. He had faith—he saw into the future. The fateful threads of the past, so inextricably woven with his error, wound out their tragic length here in this forlorn desert.

Cardashan then took the little tin box from his pocket and, opening it, removed the folded certificate. He had kept the pen, and now he wrote something upon the paper, and this time in lieu of ink he wrote with blood. The moon afforded him enough light to see, and, having replaced the paper, he laid the little box upon a shelf of rock. It would remain there unaffected by dust, moisture, heat, time. How long had those printed images been there, clear and sharp, on the dry stone wall? There were no trails in that desert, and always there were incalculable changes. Cardashan saw this mutable mood of Nature—the sands would fly and seep and carve and bury; the floods would dig and cut; the ledges would weather in the heat and rain; the avalanches would slide; the cactus seeds would roll in the wind to catch in a niche and split the soil with thirsty roots. Years would pass. Cardashan seemed to see them, too, and likewise destiny leading a child down into this forlorn waste, where she would find love and a name.

Cardashan covered the dark, still face of his comrade from the light of the waning moon. That action was the severing of his hold on realities. They fell away from him in final separation. Vaguely, dreamily he seemed to behold his soul. Night merged into gray day—and night came again, weird and dark. Then up out of the vast void of the desert, from the silence and illimitableness, trooped his phantoms of peace. Majestically they formed around him, marshalling and mustering in ceremonious state, and moved to lay upon him their passionless serenity.

CHAPTER ONE:
OLD FRIENDS

Richard Gale reflected that his sojourn in the West had been exactly what his disgusted father had predicted—an idling here and a dreaming there, with no objective point or purpose. It was reflection such as this, only more serious and perhaps somewhat desperate, that had brought Gale down to the border. For some time the newspapers had been printing news of Mexican revolution, guerrilla warfare, United States cavalry patrolling the international line, American cowboys fighting with the rebels, and wild stories of bold raiders and bandits. Regarding these rumors Gale was skeptical. But as opportunity, and adventure, too, had apparently given him a wide berth in Montana, Wyoming, Colorado, he had struck southwest for the Arizona border, where he hoped to see some stirring life. He did not care very much what happened. Months of futile wandering in the hope of finding a place where he fitted had inclined Richard to his father's opinion.

It was after dark one evening in early October that Richard arrived in Casita. He was surprised to find that it was evidently a town of importance. There was a jostling, jabbering, sombreroed crowd of Mexicans around the railroad station. He felt as if he were in a foreign country. After a while he saw several men of his own nationality, one of whom he engaged to carry his baggage to a hotel. They walked up a wide, well-lighted street, lined with buildings in which were bright windows. Of the many people encountered by Gale, most were Mexicans. His guide explained that the smaller half of Casita lay in Arizona, the other half in Mexico, and of several thousand inhabitants the majority belonged on the southern side of the street, which was the boundary line. He also said that rebels had entered the town that day, causing a good deal of excitement.

Gale was almost at the end of his financial resources, which fact occasioned him to turn away from a potential hotel and to ask his guide for a cheaper lodging house. When this was found, a sight of the loungers in the office, and also a desire for comfort, persuaded Gale to change his traveling clothes for rough outing garb and boots.

Well, I'm almost broke, he soliloquized thoughtfully. *The governor said I wouldn't make any money. He's right . . . so far. And he said I'd be coming home beaten. There he's wrong. . . . I've got a hunch that something'll happen to me in this greaser town.*

He went out into a wide, whitewashed, high-ceilinged corridor and from that into an immense room that, but for pool tables, bar, and benches, would have been like a courtyard. The floor was cobble-stoned, the walls were of adobe, and the large windows opened like doors. A blue cloud of smoke filled the place. Gale heard the *click* of pool balls and the *clink* of glasses along the crowded bar. Bare-legged, sandal-footed Mexicans in white rubbed shoulders with Mexicans mantled in black and red. There were others in tight-fitting blue uniforms with gold fringe or tassels at the shoulders. These men wore belts with heavy, bone-handled guns and evidently were the *rurales*, or native policemen. There were black-bearded, coarse-visaged Americans, some gambling around the little tables, others drinking. The pool tables were the center of a noisy crowd of younger men, several of whom were unsteady on their feet. There were khaki-clad cavalrymen strutting in and out.

At one end of the room, somewhat apart from the general mêlée, was a group of six men around a little table, four of whom were seated, the other two standing. These last two drew a second glance from Gale. The sharp-featured, bronzed faces and piercing eyes, the tall, slender, loosely-jointed bodies, the quiet, easy, reckless air that seemed to be a part of the men—these things would plainly have stamped them as cowboys, without the buckled sombreros, the colored scarves, the high-topped, high-heeled boots with great silver-rowelled spurs. Gale did not fail to note, also, that these cowboys wore guns, and this fact was rather a shock to his idea of the modern West. It caused him to give some credence to the rumors of fighting along the border, and he sustained a thrill.

He satisfied his hunger in a restaurant adjoining, and, as he stepped back into the saloon, a man wearing a military cape jostled him. Apologies from both were instant. Gale was moving on when the other stopped short, as if startled, and, leaning forward, exclaimed: "Dick Gale?"

"You've got me," replied Gale in surprise. "But I don't know you."

He could not see the fellow's face because it was wholly shaded by a wide-brimmed hat, pulled well down.

"By Jove! It's Dick! If this isn't great! Don't you know me?"

"I've heard your voice somewhere," replied Gale. "Maybe I'll recognize you if you come out from under that bonnet."

For answer the man hurriedly drew Gale into the restaurant, where he thrust back his hat to disclose a handsome, sunburned face.

"George Thorne. So help me. . . ."

"S-sssh. You needn't yell," interrupted the other as he met Gale's outstretched hands. There was a close, hard, straining grip. "I must not be recognized here. There are reasons. I'll explain in a minute. Come on, let's sit down at this table."

There was a vacant table nearby, and they pulled out chairs and sat down.

"Say, but it's fine to see you," Thorne continued. "Five years, Dick, five years since I saw you run down University Field and spread-eagle the whole Wisconsin football team."

"Don't recollect that," replied Dick, laughing. "George, I'll bet you I'm gladder to see you than you are to see me. It seems so long. You went into the Army, didn't you?"

"I did. I'm here now with the Ninth Cavalry. But . . . never mind me. What're you doing 'way down here? Say, I just noticed your togs. Dick, you can't be going in for mining or ranching, not in this god-forsaken desert?"

"On the square, George, I don't know any more why I'm here than . . . than you know."

"Well, that beats me," ejaculated Thorne, sitting back in his chair, amazement and concern in his expression. "What the devil's wrong? Your old man has too much money for you ever to be up against it. Dick, you couldn't have gone to the bad."

A tide of emotion moved over Gale. How good it was to meet a friend—someone to whom he could talk! He had never appreciated his loneliness until that moment. "George, how I ever drifted down here I don't know. I didn't exactly quarrel with the governor. But . . . damn it, Dad hurt me . . . shamed me, and I dug out for the West. It was this way. After leaving college, I tried to please him by tackling one thing after another that he set me to do. On the square I had no head for business. I made a mess of everything and the governor got sore. He kept ramming the harpoon into me till I just couldn't stand it. What little ability I possessed deserted me when I got my back up, and there you are. Dad and I had a rather uncomfortable half hour. When I quit . . . when I told him straight out that I was going West to fare for myself, why it wouldn't have been so tough if he hadn't laughed at me. He called me a rich man's son . . . an idle, easy-going, spineless swell. He said I didn't even have character enough to be out and out bad. He said I didn't have sense enough to marry one of the nice girls in my sister's crowd. He said I couldn't earn a dollar . . . that I'd starve out West and couldn't get back home unless I sent to him for money. He said he didn't believe I could fight . . . could really make a fight for anything under the sun. Oh, he shot it into me, all right."

Dick dropped his head, somewhat ashamed of the smarting dimness in his eyes. He had not meant to say so much. Yet what a relief to let out that long-congested burden.

"Fight!" cried Thorne hotly. "What's ailing him? Didn't they call you Biff Gale in college? Dick, you were one of the best men Stagg ever developed. I heard him say so . . . that you were the fastest one-hundred-and-seventy-five-pound man he'd ever trained, the hardest to stop."

"The governor didn't count football," said Dick, his face coming up again. "He didn't mean that kind of a fight. When I left home, I don't think I had an idea what was wrong with me. But, George, I think I know now. I was a rich man's son . . . spoiled, dependent, absolutely ignorant of the value of money. I haven't yet discovered any earning capacity in me. I seem to be unable to do anything with my hands. That's the trouble. But I'm at the end of my tether now. And I'm going to punch cattle or be a miner or do some real stunt . . . like joining the rebels."

"Aha! I thought you'd spring that last one on me," declared Thorne, wagging his head. "Well, you just forget it. Say, old boy, there's something doing in Mexico. The U.S. in general doesn't realize it. But across that line there are crazy revolutionists, ill-paid soldiers, guerrilla leaders, raiders, robbers, outlaws, bandits galore, starving peons by the thousand, girls and women in terror. Mexico is like some of her volcanoes . . . ready to erupt fire and hell. Don't make the awful mistake of joining the rebel forces. Americans are hated by Mexicans of the lower class . . . the fighting class, both rebel and Federal. Half the time these crazy greasers are on one side, then on the other. If you didn't starve or get shot in ambush or die of thirst, some greaser would knife you in the back for your belt buckle or your boots. There are a good many Americans with the rebels eastward toward Agua Prieta and Juárez. Orozco is operating in Chihuahua, and I guess he has some idea of warfare. But this is Sonora, a mountainous desert, the home of the slave and the Yaqui. There's unorganized revolt everywhere. The American miners and ranchers, those who could get away, have fled across into the States, leaving property. Those who couldn't or wouldn't come must fight for their lives, are fighting now."

"That's bad," said Gale. "It's news to me. Why doesn't the government take action, do something?"

"Afraid of international complications. Don't want to offend the Maderists, or be criticized by jealous foreign nations. It's a delicate situation, Dick. The Washington officials know the gravity of it, you can bet. But the U.S. in general is in the dark, and the Army . . . well, you ought to hear the inside talk back at San Antonio. We're patrolling the boundary line. We're making one grand bluff. I could tell you of a dozen instances where cavalry should have pursued raiders on the other side of the line. But we don't do it. The officers are a grouchy lot these days. You see, of course, what significance would attach to U.S. Cavalry going into Mexican territory. There would simply be hell. My own colonel is the sorest man on the job. We're all sore. It's like sitting on a powder magazine. We can't keep the rebels and raiders from crossing the line. Yet we don't fight. My commission expires soon. I'll be discharged in three months. You can bet I'm glad for more reasons than I've mentioned."

Thorne was evidently laboring under strong, suppressed excitement. His face showed pale under the tan and his eyes gleamed with a dark fire. Occasionally his delight at meeting, talking with Gale dominated the other emotion, but not for long. The table where they were seated was near one of the door-like windows leading into the street, and every little while he would glance out sharply. Also he kept consulting his watch. These details gradually grew upon Gale, as Thorne talked.

"George, it strikes me that you're upset," said Dick. "I

seem to remember you as a cool-headed fellow who nothing could disturb. Has the Army changed you?"

Thorne laughed. It was a laugh with a strange high
note. It was reckless—it hinted of exaltation. He rose
abruptly; he gave the waiter money to go for drinks; he
looked into the saloon, and then into the street. On this
side of the house there was a porch opening on a plaza
with trees and shrubbery and benches. Thorne peered out
one window, then another. His actions were rapid. Returning to the table, he put his hands upon it and leaned
over to look closely into Gale's face.

"I'm away from camp without leave," he said.

"Isn't that a serious offense?" asked Dick.

"Serious? For me, if I'm discovered, it means ruin.
There are rebels in town. Any moment we might have
trouble. I ought to be ready for duty . . . within call. If I'm
discovered, it means arrest. That means delay . . . the failure of my plans . . . ruin."

Gale was silenced by his friend's intensity. Thorne bent
over closer with his dark eyes searchingly bright.

"We were old pals . . . once?"

"Surely," replied Dick.

"What would you say, Dick Gale . . . if I told you that
you're the one now I'd rather have had come along than
any other . . . at this crisis of my life?"

The earnest gaze, the passionate voice with its deep
tremor, drew Dick upright, thrilling and eager, conscious
of a strange, unfamiliar impetuosity.

"Thorne, I should say I was damn glad to be the fellow," replied Dick.

Their hands locked for a moment, then Thorne sat
down again, with his head close over the table.

"Listen," he began in low swift whisper. "A few days, a
week ago . . . it seems like a year . . . I was of some assistance to refugees fleeing from Mexico into the States.
They were all women and one of them was dressed as a
nun. Quite by accident I saw her face. It was that of a
beautiful girl. I observed she kept aloof from the others. I

suspected a disguise and, when opportunity afforded, spoke to her, offered my services. She replied to my poor efforts at Spanish in fluent English. She had fled in terror from her home, some place down in Sinaloa. Rebels are active there. Her father was captured and held for ransom. When the ransom was paid, the rebels killed him. The leader of these rebels was a bandit named Rojas. Long before the revolution began, he had been feared by the people of class . . . loved by the peons. Bandits are worshipped by the peons. All of the famous bandits have robbed the rich and have given to the poor. Rojas saw the daughter, made off with her. But she contrived to bribe her guards, and escaped almost immediately, before any harm befell her. She hid among friends. Rojas nearly tore down the town in his efforts to find her. Then she disguised herself, and traveled by horseback, stage, and train to Casita.

"Her story fascinated me, and that one fleeting glimpse I had of her face I couldn't forget. She had no friends here, no money. She knew Rojas was trailing her. This talk I had with her was at the railroad station, where all was bustle and confusion. No one noticed us, so I thought. I advised her to remove the disguise of a nun before she left the waiting room. And I got a boy to guide her. He fetched her right here to this place. I had promised to come in the evening to talk over the situation with her. I found her, Dick . . . and, when I saw her, I went stark, staring, raving mad over her. She is the most beautiful, wonderful girl I ever saw. Her name is Mercedes Castañeda and she belongs to one of the old wealthy Spanish families. She has lived abroad, and in Havana. She speaks French as well as English. She is . . . but I must try to be brief. Dick, think. Think. With Mercedes, also, it was love at first sight. My plan is to marry her and get her farther into the interior, away from the border. It may not be easy. She's watched. So am I. It was impossible to see her without the women of this place knowing. At first perhaps they had only curiosity . . . an itch to gossip. But the last two days there has been a change. Since last night, there's some powerful influence at work. Oh, these Mexicans are subtle, mysterious. After all, they're Spaniards. They work in secret, in the dark. They are dominated first by religion, then by gold, then by passion for a woman. Rojas must have got word to his friends here. Yesterday his gang of cut-throat rebels arrived, and today he came. When I learned that, I took my chance and left camp. I hunted up a priest. He promised to come here. It's time he's due. But I'm afraid he'll be stopped."

"Thorne, why don't you take the girl and get married without waiting, without running these risks?" said Dick.

"I fear it's too late now. I should have done that last night. You see, we're still not over the line. . . ."

"Then this is Mexican territory now?" queried Gale sharply.

"I guess, yes, old boy. That's what complicates it. Rojas and his rebels have Casita in their hands. But Rojas, even without his rebels, would be able to stop me, get the girl, and make for his mountain haunts. If Mercedes is really watched . . . if her identity is known, which I am sure is the case, we couldn't get far from here before I'd be knifed and she seized."

"Good heavens, Thorne, can that sort of thing happen less then a stone's throw from the U.S. line?" asked Gale incredulously.

"It can happen and don't you forget it. You don't seem to realize the power these guerrilla leaders, these rebel captains, and particularly these bandits exercise over the mass of Mexicans. A bandit is a man of honor in Mexico. He is feared, envied, loved. In the hearts of the people he stands next to the national idol . . . the bullfighter, the matador. The race has a wild, barbarian, bloody strain. Take Quinteros, for instance. He was a peon, a slave. He became a famous bandit. At the outbreak of the revolution he proclaimed himself a leader, and with a band of followers he devastated whole counties. The opposition to Federal forces was only a blind for his band to rob and riot, and carry off women. The motto of this man and his followers was . . . 'Let us enjoy ourselves while we may.'

"There are other bandits besides Quinteros, not so famous or such great leaders, but just as bloodthirsty. I've seen Rojas. He's a handsome, bold, sneering devil, vainer than any peacock. He decks himself in gold lace, silver trappings, in all the finery he can steal. He was one of the rebels who helped sack Sinaloa and carry off half a million in money and valuables. Rojas spends gold like he spills blood. But he is chiefly famous for abducting women. The peon girls consider it an honor to be ridden off with. Rojas has shown a penchant for girls of the better class."

Thorne wiped the perspiration from his pale face and bent a dark gaze out of the window before he resumed his talk.

"Consider what the position of Mercedes really is. I can't get any help from our side of the line. If so, I don't know where. The population on that side is mostly Mexican, absolutely in sympathy with whatever actuates those on this side. The whole caboodle of greasers on both sides belong to the class in sympathy with the rebels, the class that secretly respects men like Rojas and hates an aristocrat like Mercedes. They would conspire to throw her into his power. Rojas can turn all the hidden underground influences to his ends. Unless I thwart him, he'll get Mercedes as easily as he can light a cigarette. But I'll kill him or some of his gang or her, before I let him get her. This is the situation, old friend. I've little time to spare. I face arrest for desertion. Rojas is in town. I think I was followed to this hotel. The priest has betrayed me or has been stopped. Mercedes is here alone, waiting, absolutely dependent upon me to save her from . . . from . . . she's the sweetest, liveliest girl! In a few moments . . . sooner or later there'll be hell here . . . Dick, are you with me?"

Dick Gale drew a long deep breath. A coldness, a lethargy, an indifference that had weighed upon him for months had passed out of his being. On the instant he could not speak, but his hand closed powerfully upon his friend's. Thorne's face changed wonderfully, the distress, the fear, the appeal all vanishing in a smile of passionate gratefulness.

Then Dick's gaze, attracted by some slight sound, shot over his friend's shoulder to see a face at the window—a handsome, bold, sneering face with glittering dark eyes that flashed in sinister intentions.

Dick stiffened in his seat. Thorne with sudden clenching of hands wheeled toward the window.

"Rojas," he whispered.

Chapter Two:
Mercedes Castañeda

The dark face vanished. Dick Gale heard footsteps and the *tinkle* of spurs. He strode to the window and was in time to see a Mexican swagger into the front door of the saloon. Dick had only a glimpse, but in that he saw a huge black sombrero with a gaudy band, the back of a short, tight-fitting jacket, a heavy pearl-handled gun swinging with a fringe of sash, and close-fitting trousers spreading wide at the bottom. There were men passing in the street, also several Mexicans lounging against the hitching rail at the curb.

"Did you see him? Where did he go?" whispered Thorne as he joined Gale. "Those greasers out there with the cartridge belts crossed over their breasts . . . they are rebels."

"I think he went into the saloon," replied Dick. "He had a gun, but, for all I can see, the greasers out there are unarmed."

"Never believe it. There. Look, Dick, that fellow's a guard, for all he seems so unconcerned. See, he has a short carbine, almost concealed. There's another greaser farther down the path. I'm afraid Rojas has this place spotted."

"If we could only be sure."

"I'm sure, Dick . . . let's cross the hall. I want to see how it looks from the other side of the bend."

Gale followed Thorne out of the restaurant into the

high-ceilinged corridor that evidently divided the hotel, opening into the street and running back to a patio. A few dim yellow lamps flickered. A Mexican, with a blanket around his shoulders, stood in the front entrance. Back toward the patio there were sounds of boots on the stone floor. Shadows flitted across that end of the corridor. Thorne entered a huge chamber, which was even more poorly lighted than the hall. It contained a table littered with papers, a few high-backed chairs, a couple of couches, and was evidently a parlor.

"Mercedes has been meeting me here," said Thorne. "At this hour she comes every moment or so to the head of the stairs there, and, if I am here, she comes down. Mostly there are people in this room, a little later. We go out into the plaza. It faces the dark side of this place, and that's where I must slip out with her, if there's any chance at all to get away."

They peered out of the open window. The plaza was gloomy and at first glance apparently deserted. In a moment, however, Gale discovered a slow-pacing dark form on the path. Farther down there was another. No particular keenness was required to see in these forms a sentinel-like stealthiness.

Gripping Gale's arm, Thorne pulled him back from the window.

"You saw them," he whispered. "It's just as I feared. Rojas has the place surrounded. I should have taken Mercedes away. But . . . I had no time . . . no chance. I'm bound . . . there's Mercedes now. My God. Dick, think, think, if there's a way to get her out of this trap."

Gale turned as his friend went down the room. In the dim light at the head of the stairs stood the slim, muffled figure of a woman. When she saw Thorne, she flew noiselessly down the stairway to him, then he caught her in his arms. She spoke softly, brokenly, in a low, swift voice. It was a mingling of incoherent Spanish and English, but to Gale it was mellow, deep, utterly tender, a voice full of joy, fear, passion, hope, and loss. Upon Gale it had an unaccountable effect. He found himself thrilling, wondering.

Thorne led the girl to the center of the room, under the light where Gale stood. She had raised a white hand, holding a black lace mantilla half aside. Dick saw a small dark head, proudly held, an oval face half hidden, white as a flower, and magnificent eyes.

Then Thorne spoke.

"Mercedes . . . Dick Gale, an old friend, the best friend I ever had."

She swept the mantilla back over her head, disclosing a lovely face, strange and striking to Gale in its pride and fire, its intensity.

"*Señor* Gale . . . ah, I cannot speak of my happiness. His friend."

"Yes, Mercedes, my friend and yours," said Thorne, speaking rapidly. "We'll have need of him. Dear, there's bad news and no time to break it gently. The priest did not come. He must have been detained. And listen . . . be brave, dear Mercedes . . . Rojas is here."

She uttered an inarticulate cry, the poignant terror of which shook Gale's nerve, and swayed as if she would faint. Thorne caught her and a husky voice importuned her to bear up. "My darling, for God's sake, don't faint . . . don't go to pieces. We'd be lost. We've got a chance. We'll think of something. Be strong. Fight."

Plain it was to Gale that Thorne was distracted. He scarcely knew what he was saying. Pale, and shaking, he clasped Mercedes to him. Her terror had struck him helpless. It was such strange terrible wildness—it was so full of horrible certainty of what fate awaited her.

She cried out in Spanish, beseeching him, and, as he shook his head, she changed to English: "*Señor*, my lover. I will be strong . . . I will fight . . . I will obey. But swear by my Virgin if need be, to save me from Rojas . . . you will kill me!"

"Mercedes . . . yes, I'll swear," he replied hoarsely. "I

know . . . I'd rather have you dead than . . . but don't give up. Rojas can't be sure of you or he wouldn't wait. He's in there. He's got his men there . . . all around us. But he hesitates. A beast like Rojas doesn't stand idle for nothing. I tell you we've a chance. Dick here will think of something. We'll slip away. Then he'll take you somewhere. Only . . . speak to him . . . show him you won't weaken . . . Mercedes, this is more than love and happiness for us. It's life or death."

She became quiet and recovered control of herself. Suddenly she wheeled to face Gale with proud dark eyes, tragic sweetness of appeal, an exquisite grace.

"*Señor,* I will be brave. You are an American. You cannot know the Spanish blood . . . the peon bandit's hate and cruelty. I wish to die before Rojas's hand touches me. If he takes me alive, then the hour, the little day that my life lasts afterward will be torture . . . torture of hell. If I live two days, his brutal men will have me. If I live three . . . the dogs of his camp! *Señor,* have you a sister who you love? Help *Señor* Thorne to save me. He is a soldier. He is bound. He must not betray his honor, his duty, for me . . . ah, you two splendid Americans . . . so big, so strong, so fierce. What is that little black half-breed slave Rojas to such men? Rojas is a coward. Now, let me waste no more precious time. I am ready. I will be brave."

She came close to Gale, holding out her white hands, a woman all fire and soul and passion. To Gale she was wonderful. His heart leaped. As he bent over her hands and kissed them, he seemed to feel himself renewed, remade.

"*Señorita,*" he said, "I am happy to be your servant. I can conceive of no greater pleasure than giving the service you require."

"And what is that?" inquired Thorne hurriedly.

"That of incapacitating *Señor* Rojas for tonight and perhaps several nights to come," replied Gale.

"Dick, what will you do?" asked Thorne, now in alarm.

"I'll make a row in that saloon," returned Dick bluntly.

"I'll start something. I'll rush Rojas and his crowd. I'll. . . ."

"Lord! No, you mustn't, Dick, you'll be knifed!" cried Thorne. He was in distress, yet his eyes were shining.

"I'll take a chance. Maybe I can surprise that slow greaser bunch, and yet get away before they know what's happened. You be ready, watching out the windows when the row starts. Those fellows out there in the plaza will run into the saloon. Then you slip out, go straight through the plaza, down the street. It's a dark street, I remember. I'll catch up with you before you get far."

Thorne gasped, but did not say a word. Mercedes leaned against him, her white hands now at her breast, her great eyes watching Gale as he went out.

In the corridor Gale stopped long enough to pull on a pair of heavy gloves, to muss his hair and disarrange his collar. Then he stepped into the restaurant, went through, and halted in the door leading into the saloon. His 5'11' and 180 pounds were more noticeable there, and it was part of his plan to attract attention to himself. No one, however, appeared to notice him. The pool players were noisily intent on their game; the same crowd of motley robed Mexicans hung over the reeking bar. Gale's roving glance soon fixed upon the man he took to be Rojas. He recognized the huge, high-peaked black sombrero with its ornamented band. The Mexican's face was turned aside. He was in earnest, excited colloquy with a dozen or more comrades, most of whom were sitting around a table. They were listening, talking, drinking. The fact that they wore cartridge belts crossed over their breasts satisfied Gale that these were the rebels. He had noted that feature on the outside Mexicans he and Thorne had taken for guards. A waiter brought more drinks to this group at the table, and this caused the leader to turn so Gale could see his face. It was, indeed, the sinister, sneering face of the bandit, Rojas. Gale gazed at the man with curiosity. He was under medium height, and striking in appearance only because of his dandified dress and evil visage. He wore a lace scarf, a tight bright-buttoned jacket, a buckskin vest embroidered in red, a sash and belt joined by an enormous silver buckle. Gale saw again the pearl-handled gun swinging at the bandit's hip. Jewels flashed in his scarf. There were gold rings in his ears, and diamonds on his fingers.

Gale became conscious of an inward fire that threatened to counteract his coolness. Other emotions harried his self-control. It seemed as if sight of the man liberated or created a devil in Gale. And at the bottom of his feelings there seemed to be a wonder at himself, a strange satisfaction for the something that had come to him.

He stepped out of the doorway, down the couple of steps to the floor of the saloon, and he staggered a little, simulating drunkenness. He fell over the pool tables, jostled Mexicans at the bar, laughed like a maudlin fool, and, with his hat slouched down, crowded here and there. Presently his eye caught sight of the group of cowboys who he had before noticed with such interest.

They were still in a corner somewhat isolated. With fertile mind working, Gale lurched over to them. He remembered his many unsuccessful attempts to get acquainted with cowboys. If he were to get any help from these silent aloof rangers, it must be by striking fire from them in one swift stroke. Planting himself squarely before the two tall cowboys who were standing, he looked straight into their lean, bronzed faces. He spared a full moment of that keen cool gaze before he spoke.

"I'm not drunk. I'm throwing a bluff and I mean to start a rough house. I'm going to rush that damned bandit, Rojas. It's to save a girl . . . to give her lover a chance to escape with her. She's in the hotel. Rojas is here to get her. When I start a row, he's to try to slip out with her. Every door and window is watched. I've got to raise hell to draw the guards in. Well, you're my countrymen. We're in Mexico. A beautiful girl's honor, soul, life lie in the balance. Now, gentlemen, watch me!"

One cowboy's eyes narrowed, blinking a little, and his lean jaw dropped; the other's hard face rippled with a fleeting smile.

Gale backed away, and his pulse took to leaping when he saw the two cowboys, as if one mind actuated both, slowly stride after him. Then Gale swerved, staggering along, brushed against the tables, kicked over the empty chairs. He passed Rojas and his gang, and out of the tail of his eye saw that the bandit was watching him, waving his hands, talking fiercely. The hum of the many voices grew louder, and, when Dick lurched against a table, overturning it and spilling glasses into the laps of several Mexicans, there arose a shrill united jabber. He had succeeded in attracting attention; almost every face turned his way. One of the insulted men, a little tawny fellow, leaped up to confront Gale, and in a frenzy screamed a volley of Spanish, of which Gale distinguished *gringo*. The Mexican stamped and made a threatening move with his right hand. Dick swung his leg and, with a swift side kick, knocked the fellow's feet from under him, whirling him down with a *thud*.

The action was performed so suddenly, so adroitly, it made the Mexican such a weakling, so like a tumbled tenpin, that the shrill jabber hushed. Gale knew this to be the significant moment.

Wheeling, he rushed at Rojas. It was his old line-breaking plunge. Neither Rojas nor his men had time to move. The black-skinned bandit's face turned a dirty white; his jaw dropped; he might have shrieked if Gale had not hit him. The blow swept him backward against his men. Then Gale's heavy body, swiftly following with the momentum of that rush, struck the little group of rebels. They went down, with table and chairs, in a sliding crash.

Gale, carried by his plunge, went with them. Like a cat he landed on top. As he rose, his powerful hands fastened on Rojas. He jerked the little bandit off the tangled pile of struggling, yelling men, swinging him with terrific force, then let go his hold. Rojas slid along the floor, knocking over tables and chairs. Gale bounded back, dragged Rojas up, handling him as if he were a limp sack.

A shot rang out above the yells. Gale heard the *jingle* of breaking glass. The room darkened perceptibly. He flashed a glance backward. The two cowboys were between him and the crowd of frantic rebels. One cowboy held two guns low down, level in front of him. The other had his gun raised, aimed. On the instant it spouted red and white, and with the *crack* came the crashing of glass, another darkening shade over the room. With a cry Gale slung the bleeding Rojas from him. The bandit struck a table, toppled over it, fell, and lay prone.

Another shot made the room full of moving shadows, with light only back of the bar. A white-clad figure rushed at Gale. He tripped the man, but had to kick hard to disengage himself from grasping hands. Another figure closed in on Gale. This one was dark, swift. A blade glinted—described a circle aloft. Simultaneously with a close red flash the knife wavered—the man wielding it stumbled backward. In the din Gale did not hear a report, but the Mexican's fall was significant. Then pandemonium broke loose. The din became a roar. Gale heard shots that sounded like dull spats in the distance. The big lamp behind the bar seemingly split, then sputtered, and went out, leaving the room in darkness.

Gale leaped toward the restaurant door, which was outlined faintly by the yellow light within. Right and left he pushed the groping men who jostled with him. He vaulted a pool table, sent tables and chairs flying, and gained the door, to be the first of a wedging mob to squeeze through. One sweep of his arm knocked the restaurant lamp from its stand, and he ran out, leaving darkness behind him. A few bounds took him into the parlor. It was deserted. Thorne had gotten away with Mercedes!

It was then Gale slowed up. For the space of perhaps sixty seconds or less he had been moving with startling velocity. He peered cautiously out into the plaza. The paths, the benches, the shady places under the trees contained no skulking men. He ran out, keeping to the shade, and did not go into the path till he was halfway through the plaza. Under a street lamp, at the far end of the path, he thought he saw two dark figures. He ran faster—soon reached the street. The uproar back in the hotel began to diminish or else he was getting out of hearing. The few people he saw close at hand were all coming his way, and only the foremost showed any excitement. Gale walked swiftly, peering ahead for two figures. Presently he saw them—one tall, wearing a cape—the other slight, mantled. Gale drew a sharp breath of relief. Thorne and Mercedes were not far ahead.

From time to time Thorne looked back. He strode swiftly, almost carrying Mercedes, who clung closely to him. She, too, looked back. Once Gale saw her white face flash in the light of a street lamp. He began to overhaul them, and soon, when the last lamp had been passed and the street was dark, he ventured a whistle. Thorne heard it, for he turned, whistled a low reply, and went on. Not for some distance beyond did they halt to wait. The desert began here; Gale felt the soft sand under his feet, saw the grotesque forms of cactus. Then he came up with the fugitives.

"Dick . . . are . . . you . . . all right?" panted Thorne, grasping Gale.

"I'm . . . out of . . . breath but . . . OK," replied Gale.

"Say . . . I'm glad!" choked Thorne. "I was scared . . . helpless. Dick, it worked splendidly. We had no trouble. What on earth did you do?"

"I made the row all right," said Dick.

"Good heavens, it was like a row I once heard made by a mob. But the shots . . . Dick . . . were they at you? They paralyzed me. Then the yells. What happened? Those guards of Rojas ran around in front at the first shot. Tell me what happened."

"While I was rushing Rojas, a couple of cowboys shot out the lamps. A Mexican who pulled a knife on me got hurt . . . I guess. Then I think there was some shouting from the rebels, after the room was dark."

"Rushing Rojas?" queried Thorne, leaning close to Dick. His voice was thrilling, exultant, deep with certainty that yet needed confirmation. "What did you do to him?"

"I handed him one off side . . . tackled . . . they tried a forward pass," replied Dick, lightly speaking the football vernacular so familiar to Thorne.

Thorne leaned closer, wagging his head, his fine face showing, fierce and corded, in the starlight. "Tell me straight," he demanded in thick voice.

Gale divined then something of the suffering Thorne had undergone—something of the hot, wild, vengeful passion of a lover who must have brutal truth.

It stilled Dick's lighter mood and he was about to reply when Mercedes pressed close to him, touched his hands, looked up into his face with wonderful eyes. He thought he would not soon forget their beauty—the shadow and pain that had been the hope dawning so fugitively.

"Dear lady," said Gale with voice not wholly steady, "Rojas himself will hound you no more tonight . . . nor for many nights."

She seemed to shake, to thrill, to rise with the intelligence. She pressed his hand close over her heaving breast. Gale felt the quick throb of her heart.

"*Señor* . . . *Señor* Dick!" she cried. Then her voice failed. But her hands flew up, quick as a flash she raised her face, kissed him. Then she turned and with a sob fell into Thorne's arms.

There ensued a silence broken only by Mercedes's low sobbing. Gale walked some paces away. If he were not stunned, he certainly was powerfully agitated. The strange sweet fire of that girl's lips! It remained with him. On the spur of the moment he imagined he had a jealousy of Thorne. But presently this passed. It was only that he had been deeply moved—stirred to the depths during the last hour—had become conscious of the awakening of a spirit. What remained with him now was the splendid glow of gladness that he had been of service to Thorne. And by the intensity of Mercedes's abandon of relief and gratitude he measured her agony of terror and the hellish fate he had spared her.

"Dick, Dick . . . come here!" called Thorne softly. "Let's pull ourselves together now. We've got a problem yet. What to do? Where to go? How to get any place? We don't dare risk the station . . . the corrals where Mexicans hire out horses. We're on good old U.S. ground this minute, but we're not out of danger."

As he paused, evidently hoping for a suggestion from Gale, the silence was broken by the clear ringing peal of a bugle. Thorne gave a violent start. Then he bent over, listening. The beautiful notes of the bugle floated out of the darkness, clearer, sharper, faster. "It's a call, Dick. It's a call!" he cried.

Gale had no answer to make. Mercedes stood as if stricken. The bugle call ended. From a distance another faintly pealed. There were other sounds too remote to recognize. Then scattering shots rattled out.

"Dick, the rebels are fighting somebody," burst out Thorne excitedly. "The little Federal garrison still holds its stand. Perhaps it is attacked again. Anyway, there's something doing over the line. Maybe the crazy greasers are firing on our camp. We've feared it . . . in the dark . . . and here I am, away without leave . . . practically a deserter!"

"Go back! Go back, before you're too late!" cried Mercedes.

"Better make tracks, Thorne," added Gale. "It can't help our predicament for you to be arrested. I'll take care of Mercedes."

"No . . . no . . . no," replied Thorne. "I can get away . . . avoid arrest."

"That'd be all right for the immediate present. But it's not best for the future. George, a deserter is a deserter! Better hurry. Leave the girl to me till tomorrow."

Mercedes embraced her lover, begged him to go. Thorne wavered.

"Dick, I'm up against it," he said. "You're right. If only I can run back in time . . . but, oh, I hate to leave her. Old fellow, you've saved her. I already owe you everlasting gratitude. Keep out of Casita, Dick. The U.S. side might be safe, but I'm afraid to trust it at night. Go out in the desert, up in the mountains, in some safe place. Then come to me in camp. We'll plan. I'll have to confide in Colonel Weede. Maybe he'll help us. Hide her from the rebels, that's all."

He wrung Dick's hand, clasped Mercedes tightly in his arms, kissed her, and murmured low over her, then released her to rush off into the darkness. He disappeared in the gloom. The sound of his dull footfalls gradually died away.

For a moment the desert silence oppressed Gale. He was unaccustomed to such strange stillness. There was a low stir of sand, a rustle of stiff leaves in the wind. How white the stars burned. Then a coyote barked, to be bayed by a dog. Gale realized that he was between the edge of an unknown desert and the edge of a hostile town. He had to choose the desert, because, although he had no doubt that in Casita there were many Americans who might befriend him, he could not chance the risks of seeking them at night.

He felt a slight touch on his arm, felt it move down, felt Mercedes slip a trembling cold little hand into his. Dick looked at her. She seemed a white-faced girl now with staring, frightened black eyes that flashed up at him. If the loneliness, the silence, the desert, the unknown dangers of the night affected him, what must they be to this hunted, driven girl? Gale's heart swelled. He was alone with her. He had no weapon, no money, no food, no drink, no covering, nothing except his two hands. He had absolutely no knowledge of the desert, of the direction or whereabouts of the boundary line between the republics; he did not know where to find the railroad, or any road or trail, or whether or not there were towns near or far. It was a critical, desperate situation. He thought first of the girl, and groaned in spirit, prayed that it would be given him to save her. When he remembered himself, it was with the stunning consciousness that he could conceive of no situation which he would have exchanged for this one—where fortune had set him a perilous task of loyalty to a friend, to a helpless girl.

"*Señor . . . señor,*" suddenly whispered Mercedes, clinging to him. "Listen. I hear horses coming."

CHAPTER THREE:
A FLIGHT INTO THE DESERT

Uneasy and startled, Gale listened and, hearing nothing, wondered if Mercedes's fears had not worked upon her imagination. He felt a trembling seize her and he held her hands tightly.

"You were mistaken, I guess," he whispered.

"No, no, *señor*."

Dick turned his ear to the soft wind. Presently he heard, or imagined he heard, low beats. Like the first faint far-off beats of a drumming grouse they recalled to him the Illinois forests of his boyhood. In a moment he was certain the sounds were the pad-like steps of hoofs in yielding sand. The regular tramp was not that of grazing horses.

On the instant, made cautious and stealthy by alarm, Gale drew Mercedes deeper into the gloom of the shrubbery. Sharp pricks from thorns warned him that he was pressing into a cactus growth, and he protected Mercedes as best he could. She was shaking as one with a severe chill. She breathed with little hurried pants and leaned upon him, almost in collapse. Gale ground his teeth in helpless rage at the girl's fate. If she had not been beautiful, she might still have been free and happy in her home. What a strange world to live in—how unfair was fate!

The sounds of hoof beats grew louder. Gale made out a dark moving mass against a background of dull gray. There was a line of horses. He could not discern whether or not all the horses carried riders. The murmur of voices struck his ear—then a low laugh. It made him tingle, for it sounded American. Eagerly he listened. There was an interval where only the hoof beats could be heard.

"It shore was, Laddy, it shore was," came a voice out of the darkness. "Rough house! Laddy, since wire fences drove us out of Texas, we ain't seen the like of that. An' we never had such a call."

"Call? It was a burnin' roast," replied another voice. "I felt low-down. He vamoosed some sudden, an' I hope he an' his friends shook the dust of Casita. That's a rotten town, Jim."

Gale leaped up in joy. What luck! The speakers were none other than the two cowboys who he had accosted in the Mexican hotel.

"Hold on, fellows!" he called out, and strode into the road.

The horses snorted and stamped. There followed swift rustling sounds—a *clinking* of spurs, then silence. The figures loomed clearer in the gloom. Gale saw five or six horses, two with riders, and one other, at least, carrying a pack. When Gale got within fifteen feet of the group, the foremost horseman said: "I reckon that's close enough, stranger."

Something in the cowboy's hand glinted darkly bright in the starlight.

"You'd recognize me, if it wasn't so dark," replied Gale, halting. "I spoke to you a little while ago . . . in the saloon back there."

"Come over an' let's see you," said the cowboy curtly.

Gale advanced till he was close to the horse. The cowboy leaned over in the saddle and peered into Gale's face. Then without a word he sheathed the gun and held out his hand. Gale met a grip of steel that warmed his blood. The other cowboy got off his nervous, spirited horse and threw the bridle. He, too, peered closely into Gale's face.

"My name's Ladd," he said. "Reckon I'm some glad to meet you again."

Gale felt another grip as hard and strong as the other

had been. He realized he had formed friends who belonged to a class of men who he had despaired of ever knowing.

"Gale . . . Dick Gale is my name," he began swiftly. "I dropped into Casita tonight, hardly knowing where I was. A boy took me to that hotel. There I met an old friend who I had not seen for years. He belongs to the cavalry stationed here. He had befriended a Spanish girl . . . fallen in love with her. Rojas had killed this girl's father . . . tried to abduct her. You know what took place at the hotel. Gentlemen, if it's ever possible, I'll show you how I appreciate what you did for me there. I got away, found my friend with the girl. We hurried out here beyond the edge of town. Then Thorne had to make a break for camp. We heard bugle calls, shots. And he was away without leave. That left the girl with me. I don't know what to do. Thorne swears Casita is no place for Mercedes at night. I. . . ."

"The girl ain't no peon . . . no common greaser?" interrupted Ladd.

"No. Her name is Castañeda. She belongs to an old Spanish family, once rich and influential."

"Reckoned as much," replied the cowboy. "There's more than Rojas's wantin' to kidnap a pretty girl. Shore he does that every day or so. Must be somethin' political or feelin' against class. Well, Casita ain't no place for your friend's girl at night or day, or any time. Shore there's Americans who'd take her in an' fight for her, if necessary. But, it ain't wise to risk that. Lash, what do you say?"

"It's been gettin' hotter 'round this greaser corral for some weeks," replied the other cowboy. "If that two-bit of a garrison surrenders, there's no tellin' what'll happen. Orozco is headin' west from Agua Prieta with his guerrillas. Campo is burnin' bridges, an' tearin' up the railroad south of Nogales. Then there's all these bandits callin' themselves revolutionists just for an excuse to steal, burn, kill, an' ride off with women. It's plain facts, Lash, an' bein' across the U.S. line a few inches or so don't make no hell of a difference. My advice is . . . don't let Miss Castañeda ever set foot in Casita again."

"Looks like you've shore spoke sense," said Lash. "I
reckon, Gale, you an' the girl ought to come with us. Casita shore would be a little warm for us tomorrow. We
didn't kill anybody, but I shot a greaser's arm off an' Ladd
strained friendly relations by destroyin' property. We
know people who'll take care of the *señorita* till your
friend can come for her."

Dick warmly spoke his gratefulness, and, inexpressibly
relieved and happy for Mercedes, he went toward the
clump of cactus where he had left her. She stood erect,
waiting, and, dark as it was, he could tell she had lost the
terror that had so shaken her.

"*Señor* Gale, you are my good angel," she said tremulously.

"I've been lucky to fall in with these men, and I'm glad
with all my heart," he replied. "Come."

He led her into the road up to the cowboys, who now
stood bareheaded in the starlight. They seemed shy, and
Lash was silent while Ladd made embarrassed, unintelligible reply to Mercedes's thanks.

There were five horses, two saddled, two packed, and
the remaining one carried only a blanket. Ladd shortened
the stirrups on his mount and helped Mercedes up into
the saddle. From the way she settled herself and took the
few restive prances of the mettlesome horse, Gale judged
that she could ride. Lash then urged Gale to take his
horse. But this Gale refused to do.

"I'll walk," he said. "I'm used to walking. I know cowboys are not."

They tried again to persuade him, without avail. Then
Ladd started off, riding bareback. Mercedes fell in behind
with Gale walking beside her. The two pack animals came
next, and Lash brought up the rear.

Once started with protection assured for the girl and a
real objective point in view, Gale relaxed from the tense
strain he had been laboring under. How glad he would

have been to acquaint Thorne with their good fortune. Later, of course, there would be some way to get word to the cavalryman. But till then, what torments his friend would suffer.

It seemed to Dick that a very long time had elapsed since he stepped off the train, and one by one he went over every detail of incident that had occurred between that arrival and the present moment. Strange as the facts were he had no doubts. He realized that before that night he had never known the depths of wrath undisturbed in him—had never conceived even a passing idea that it was possible for him to try to kill a man.

His right hand was swollen, stiff, so sore that he could scarcely close it. His knuckles were bruised and bleeding, and ached with a sharp pain. Considering the thickness of his heavy glove, Gale was of the opinion that to bruise his hand so he must have struck Rojas a powerful blow. He remembered that for him to give or take a blow had been nothing. This blow to Rojas, however, had been a different matter. The hot wrath that had been his motive was not puzzling, but the effect in him after he had cooled off was a subtle difference that puzzled and eluded him. The more it baffled him, the more he pondered. All those wandering months of his had been filled with dissatisfaction, yet he had been too apathetic in thought to understand himself. So he had not been much of a hand to try. Perhaps it had not been the blow to Rojas any more than other things that had wrought some change in him.

His meeting with Thorne; the wonderful black eyes of a Spanish girl; her appeal to him; the hate inspired by Rojas, and the rush, the blow, the action; sight of Thorne and Mercedes hurrying safely away; the girl's hands pressing his to her heaving breast; the sweet fire of her kiss; the fact of her being alone with him, dependent upon him—all these things Gale turned over and over in his mind, only to fail of any definite conclusion as to which had affected him so remarkably, or to tell what had really happened to him.

Had he fallen in love with Thorne's sweetheart? The
idea came in a flash. Was he, all in an instant, and by one
of those incomprehensible reversals of character, jealous
of his friend? Dick was almost afraid to look up at Mercedes. Still he forced himself to do so, and, as it chanced,
Mercedes was looking down at him. Somehow the light
was better, and he clearly saw her white face, her black
and starry eyes, her perfect mouth. With a quick, graceful impulsiveness she put her hand upon his shoulder.
Like her appearance, the action was new, strange, striking to Gale, but it brought home suddenly to him the nature of gratitude and affection in a girl of her blood. It
was sweet and sisterly. He knew then that he had not
fallen in love with her. The feeling that was akin to jealousy seemed to be of the beautiful something for which
Mercedes stood in Thorne's life. Gale then grasped the
bewildering possibilities, the infinite wonder of what a
girl could mean to a man.

The other haunting intimations of change seemed to be
elusively blended—with sensations—the heat and thrill
of action, the sense of something done and more to do,
the utter vanishing of an old weary hunt for he knew not
what. Maybe it had been a hunt for work, for energy, for
spirit, for love, for his real self. Whatever it might be, there
appeared to be now some hope of finding it.

The desert began to lighten. Gray openings in the border of shrubby growths changed to paler hue. The road
could be seen some distance ahead and it had become a
stony descent down, steadily down. Dark-ridged backs of
mountains bounded the horizon, and all seemed near at
hand, hemming in the plain. In the east a white glow
grew brighter and brighter, reaching up to a line of cloud,
defined sharply below by a rugged, notched range.
Presently a silver circle slid up behind the black mountain, and the gloom of the desert underwent a transfor-
mation. From a gray mantle it changed to a transparent
haze. The moon was rising.

"*Señor*, I am cold," said Mercedes.

Dick had been carrying his coat upon his arm. He had felt warm, even hot, and had imagined that the steady walk had occasioned it. But his skin was cool. The heat came from an inward burning. He stopped the horse and raised the coat up, and helped Mercedes put it on.

"I should have thought of you," he said. "But I seemed to feel warm. The coat's a little large . . . we might wrap it around you twice."

Mercedes smiled and lightly thanked him in Spanish. The flash of mood was in direct contrast to the appealing, passionate, and tragic states in which he had necessarily viewed her, and it gave him a vivid impression of what vivacity and charm she might possess under happy conditions. He was about to start when he observed that Ladd had halted, and was peering ahead in evident caution. Mercedes's horse began to stamp impatiently, raised his ears and head, and acted as if he were about to neigh.

A warning—"*Hist!*"—from Ladd bade Dick put a quieting hand on the horse. Lash came noiselessly forward to join his companion. The two then listened and watched.

An uneasy yet mounting stir ran through Gale's veins. This scene was not fancy. These men of the ranges had heard or seen or scented danger. It was all real, as tangible and sure as the touch of Mercedes's hand upon his arm. Probably for her the night had terrors beyond Gale's power to comprehend. He looked down into the desert and would have felt no surprise at anything hidden among the whorled and demon-armed cacti, the dark, winding arroyos, the shadowed rocks with their moonlit tips, the ragged plain leading to black bold mountains. The wind appeared to blow softly with an almost imperceptible moan over the desert. That was a new sound to Gale. But he heard nothing more.

Presently Lash went to the rear and Ladd started ahead. The progress now, however, was considerably slower, not owing to a bad road, for that became better, but probably owing to caution exercised by the cowboy guide. At the end of a half hour this marked deliberation changed, and the horses followed Ladd's at a gait that put Gale to his best walking paces.

Meanwhile, the moon soared high above the black, corrugated peaks. The gray, the gloom, the shadow whitened. The clearing of the dark foreground appeared to lift a distant veil and show endless aisles of desert reaching down between dim horizon-bounding ranges.

Gale gazed abroad, knowing that as this night was the first time for him to awake to consciousness of a vague, indefinite, wonderful other self, so it was one wherein he began to be aware of an encroaching presence of physical things—the immensity of the star-studded sky, the grand soaring moon, the bleak, cold, mysterious mountain and limitless slope, and plain and ridge and valley. Those things in all their magnificence had not heretofore been unnoticed by him; only they spoke a different meaning, a voice that he had never heard called for him to see, to feel the vast, hard externals of the heavens and earth—all that represented the open, the free, silence and solitude and space.

Once more his meditations, like his steps, were halted by Ladd's actions. The cowboy reined in his horse, listened a moment, then swung down out of the saddle. He raised a cautioning hand to the others, then slipped into the gloom and disappeared. Gale marked that the halt had been made in a ridged and cut-up pass between low mesas. He could see the columns of cactus standing out, black against the moon-white sky. The horses were evidently tiring, for they did not manifest impatience. Gale heard their short heaves, also the bark of some animal, a dog or a coyote. It sounded like a dog, and this led Gale to wonder if there was any human habitation near at hand. To the right, up under the ledges some distance away, stood two square black objects, too uniform he thought to be rocks. While he was peering at them, uncertain what to think, the shrill whistle of a horse pealed out, to be followed by a hard rattle of hoofs on hard stone. Then a dog barked. At the same moment that Ladd hurriedly appeared in the road a light shone out and danced before one of the square black objects.

"Keep close, an' don't make no noise," he whispered, and led his horse at right angles off the road. Gale followed, leading Mercedes's horse. As he turned, he observed that Lash also had dismounted.

Keeping closely at Ladd's heels without brushing the cacti or stumbling over rocks and depressions was a task Gale found impossible. After he had been stabbed several times by the bayonet-like spikes that seemed to be invisible, the matter of caution became equally one of self-preservation. Both the cowboys, Dick had observed, wore leather chaps. It was no easy matter to lead a spirited horse through the dark, winding lanes walled by thorns. Mercedes's horse often balked and had to be coaxed and carefully guided. Dick concluded that Ladd was making a wide detour. The position of certain stars, grown familiar during the march, veered around from one side to another. Dick saw that the travel was fast, but by no means noiseless. The pack animals at times crashed and ripped through the narrow places. It seemed to Gale that anyone within a mile could have heard these sounds. From the tops of knolls or ridges he looked back, trying to locate the mesas where the light had danced, and the dog had barked alarm. He could not distinguish these two rocky eminences from among many rising in the background.

Presently Ladd led out into a wider lane that appeared to run straight. The cowboy mounted his horse and this fact convinced Gale that they had circled back to the road. The march proceeded then, once more at a good, steady, silent walk. When Dick consulted his watch, he was amazed to see that the hour was still early. How much had happened in little time! He now began to be aware that the night was growing colder, and, strange to him, he felt something damp that in a country he knew he would have recognized as dew. He had not been aware there was dew on the desert. The wind blew stronger, the stars shone whiter, the sky grew darker, and the moon climbed toward the zenith. The road stretched level for miles, then crossed arroyos and ridges, wound between mounds of broken, ruined rock, found a level again, and then began a long ascent. Dick asked Mercedes if she was cold and she replied in the affirmative, speaking especially of her feet, which were growing numb. Then she asked to be helped down, to walk a while. At first she was cold and lame, and accepted the helping hand Dick proferred. After a little, however, she recovered and went on without assistance. Dick could scarcely believe his eyes, as from time to time he stole a side-long glance at this silent girl who walked with lithe and rapid stride. She was wrapped in his long coat yet it did not hide her slender grace. He could not see her face that was concealed by the black mantle.

A low-spoken word from Ladd recalled Gale to the question of surroundings and of possible dangers. Ladd had halted a few yards ahead. They had reached the summit of what was evidently a high ridge that sloped with much greater steepness on the far side. It was only after a few more broad steps, however, that Dick could see down the slope. Sharply greeting his sight was a bright campfire around which clustered a group of dark figures. They were encamped in a wide arroyo where horses could be seen grazing in black patches of grass between clusters of trees. The scene had an undeniable hint of wildness. A second look at the campers told Gale they were Mexicans. At this moment Lash came forward to join Ladd, and the two spent a large, uninterrupted moment studying the arroyo. A hoarse laugh, faint yet distinct, floated up on the cool wind.

"Well, Laddy, what're you makin' of that outfit?" inquired Lash, speaking softly.

"Same as any of them other raider outfits," replied Ladd, "they've crossed the line for beef. But they'll run off any good stock. As hoss thieves these rebels have got 'em all beat. That outfit is waitin' till it's late. There's a ranch up the arroyo."

Gale heard Lash curse under his breath.

"Shore, I feel the same," said Ladd. "But we've got a girl an' the young man to look after, not to mention our pack outfit. An' we're huntin' for a job, not a fight, old hoss. Keep on your chaps."

"Nothin' to it but head south for the Río Forlorn?"

"You're talkin' sense now, Jim. I wish we'd headed that way long ago. But it ain't strange I'd want to travel away from the border, thinkin' of the girl. Jim, we can't go around this greaser outfit an' strike the road again. Too rough. So we'll have to give up gettin' to San Felipe."

"Perhaps it's just as well, Laddy. Río Forlorn is on the borderline, but it's country where these rebels ain't been yet."

"Wait till they learn of the oasis an' Belding's horses!" exclaimed Laddy. "I'm not anticipatin' peace anywhere along the border, Jim. But we can't go ahead . . . we can't go back."

"What'll we do, Laddy? It's a hike to Belding's ranch. An' if we get there in daylight, some greaser will see the girl before Belding can hide her. It'll get talked about. The news'll travel to Casita like sage balls before the wind."

"Shore we won't ride into Río Forlorn in the daytime. Let's slip the packs, Jim. We can hide them off in the cactus an' come back after them. With the young man ridin' we. . . ."

The whispering was interrupted by a loud, ringing neigh that whistled up from the arroyo. One of the horses had scented the travelers on the ridge top. The lolling manner of the Mexicans changed to one of uneasy attention.

Ladd and Lash turned back, and led the horses into the first opening on the south side of the road. There was nothing more said at the moment, and manifestly the cowboys were in a hurry. Gale had to run in the open places to keep up. When they did stop, it was welcome to Gale, for he had begun to fall behind.

The packs were slipped, securely tied, and hidden in a

mesquite clump. Ladd strapped a blanket around one of the horses. His next move was to take off his chaps.

"Gale, you're wearin' boots an' by liftin' your feet you can beat the cactus," he whispered. "But the . . . the . . . Miss Castañeda, she'll be torn all to pieces unless she puts these on. Please tell her . . . an' hurry."

Dick took the chaps, and, going up to Mercedes, he explained the situation. She laughed, evidently at his embarrassed earnestness, and slipped out of the saddle.

"*Señor, chaparejos* and I are not strangers," she said.

That fact was deftly manifested to Gale as with little assistance she got into them, and they were the kind that had to be pulled up, not buckled at the side. Gale helped her into the saddle, and then Ladd told her to follow him, called to her horse, and started off. Lash directed Gale to mount the other saddled horse and go next.

Dick had not ridden 100 yards behind the trotting leaders before he had sundry painful encounters with reaching cacti arms. His horse seemed to miss these by a narrow margin. Dick's knees appeared to be in line, and it became necessary for him to lift them high and let his boots take the onslaught of spikes. He was at home in the saddle, and this accomplishment was about the only one he possessed that had been of any advantage during his sojourn in the West.

Ladd pursued a zigzag course southward across the desert, trotting down the aisles, cantering in wide bare patches, walking through the clumps of cacti. The desert seemed all of a sameness to Dick—a wilderness of rock and jagged growths hemmed in by lowering ranges always looking close yet never growing any nearer. The moon slanted back toward the west, losing its white radiance, and the gloom of the earlier evening began to creep into the washes and to darken under the mesas. By and by Ladd entered an arroyo, and here the traveler turned and twisted with the meanderings of a dry streambed. At the head of a cañon they had to take once more to the rougher ground. Always it led down, always it grew rougher, more rolling, with wider bare spaces, always the black ranges loomed close.

Gale became chilled to the bone and his clothes were coldly damp. His knees smarted from the countless jabs of the poisoned thorns, and his right hand was either swollen stiff or too numb to move. Moreover, he was tiring. The excitement, as the long walk, the miles on miles of jolting trot—these had wearied him. Mercedes must be made of steel, he thought, to stand all that she had been subjected to and yet, when the stars were paling and dawn perhaps not far away, to have stayed in the saddle.

So Dick Gale rode on, drowsier for each mile, and more and more giving the horse a choice of ground. Sometimes a prod from a murderous spine roused Dick. A grayness had blotted out the waning moon in the west and the clear dark starry sky overhead. Once when Gale, thinking to fight his weariness, raised his head, he saw that one of the horses in the lead was riderless. Ladd was carrying Mercedes. Dick marveled that her collapse had not come sooner. Another time, rousing himself again, he imagined they were now on a good hard road.

It seemed that hours passed, although he knew only little time had elapsed, when once more he threw off the spell of weariness. He heard a dog bark. Tall trees lined the open lane down which he was riding. Presently in the gray gloom he saw low, square houses with flat roofs. Ladd turned off to the left down another lane, gloomy between trees. Every few rods there was one of the squat houses. This lane opened into wider lighter space. The cold air bore a sweet perfume whether of flowers or fruit, Dick could not tell. Ladd rode on for perhaps a quarter of a mile although it seemed interminably long to Dick. A grove of trees loomed, dark in the gray of morning. Ladd entered it and was lost in the shade. Dick rode on among trees. Presently he heard voices, and soon another house, low and flat like the others but so long he could not see the farther end, stood up blacker than the trees. As he dismounted, cramped and sore, he could scarcely stand. Lash came alongside. He spoke and someone with a big hearty voice replied to him. Then it seemed to Dick that he was led into a blackness like pitch where with the feel of blankets his drowsy faculties faded.

CHAPTER FOUR:
FORLORN RIVER

When Dick opened his eyes, a flood of golden sunshine streamed in at the open window under which he lay. His first thought was one of blank wonder as to where in the world he happened to be. The room was large, square, adobe-walled. It was littered with saddles, harness, blankets. Upon the floor was a bed spread out upon a tarpaulin. Probably this was where someone had slept. The sight of huge dusty spurs, a gun belt with sheath and gun, and a pair of leather chaps all stuck over with broken cactus thorns recalled to Dick the cowboys, the ride, Mercedes, and the whole strange adventure that had brought him there.

He did not recollect having removed his boots; indeed, upon second thought, he knew he had not done so. But there they stood upon the floor. Ladd or Lash must have taken them off when he was so exhausted and sleepy that he could not tell what was happening. He felt a dead weight of complete lassitude, and did not want to move. A sudden pain in his hand caused him to hold it up. It was black and blue, swollen to almost twice its normal size, and stiff as a board. The knuckles were skinned and crusted with dried blood. Dick soliloquized that it was the worst-looking hand he had seen since football days, and that it would inconvenience him for some time.

A warm, dry, fragrant breeze came through the window. Dick caught again the sweet smell of flowers or fruit.

He heard the fluttering of leaves, the murmur of running water, the twittering of birds, then the sound of approaching footsteps and voices. The door at the far end of the room was open. Through it he saw poles of peeled wood upholding a porch roof, a bench, rose bushes in bloom, grass, and beyond these bright green foliage of trees.

"He shore was sleepin' when I looked in an hour ago," said a voice that Dick recognized as Ladd's.

"Let him sleep," came the reply in deep good-natured tones. "Missus B. says the girl's never moved. Must have been a tough ride for them both. Forty miles through cactus."

"Young Gale hoofed it darn' near half the way," replied Ladd. "We tried to make him ride one of our horses. If he had, we'd never've got here. A walk like that'd've killed me an' Jim."

"Well, Laddy, I'm right down glad to see you boys and I'll do all I can for the young couple," said the other. "But I'm doing some worrying here, don't mistake me."

"About your stock?"

"I've got only a few head of cattle at the oasis now. I'm worrying some, mostly about my horses. The U.S. is doing some worrying, too, don't mistake me. The rebels have worked west and north as far as Casita. There are no cavalrymen along the line beyond Casita, and there can't be. It's practically waterless desert. But these rebels are desert men. They could cross the line beyond the Río Forlorn and smuggle arms into Mexico. Of course, my job is to keep tab on Chinese and Japs trying to get into the U.S. from Magdalena Bay. But I'm supposed to patrol the borderline. I'm going to hire some rangers. Now I'm not so afraid of being shot up, though out in this lonely place there's danger of it . . . what I'm afraid of most is losing that bunch of horses. If any rebels come this far . . . or if they ever hear of my horses, they're going to raid me. You know what these guerrilla Mexicans will do for horses. They're crazy on horseflesh. They know fine horses . . . breed the finest in the world. So I don't sleep nights any more."

"Reckon me an' Jim might as well tie up with you for a spell, Belding. We've been ridin' up an' down Arizona, tryin' to keep out of sight of wire fences."

"Laddy, it's open enough around Forlorn River to satisfy even an old-time cowpuncher like you." Belding laughed. "I'd take your staying on as some favor, don't mistake me. Perhaps I can persuade the young man, Gale, to take a job with me."

"That's shore likely. He said he had no money . . . no friends. An', if a scrapper's all you're lookin' for, he'll do," replied Ladd with a dry chuckle.

"Missus B. will throw some bronco capers 'round this ranch when she hears I'm going to hire a stranger."

"Why?"

"Well, there's Nell . . . and you said this Gale was a young American. My wife will be scared to death for fear Nell will fall in love with him."

Laddy choked off a laugh, then evidently slapped his knee, or Belding, for there was a resounding smack.

"He's a fine-spoken, good-looking chap, you said," went on Belding.

"Shore he is," said Ladd warmly. "What do you say, Jim?"

By this time Dick Gale's ears began to burn and he was trying to make himself deaf when he wanted to hear every little word.

"Husky young fellow, nice voice, steady clear eyes, kinda proud, I thought, an' some handsome, he was," replied Jim Lash.

"Maybe I ought to think twice before taking a stranger into my family," said Belding seriously. "*Aw*, he must be all right, Laddy, being the cavalryman's friend. No bum or lunger? He must be all right?"

"Bum? Lunger? Say, didn't I tell you I shook hands with this boy an' was plumb glad to meet him?" demanded Laddy with considerable heat. Manifestly he had been affronted. "Tom Belding, he's a gentleman, an' he could lick you in . . . in half a second. How about that, Jim?"

"Less time," replied Lash. "Tom, here's my stand. Young Gale can have my hoss, my gun, anythin' of mine."

"*Aw*, I didn't mean to insult you, boys, don't mistake me," said Belding. " 'Course he's all right."

The object of this conversation lay quietly upon his bed, thrilling and amazed at being so championed by the cowboys, delighted with Belding's idea of employing him, and much amused with the quaint seriousness of the three.

"How's the young man?" called a woman's voice. It was kind and mellow and earnest. Gale heard footsteps on flagstones.

"He's asleep yet, Wife," replied Belding. "Guess he was pretty much knocked out. I'll close the door there, so we won't wake him."

There were slow, soft steps, then the door softly closed. But that fact scarcely made a perceptible difference in the sound of the voices outside.

"Laddy an' Jim are going to stay," went on Belding. "It'll be like the old Panhandle days a little. I'm powerful glad to have the boys, Nellie. You know I meant to send to Casita to ask them. We'll see some trouble before the revolution is ended. I think I'll make this young Gale an offer."

"He isn't a cowboy?" asked Mrs. Belding quietly.

"No."

"Shore he'd make a darn' good one," put in Laddy.

"What is he? Who is he? Where did he come from? Surely you must be. . . ."

"Laddy swears he's all right," interrupted the husband. "That's enough reference for me. Isn't it enough for you?"

"*Humph!* Laddy knows a lot about young men, now, doesn't he, especially strangers from the East? Tom, you must be careful."

"Wife, I'm only too glad to have a noisy young chap come along. What sense is there in your objection, if Jim and Laddy stick up for him?"

"But Tom . . . he'll fall in love with Nell," protested Mrs. Belding.

"Well, wouldn't that be regular? Doesn't every man who comes along fall in love with Nell? Hasn't it always happened? When she was a schoolgirl in Kansas, didn't it happen? Didn't she have a hundred moon-eyed ninnies after her in Texas? I've had some peace out here in the desert, except when a greaser or a prospector or a Yaqui would come along. Then same old story . . . in love with Nell."

"But Tom . . . Nell might fall in love with this young man!" exclaimed his wife in distress.

"Laddy, Jim, didn't I tell you?" cried Belding. "I knew she'd say that. My dear wife, I would be simply overcome with joy if Nell did fall in love once. Real good and hard. She's wilder than any antelope out there in the desert. Nell's nearly twenty now and so far as we know she's never cared a rap for any fellow, and she's just as gay and full of the devil as she was at fourteen. Nell's as good and lovable as she is pretty, but I'm afraid she'll never grow into a woman while we live out in this lonely land. And you've always hated towns where there was a chance for the girl . . . just because you were afraid she'd fall in love. You've always been strange, even silly about that. I've done my best for Nell . . . loved her as if she were my own daughter. I've changed many business plans to suit your whims. There are rough times ahead, maybe. I need men. I'll hire this chap, Gale, if he'll stay. Let Nell take her chance with him, just as she'll have to take chances with men when we get out of this desert. She'll be all the better for it."

"I hope Laddy's not mistaken in his opinion of this newcomer," replied Mrs. Belding with a sigh of resignation.

"Shore I never made a mistake in my life figgerin' people," said Laddy stoutly.

"Yes, you have, Laddy," replied Mrs. Belding. "You're wrong about Tom. Well, supper is to be got. That young man and the girl will be starved. I'll go in now. If Nell happens around, don't . . . don't flatter her, Laddy, like you did at dinner. Don't make her think of her looks."

Dick heard Mrs. Belding walk away.

"Shore she's powerful particular about that girl," observed Laddy. "Say, Tom, Nell knows she's pretty, doesn't she?"

"She's liable to find it out unless you shut up, Laddy. When you visited us out here some weeks ago, you kept paying cowboy compliments to her."

"An' it's your idee that cowboy compliments are plumb bad for girls?"

"Downright bad, Laddy, so my wife says."

"I'll be darned if I believe any girl can be hurt by a little sweet talk. It pleases 'em. But say, Belding, speakin' of looks, have you got a peek yet at the Spanish girl?"

"Not in the light."

"Well, neither have I in daytime. I had enough by moonlight. Nell is some on looks, but I'm regretfully passin' the ribbon to the lady from Mex. Jim, where are you?"

"My money's on Nell," replied Lash. "Gimme a girl with flesh an' color, an' blue eyes a-laughin'. Miss Castañeda is some peach, I'll not gainsay. But her face seemed too white. An' when she flashed those eyes on me, I thought I was shot. When she stood up there at first, thankin' us, I felt as if a . . . a princess was 'round somewhere. Now, Nell is kiddish an'sweet an'. . . ."

"Chop it," interrupted Belding. "Here comes Nell now."

Dick's tingling ears took in the pattering of light footsteps, the rush of someone running.

"Here you are!" cried a sweet, happy voice. "Dad, the *señorita* is perfectly lovely. I've been peeping at her. She sleeps like . . . like death. She's so white. Oh, I hope she won't be ill."

"Shore she's only played out," said Laddy. "But she had spunk while it lasted. I was just arguin' with Jim an' Tom about Miss Castañeda. I'm powerful sorry I have to pass the ribbon to her."

"Gracious! Why, she is beautiful. I never saw anyone so beautiful. How strange and sad, that about her! Tell me more, Laddy. You promised. I'm dying to know. I never hear anything in this awful place. Didn't you say the *señorita* had a sweetheart?"

"Shore I did."

"And he's a cavalryman?"

"Yes."

"Is he the young man who came with you?"

"Nope. That fellow's the one who saved the girl from Rojas."

"Ah! Where is he, Laddy?"

"He's in there, asleep."

"Is he hurt?"

"I reckon not. He walked about fifteen miles."

"Is he . . . nice, Laddy?"

"Shore."

"What is he like?"

"Well, I'm not long acquainted, never saw him by day, but I was some tolerable took with him. An' Jim here, Jim says the young man can have his gun an' his hoss."

"Wonderful! Laddy, what on earth did this stranger do to win you cowboys in just one night?"

"I'll shore have to tell you. Me an' Jim were watchin' a game of cards in the Del Sol saloon in Casita. That's across the line. We had acquaintances, four fellows from the Cross Bar outfit, where we worked a while back. This Del Sol is a billiard hall, saloon, restaurant, an' the like. An' it was full of greasers. Some of Campo's rebels were there, drinkin' an' playin' games. Then pretty soon in came Rojas with some of his outfit. They were packin' guns an' kept to themselves off to the side. I didn't give them a second look till Jim said he reckoned there was somethin' in the wind. Then, careless like, I began to peek at Rojas. They call Rojas the 'dandy rebel,' an' he shore looked the part. It made me sick to see him in all that fine lace an' glitter, knowin' him to be the cut-throat robber he is. It's no uncommon sight to see excited greasers. They're all crazy. But this bandit was shore some agitated. He kept his men in a tight bunch 'round a table. He talked an' waved his hands. He was actually shakin'. His eyes had a wild glare . . . now, I figgered that trouble was brewin', most likely for the little Casita garrison. People seemed to think Campo an' Rojas would join forces to oust the Federals. Jim thought Rojas's excitement was at the hatchin' of some plot. Anyway, we didn't join no card games, an' without pretendin' to we was some watchful.

"A little while afterward I seen a fellow standin' in the restaurant door. He was a young American, dressed in corduroys an' boots, like a prospector. You know it's no unusual fact to see prospectors in these parts. What made me think twice about this one was how big he seemed, how he filled up that door. He looked 'round the saloon, an', when he spotted Rojas, he sorta jerked up. Then he pulled his slouch hat lop-sided, an' begun to stagger down the steps. First off I figgered he was drunk. But I remembered he didn't seem drunk before. It was some queer. So I watched that young man.

"He reeled 'round the room like a fellow who was drunker'n a lord. Nobody but me seemed to notice him. Then he began to stumble over pool players an' get his feet tangled up in chairs an' bump against tables. He got some pretty hard looks. He came 'round our way, an' all of a sudden he seen us cowboys. He gave another start, like the one when he first seen Rojas, then he made for us. I tipped Jim off that somethin' was doin'.

"When he got close, he straightened up, put back his slouch hat, an' looked at us. Then I seen his face. It sorta electrified yours truly. It was white, with veins standin' out, an' eyes flamin' . . . a face of fury. I was plumb amazed, didn't know what to think. Then this queer young man shot some cool polite words at me an' Jim. He was only bluffin' at bein' drunk . . . he meant to rush Rojas, to start a rough house . . . the bandit was after a girl . . . this girl was in the hotel an' she was the sweetheart of a soldier, the young fellow's friend . . . the hotel was watched by Rojas's guards . . . an' the plan was to make a fuss an' get the girl away in the excitement. Well,

Jim an' me was reminded of bein' Americans . . . that cowboys generally had a name for loyalty to women. Then this amazin' chap . . . you can't imagine how scornful . . . said he was alone, an' for me an' Jim to watch him.

"Before I could catch my breath, an' figger out what he meant by rush an' rough house, he had knocked over a table an' crowded some greasers half off the map. One little funny man leaped up like a wild monkey an' began to screech. An' in another second he was in the air upside down. When he lit, he laid there. Then, quicker 'n I can tell you, the young man dived at Rojas. Like a mad steer on the rampage he charged Rojas, an' his men. The whole outfit went down . . . smash! I figgered then what rush meant. The young fellow came up out of the pile with Rojas, an' just like I'd sling an empty sack along the floor, he sent the bandit. But swift as that went he was on top of Rojas before the chairs an' tables had stopped rollin'.

"I woke up then, an' made for the center of the room, Jim with me. I began to shoot out the lamps. Jim throwed his guns on the crazy rebels, an' I was afraid there'd be blood spilled before I could get the room dark. Bein' shore busy, I lost sight of the young fellow for a second or so, an', when I got an eye free for him, I seen a greaser about to knife him. Think I was some considerate of the greaser by only shootin' his arm off. Then I cracked the last lamp, an' in the hullabaloo me an' Jim vamoosed.

"We made tracks for our hosses an' packs, an' was hittin' the San Felipe road when we run right plumb into the young man. Well, he said his name was Gale, Dick Gale. The girl was with him, safe an' well, but her sweetheart, the soldier, bein' away without leave, had to go back sudden. There shore was some trouble, for Jim an' me heard shootin'. Gale said he had no money, no friends, was a stranger in a desert country, an' he was distracted to know how to help the girl. So me an' Jim started off with them for San Felipe, got switched, an' then we headed for the Río Forlorn."

"Oh, I think he was perfectly splendid!" exclaimed the girl.

"Shore he was. Only, Nell, you can't lay no claim to bein' the original discoverer of that fact."

"But Laddy, you haven't told me what he looks like."

At this juncture Dick Gale felt it absolutely impossible for him to play the eavesdropper any longer. Quietly he rolled out of bed. The voices still sounded close outside, and it was only by effort that he kept from further listening. Belding's kindly interest, Laddy's blunt and sincere cowboy eulogy, the girl's sweet eagerness and praise—these warmed Gale's heart. He had fallen among simple people into whose lives the advent of an unknown man was welcome. He found himself in a singularly agitated mood. The excitement, the thrill, the difference felt in himself, experienced the preceding night, had extended on into his present. And the possibilities suggested by the conversation he had unwittingly overheard added sufficiently to the other feelings to put him into a peculiarly receptive state of mind. He was wild to be one of Belding's rangers. The idea of riding a horse, in the open desert with a dangerous duty to perform, seemed to strike him with an appealing force. Something within him went out to the cowboys, to this blunt and kind Belding. He was afraid to meet the girl. If every man who came along fell in love with this sweet-voiced Nell, then what hope had he to escape—now—when his whole inner awakening betokened a change of spirit, hope, a finding of real worth, real good, real power in himself? He did not understand wholly, yet he felt ready to ride, to fight, to love the desert, to love these outdoor men, to love a woman. That beautiful Spanish girl had spoken to something dead in him, and it had quickened to life. The onset voice of an audacious, unseen girl warned him that presently the still more wonderful thing would happen to him.

Gale imagined he made noise enough as he clumsily pulled on his boots, yet the voices, split by a merry laugh, kept on murmuring outside the door. It was awkward for him, having only one hand available, to lace up his boots. He looked out of the window. Evidently this was at the end of the house. There was a flagstone walk beside which ran a ditch full of swift muddy water. It made a pleasant sound. There were trees strange of form and color to him. He heard bees, birds, chickens, saw the red of roses and green of grass. Then he saw, close to the wall, a tub full of water, and a bench upon which lay basin, soap, towel, comb, and brush. The window was also a door, for under it there was a step.

Gale hesitated a moment, then went out. He stepped naturally, hoping and expecting that the cowboys would hear him. But nobody came. Awkwardly, with left hand, he washed his face. Upon a nail in the wall hung a little mirror by the aid of which Dick combed and brushed his hair. He imagined he looked a most haggard and unshaven wretch. With that, he faced forward, meaning to go around the corner of the house to greet the cowboys and these new-found friends.

Dick had taken but one step when he was halted by laughter and the patter of light feet.

From close around the corner pealed out that sweet voice. "Dad, you'll have your wish and Mama will be wild!"

Dick saw a little foot sweep into view, a white dress, then the swift-moving form of a girl. She was looking backward.

"Dad, I shall fall in love with your new ranger. I will . . . I have. . . ."

Then she plumped squarely into Dick's arms. She started back violently.

Dick saw a fair face, and dark blue, audaciously flashing eyes. Swift as lightning their expression changed to surprise—fear—wonder. For an instant they were level with Dick's, grave, questioning. Suddenly, sweetly she blushed.

"Oh-h!" she faltered.

Then the blush turned to a scarlet fire. She whirled past him and, like a white gleam, was gone.

Dick became conscious of the stronger, thicker beat of his heart. He experienced a singular elevation of spirit. The moment just elapsed had been the one for which he had been ripe, the event upon which strange circumstances had been rushing him.

With a couple of strides he turned the corner. Laddy and Lash were there, talking to a man of burly form. Seen by day both cowboys were gray-haired, red-skinned, and weather-beaten with lean, sharp features and gray eyes so much alike that they might have been brothers.

"Hello, there's the young fellow," spoke up the burly man. "Mister Gale, I'm glad to meet you. My name's Belding."

His greeting was as warm as his hand clasp was long and hard. Gale saw a heavy man of medium height. His head was large and covered with grizzled locks. He wore a short-cropped mustache and chin beard. His skin was brown, and his dark eyes beamed with a genial light.

The cowboys were as cordial as if Dick had been their friend for years.

"Young man, did you run into anything as you came out?" asked Belding with twinkling eyes.

"Why, yes, I met something white and swift, flying by," replied Dick.

"Did she see you?" asked Laddy.

"I think so, but she didn't wait for me to introduce myself."

"That was Nell Burton, my girl, stepdaughter, I should say," said Belding. "She's sure some whirlwind, as Laddy calls her. Come, let's go in and meet the wife."

The house was long, like a barracks, with porch extending all the way, and doors every dozen paces. When Dick was ushered into a sitting room, he was amazed at the light and comfort. This room had two big windows and a door opening into a patio where there were luxuriant grass, roses in bloom, and flowering trees. He heard the slow splashing of water.

In Mrs. Belding, Gale found a woman of noble proportions and striking appearance. Her hair was white. She had a strong, serious, lined face that bore haunting evidences of past beauty. The gaze she bent upon him was almost piercing in its intensity. Her greeting, which seemed to Dick rather slow in coming, was kind but not cordial. Gale's first thought, after he had thanked these good people for their hospitality, was to inquire about Mercedes. He was informed that the Spanish girl had awakened with a considerable fever and nervousness. When, however, her anxiety had been allayed, and her thirst relieved, she had fallen asleep again. Mrs. Belding said the girl had suffered no great hardship, other than mental, and would very soon be rested and well.

"Now, Gale," said Belding, as they sat down while his wife had excused herself to get supper, "the boys, Jim and Laddy, told me about you, and the mix-up at Casita. I'll be glad to take care of the girl till it's safe for your soldier friend to get her out of the country. That won't be very soon, don't mistake me. I don't want to seem over-curious about you. Laddy has interested me in you . . . and straight out I'd like to know what you propose to do now."

"I haven't any plans," replied Dick, and, taking the moment as propitious, he decided to speak frankly concerning himself. "I just drifted down here. My home is in Chicago. When I left school some years ago . . . I'm twenty-five now . . . I went to work for my father. He's . . . he has business interests there. I tried all kinds of inside jobs. I couldn't please my father. I guess I put no real heart in my work. The fact was I didn't know how to work. The governor and I didn't exactly quarrel, but he hurt my feelings, and I quit. Six months or more ago, I came West, and have knocked about from Wyoming southwest to the border. I tried to find congenial work, but nothing ever came my way. To tell you frankly, Mister Belding, I confess indifference, indolence. I believe, though, that all the time I didn't know what I wanted. I've learned . . . well, just lately. . . ."

"What do you want to do?" interposed Belding.

"I want a man's job. I want to do things with my hands. I want action. I want to be outdoors."

Belding nodded his head as if he understood that, and he began to speak again, cut something short, then went on hesitatingly. "Gale . . . you could go home again . . . to the old man . . . it'd be all right?"

"Mister Belding, there's nothing shady in my past. The governor would be glad to have me home. That's the only consolation I've got. But I'm not going. I'm broke. I won't be a tramp. And it's up to me to do something."

"How'd you like to be a border ranger?" asked Belding, laying a hand on Dick's knee. "Part of my job here is United States Inspector of Immigration. I've got that boundary line to patrol . . . to keep out Chinamen and Japs. This revolution has added complications, and I'm looking for smugglers and raiders here any day. You'll not be hired by the U.S. You'll simply be my ranger, same as Laddy and Jim, who have promised to work for me. I'll pay you well, give you a room here, furnish everything down to guns, and the finest horse you ever saw in your life. Your job won't be safe and healthy, sometimes, but it'll be a man's job . . . don't mistake me. You can gamble on having things to do outdoors. Now, what do you say?"

"I accept, and I thank you. I can't say how much," replied Gale earnestly.

"Good. That's settled. Let's go out and tell Laddy and Jim."

Both cowboys expressed satisfaction at the turn of affairs, and then with Belding they set out to take Gale around the ranch. The house, and several outbuildings, were constructed of adobe, which, according to Belding, retained the summer heat on into winter and the winter cold on into summer. These gray-red mud habitations were hideous to look at, and this fact, perhaps, made their really comfortable interiors more vividly a contrast. The wide grounds were covered with luxuriant grass and flowers and different kinds of trees. Gale's interest led him to ask about fig trees and pomegranates, and especially about a beautiful specimen that Belding called paloverde.

Belding explained that the luxuriance of this desert place was due to a few springs and the dammed-up waters of the Río Forlorn. Before he had come to the oasis, it had been inhabited by a Papago Indian tribe, and a few peon families. The oasis lay in an arroyo, a mile wide, and sloped southwest for some ten miles or more. The river went dry most of the year, but enough water was stored in flood season to irrigate the gardens and alfalfa fields.

"I've got one never-failing spring on my place," said Belding. "Fine sweet water. You know what that means in the desert. I like this oasis. The longer I live here the better I like it. There's not a spot in southern Arizona that'll compare with this valley for water or grass or wood. It's beautiful and healthy. Forlorn and lonely, yes, especially for women like my wife and Nell, but I like it. And between you and me, boys, I've something up my sleeve. There's gold dust in the arroyos and there's mineral up in the mountains. If we only had water! This little hamlet has steadily grown since I took up a station here. Why, Casita is no place beside Forlorn River. Pretty soon the Southern Pacific will shoot a railroad branch out here. There are possibilities, and I want you boys to stay with me, and get in on the ground floor. I wish this damn' rebel war was over. . . . Well, here are the corrals and the fields. Gale, take a look at that bunch of horses."

Belding's last remark was made as he led his companions out of shady gardens into the open. Gale saw an adobe shed and a huge pen fenced by strangely twisted and contorted branches or trunks of mesquite, and beyond these wide flat fields, green—a dark rich green— and dotted with beautiful horses. There were whites and blacks and bays and grays. In his admiration Gale searched his memory to see if he could remember the like of these magnificent animals, and had to admit that the only ones he could compare with them were the Arabian steeds.

"Every rancher loves his horses," said Belding. "When I was in the Panhandle, I had some fine stock. But these are Mexican. They came from Durango where they were bred. Mexican horses are the finest in the world, bar none."

"Shore I reckon I savvy why you don't sleep nights," drawled Laddy. "I see a greaser out there . . . no, it's an Indian."

"That's my Papago herdsman. I keep strict watch over the horses now, day and night. Lord, how I'd hate to have Rojas or Salazar . . . any of those bandit rebels . . . find my horses. Gale, can you ride?"

Dick modestly replied that he could, according to the Eastern idea of horsemanship.

"You don't need to be half horse to ride one of that bunch. But over there in the other field I've iron-jawed broncos I wouldn't want you to tackle . . . except to see the fun. I've an outlaw I'll gamble even Laddy can't ride."

"So. How much'll you gamble?" asked Laddy instantly.

The ringing of a bell, which Belding said was a call to supper, turned the men back toward the house. Facing that way, Gale saw dark, beetling ridges rising from the oasis and leading up to bare black mountains. He had heard Belding call them the No Name Mountains and somehow the appellation suited these lofty, mysterious, frowning peaks.

It was not until they reached the house, and were about to go in, that Belding chanced to discover Gale's crippled hand.

"What an awful injury!" he exclaimed. "Where the devil did you get that?"

"I stove in my knuckles on Rojas," replied Dick.

"You did that in one punch? Say, I'm glad it wasn't me you hit! Why didn't you tell me? That's a bad hand. Those cuts are full of dirt and sand. Inflammation's setting in. It's got to be dressed . . . Nell!" he called.

There was no answer. He called again, louder.

"Mother, where's the girl?"

"She's there in the dining room," replied Mrs. Belding.

"Did she hear me?" he inquired impatiently.

"Of course."

"Nell!" roared Belding.

This brought results. Dick saw a glimpse of golden hair and a white dress in the door. But they were not visible longer than a second.

"Dad, what's the matter?" asked a voice that was still as sweet as formerly but now rather small and constrained.

"Bring the antiseptics, cotton, bandages . . . and things out here. Hurry now."

Belding fetched a pail of water and a basin from the kitchen. His wife followed him out and, upon seeing Dick's hand, was all solicitude. Then Dick heard light, quick footsteps, but he did not look up.

"Nell, this is Dick Gale, who came with the boys last night," said Belding. "He's got an awful hand. Got it pummeling that greaser, Rojas. I want you to dress it. Gale, this is my stepdaughter, Nell Burton, of whom I spoke. She's some good when there's anybody sick or hurt. Shove out your fist, my boy, and let her get at it. Supper's nearly ready."

Dick felt that same strange thick beat of his heart, yet he had never been cooler in his life. More than anything else in the world he wanted to look at Nell Burton; however, divining that the situation might be embarrassing for her, he refrained from looking up. She began to bathe his injured knuckles. He noted the softness, the deftness of her touch, and then it seemed her fingers were not quite so steady as they might have been. Still, in a moment, they appeared to become surer in their work. She had beautiful hands, not too large, although certainly not small, and they were strong, brown, supple. He observed next, with a stealthy upward-stealing glance, that she had rolled up her sleeves, exposing fine round arms, graceful in line. Her skin was brown—no, it was more gold than brown. It had a wonderful clear tint. Dick stoically lowered his eyes then, putting off as long as possible the alluring moment when he was to look into her face. That would be a fateful moment. He played with a certain strange joy of anticipation. When, however, she sat down beside him and rested his injured hand in her lap as she cut bandages, she was so thrillingly near that he yielded to an irrepressible desire to look up. She had a sweet fair face, warmly tinted with that same healthy golden-brown sunburn. Her hair was light gold and abundant, a waving mass. Her eyes were shaded by long downcast lashes, yet through them he caught a gleam of blue.

Despite the stir within him, Gale, seeing she was now absorbed in her task, critically studied her with a second, closer gaze. She was a sweet, wholesome, joyous, pretty girl.

"Shore it must've hurt?" required Laddy, who sat an interested spectator.

"Yes, I confirm it did," replied Dick slowly, with his eyes on Nell's face. "But I didn't mind. . . ."

The girl's lashes swept up swiftly in surprise. She had taken his words literally. But the dark blue eyes met his for only a fleeting second. Then the warm tint in her cheeks turned as red as her lips. Hurriedly she finished tying the bandage and rose to her feet. She was tall, superb of build.

"I thank you," said Gale, also rising.

With that Belding appeared in the doorway and, finding the operation concluded, called them in to supper. Dick had the use of only one arm, and he certainly was keenly aware of the shy, silent girl across the table, but in spite of these considerable handicaps he eclipsed both hungry cowboys in the assault upon Mrs. Belding's bounteous supper. Belding talked, the cowboys talked more or less, Mrs. Belding put in a word now and then, and Dick managed to find brief intervals when it was possible for him to say "yes" or "no." He observed gratefully that no one around the table seemed to be aware of his enormous appetite.

After supper, having a favorable opportunity when for the moment no one was at hand, Dick went out through the yard, past the gardens and fields, and climbed the first knoll. From that vantage point he looked out on the little hamlet, somewhat to his right, and was surprised at its extent, its considerable number of adobe houses. The overhanging mountains, ragged and darkening, a great heave of splintered, sundered rock, rather chilled and affronted him.

Westward the setting sun gilded a spiked, frost-colored, limitless expanse of desert. It awed Gale. Everywhere rose blunt broken ranges or isolated groups of mountains. Yet the desert stretched away and down between and beyond them. When the sun set and Gale could not see so far, he felt a relief.

That grand and austere attraction of distance gone, he saw the desert nearer at hand—the valley at his feet. What a strange, gray, somber place! There was a lighter strip of gray winding down between darker hues. This, he realized presently, was the riverbed, and he saw how the pools of water narrowed and diminished in size till he lost them—ashes in gray sand. This was the rainy season, near its end, and here a little river struggled hopelessly, forlornly to live on the desert. He received a potent impression of the nature of that blasted age-worn waste that he had divined was to give him strength and work and love.

CHAPTER FIVE:
A DESERT ROSE

Belding assigned Dick to a little room that had no windows, but two doors, one opening into the patio, the other into the yard on the west side of the house. It contained only the barest necessities for comfort. Dick mentioned the baggage he had left in the hotel at Casita, and it was Belding's opinion that a try to recover this property would be rather risky. On the moment, Richard Gale was probably not popular with the Mexicans at Casita. So Dick bade good bye to fine suits of clothes and linen, with a feeling that, as he had said farewell to an idle and useless past, it was just as well not to have any old luxuries as reminders. As he possessed, however, not a thing save the clothes on his back, and not even a handkerchief, he expressed regret that he did come to Forlorn River a beggar.

"Beggar, hell!" exploded Belding with his eyes snapping in the lamplight. "Money's the last thing we think of out here. All the same, Gale, if you stick, you'll be rich."

"It wouldn't surprise me," replied Dick thoughtfully. But he was not thinking of material wealth. Then, as he viewed his stained and torn shirt, he laughed and said: "Belding, long as there are girls like Mercedes and Miss Nell around, while I'm getting rich, I'd rather have a clean shirt . . . and such."

"We've a little Mex store in town, and what you can't get there the womenfolks will make for you."

When Dick lay down, he was dully conscious of pain

and headache, that he did not feel well. Despite this, and a mind thronging with memories and anticipation, he succumbed to weariness, and soon fell asleep.

It was light when he awoke but a strange brightness seen through what seemed blurred eyes. A moment passed before his mind worked clearly, and then he had to make an effort to think. He was dizzy. When he essayed to lift his right arm, an excruciating pain made him desist. Then he discovered that his arm was badly swollen, and the hand had burst its bandages. The injured member was red, angry, inflamed, and twice its normal size. He felt hot all over, and a raging headache consumed him.

Belding came stamping into the room.

"Hello, Dick. Do you know it's late? How's the busted fist this morning?"

Dick tried to sit up, but his effort was a failure. He got about half up, then felt himself weakly sliding back.

"I guess . . . I'm pretty sick," he said.

He saw Belding lean over him, feel his face, and speak, and then everything seemed to drift, not into darkness, but into some region where he had dim perceptions of gray, moving things and of voices that were remote. Then there came an interval when all was blank. He knew not whether it was one of minutes or hours, but, after it, he had a clearer mind. He slept, awakened during night time, and slept again. When he again opened his eyes, the room was sunny, and cool with a fragrant breeze that blew through the open door. Dick felt better, but he had no particular desire to move or talk or eat. He had, however, a burning thirst. Mrs. Belding visited him often; her husband came in several times, and once Nell slipped in noiselessly. Even this last event aroused no interest in Dick.

On the next day he was very much improved.

"We've been afraid of blood poisoning," said Belding. "But my wife thinks the danger's past. You'll have to rest that arm for a while."

Ladd and Jim came peeping in at the door.

"Come in, boys. He can have company, the more the better, if it'll keep him content. He mustn't move, that's all."

The cowboys entered, slow, easy, cool, kind-voiced.

"Shore it's tough," said Ladd, after he had greeted Dick. "You look used up."

Jim Lash wagged his half bald, sunburned head. "Must've been more'n tough for Rojas."

"Gale, Laddy tells me one of our neighbors, fellow named Carter, is going to Casita," put in Belding. "Here's a chance to get word to your friend, the soldier."

"Oh, that will be fine!" exclaimed Dick. "I declare I'd forgotten Thorne. How is Miss Castañeda? I hope. . . ."

"She's all right, Gale. Been up and around the patio for two days. Like all the Spanish . . . the real thing . . . she's made of Damascus steel. We've been getting acquainted. She and Nell made friends at once. I'll call them in."

He closed the door leading out into the yard, explaining that he did not want to take chances of Mercedes's presence becoming known to neighbors. Then he went to the patio and called.

Both girls came in, Mercedes leading. Like Nell she wore white and she had a red rose in her hand. Dick would scarcely have recognized anything about her except her eyes, and the way she carried her little head, and her beauty burst upon him, strange and anew. She was swift, impatient in her movements to reach his side.

"*Señor*, I am so sorry you were ill . . . so happy you are better."

Dick greeted her, offering his left hand gravely, apologizing for the fact that owing to a late infirmity he could not offer the right. Her smile exquisitely combined sympathy, gratitude, admiration. Then Dick spoke to Nell, likewise offering his hand, which she took shyly. Her reply was a murmured, unintelligible one, but her eyes were glad, and the tint in her cheeks threatened to rival the hue of the rose she carried.

Everybody chatted then, except Nell, who had apparently lost her voice. Presently Dick remembered to speak of the matter of getting news to Thorne.

"*Señor*, may I write to him? Will someone take a letter? I shall hear from him," she said with her white hands moving.

"Assuredly. I guess poor Thorne is almost crazy. I'll write to him. No, I can't, with this crippled hand."

"That'll be all right, Gale," said Belding. "Nell will write for you. She writes all my letters."

So Belding arranged it, and Mercedes flew away to her room to write, while Nell fetched pen and paper and seated herself beside Gale's bed to take his dictation.

What with watching Nell and trying to catch her glance, and listening to Belding's talk with the cowboys, Dick was hard put to dictate any kind of a creditable letter. Nell met his gaze once—then no more. The color came and went in her cheeks, and sometimes, when he told her to write so and so, there was a demure smile on her lips. She was laughing at him. And Belding was talking over the risks involved in a trip to Casita.

"Shore I'll ride in with the letters," Ladd said.

"No you won't," replied Belding. "That bandit outfit will be laying for you."

"Well, I reckon, if they was, I wouldn't be uncommon grieved."

"I'll tell you, boys, I'll ride in myself with Carter. There's business I can see to, and I'm curious to know what the rebels are doing. Laddy, keep one eye open while I'm gone. See the horses are locked up. Gale, I'm going to Casita myself. Ought to get back tomorrow sometime. I'll be ready to start in an hour. Have your letter ready, and say . . . if you want to write home, it's a chance. Sometimes we don't go to the P.O. in a month."

He tramped out, followed by the tall cowboys, and then Dick was able to bring his letter to a close. Mercedes came back and her eyes were shining. Dick imagined a letter received from her would be something of an event for a fellow. Then, remembering Belding's suggestion, he decided to profit by it.

"May I trouble you to write another for me?" asked Dick, as he received the letter from Nell.

"It's no trouble. I'm sure . . . I'd be pleased," she replied.

That was altogether a wonderful speech of hers, Dick thought, because the words were the first coherent ones she had spoken to him.

"May I stay?" asked Mercedes, smiling.

"By all means," he answered, and then he settled back, and began. Presently he paused, partly because of genuine emotion, and stole a look from under his hand at Nell. She wrote swiftly and her downcast face seemed to be softer in its expression of sweetness. If she had in the very least been drawn to him—but that was absurd, impossible! It dawned on him that for the brief instant when Nell had met his gaze she had lost her shyness. It was a woman's questioning eyes that had pierced through him.

During the rest of the day Gale was content to lie still on his bed, thinking and dreaming, dozing at intervals, and watching the lights change on the mountain peaks, feeling the warm, fragrant desert wind that blew in upon him. He seemed to have lost the faculty of estimating time. A long while, strong in its effect upon him, appeared to have passed since he had met Thorne. He accepted things as he felt them, and repudiated his intelligence. His old inquisitive habit of mind returned. Did he love Nell? Was he only attracted for the moment? What was the use of worrying about her or himself? He refused to answer, and deliberately gave himself up to dreams of her sweet face, her red lips, her strong and beautiful body, and of that last dark-blue glance.

Next day he believed he was well enough to leave his room, but Mrs. Belding would not permit him to do so. She was kind, soft-handed, motherly, and she was always coming in to minister to his comfort. This attention was sincere, not in the least forced, yet Gale felt that the friendliness so manifest in the others of the household did not extend to her. He sensed something that a little thought persuaded him was antagonism. It surprised him, perplexed him, hurt him. He had never been much of a success with girls and young married women, but their mothers and old people had generally been fond of him. Still, although Mrs. Belding's hair was snow-white, she did not impress him as being old. He reflected that there might come a time when it would be desirable, far beyond any ground of everyday friendly kindliness, to have Mrs. Belding be well disposed toward him. So he thought about her, and pondered how to make her like him. It did not take very long for Dick to discover that he liked her. Her face, except when she smiled, was thought-ful and sad. But it seemed too strong, too intense, too nobly lined. It was a face to make one serious. Like a haunting shadow, like a phantom of happier years, the sweetness of Nell's face was there, an infinite mark of beauty that had been transmitted to the daughter. Dick believed Mrs. Belding's friendship and motherly love were worth much striving to win, entirely aside from any more selfish motive. He decided both would be hard to get. Often he felt her deep, penetrating gaze upon him, and although this in no wise embarrassed him—for he had no shameful secrets of past or present—it showed him how useless it would be to try to conceal anything from her. Naturally, on first impulse, he wanted to hide his interest in the daughter, but he resolved to be ab-solutely frank and true, and through that win or lose. Moreover, if Mrs. Belding asked him any questions about his home, his family, his connections, he would not avoid direct and truthful answers.

Toward evening Gale heard the tramp of horses, and Belding's hearty voice. Presently the rancher strode in upon Gale, shaking the gray dust from his broad shoul-ders, and waving a letter.

"Hello Dick. Good news and bad!" he said, putting the

letter in Dick's hand. "Had no trouble finding your friend, Thorne. Looked like he'd been drunk for a week! Say, he nearly threw a fit. I never saw a fellow so wild with joy. He was sure you and Mercedes were lost in the desert. He wrote two letters that I brought. Don't mistake me, boy, it was some fun with Mercedes just now. I teased her, wouldn't give her the letter. You ought to have seen her eyes. If ever you see a black and white desert hawk swoop down upon a quail, then you'll know how Mercedes pounced upon her letter. Well, Casita is one hell of a place these days. I tried to get your baggage, and think I made a mistake. We're going to see travel toward Forlorn River. The Federal garrison got reinforcements from somewhere and is holding out. There's been fighting for three days. The rebels have a string of flat railroad cars, all iron, and they ran this up within range of the barricades. They've got some machine-guns, and they're going to lick the Federals sure. There are dead soldiers in the ditches. Mexican non-combatants lying dead in the streets . . . and buzzards everywhere. It's reported that Campo, the rebel leader, is on the way up from Sinaloa, and that Huerta, a Federal general, is coming to relieve the garrison. I don't take much stock in reports. But there's hell in Casita, all right."

"Do you think we'll have trouble out here?" asked Dick excitedly.

"Sure. Some kind of trouble sooner or later," replied Belding gloomily. "Why, you can stand on my ranch and step over into Mexico. Laddy says we'll lose horses and other stock in night raids. Jim Lash doesn't look for any worse. But Jim isn't as well acquainted with greasers as I am. Anyway, my boy, as soon as you can hold a bridle and a gun, you'll be on the job, don't mistake me."

"With Laddy and Jim?" asked Dick, trying to be cool.

"Sure. With them and me, and by yourself."

Dick drew a deep breath, and, even after Belding had departed, he forgot for a moment about the letter in his hand. Then he unfolded the paper and read:

Dear Dick:

You've more than saved my life. To the end of my days you'll be the one man to whom I owe everything. Words fail to express my feelings. This must be a brief note. Belding is waiting, and I used up most of the time writing to Mercedes. I like Belding. He was not unknown to me, though I never met or saw him before. You'll be interested to learn that he's the unadulterated article, the real Western goods. I've heard of some of his stunts and they made my hair curl. Dick, your luck is staggering. The way Belding spoke of you was great. But you deserve it, old man.

I'm leaving Mercedes in your charge, subject of course to advice from Belding. Take care of her, Dick, for my life is wrapped up in her. By all means, keep her from being seen by Mexicans, no matter who. We are sitting tight here, doing nothing. If some action doesn't come soon, it'll be darned strange.

Things are centering this way. There's scrapping right along and people have begun to move. We're still patrolling the line eastward of Casita. It'll be impossible to keep any tab on the line west of Casita, for it's too rough. That cactus desert is awful. Cowboys or rangers with desert-bred horses might keep raiders and smugglers from crossing. But, if cavalrymen could stand that waterless wilderness, which I much doubt, their horses would drop under them.

If things do quiet down before my commission expires, I'll get leave of absence, run out to Forlorn River, marry my beautiful Spanish princess, and take her to a civilized country, where, I opine, every son-of-a-gun who sees her will lose his head, and drive me mad. It's my great luck, old pal, that you are a fellow who never seemed to care a damn about pretty girls. So you won't give me the double-cross and run off with Mercedes . . . carry her off, like the villain in the play, I mean.

That reminds me of Rojas. Oh, Dick, it was glorious!

*You didn't do anything to the dandy rebel! Not at all!
You merely caressed him . . . gently moved him to one
side. Dick, harken to these glad words. Rojas is in the
hospital. I was interested to inquire. He had a smashed
finger, a dislocated collar bone, three broken ribs, and a
fearful gash on his face. He'll be in the hospital for a
month. Dick, when I meet that pig-headed dad of yours,
I'm going to give him the surprise of his life.*

*Send me a line whenever anyone comes in from F.R.
and enclose Mercedes's letter in yours. Take care of her,
Dick, and may the future hold in store for you some of the
sweetness I know now!*

Faithfully yours,
Thorne

Dick reread the letter, then folded it, and placed it under his pillow.

"Never care for pretty girls, huh?" he soliloquized.
"George, I never saw any till I struck southern Arizona.
Guess I'd better make up for lost time."

While he was eating his supper, with appetite rapidly returning to normal, Ladd and Jim came in, bowing their
tall heads to get in the door. Their friendly advances were
singularly welcome to Gale, and he listened. Jim Lash
had heard from Belding the result of the mauling given to
Rojas by Dick, and talked about what a grand thing that
was. Ladd had a good deal to say about Belding's horses.
It took no keen judge of human nature to see that horses
constituted Ladd's ruling passion.

"I've had wimmin go back on me, but never no hoss!"
declared Ladd, and manifestly that was a controlling
truth with him. "Shore it's a cinch Belding is a-goin' to
lose some of them hosses. You can search me if I don't
think there'll be more doin' on the border here than along
the Río Grande. We're just the same as on greaser soil.
Mebbe we don't stand no such chance of bein' shot up as

we would across the line. But who's goin' to give up his hosses without a fight? Half the time, when Belding's stock is out of the alfalfa, it's grazin' over the line. He thinks he's careful about them hosses, but he ain't."

"Looka here, Laddy, you cain't believe all you hear," replied Jim seriously. "I reckon we mightn't have any trouble."

"Back up, Jim. Shore you're standin' on your bridle. I ain't goin' much on reports. Remember that American we met in Casita, the prospector who'd just gotten out of Sonora? He had some story, he had. Swore he'd killed seventeen greasers, breakin' through the rebel line 'round the mine where he an' other Americans were corralled. The next day, when I met him again, he was drunk an' then he told me he'd shot thirty greasers. The chances are he did kill some. But reports are exaggerated. There are miners fightin' for life down in Sonora, you can gamble on that. An' the truth is bad enough. Take Rojas's harryin' of the *señorita*, for instance. Can you beat that? Shore, Jim, there's more doin' than the raidin' of a few hosses. An' Forlorn River is goin' to get hers."

Another dawn found Gale so much recovered that he arose and looked after himself, not, however, without considerable difficulty and rather disheartening twinges of pain. Sometime during the morning he heard the girls in the patio and called to ask if he might join them. He received one response, a mellow: "*Si, señor.*" It was not as much as he wanted, but, considering that it was enough, he went out. He had not as yet visited the patio, and surprise and delight were in store for him. He found himself lost in a labyrinth of green and rose-bordered walks. He strolled around, discovering that the patio was a courtyard, open at one end, but he failed to discover the young ladies. So he called again. The answer came from the center of the square. After stooping to get under shrubs and wading through bushes, he entered an open sandy circle, full of magnificent and murderous-looking cactus plants, strange to him; on the other side, in the shade of a beautiful tree, he found the girls—Mercedes sitting in a hammock, Nell upon a blanket.

"What a beautiful tree!" he exclaimed. "I never saw one like that. What is it?"

"Paloverde," replied Nell.

"*Señor*, paloverde means green tree," added Mercedes.

This desert tree, which had struck Dick as so new and strange and beautiful, was not striking on account of size, for it was small, scarcely reaching higher than the roof, but rather because of its exquisite color of green, trunk and branch alike, and owing to the odd fact that it seemed not to possess leaves. All the tree from ground to tiny flat twigs was a soft polished green. It bore no thorns.

Right then and there began Dick's education in desert growths, and he felt that, even if he had not had such charming teachers, he would still have been absorbed, for the patio was full of desert wonders. A twisting-trunked tree with full foliage of small gray leaves Nell called a mesquite. Then Dick remembered the name and now he saw where the desert got its pale gray color. A huge, lofty, fluted column of green was a saguaro, or giant cactus. Another odd-shaped cactus, resembling the legs of an inverted devil fish, bore the name ocotillo. Each branch rose, high and symmetrical, furnished with sharp blades that seemed to be at once leaves and thorns. Yet another cactus interested Gale, and it looked like a huge, low barrel covered with green-ribbed cloth and long thorns. This was the *bisnaga*, or barrel cactus. According to Nell and Mercedes, this plant was a happy exception to its desert neighbors, for it secreted water that had many times saved the lives of men. Last of the cacti to attract Gale, and the one to make him shiver, was a low plant, consisting of stem and many rounded protuberances of a frosty steely white and covered with long, murderous spikes. From this plant the desert got its frosty glitter. It was as stiff, as unyielding as steel, and bore the name cholla.

Dick's enthusiasm was contagious and his earnest de-

sire to learn was flattering to his teachers. When it came to
assimilating Spanish, however, he did not appear to be so
apt a pupil. He managed, after many trials, to acquire
"*buenos días*" and "*buenas tardes*" and "*señorita*" and "*gra-
cias,*" and a few other short terms. Dick was indeed eager
to get a little smattering of Spanish, and perhaps he was
not really quite so stupid as he pretended to be. It was delightful to be taught by a beautiful Spaniard, who was so
gracious and intense and magnetic of personality, and by
a sweet American girl who moment by moment forgot her
shyness. Gale wished to prolong the lessons.

So that was the beginning of many afternoons in which
he learned desert lore and Spanish verbs, and something
else that he dared not name.

Nell Burton had never shown to Gale that daring side
of her character that had been so suggestively defined in
Belding's terse description and Ladd's encomiums, and
in her own audacious speech and merry laugh and flashing eye of that never to be forgotten first meeting. She
might have been an entirely different girl. But Gale remembered, and, when the ice had been broken between
them, he was always trying to surprise her into her real
self. There were moments that fairly made him tingle
with expectation. Yet he saw little more than a ghost of
her vivacity and never a gleam of that individuality that
Belding had called a devil. The few times Dick had been
left alone with her in the patio, upon occasion when Mercedes absented herself for a few moments, were ones
wherein Nell grew suddenly unresponsive and restrained, or else left him upon some trifling and transparent pretext. On the last occasion of this kind, Mercedes
returned to find Dick staring disconsolately at the rose-
bordered path where Nell had evidently vanished. The
Spanish girl was wonderful in her divination. Her magnificent eyes burned him.

"*Señor* Dick!" she cried.

Dick looked at her, soberly nodded his head, and then
he laughed. Mercedes had seen through him in one swift

glance. Her white hand touched his in wordless sympathy and thrilled him. This Spanish girl was all fire and passion and love. She understood him; she was his friend; she pledged him what he felt would be the most subtle and powerful influence.

Little by little he learned details of Nell's varied yet uneventful life. She had lived in many places. As a child she remembered moving from town to town, of going to school among schoolmates who she never had time to know. Lawrence, Kansas, where she studied for several years, was the later exception to this changeful nature of her schooling. Then she moved to Still-water, Oklahoma, from there to Austin, Texas, and on to Waco, where her mother met and married Belding. They lived in New Mexico a while, in Tucson, Arizona, in Douglas, and finally had come to lonely Forlorn River.

"Mother could never live in one place any length of time," said Nell, "and, since we've been in the Southwest, she has never ceased trying to find some trace of her father. He was last heard of in Nogales fourteen years ago. She thinks Grandfather was lost in the Sonora Desert. And every place we go is worse. Oh, I love the desert. But I'd like to go back to Lawrence . . . or to see Chicago or New York . . . some of the places I've heard about. I remember the college at Lawrence, though I was only twelve. I saw races . . . and once a real football game. Since then, I've read magazines and papers about big football games and I was always fascinated. Mister Gale, of course you've seen games?"

"Yes, a few," replied Dick, and he laughed a little. It was on his lips then to tell her about some of the famous games in which he had participated. But he refrained from exploiting himself. There was little, however, of the color and sound and cheer, of the violent action and rush and battle incidental to a big college football game that he did not succeed in making Mercedes and Nell feel just as if they had been there. They hung, breathless and wide-eyed, upon his words.

Someone else was present at the latter part of Dick's narrative. The moment he became aware of Mrs. Belding's presence, he remembered fancying he had heard her call, and now he was certain she had done so. Mercedes and Nell, however, had been and still were oblivious to everything except Dick's recital. He saw Mrs. Belding cast a strange, intent glance upon Nell, then turn and go silently back through the patio. Dick concluded his talk, somewhat at the expense of the brilliant beginning.

Dick was haunted by the strange expression he had caught on Mrs. Belding's face, especially the look in her eyes. It had been one of repressed pain liberated in a flash of certainty. The mother had seen just as quickly as Mercedes how far he had gone on the road of love. Perhaps she had seen more— even more than he dared hope. The incident roused Gale. He could not understand Mrs. Belding, nor why that look of hers, that seemingly baffled, hopeless look of a woman who saw the inevitable forces of life and could not thwart them, should cause him perplexity and distress. He wanted to go to her and tell her how he felt about Nell, but fear of absolute destruction of his hopes held him back. He would wait. Nevertheless, an instinct that was perhaps akin to self-preservation prompted him to want to let Nell know the state of his mind. A million words crowded his brain, seeking utterance. Who and what he was, how he loved her, the work he expected to take up soon, his longings, hopes, and plans— all these things he wanted to tell of, at length. But something checked him. And the repression made him so thoughtful and quiet, even melancholy, that he went outdoors to try to throw off the mood. The sun was yet high and a dazzling white light enveloped valley and peaks. He felt that the wonderful sunshine was the dominant feature of that arid region. It was like white gold. It had burned its color in a face he knew. It was going to warm his blood, brown his skin. A hot languid breeze, so dry that he felt his lips shrink with its contact, came from the desert, and it seemed to smell of wide-open untainted places where sand blew and strange pungent plants gave a bittersweet tang to the air.

When he returned to the house, some hours later, his room had been put in order. In the middle of the white coverlet on his table lay a fresh red rose. Nell had dropped it there. Dick picked it up, feeling a surge in his breast. It was a bud just beginning to open, to show down between its petals a dark-red, unfolding heart. How fragrant it was, how exquisitely delicate, how beautiful its inner hue of red, deep and dark, the crimson of life blood. Had Nell left it there by accident or by intent? Was it merely kindness or a girl's subtlety? Was it a message couched elusively, a symbol, a hope, in a half-blown desert rose?

CHAPTER SIX:
THE YAQUI

It was evening of a lowering December day. Some fifty miles west of Forlorn River a horseman rode along an old, dimly defined trail. From time to time he halted to study the lay of the land ahead. It was bare, somber, ridged desert, covered with dim-colored greasewood and stunted prickly pear. Distant mountains hemmed in the valley, raising black spurs above the round lomas and the square-walled mesas.

This lonely horseman bestrode a steed of magnificent build, perfectly white except for a dark bar of color running down the noble head from ears to nose. Sweat-caked dust stained the long flanks. The horse had been running. His mane and tail were laced and knotted to keep their length out of reach of grasping cactus and brush. Clumsy, homemade leather shields covered the front of his forelegs and ran up well to his wide breast. What other-wise would have been muscular symmetry of limb was marred by many a scar and many a bump. He was lean, gaunt, worn, a huge machine of muscle and bone, beautiful only in head and mane, a weight carrier, a horse strong and fierce like the desert that had bred him.

The rider fitted the horse as he fitted the saddle. He was a young man of exceedingly powerful physique, wide-shouldered, long-armed, big-legged. His lean face, where it was not red, blistered, and peeling, was the hue of bronze. He had a dark eye, a falcon gaze, roving and keen. His jaw was prominent and set, mastiff-like; his lips were stern. It was youth, with its softness not yet quite burned and hardened away, that kept the whole cast of his face from being ruthless.

This young man was Dick Gale, but not the listless traveler, not the lounging wanderer who two months before had by chance dropped into Casita. Friendship, chivalry, love—the deep-seated, unplumbed emotions that had been stirred into being with all their incalculable power for spiritual change had rendered different the meaning of life. In the moment almost of their realization the desert had claimed Gale and had drawn him into its crucible. The desert had multiplied weeks into years. Heat, thirst, hunger, loneliness, toil, fear, ferocity, pain—he knew them all. He had felt them all, the white sun with its glazed, coalescing, lurid fire; the caked, split lips and rasping, dry-puffed tongue; the sickening ache in the pit of the stomach; the insupportable silence, the empty space, the utter desolation, the contempt of life; the weary ride, the long climb, the plod in sand, the search, search, search for water; the sleepless night alone, the watch and wait, the dread of ambush, the swift flight; the fierce pursuit of men wild as Bedouins and as fleet, the willingness to deal sudden death; the pain of poison thorn, the stinging tear of lead through flesh, and that strange paradox of the burning desert, the cold at night, the piercing icy wind, the dew that penetrated to the marrow, the numbing desert cold of the dawn.

Beyond any dream of adventure he had ever had, beyond any wild story he had ever read, had been his experience with those hard-riding rangers, Ladd and Lash. Then he had traveled alone the 100 miles of desert between Forlorn River and the Sonoyta Oasis. Ladd's prophecy of trouble on the border had been mild compared to what had become the actuality. With rebel occupancy of the garrison at Casita, outlaws, bandits, raiders in rioting bands had spread westward. Like troops of Arabs, magnificently mounted, they were here, there, everywhere along the line, and, if murder and worse were confined to the Mexican side, pillage and raiding were perpetuated across the border.

Many a dark-skinned raider bestrode one of Belding's fast horses, and, indeed, all except his selected white thoroughbreds had been stolen. So the job of the rangers had become greatly more than a patrolling of the boundary line to keep Japanese and Chinese from being smuggled into the United States. Belding kept close at home to protect his family and to hold his property. But the three rangers, in fulfilling their duty, had incurred risks on their own side of the line, had been outraged, pursued, and injured on the other. Some of the few water holes that had to be reached lay far across the border in Mexican territory. Horses had to drink, men had to drink, and Ladd and Lash were not of the stripe that forsook a task because of danger. Slow to wrath at first, as became men who had long lived peaceful lives, they had at length revolted, and desert vultures could have told a gruesome story. Made a comrade and ally of these border men, Dick Gale had leaped at the desert action and strife with an intensity of heart and a rare physical ability that accounted for the remarkable fact that he had not yet fallen by the way.

On this December afternoon the three rangers, as often, were separated. Lash was far to the westward of Sonoyta, somewhere along Camino del Diablo, that terrible Devil's Road where many desert wayfarers had perished. Ladd had long been overdue in a prearranged meeting with Gale. The fact that Ladd had not shown up miles west of the Papago Well was significant.

The sun had hidden behind clouds all the latter part of that day, an unusual occurrence for that region even in winter. And now, as the light waned suddenly, telling of the hidden sunset, a cold, dry, penetrating wind sprang up and blew in Gale's face. Not at first but by imperceptible degrees it chilled him. He untied his coat from the back of the saddle and put it on. A few cold drops of rain touched his cheek.

He halted upon the edge of a low escarpment. Below him the narrowing valley showed bare black ribs of rock, long, winding gray lines leading down to a central floor where mesquite and cactus dotted the barren landscape. Moving objects, diminutive in size, gray and white in color, arrested Gale's roving sight. They bobbed away for a while, then stopped. They were antelope and they had seen his horse. When he rode on, they started once more, keeping to the lowest level. These wary animals were often desert watchdogs for the ranger: they would betray the proximity of horse or man. With them trotting forward, he made better time for some miles across the valley. When he lost them, caution once more slowed his advance.

The valley sloped up and narrowed, to head into an arroyo where grass began to show gray between the clumps of mesquite. Shadows formed ahead in the hollows, along the walls of the arroyo, under the trees, and they seemed to creep, to rise, to float into a veil cast by the background of bold mountains, at last to claim the skyline. Night was not close at hand, but it was there in the east, lifting upward, drooping downward, encroaching upon the west.

Gale dismounted to lead his horse, to go forward more slowly. He had ridden sixty miles since morning, and he was tired, and a not entirely healed wound in his hip made one leg drag a little. A mile up the arroyo, near its head, lay the Papago Well. The need of water for his horse entailed a risk that otherwise he could have avoided. The well was on Mexican soil. Gale distinguished a faint light flickering through the thin, sharp foliage. Campers were at the well, and, whoever they were, no doubt they had prevented Ladd from meeting Gale. Ladd had gone back to the next water hole, or maybe he was hiding in an arroyo to the eastward, awaiting developments.

Gale turned his horse, not without urge of iron arm and persuasive speech, for the desert steed scented water, and plodded back to the edge of the arroyo, where in a secluded circle of mesquite he halted. The horse snorted his relief at the removal of the heavy-burdened saddle and accoutrements, and, sagging, bent his knees, lowered himself with slow heave, and plunged down to roll in the sand. Gale poured the contents of his larger canteen into his hat and held it to the horse's nose.

"Drink, Sol," he said.

It was but a drop for a thirsty horse, yet Blanco Sol rubbed a wet muzzle against Gale's hand in appreciation. Gale loved the horse and was loved in return. They had saved each other's lives, and had spent long days and nights of desert solitude together. Sol had known other masters, although none so kind as this new one, but it was certain that Gale had never before known a horse.

The spot of secluded ground was covered with bunches of galleta grass upon which Sol began to graze. Gale made a long halter of his lariat to keep the horse from wandering in search of water. Next Gale kicked off the cumbersome *chaparejos* with their flapping, tripping folds of leather over his feet, and, drawing a long rifle from its saddle sheath, he slipped away into the shadows.

The coyotes were howling, not here and there, but in concerted volume at the head of the arroyo. To Dick this was no more reassuring than had been the flickering light of campfire. The wild desert dogs, with their characteristic insolent curiosity, were baying men around a campfire. Gale proceeded slowly, halting every few steps, careful not to brush against the stiff greasewood. In the soft sand his steps made no sound. The twinkling light vanished occasionally, like a jack-o'-lantern, and, when it did show, it seemed still a long way off. Gale was not seeking trouble or inviting danger. Water was the thing that drove him. He must see who these campers were, and then decide how to give Blanco Sol a drink.

A rabbit rustled out of brush at Gale's feet and *thumped* away over the sand. The wind pattered among dry, broken stalks of dead ocotillo. Every little sound brought Gale to a listening pause. The gloom was thickening fast into darkness. It would be a night without starlight. He moved forward, up the pale zigzag aisles between the mesquite. He lost the light for a while, but the coyote chorus told him he was approaching the campfire. Presently the light danced through the black branches, and soon grew into a flame. Stooping low with bushy mesquites between him and the fire, Gale advanced. The coyotes were in full cry. Gale heard the trampling, stamping *thumps* of many hoofs. The sound worried him. Foot by foot he advanced, and finally began to crawl. The wind favored his position so that neither coyotes nor horses could scent him. The nearer he approached the head of the arroyo, where the well was located, the thicker grew the desert vegetation. At length a dead paloverde, with huge black clumps of its parasite mistletoes thick in the branches, marked a distance from the well that Gale considered close enough. Noiselessly he crawled here and there until he secured a favorable position, and then rose to peep from behind his covert.

He saw a bright fire, not a cooking fire, for that would have been low and red, but a crackling blaze of mesquite. Three men were in sight, all close to the burning sticks. They were Mexicans and of the coarse type of raiders, rebels, bandits that Gale had expected to see. One stood up, his back to the fire; another sat with shoulders enveloped in a blanket, and the third lounged in the sand, his feet almost in the blaze. They had cast off belts and weapons. A glint of steel caught Gale's eye. Three short, shiny carbines leaned against a rock. A little to the left, within the circle of light, stood a square house made of adobe bricks. Several untrimmed poles upheld a roof of brush that was partly fallen in. This house was a Papago Indian habitation, and a month before had been occupied by a family that had been murdered or driven off by a roving band of outlaws. A rude corral showed dimly in the edge of firelight, and from a black mass within came the snort and stamp and whinny of horses.

Gale took in the scene in one quick glance, then sank down at the foot of the mesquite. He had naturally ex-

pected to see more men. But the situation was by no
means new. This was one, or part of one of the raider
bands harrying the border. They were stealing horses, or
driving a herd already stolen. These bands were more numerous than the water holes of northern Sonora; they
never camped long at one place; like Arabs they roamed
over the desert all the way from Nogales to Casita. If Gale
had gone peaceably up to this campfire, there were 100
chances that the raiders would kill and rob him to one
chance that they might not. If they recognized him as a
ranger comrade of Ladd and Lash—if they got a glimpse
of Blanco Sol—then Gale would have no chance.

These Mexicans had evidently been at the well some
time. Their horses being in the corral meant that grazing
had been done by day. Gale revolved questions in his
mind. Had this trio of outlaws run across Ladd? It was
not likely, for in that event they might not have been so
comfortable and carefree in camp. Were they waiting for
more members of their gang? That was very probable.
With Gale, however, the most important consideration
was to get his horse to water. Sol must have a drink if it
cost a fight. There was stern reason for Gale to hurry eastward along the trail. He thought it best to go back to
where he had left his horse and not make any decisive
move until daylight.

With the same noiseless care he had exercised in the advance, Gale retreated until it was safe for him to rise and
walk on down the arroyo. He found Blanco Sol contentedly grazing. A heavy dew was falling, and, as the grass
was abundant, the horse did not show the usual restlessness and distress after a dry and exhausting day. Gale carried his saddle, blankets, and bags into the lee of a little
greasewood-covered mound, from around which the
wind had cut the soil, and here in a wash he risked build-
ing a small fire. By this time the wind was piercingly cold.
Gale's hands were numb and he moved them to and fro
over the little blaze. Then he made coffee in a cup, cooked
some slices of bacon on the end of a stick, and took a cou-

ple of hard biscuits from a saddlebag. Of these his meal consisted. After that, he removed the halter from Blanco Sol, intending to leave him free to graze for a while.

Then Gale returned to his little fire, replenished it with short sticks of dead greasewood and mesquite, and, wrapping his blanket around his shoulders, he sat down to warm himself and to wait till it was time to bring in the horse and tie him up.

The fire was inadequate, and Gale was cold, and wet with dew. Hunger and thirst were with him. His bones ached and there was a dull, deep-seated pain throbbing in his unhealed wound. For days unshaven, his beard seemed like a million pricking needles in his blistered skin. He was so tired that, once having settled himself, he did not move hand or foot. The night was dark, dismal, cloudy, windy, growing colder. A moan of wind in the mesquites was occasionally pierced by the high-keyed yelp of a coyote. There were lulls in which the silence seemed to be a thing of stifling, encroaching substance— a thing that enveloped, buried the desert.

Judged by the great average of ideals and conventional standards of life Dick Gale was a starved, lonely, suffering, miserable wretch. But in his case the judgment would have hit only externals, would have missed the vital inner truth. For Gale was happy with a kind of strange wild glory in the privations, the panic, the perils, and the silence and solitude to be endured on this desert land. In the past he had not been of any use to himself or others, and he had never known what it meant to be hungry, cold, tired, lonely. He had never worked for anything. The needs of the day had been provided, and tomorrow and the future looked the same. Danger—peril—toil—these had been words read in books and papers.

In the present he used his hands, his senses, and his wits. He had a duty to a man who relied on his services. He was a comrade, a friend, a valuable ally to riding, fighting rangers. He had spent endless days, weeks that seemed years, alone with a horse, trailing over, climbing

over, hunting over a desert that was harsh and hostile by
nature, and made perilous by the invasion of savage men.
That horse had become human to Gale. And with him
Gale had learned to know the simple needs of existence.
Like dead scales, the superficialities, the falsities, the
habits that had once meant all of life dropped off, useless
things in this stern waste of rock and sand.

Gale's happiness, as far as it concerned the toil and
strife, was perhaps a grim and stoical one. But love abided
with him, and it had engendered and fostered other un-
developed traits—romance and a feeling for beauty and a
keen observance of Nature. He felt pain, but he was never
miserable. He felt the solitude, but he was never lonely.

As he rode across the desert, even though keen eyes
searched for the moving black dots, the rising puffs of
white dust that were warnings, he saw Nell's face in every
cloud. The clean-cut mesas took on the shape of her
straight profile with its strong chin and lips, its fine nose
and forehead. There was always a glint of gold or touch of
red or graceful line or gleam of blue to remind him of her.
Then, at night, her face shone, warm and glowing, flush-
ing and paling in the campfire.

Tonight, as usual, with a keen ear to the wind, Gale listened as one on guard, yet he watched the changing phantom of a sweet face in the embers, and, as he watched, he
thought. The desert developed and multiplied thought. A
thousand sweet faces glowed in the pink and white ashes
of his campfire, the faces of other sweethearts or wives
that had gleamed for other men. Gale was happy in his
thought of Nell, for something, when he was alone this
way in the wilderness, told him she was near him, she
thought of him, she loved him. But there were many men
alone on that vast Southwestern plateau, and where they
saw dream faces, surely for many it was a fleeting flash, a
gleam soon gone, like the hope and the name and the
happiness that had been and was now no more. Often
Gale thought of these hundreds of desert travelers, prospectors, wanderers who had ventured down the Camino

del Diablo, never to be heard of again. Belding had told him of that most terrible of all desert trails—a trail of shifting sands. Lash had traversed it, and brought back stories of buried water holes, of bones bleaching white in the sun, of gold mines as lost as were the prospectors who had sought them, of the merciless Yaqui and his hatred for the Mexican. Gale thought of this trail and the men who had camped along it. For many there had been one night, one campfire that had been the last. This idea seemed to creep in out of the darkness, the loneliness, the silence, and to find a place in Gale's mind, so that it had strange fascination for him. He knew now, as he had never dreamed before, how men drifted into the desert, leaving behind graves, wrecked homes, ruined lives, lost wives and sweethearts. And for every wanderer, every campfire had a phantom face. Gale measured the agony of these men at their last campfire by the joy and promise he traced in the ruddy heart of his own.

By and by Gale remembered what he was waiting for, and, getting up, he took the halter and went out to find Blanco Sol. It was pitch dark now and Gale could not see a rod ahead. He felt his way, and presently, as he rounded a mesquite, he saw Sol's white shape outlined against the blackness. The horse jumped and wheeled, ready to run. It was doubtful if anyone unknown to Sol could ever have caught him. Gale's low call reassured him and he went on grazing. Gale haltered him in the likeliest patch of grass and returned to his camp. There he lifted his saddle into a protected spot, under a low wall of the mound, and laying one blanket on the sand he covered himself with the other and stretched himself for the night.

Here he was out of reach of the wind, but he heard its melancholy moan in the mesquites. There was no other sound. The coyotes had ceased their hungry cries. Gale dropped to sleep, and slept soundly during the first half of the night, and after that he seemed always to be partially awake, aware of increasing cold and damp. The dark mantle turned gray, and then daylight came quickly.

The morning was clear and nipping cold. He threw off the wet blanket, and got up, cramped and half-frozen. A little brisk action was all that was necessary to warm his blood and loosen his muscles, and then he was fresh, tingling, eager. The sun rose in a golden blaze, and the descending valley took on wondrous, changing lines. Then he fetched up Blanco Sol, saddled him, and tied him in the thickest clump of mesquite.

"Sol, we'll have a drink pretty soon," he said, patting the splendid neck.

Gale meant it. He would not eat till he had watered his horse. Sol had gone nearly forty-eight hours without a sufficient drink, and that was long enough, even for a desert-bred beast. No three raiders could keep Gale away from that well. Taking his rifle in hand, he faced up the arroyo. Rabbits were frisking in the short willows and some were so tame he could have kicked them. Gale walked swiftly for a goodly part of the distance, and then, when he saw blue smoke curling up above the trees, he proceeded slowly, with alert eye and ear. From the lay of the land and position of trees seen by daylight he found an easier and safer course than the one he had taken in the dark. And by careful work he was enabled to get closer to the well, and somewhat above it.

The Mexicans were leisurely cooking their morning meal. They had two fires, one for warmth, the other to cook over. Gale had an idea these raiders were familiar to him. It seemed all these border hawks resembled one another—being mostly small of build, wiry, angular, sweaty-faced, and black-haired, and they wore the oddly styled Mexican clothes and sombreros. A slow wrath stirred in Gale as he watched the trio. They showed not the slightest indication of breaking camp. One fellow, evidently the leader, packed a gun at his hip, the only weapon in sight. Gale noted this with speculative eyes. The raiders had slept inside the little adobe house and had not yet brought out the carbines. Next Gale swept his gaze to the corral in which he saw more than a dozen horses, some of them fine animals. They were stamping and whistling, fighting one another, and pawing the dirt. This was entirely natural behavior for desert horses penned in when they wanted to get at water and grass.

But suddenly one of the blacks, a big shaggy fellow, shot up his ears and pointed his nose over the top of the fence. He whistled. Other horses looked in the same direction, and their ears went up, and they, too, whistled. Gale knew that other horses or men, very likely both, were approaching. But the Mexicans did not hear the alarm, or show any interest if they did. These mescal-drinking raiders were not scouts. It was notorious how easily they could be surprised or ambushed. Mostly they were ignorant thick-skulled peons. They were wonderful horsemen, and could go along without food or water, but they had no other accomplishments or attributes calculated to help them in desert warfare. They had poor sight, poor hearing, poor judgment, and, when excited, they resembled crazed ants running wild.

Gale saw two Indians on burros come riding up the other side of the knoll upon which the adobe house stood, and apparently they were not aware of the presence of the Mexicans, for they came on up the path. One Indian was a Papago. The other man, striking in appearance for other reasons than that he seemed to be about to fall from the burro, Gale took to be a Yaqui. These travelers had absolutely nothing for an outfit except a blanket and a half empty bag. They came over the knoll and down the path toward the well, turned a corner of the house, and completely surprised the raiders.

Gale heard a short, shrill cry, strangely high and wild, and this came from one of the Indians. It was answered by hoarse shouts. Then the leader of the trio, the Mexican who packed a gun, pulled it and fired point-blank. He missed once—and again. At the third shot the Papago shrieked and tumbled off his burro to fall in a heap. The other Indian swayed, as if the taking away of the support lent by his comrade had brought collapse, and with the fourth shot he, too, slipped to the ground.

The reports had frightened the horses in the corral, and the vicious black, crowding the rickety bars, broke them down. He came plunging out. Two of the Mexicans ran for him, catching him by nose and mane, and the third ran to block the gateway.

Then with a splendid vaulting mount the Mexican with the gun leaped to the back of the horse. He yelled and waved his gun, and urged the black forward. The other raiders yelled likewise. The manner of all three was savagely jocose. They were having sport. The two on the ground began to dance and jabber. The mounted leader shot again, and then stuck like a leech upon the bare back of the rearing black. It was a vain show of horsemanship. Then this Mexican, by some strange grip, brought the horse down, plunging almost upon the body of the Indian that had fallen last.

Gale stood aghast, with his rifle clutched tightly. He could not divine the intention of the raider, but he suspected something strikingly brutal. The horse answered to that cruel guiding hand, yet he swerved and bucked. He reared aloft, pawing the air, wildly snorting, then he plunged down upon the prostrate Indian. Even in the act, the intelligent animal tried to keep from striking the body with his hoofs. But that was not possible. A yell hideous in its passion signaled this feat of horsemanship.

The Mexican made no move to trample the body of the Papago. He turned the black to ride, again, over the other Indian. That brought into Gale's mind what he had heard—of a Mexican's hate for a Yaqui. It recalled the barbarism of these savage peons, and the war of extermination being waged upon the Yaquis.

Suddenly Gale was horrified to see the Yaqui writhe and raise a feeble hand. The action brought renewed and more savage cries from the Mexicans. The horse snorted in terror.

Gale could bear no more. He took a quick shot at the rider. He missed the moving figure, but hit the horse. There was a bound, a horrid scream, a mighty plunge, then the horse went down, giving the Mexican a stunning fall. Both beast and man lay still.

Gale rushed from his cover to intercept the other raiders before they could reach the house and their weapons. One fellow yelled and ran wildly in the opposite direction; the other stood stricken in his tracks. Gale ran in close, and picked up the gun that had dropped from the raider leader's hand. This fellow had begun to stir, to come out of his stunned condition. Then the frightened horses burst the corral bars and in a thundering, dust-mantled stream fled up the arroyo.

The fallen raider sat up, mumbling to his saints in one breath, cursing in his next. The other Mexican kept his stand, intimidated by the threatening rifle.

"Go, greasers! Run!" yelled Gale. Then he yelled it in Spanish. At the point of his rifle he drove the two raiders out of the camp. His next move was to run into the house and fetch out the carbines. With a heavy stone he dismantled each weapon. That done, he set out on a run for his horse. He took the shortest cut down the arroyo, with no concern as to whether or not he would encounter the raiders. Probably such a meeting would be all the worse for them and they knew it. Blanco Sol heard him coming and whistled a welcome, and, when Gale ran up, the horse was snorting war. Mounting, Gale rode rapidly back to the scene of the action, and his first thought, when he arrived at the well, was to give Sol a drink and to fill his canteens.

Then Gale led his horse away from the water hole, and decided, before remounting, to have a look at the Indians. The Papago had been shot through the heart, but the Yaqui was still alive. Moreover, he was conscious and staring up at Gale with great, strange, somber eyes, black as volcanic slag.

"*Gringo* good . . . no kill?" he said in husky whisper. His speech was not affirmative so much as questioning.

"Yaqui, you're done for," said Gale, and his words were positive. He was simply speaking aloud his mind.

"Yaqui . . . no hurt much," replied the Indian, and then he spoke a strange word, repeated it again and again. An instinct of Gale's, or perhaps some suggestion in the husky thick whisper or dark face, told Gale to reach for his canteen. He lifted the Indian and gave him to drink, and, if ever in all his life he saw gratitude in human eyes, he saw it then. Then he examined the injured Yaqui, not forgetting for an instant to send wary fugitive glances on all sides. Gale was not to be surprised. The Indian had three wounds—a bullet hole in his shoulder, a crushed arm, and a badly lacerated leg. What had been the matter with him before being set upon by the raider Gale could not be certain.

The ranger thought rapidly. This Yaqui would live unless left there to die or be murdered by the Mexicans when they found courage to sneak back to the well. It never occurred to Gale to abandon the poor fellow. That was where his old training, the higher order of human feeling, made impossible the following of any elemental instinct of self-preservation. All the same Gale knew he multiplied his perils a hundredfold by burdening himself with a crippled Indian. Swiftly he set to work, and with rifle ever under his hand and shifting glance spared from his task, he bound up the Yaqui's wounds at the same time that he kept keen watch.

The Indians' burros and the horses of the raiders were all out of sight. Time was too valuable for Gale to use any in what might be vain search. Therefore, he lifted the Yaqui upon Sol's broad shoulders and climbed into the saddle. At a word Sol dropped his head and started eastward up the trail, walking swiftly without resentment for his double burden.

Far ahead, between two huge mesas where the trail mounted over a pass, a long line of dust clouds marked the position of the horses that had escaped from the corral. Those that had been stolen would travel straight and true for home and perhaps would lead the others with them. The raiders were left on the desert without guns or mounts.

Blanco Sol walked or jog-trotted six miles to the hour. At that gait fifty miles would not have wet or turned a hair of his dazzling white coat. Gale, bearing in mind the ever-present possibility of encountering more raiders and of being pursued, saved the strength of the horse. Once out of sight of Papago Well, Gale dismounted and walked beside the horse, steadying with one firm hand the helpless, dangling Yaqui.

The sun cleared the eastern ramparts and the coolness of morning fled as if before a magic foe. The whole desert changed. The grays and blacks wore bright; the mesquites glistened; the cactus took the silver line of frost, and the rocks gleamed gold and red. Then, as the heat increased, a wind rushed up out of the valley behind Gale, and the hotter the sun blazed down, the swifter rushed the wind. The wonderful, transparent haze of distance lost its bluish line for one with tinge of yellow. Flying sand made the peaks dimly outlined.

Gale kept pace with his horse. He bore the twinge of pain that darted through his injured hip at every stride. His eye roved over the wide, smoky prospect, seeking the landmarks he knew. When the wild and bold spurs of No Name Mountains loomed through a rent in flying clouds of sand, he felt nearer home. Another hour brought him abreast of a dark, straight shaft rising clearly from a beetling escarpment. This was a monument marking the international boundary line. When he had passed it, he had his own country underfoot. In the heat of midday he halted in the shade of a rock and, lifting the Yaqui down, gave him a drink. Then, after a long sweeping survey of the surrounding desert, he removed Sol's saddle and let him roll, and took for himself a welcome rest, a bite to eat.

The Yaqui was tenacious of life. He was still holding his own. For the first time Gale really looked at the Indian to study him. He had a large head, nobly cast, and a face that resembled a shrunken mask. It seemed chiseled in the dark-red volcanic lava of his Sonora wilderness. The Indian's eyes were always black and mystic, but this Yaqui's encompassed all the tragic desolation of the desert. They were fixed upon Gale, moved only when he moved. The Indian was short and broad, and his body showed unusual muscular development, although he seemed greatly emaciated from starvation or illness.

Gale resumed his homeward journey. When he got through the pass, he faced a great depression as rough as if millions upon millions of gigantic spikes had been driven by the hammer of Thor into a seamed and cracked floor. This was Altar Valley. It was a chaos of arroyos, cañons, rocks, and ridges all mantled with cactus, and at its eastern end it claimed the dry bed of Forlorn River and water when there was any.

With a wounded helpless man across the saddle, this stretch of thorny and contorted desert was practically impassable. Yet Gale headed into it unflinchingly. He would carry the Yaqui as far as possible, or until death made the burden no longer a duty. Blanco Sol plodded on over the dragging sand, up and down the steep loose banks of washes, out in the rocks, and through the rows of white-toothed chollas.

The sun sloped westward, bending fiercer heat in vengeful parting reluctance. The wind slackened. The dust settled. And the bold forbidding front of No Name Mountains changed to red and gold. Gale held grimly by the side of the tireless, implacable horse, holding the Yaqui on the saddle, taking the brunt of the merciless thorns. In the end it became heartrending toil. His heavy chaps dragged him down, but he dared not go on without them, for, thick and stiff as they were, the terrible, steel-bayoneted spikes of the chollas pierced through to sting his legs.

To the last mile Gale held to Blanco Sol's gait and kept ever-watchful gaze ahead on the trail. Then with the low, flat houses of Forlorn River shining redly in the sunset,

Gale flagged and rapidly weakened. The Yaqui slipped out of the saddle and dropped limply in the sand. Gale could not mount his horse. He clutched Sol's long tail and twisted his hand in it and staggered on.

Blanco Sol whistled a piercing blast. He scented cool water and sweet alfalfa hay. Twinkling lights ahead meant rest. The melancholy desert twilight rapidly succeeded the sunset. It accentuated the forlorn loneliness of the gray winding river of sand and its grayer shores. Night shadows trooped down from the black and looming mountains.

CHAPTER SEVEN:
WHITE HORSES

"A crippled Yaqui! Why the hell did you saddle yourself with him?" roared Belding as he laid Gale upon the bed.

Belding had grown hard these late violent weeks.

"Because I chose," whispered Gale in reply. "Go after him . . . he dropped in the trail . . . across the river . . . near the first big saguaro."

Belding began to swear as he fumbled with matches and the lamp, but, as the light flared up, he stopped short in the middle of a word.

"You said you weren't hurt?" he demanded in sharp anxiety, as he bent over Gale.

"I'm only . . . all in . . . . Will you go . . . or send someone . . . for the Yaqui?"

"Sure, Dick, sure," Belding replied in softer tones. Then he stalked out; his heels rang on the flagstones; he opened a door and called: "Mother . . . girls, here's Dick back! He's done up. Now, no, no, he's not hurt or in bad shape. You women . . . do what you can to make him comfortable. I've got a little job on hand."

There were quick replies that Gale's dulling ears did not distinguish. Then it seemed Mrs. Belding was beside his bed, her very presence so cool and soothing and helpful, and Mercedes and Nell, wide-eyed and white-faced, were fluttering around him. He drank thirstily but refused food. He wanted rest. And with their faces drifting away in a kind of haze, with the feeling of gentle hands about him, he lost consciousness.

He slept twenty hours. Then he arose, thirsty, hungry, lame, over-worn, and presently went in search of Belding and the business of the day.

"Your Yaqui was damn' near dead, but guess we'll pull him through," said Belding. "Dick, that Indian came here by rail and foot and Lord only knows how else, all the way from New Orleans! He spoke English better than most Indians and I know a little Yaqui. I got some of his story and guessed the rest. The Mexican government is trying to root out the Yaquis. A year ago his tribe was taken in chains to a Mexican port on the Gulf. The fathers, mothers, children were separated and put on ships bound for Yucatán. There they were made slaves on the great henequen plantations. They were driven, beaten, starved. Each slave had for a day's returns a hunk of sourdough, no more. Yucatán is low, marshy, damp, hot. The Yaquis were bred on the high dry Sonoran plateau where the air is like a knife. They dropped dead in the henequen fields and their places were taken by more. You see the Mexicans won't kill outright in their war of extermination of the Yaquis. They get use out of them. It's a horrible thing. Well, this Yaqui you brought in escaped from his captors, got aboard a ship, and eventually reached New Orleans. Somehow he traveled 'way out here. He was a sick man, then. And he must have fallen foul of some greasers."

Gale told of his experience at Papago Well.

"That raider who tried to grind the Yaqui under a horse's hoofs . . . he was a hyena!" concluded Gale, shuddering. "I've seen some blood spilled and some hard sights, but that inhuman devil took my nerve. Why, as I told you, Belding, I missed a shot at him . . . not twenty paces."

"Dick, in a case like that the sooner you clean up the bunch the better," said Belding grimly. "As for hard sights . . . wait till you've seen a Yaqui do up a Mexican.

Bar none, that is the limit! It's blood lust, that is the limit! It's blood lust, a racial hate, deep as life, and terrible. The Spaniards crushed the Aztecs four or five hundred years ago. That hate has had time to grow as deep as a cactus root. The Yaquis are mountain Aztecs. Personally I think they are noble and intelligent, and if let alone would be peaceable and industrious. I like the few I've known. But they are a doomed race. Have you any idea what ailed this Yaqui, before the raider got in his work?"

"No, I haven't. I noticed the Indian seemed in bad shape, but I couldn't tell what was the matter with him."

"Well, my idea is another personal one. Maybe it's off-color. I think that Yaqui was, or is, for that matter, dying of a broken heart. All he wanted was to get back to his mountains and die. There are no Yaquis left in that part of Sonora he was bound for."

"He had a strange look in his eyes," said Gale thoughtfully.

"Yes, I noticed that. But all Yaquis have a wild look. Dick, if I'm not mistaken, this fellow was a chief. It was a waste of strength, a needless risk for you to save him, pack him back here. But, damn the whole greaser outfit generally, I'm glad you did. He can stay here long as he needs to."

Gale remembered then to speak of his concern for Ladd.

"Laddy didn't go out to meet you," replied Belding. "I knew you were due in any day, and, as there's been trouble between here and Casita, I sent him that way. Since you've been out, our friend Carter lost a bunch of horses and a few steers. Did you get a good look at the horses those raiders had at Papago Well?"

Dick had learned, since he had become a ranger, to see everything with keen, sure, photographic eyes, and, being put to the test so often required of him, he described the horses as a dark-colored drove, mostly bays and blacks, with one spotted sorrel.

"Some of Carter's . . . sure as you're born!" exclaimed Belding. "His bunch has been split up, divided among several bands of raiders. He has a grass ranch up here in Three Mile Arroyo. It's a good long ride in U.S. territory from the border."

"Those horses I saw will go home, don't you think?" asked Dick.

"Sure. They can't be caught or stopped."

"Well, what shall I do now?"

"Stay here and rest," bluntly replied Belding. "You need it. Let the women fuss over you . . . doctor you a little. When Jim gets back from Sonoyta, I'll know more about what we ought to do. My Lord, it seems our job now isn't keeping Japs and Chinamen out of the U.S. It's keeping our property from going into Mexico."

"Are there any letters for me?" asked Gale.

"Letters! Say, my boy, it'd take something pretty important to get me or any man here back Casita way. If the town is safe these days, the road isn't. It's a month now since anyone went to Casita."

Gale had received several letters from his sister Elsie, the last of which he had not answered. There had not been much opportunity for writing on his frequent returns to Forlorn River, and, besides, Elsie had written that her father had stormed over what he considered Dick's falling into wild and evil ways.

"Time flies," said Dick. "George Thorne will be free before long and he'll be coming out. I wonder if he'll stay here or try to take Mercedes away."

"Well, he'll stay right in Forlorn River, if I have any say," replied Belding. "I'd like to know how he'd ever get that Spanish girl out of the country now, with all the trails overrun by rebels and raiders. It'd be hard to disguise her. Say, Dick, maybe we *can* get Thorne to stay here. You know, since you discovered the possibility of a big water supply, I've had dreams of a future for Forlorn River. If only this damned war was over! Dick, that is what it is . . . war . . . scattered along the northern border of Mexico from gulf to gulf. What if it isn't our war? We're on the fringe. No, we can't develop Forlorn River until there's peace."

The discovery Belding alluded to was one that might very well lead to the making of a wonderful mining and agricultural district of Altar Valley. While in college Dick Gale had studied engineering, but he had not set the scientific college world afire with his brilliance. Nor, after leaving college, had he been able to satisfy his father that he could hold a job. Nevertheless, his smattering of engineering skill bore fruit in the last place on earth when anything might have been expected of it—in the desert. Gale had always wondered about the source of Forlorn River. No white man or Mexican, or so far as known no Indian, had climbed those mighty broken steps of rock called No Name Mountains, from which Forlorn River was supposed to come. Gale had discovered a long, narrow, rock-bottomed and rock-walled gulch that could be dammed at the lower end by the dynamiting of leaning cliffs above. An inexhaustible supply of water could be stored there. Furthermore, he had worked out an irrigation plan to bring water down for mining uses, and to make a paradise out of that part of Altar Valley that lay in the United States. Belding claimed there was gold in the arroyos, gold in the gulches, not in quantities to make a prospector rejoice, but enough to work for, and the soil on the higher levels of Altar Valley needed only water to make it grow anything all the year around. Gale, too, had come to have dreams of a future for Forlorn River.

On the afternoon of the following day, Ladd unexpectedly appeared, leading a lame and lathered horse into the yard. Belding and Gale, who were at work in the forge, looked up and were surprised out of speech. The legs of the horse were raw and red, and he seemed about to drop. Ladd's sombrero was missing; he wore a bloody scarf around his head; sweat and blood and dust had formed a crust on his face; little streams of powdery dust slid from him, and the lower half of his scarred chaps were full of broken white thorns.

"Howdy, boys," he drawled. "I shore am glad to see you all."

"Where'n hell's your hat?" demanded Belding furiously. It was a ridiculous greeting. But Belding's words signified little. The dark shade of worry and solicitude crossing his face told more than his blank amaze.

The ranger stopped unbuckling the saddle girths and, looking at Belding, broke into his slow cool laugh.

"Tom, you recollect that whopper of a saguaro up there where Carter's trail branches off the main trail to Casita? Well, I climbed it an' left my hat on top for a woodpecker's nest."

"You've been running . . . fighting?" queried Belding, as if Ladd had not spoken at all.

"I reckon it'll dawn on you after a while," replied Ladd, slipping the saddle.

"Laddy, go in the house to the women," said Belding. "I'll tend to your horse."

"Shore, Tom, in a minute. I've been down the road. An' I found hoss tracks an' steer tracks goin' across the line. But I seen no sign of raiders till this mornin'. Slept at Carter's last night. That raid the other day cleaned him out. He's shootin' mad. Well, this mornin' I rode plumb into a bunch of Carter's hosses, runnin' wild for home. Some greasers were tryin' to head them 'round an' chase them back across the line. I rode in between an' made matters embarrassin'. Carter's hosses got away. Then me an' the greasers had a little game of hide-an'-seek in the cactus. I was on the wrong side, an' had to break through their line to head toward home. We run some. But I had a closer call than I'm stuck on havin'."

"Laddy, you wouldn't have any such close calls if you'd ride one of my horses," expostulated Belding. "This bronco of yours can run, and, Lord knows, he's game. But you want a big strong horse, Mexican-bred, with cactus in his blood. Take one of the bunch. Bull . . . White Woman . . . Blanco José."

"I had a big fast hoss a while back, but I lost him," said Ladd. "This bronco ain't so bad. Shore, Bull and that white devil with his greaser name . . . they could run down my bronc', kill him in a mile of cactus. But somehow, Tom, I can't make up my mind to take one of them grand white hosses. Shore, I reckon I'm kinda soft. An' mebbe I'd better take one before the raiders clean up Forlorn River."

Belding cursed, low and deep, in his throat and the sound resembled muttering thunder. The shade of anxiety on his face changed to one of dark gloom and passion. Next to his wife and daughter there was nothing so dear to him as those white horses. His father and his grandfather—all his progenitors of whom he had trace—had been lovers of horses. It was in the Beldings' blood.

"Laddy, before it's too late can't I get the whites away from the border?"

"Mebbe it ain't too late, but where can we take them?"

"To San Felipe?"

"No. We've more chance to hold them here."

"To Casita, and the railroad?"

"Afraid to risk gettin' there. An' the town's full of rebels who need hosses."

"Then straight north?"

"Shore, man, you're crazy. There's no water, no grass for a hundred miles. I'll tell you, Tom, the safest plan would be to take the white bunch south into Sonora, into some wild mountain valley. Keep them there till the raiders have traveled on back east. Pretty soon there won't be any rich pickin' left for these greasers. An' then they'll ride on to new ranges."

"Laddy, I don't know the trails into Sonora. An' I can't trust a Mexican or a Papago. Between you and me I'm afraid of this Indian who herds for me."

"I reckon we'd better stick here, Tom. Dick, it's some good to see you again. But you seem kinda quiet. Shore you get quieter all the time. Did you see any sign of Jim out Sonoyta way?"

Then Belding led the lame horse to the watering trough while the two rangers went toward the house. Dick was telling Ladd about the affair at Papago Well when they turned the corner under the porch. Nell was sitting in the door. She rose with a little scream and came flying toward them.

"Now I'll get it," whispered Ladd. "The women'll make a baby of me. An' shore I can't help myself."

"Oh, Laddy, you've been hurt!" cried Nell, as with white cheeks and dilating eyes she ran to him, caught his arm.

"Nell, I only run a thorn in my ear."

"Oh, Laddy, don't lie! You've lied before. I know you're hurt. Come in to Mother."

"Shore, Nell, it's only a scratch. My bronc' threwed me."

"Laddy, no horse ever threw you." The girl's words and accusing eyes only hurried the ranger on to further duplicity.

"Mebbe I got it when I was ridin' hard under a mesquite, an' a sharp snag. . . ."

"You've been shot! Mama, here's Laddy, and he's been shot. Oh, these dreadful days we're having! I can't bear them. Forlorn River used to be so safe and quiet. Nothing happened. But now! Jim comes home with such a bloody hole in him . . . then Dick . . . then Laddy! Oh, I'm afraid someday they'll *never* come home."

The morning was bright, still, and clear as crystal. The heat waves had not yet begun to rise from the desert. A soft gray, white, and green tint, perfectly blended, lay like a darker mantle over mesquite and sand and cactus. The cañons of distant mountains showed, deep and full of lilac haze.

Nell sat perched high upon the topmost bar of the corral gate. Dick leaned beside her, now with his eyes on her face, now gazing out into the alfalfa field where Belding's thoroughbreds grazed and pranced and romped and whistled. Nell watched the horses. She loved them, never tired of watching them. But her gaze was too persistently fixed upon them, too consciously averted from the yearning eyes that tried to meet hers, to be altogether natural.

A great fenced field of dark velvety green alfalfa fur-

nished a rich background for the drove of about twenty
white horses. Even without the horses the field would
have presented a striking contrast at the surrounding hot,
glaring blaze of rock and sand. Belding had bred 100 or
more horses from the original stock he had brought up
from Durango. His particular interest was in the almost
unblemished whites, and these he had given especial
care. He had made a good deal of money selling this
strain to friends among the ranchers back in Texas. No
mercenary consideration, however, could have made him
part with the great rangy white horses he had gotten from
the Durango breeder. They were named Blanco Diablo
(White Devil), Blanco Sol (White Sun), Blanca Reina
(White Queen), Blanca Mujer (White Woman), and El
Gran Toro Blanco (The Great White Bull). Belding had
been laughed at by ranchers for preserving the sentimental Durango names, and he had been unmercifully
ridiculed by cowboys. But the names had never been
changed.

Blanco Diablo was the only horse in the field that was
not free to roam and graze where he listed. A stake and a
halter held him to one corner where he was severely let
alone by the other horses. He did not like this isolation.
Blanco Diablo was not happy unless he was running, or
fighting a rival. Of the two he would rather fight. If anything white could resemble a devil, this horse surely did.
He had nothing beautiful about him yet he drew the gaze
and held it. The look of him suggested discontent, anger,
revolt, viciousness. When he was not grazing or prancing,
he held his long lean head level, pointing his nose and
showing his teeth. Belding's favorite was almost all the
world to him, and he swore Diablo could stand more heat
and thirst and cactus than any horse he owned, and could
run down and kill any horse in the Southwest. The fact
that Ladd did not agree with Belding on these salient
points was a great disappointment to him and also a per-
petual source for argument. Ladd and Lash both hated
Diablo, and Dick Gale, after one or two narrow escapes

from being brained, had inclined to the cowboys' side of the question.

El Gran Toro Blanco upheld his name. He was a huge, massive, thick-flanked stallion, a kingly mate for his full-bodied glossy consort Blanca Reina. The other mare, Blanca Mujer, was dazzling white, without a spot, perfectly pointed, racy, graceful, elegant, yet carrying weight and brawn and range that suggested her relation to her forebears.

The cowboys admitted some of Belding's claims for Diablo, but they pinned loyal and unshakable allegiance to Blanco Sol. As for Dick, he had to fight himself to keep out of arguments, for he sometimes imagined he was unreasonable about the horse. Although he could not understand himself, he knew he loved Sol as a man loved a friend, a brother. Free of heavy saddle and the clumsy leg shields, Blanco Sol was sometimes all-satisfying to the eyes of the rangers. As long and big as Diablo was, Sol was longer and bigger. Also he was higher, more powerful. He looked more a thing for action—speedier. At a distance the honorable scars and lumps that marred his muscular legs were not visible. He grazed aloof from the others, and did not cavort, or prance, but when he lifted his head to whistle, how wild he appeared, and proud and splendid! The dazzling whiteness of the desert sun shone from his coat; he had the fire and spirit of the desert in his noble head, its strength and power in his gigantic frame.

"Belding swears Sol never beat Diablo," Dick was saying.

"He believes it," replied Nell. "Dad is queer about that horse."

"But Laddy rode Sol once . . . made him beat Diablo. Jim saw the race."

Nell laughed. "I saw it, too. For that matter even I have made Sol put his nose before Dad's favorite."

"I'd like to have seen that. Nell, aren't you ever going to ride with me?"

"Someday . . . when it's safe."

"Safe!"

"I . . . I mean when the raiders have left the border."

"Oh, I'm glad you meant that," said Dick, laughing. "Well . . . I've often wondered how Belding ever came to give Blanco Sol to me."

"He was jealous. I think he wanted to get rid of Sol."

"No? Why, Nell, he'd give Laddy or Jim one of the whites any day."

"Would he? Not Devil or Queen or White Woman. Never in this world. But Dad has lots of fast horses the boys could pick from. Dick, I tell you Dad wants Blanco Sol to run himself out . . . lose his speed on the desert. Dad is just jealous for Diablo."

"Maybe. He surely has a strange passion for horses. I think I understand better than I used to. I owned a couple of racers once. They were just animals to me, I guess. But Blanco Sol!"

"Do you love him?" asked Nell, and now a warm blue flash of eyes swept his face.

"Do I? Well, rather."

"I'm glad. Sol has been finer, a better horse since you owned him. He loves you, Dick. He's always watching for you. See him raise his head. That's for you. I know as much about horses as Dad or Laddy any day. Sol always hated Diablo and he never had much use for Dad."

Dick looked at her. "It'll be . . . be pretty hard to leave Sol . . . when I go away."

Nell sat perfectly still. "Go away?" she asked presently, with just the faintest tremor in her voice.

"Yes. Sometimes when I get blue . . . as I am today . . . I think I'll go. But, in sober truth, Nell, it's not likely that I'll spend all my life here."

There was no answer to this. Dick put his hand softly over hers, and, despite her half-hearted struggle to free it, he held on.

"Nell."

Her color fled. He saw her lips part. Then a living step on the gravel, a cheerful, complaining voice, interrupted him, and made him release Nell and draw back. Belding strode into view around the adobe shed.

"Hey, Dick, that darned Yaqui Indian can't be driven or hired or coaxed to leave Forlorn River. He's well again, well enough to travel. I offered him horse, gun, blanket, grub. But no go."

"That's funny," replied Gale with a smile. "Let him stay . . . put him to work."

"It doesn't strike me funny. But I'll tell you what I think. That poor homeless heart-broken Indian has taken a liking to you, Dick. These desert Yaquis are strange folk. I've heard strange stories about them. I'd believe 'most anything. And that's how I figure his case. You saved his life. That sort of thing counts big with any Indian, even with an Apache. With a Yaqui maybe it's of deep significance. I've heard a Yaqui say that with his tribe no debt to friend or foe ever went unpaid. Perhaps that's what ails this fellow."

"Dick, don't laugh," said Nell. "I've noticed the Yaqui. It's pathetic the way his great gloomy eyes follow you."

"You've made a friend," continued Belding. "A Yaqui could be a real friend on this desert. If he gets his strength back, he'll be of service to you, don't mistake me. He's welcome here. But you're responsible for him and you'll have trouble keeping him from massacring all the greasers in Forlorn River."

The probability of a visit from raiders, and a dash bolder than usual on the outskirts of a ranch, led Belding to build a new corral. It was not sightly to the eye, but it was high and exceedingly strong. The gate was a massive affair, swinging on huge hinges and fastened with heavy chains and padlocks. At the outside it had been completely covered with barbed wire that would make it a troublesome thing to work on in the dark.

At night Belding locked his white horses in this corral. The Papago herdsman slept in the adobe shed adjoining. Belding did not imagine that any wooden fence, however substantially built, could keep determined raiders from breaking it down. They would have to take time, however, and make considerable noise, and Belding relied on these facts. Belding did not believe a band of night raiders would hold out against a hot rifle fire. So he began to make up some of the sleep he had lost. It was noteworthy, however, that Ladd did not share Belding's sanguine hopes.

Jim Lash rode in, reporting that all was well out along the line toward the Sonoyta Oasis. Days passed, and Belding kept his rangers home. Nothing was heard of raiders near at hand. Many of the newcomers, both American and Mexican, who came with wagons and pack trains from Casita stated that property and life were cheap back in that rebel-infested town.

One January morning Dick Gale was awakened by a terrible, shrill, ringing sound that burst right into his ears. He leaped up, bewildered and frightened. He heard Belding's booming voice, answering shouts, and rapid steps on the flagstones. But these had not awakened him. Heavy breaths, almost snorts, seemed to puff in at his door. Dawn was just breaking, cold and gray. Dick saw something whiter than the gray. Gun in hand, he bounded across the room. Just outside his door stood Blanco Sol.

It was not unusual for Sol to come poking his head in at Dick's door during daylight. But now in the early dawn, when he had been locked in the corral, it meant raiders—no less. Dick called softly to the snorting horse, and, hurriedly getting into boots and clothes, he went out, with a gun in each hand. Sol was quivering in every muscle. Like a dog he followed Dick around the house. Hearing shouts in the direction of the corrals, Gale bent swift steps that way.

He caught up with Jim Lash who was also leading a white horse.

"Hello, Jim, guess it's all over but the fireworks," said Dick.

"I cain't say just what'n hell has come off," replied Lash. "I've got the Bull. Found him runnin' in the yard."

They reached the corral to find Belding shaking, raving like a madman. The gate was open; the corral was empty. Ladd stooped over the ground, evidently trying to find tracks.

"I reckon we might jest as well cool off an' wait for daylight," suggested Jim.

"Shore. They've flown the coop, you can gamble on that. Tom, where's the Papago?" said Ladd.

"He's gone, Laddy . . . gone!"

"Double-crossed us, eh? I see here's a crowbar lyin' by the gatepost. That Indian fetched it from the forge. It was used to pry out the bolts an' staples. Tom, I reckon there wasn't much time lost forcin' that gate."

Belding roared in his rage. He was in his shirt sleeves and bare feet. He said he had heard the horses running as he leaped out of bed.

"What woke you?" asked Laddy.

"Sol. He came whistling for Dick. Didn't you hear him before I called you?"

"Hear him? He came thunderin' right under my window. I jumped up in bed, an', when he let out that blast, Jim lit square in the middle of the floor, an' I was scared stiff. Dick, seein' it was your room he blew into, what did you think?"

"I couldn't think. I'm shaking yet, Laddy."

"Boys, I'll bet Sol spilled a few raiders if any got hands on him," said Jim. "Now, let's sit down an' wait for daylight. It's my idea we'll find some of the hosses runnin' loose. Tom, you go an' get some clothes on. It's freezin' cold. An' don't forget to tell the womenfolks we're all right."

Daylight made clear some details of the raid. The cowboys found tracks of eight raiders coming up from the riverbed where their horses had been left. Evidently the Papago had been false to his trust. His few personal belongings were gone. Lash was correct in his idea of finding more horses loose in the fields. The men soon rounded up eleven of the whites, all more or less frightened, and among the number were Queen and Blanca Mujer. The raiders had been unable to handle more than one horse for each man. It was bitter irony of fate that Belding should lose his favorite, the one horse more dear to him than all the others. Somewhere out on the trail a raider was fighting the iron-jawed savage Blanco Diablo.

"I reckon we're some lucky," observed Jim Lash.

"Lucky ain't enough word," replied Ladd. "You see it was this way. Some of the raiders piled over the fence while the others worked on the gate. Mebbe the Papago went inside to pick out the best hosses. But it didn't work except with Diablo, an' how'n hell they ever got him I don't know. I'd have gambled it'd take eight men to steal him. But greasers have got us all skinned on handlin' hosses."

Belding was inconsolable. He cursed and railed, and finally he declared he was going to trail the raiders.

"Tom, you just ain't a-goin' to do nothin' of the kind," said Ladd coolly.

Belding groaned and bowed his head. "Laddy, you're right," he replied presently. "I've got to stand it. I can't leave the women and my property. But it's sure tough. I'm sore way down deep and nothin' but blood would ever satisfy me."

"Leave that to me an' Jim," said Ladd.

"What do you mean to do?" demanded Belding, starting up.

"Shore, I don't know yet. Give me a light for my pipe. An', Dick, go fetch out your Yaqui."

Chapter Eight:
The Running of Blanco Sol

The Yaqui's strange, dark glance roved over the corral, the swinging gate with its broken fastenings, the tracks in the road, and then rested upon Belding.

"Malo hombre," he said, and his Spanish was clear.

"Shore, Yaqui, about eight bad men, an' a traitor Indian," said Ladd.

"I think he means my herder," added Belding. "If he does, that settles any doubt it might be decent to have . . . Yaqui, *malo* Papago . . . *sí?*"

The Yaqui spread wide his hands. Then he bent over the tracks in the road. They led every whither, but gradually he worked out of the thick net to take the trail that the cowboys had followed down to the river. Belding and the rangers kept close at his heels; occasionally Dick lent a helping hand to the still feeble Indian. He found a trampled spot where the raiders had left their horses. From this point a deeply defined narrow trail led across the dry riverbed.

Belding asked the Yaqui where the raiders would head for in the Sonora Desert. For answer the Indian followed the trail across the stream of sand, through willows and mesquite, up to the level of rock and cactus. At this point he halted. A sand-filled, almost obliterated trail led off to the left, and evidently went around to the east of No Name Mountain. To the right stretched the road toward Papago Well and the Sonoyta Oasis. The trail of the raiders took a southeasterly course over untrodden desert. The Yaqui spoke in his own tongue—then in Spanish.

"Think he means slow march," said Belding. "Laddy, from the looks of that trail the greasers are having trouble with the horses."

"Tom, shore a boy could see that," replied Laddy. "Ask Yaqui to tell us where the raiders are headin', an' if there's water."

It was wonderful to see the Yaqui point. His dark hand stretched; he sighted over his stretched finger at a low, white escarpment in the distance. Then with a stick he traced a line in the sand, and then at the end of that another line at right angles. He made crosses and marks and holes, and, as he drew the rude map, he talked in Yaqui— in Spanish—with a word here and there in English. Belding translated as best he could. The raiders were heading southeast toward the railroad that ran from Nogales down into Sonora. It was four days' travel—bad trail— good sure water hole one day out—then water not sure for two days. Raiders traveling slow—bothered by too many horses—not looking for pursuit—were never pursued—could be headed and ambushed, that night, at the first water hole, a natural trap in a valley.

The men returned to the ranch. The rangers ate and drank while making hurried preparations for travel. Blanco Sol and the cowboys' horses were fed, watered, and saddled. Ladd again refused to ride one of Belding's whites. He was quick and cold.

"Get me a long-range rifle an' lots of shells. Rustle now," he said.

"Laddy, you don't want to be weighted down?" protested Belding.

"Shore I want a gun that'll outshoot the dinky little carbines an' muskets used by the rebels. Trot one out an' be quick."

"I've got a Four-Oh-Five, a long-barreled heavy rifle

that'll shoot a mile. I use it for mountain sheep. But Laddy, it'll break that bronc's back."

"His back won't break so easy. Dick, take plenty of shells for your Remington. An' don't forget your field glass."

In less than an hour after the time of the raid the three rangers, heavily armed and superbly mounted on fresh horses, rode out on the trail. As Gale turned to look back from the far bank of Forlorn River, he saw Nell, waving a white scarf. He stood high in his stirrups and waved his sombrero. Then the mesquites hid the girl's slight figure, and Gale wheeled, grim-faced, to follow the rangers.

They rode in single file with Ladd in the lead. He did not keep to the trail of the raiders all the time. He made short cuts. The raiders were traveling leisurely and they evinced a liking for the most level and least cactus-covered stretches of ground. But the cowboy took a bee-line course for the white escarpment pointed out by the Yaqui, and nothing save deep washes and impassable patches of cactus or rocks made him swerve from it. He kept the bronco at a steady walk over the rougher places and at a swinging Indian canter over the hard and level ground. The sun grew hot and the wind began to blow. Dust clouds rolled along the blue horizon. Whirling columns of sand, like water spouts at sea, circled up out of the white arid basins, and swept aloft before the wind. The escarpment began to rise, to change color, to show breaks upon its rocky face.

Whenever the rangers rode out to the brow of a knoll or ridge or an eminence, before starting to descend, Ladd required of Gale a long, careful sweeping survey of the desert ahead through the field glass. There were streams of white dust to be seen, streaks of yellow dust, trailing low clouds of sand over the glistening dunes, but no steadily rising, uniformly shaped puffs that would tell a tale of moving horses on the desert.

At noon the rangers got out of the thick of cactus.

Moreover, the gravel-bottomed washes, the low, weathering, rotting ledges of yellow rock gave place to hard, sandy rolls and bare clay knolls. The desert resembled a rounded hummocky sea of color; all light shades of blue and pink and yellow and mauve were there, dominated by the glaring white sun. Mirages glistened, wavered, faded in the shimmering waves of heat. Dust as fine as powder whipped up from under the tireless hoofs.

The rangers rode on and the escarpment began to loom. The desert floor inclined perceptively upward. When Gale got unobstructed view of the slope of the escarpment, he located the raiders and horses. In another hour's travel the rangers could see with naked eyes a long, faint-moving streak of black and white dots.

"They're headin' for that yellow pass," said Ladd, pointing to a break in the eastern end of the escarpment. "When they get out of sight, we'll rustle. I'm thinkin' that water hole the Yaqui spoke of lays in the pass."

The rangers traveled swiftly over the remaining miles of level desert leading to the ascent of the escarpment. When they achieved the gateway of the pass, the sun was low in the west. Dwarfed mesquite and greasewood appeared among the rocks. Ladd gave the word to tie up horses and go forward on foot.

The narrow neck of the pass opened and descended into a valley half a mile wide, perhaps twice that in length. It had inherently incalculable slopes of weathered rock leading up to beetling walls. With a floor bare and hard and white, except for a patch of green mesquite near the far end, it was a lurid and desolate spot, the barren bottom of a desert bowl.

"Keep down, boys," said Ladd. "There's the water hole an' hosses have sharp eyes. Shore the Yaqui figgered this place. I never seen its like for a trap."

Both white and black horses showed against the green, and a thin, curling column of blue smoke rose lazily from amidst the mesquites.

"I reckon us'd better wait till dark . . . or mebbe daylight," said Jim Lash.

"Let me figger some. Dick, what do you make of the outlet to this hole? Looks rough to me."

With his glass Gale studied the narrow construction of the walls and roughened rising floor.

"Laddy, it's harder to get out at that end than here," he replied.

"Shore that's hard enough. Let me have a look. Well, boys, it don't take no figgerin' for this job. Jim, I'll want you at the other end, blockin' the pass when we're ready to start."

"When'll that be?" inquired Jim.

"Soon as it's light enough in the mornin'. That greaser outfit will hang till tomorrow. There's no sure water ahead for two days, you remember."

"I reckon I can slip through to the other end after dark," said Lash thoughtfully. "It might get me in bad to go around."

The rangers stole back from the vantage point and returned to their horses, which they untied and left farther around among broken sections of cliff. For the horses it was a dry, hungry camp, but the rangers built a fire and had their short though strengthening meal.

The location was high and through a break in the jumble of rocks; the great colored void of desert could be seen rolling away endlessly to the west. The sun set, and, after it had gone down, the golden tips of mountains dulled, their lower shadows creeping upward.

Jim Lash rolled in his saddle blanket, his feet near the fire, and went to sleep. Ladd told Gale to do likewise while he kept the fire up and waited until it was late enough for Jim to undertake circling around the raiders.

When Gale awakened, the night was dark, cold, windy. The stars shone with white brilliance. Jim was up, saddling his horse, and Ladd was talking low. When Gale rose to accompany them, both rangers said he need not go. But Gale wanted to go because that was the thing Ladd or Jim would have done.

With Ladd leading, they moved away into the gloom. Advance was exceedingly slow, careful, silent. Under the walls the blackness seemed impenetrable. The horse was as cautious as his master. Ladd did not lose his way; nevertheless, he wound between blocks of stone and clumps of mesquite, and often tried a passage to abandon it. Finally the trail showed pale in the gloom, and eastern stars twinkled between the lofty ramparts of the pass.

The advance here was still as stealthily made as before, but not so difficult or slow. When the dense gloom of the pass lightened and there was a wide space of sky and stars overhead, Ladd halted and stood silently a moment.

"Luck again," he whispered. "The wind's in your face, Jim. The hosses won't scent you. Go slow. Don't crack a stone. Keep close under the wall. Try to get up as high as this at the other end. Wait till daylight before riskin' a loose slope. I'll be ridin' the job early. That's all."

Ladd's cool, easy speech was scarcely significant of the perilous undertaking. Lash moved very slowly away, leading his horse. The soft pads of hoofs ceased to sound about the time the gray shape merged into the black shadows. Then Ladd touched Dick's arm and turned back up the trail.

But Dick tarried a moment. He wanted a fuller sense of that ebony-bottomed abyss, with its pale encircling walls reaching up to the dusky blue sky and the brilliant stars. There was absolutely no sound.

He retraced his steps, soon coming up with Ladd, and together they picked a way back through the winding recesses of cliff. The campfire was smoldering. Ladd replenished it and lay down to get a few hours' sleep while Gale kept watch. The after part of the night wore on till the paling of stars, the thickening of gloom indicated the dark hour before dawn. The spot was secluded from wind, but the air grew cold as ice. Gale spent the time stripping wood from a dead mesquite, in pacing to and fro, in listening. Blanco Sol stamped occasionally, which sound was all that broke the stillness. Ladd awoke before the faintest gray appeared. The rangers ate and drank. When the black did lighten to gray, they saddled the horses and led them out to the pass and down to the point where they had parted with Lash. Here they waited daylight.

To Gale it seemed long in coming. Such a delay always aggravated the slow fire within him. He had nothing of Ladd's patience. He wanted action. The gray shadow below thinned out, and the patch of mesquite made a blot upon the pale valley. Then day dawned.

Still Ladd waited. He grew more silent, grimmer as the time of action approached. Gale wondered what the plan of attack would be. Yet he did not ask. He waited ready for orders.

The valley grew clear of gray shadow except under leaning walls on the eastern side. Then a straight column of smoke rose from among the mesquite. Manifestly this was what Ladd had been awaiting. He took the long .405 from its sheath and tried the lever. Then he lifted a cartridge belt from the pommel of his saddle. Every ring held a shell and these shells were four inches long. He buckled the belt around him.

"Come on, Dick."

Ladd led the way down the slope until he reached a position that commanded the rising of the trail from a level. It was the only place a man or horse could leave the valley for the pass.

"Dick, here's your stand. If any raider rides in range, take a crack at him. Now, I want the loan of your hoss."

"Blanco Sol!" exclaimed Gale, more in amaze that Ladd should ask for the horse than in a reluctance to lend him.

"Will you let me have him?" Ladd repeated almost curtly.

"Certainly, Laddy."

A smile momentarily chased the dark, cold gloom that had set upon the ranger's lean face. "Shore I appreciate it,

Dick. I know how you care for that hoss. I guess mebbe Charlie Ladd has loved a hoss. An' one not so good as Sol. I was only tryin' your nerve, Dick, askin' you without tellin' my plan. Sol won't get a scratch . . . you can gamble on that. I'll ride him down into the valley an' pull the greasers out in the open. They've got short-ranged carbines. They can't keep out of range of the Four-Oh-Five . . . an' I'll be takin' the dust of their lead. ¿Sabe, señor?"

"Laddy, you'll run Sol away from the raiders when they chase you? Run him after them when they try to get away?"

"Shore, I'll run all the time. They can't gain on Sol an' he'll run them down when I want. Can you beat it?"

"No, it's great. But suppose a raider comes out on Blanco Diablo?"

"I reckon that's the one weak place in my plan. I'm figgerin' they'll never think of that till it's too late. But if they do . . . well, Sol can outrun Diablo. An' I can always kill the white devil."

Ladd's strange hate of the horse showed in the passion of his last words, in the bulge of jaw and grim set of his lips.

Gale's hand went swiftly to the ranger's shoulder. "Laddy, don't kill Diablo unless it's to save your life."

"All right. But, by God, if I get a chance, I'll make Blanco Sol run him off his legs."

He spoke no more and set about changing the length of Sol's stirrups. When he had them adjusted to suit, he mounted and rode down the trail and out upon the level. He rode leisurely as if merely going to water his horse. The long black rifle lying across his saddle, however, was ominous.

Gale securely tied the other horse to a mesquite at hand and took a position behind a low rock over which he could easily see, and shoot when necessary. He imagined Jim Lash in similar position at the far end of the valley, blocking the outlet. Gale had grown accustomed to danger and the hard and fierce feelings peculiar to it. The boding event about to be enacted here, however, was so

peculiarly different in promise from all he had experienced that he tinglingly, thrillingly, impatiently awaited
the moment of action. In him stirred long-brooding wrath
at these border raiders—affection for Belding and keen
desire to avenge the outrages he had suffered—warm admiration for the cold, implacable Ladd and his absolute
fearlessness—and a curious throbbing interest in the old,
much-discussed, and never-decided argument as to
whether Blanco Sol was a fleeter, stronger horse than
Blanco Diablo. Gale felt that he was to see a race between
these great rivals—the kind of race that made men and
horses terrible.

Ladd rode a quarter of a mile out upon the flat before
anything happened. Then a whistle rent the still, cold air.
A horse had seen or scented Blanco Sol. The whistle was
prolonged, faint, but clear. It made the blood thrum in
Gale's ears. Sol halted. His head shot up with the old
wild-spirited sweep. Gale leveled his glass at the patch of
mesquites. He saw the raiders running to an open place,
pointing, gesticulating. The glass brought them so close
that he saw the dark faces. Suddenly they broke and fled
back among the trees. Then he got only white and dark
gleams of moving bodies. Evidently that moment was one
of boots, guns, and saddles for the raiders.

Lowering the glass, Gale saw that Blanco Sol had
started forward again. His gait was now a canter and he
had covered another quarter of a mile before horses and
raiders appeared on the outskirts of the mesquites. Then
Blanco Sol stopped. His shrill, ringing whistle came distinctly to Gale's ears. The raiders were mounted on dark
horses and they stood abreast in a motionless line. Gale
chuckled as he appreciated what a puzzle the situation
presented for them. A lone horseman in the middle of the
valley did not perhaps seem so menacing as the possibilities his presence suggested.

Then Gale saw a raider gallop swiftly from the group
toward the farther outlet of the valley. This might have
been owing to characteristic cowardice, but it was more

likely a move of the raiders to make sure of retreat. Undoubtedly Ladd saw this galloping horseman. A few waiting moments ensued. The galloping horseman reached the slope, began to climb. With naked eyes Gale saw a puff of white smoke spring out of the rocks. Then the raider wheeled his plunging horse back to the level, and went racing wildly down the valley.

The compact bunch of bays and blacks seemed to break apart and spread rapidly from the edge of the mesquites. Puffs of white smoke indicated firing and showed the nature of the raiders' excitement. They were far out of ordinary range but they spurred toward Ladd, shooting as they rode. Ladd held his ground; the big white horse stood like a rock in his tracks. Gale saw little spouts of dust rise in front of Blanco Sol and spread swift as sight to his rear. The raiders' bullets, striking low, were skipping along the hard bare floor of the valley. Then Ladd raised the long rifle. There was no smoke, but three high, *spanging* reports rang out. A gap opened in the dark line of advancing horsemen, then a riderless steed sheered off to the right. Blanco Sol seemed to turn as on a pivot and charged back toward the lower end of the valley. He circled over to Gale's right and stretched out into his run. There were now five raiders in pursuit and they came sweeping down, yelling and shooting, evidently sure of their quarry. Ladd reserved his fire. He kept turning from back to front in his saddle.

Gale saw how the space widened between pursuers and pursued, saw distinctly when Ladd eased up Sol's running. Manifestly Ladd intended to try to lead the raiders around in front of Gale's position, and presently Gale saw he was going to succeed. The raiders, riding like *vaqueros*, swept on in a curve, cutting off what distance they could. One fellow, a small wiry rider, high on his mount's neck like a jockey, led his companions by many yards. He seemed to be getting in range of Ladd, or else he shot high, for his bullets did not strike up the dust behind Sol. Gale got ready to shoot at this raider. Blanco Sol pounded by, his rapid, rhythmic hoof beats plainly to be heard. He was running easily.

Gale tried to still the jump of heart and pulse, and turned his eyes again on the nearest pursuer. This raider was crossing in, his carbine held muzzle up in his right hand, and he was coming swiftly. It was a long shot, upward of 500 yards. Gale had no time to adjust the sights of the Remington, but he knew the gun, and, holding coarsely upon the whole, general, swiftly moving blot, he began to shoot. The first bullet sent up a great splash of dust beneath the horse's nose, making him leap as if to hurdle a fence. The rifle was automatic; Gale needed only to pull the trigger. He saw now that the raiders behind were in line. Swiftly he worked the trigger. Suddenly the leading horse sprang convulsively, not up or aside, but straight ahead, and he sailed in a wonderful fall, to hit the ground and throw his rider like a catapult, then slide and roll. He half got up, fell back, and kicked, but his rider never moved.

The other raiders sawed the reins of plunging steeds and whirled to escape the unseen battery. Gale slipped a fresh clip into the magazine of his rifle. He restrained himself from useless firing and gave eager eye to the duel below. Ladd had begun to shoot while Sol was running. The .405 rang out sharply—then again. The heavy bullets streaked the dust all the way across the valley. Ladd aimed deliberately and pulled slowly, unmindful of the kicking dust puffs behind Sol and to the side. The raiders spurred madly in pursuit, loading and firing. They shot ten times while Ladd shot once and all in vain, until on Ladd's sixth shot a raider toppled backward, threw his carbine, and fell with his foot catching in a stirrup. The frightened horse plunged away, dragging him in a streak of dust.

Gale had set himself to miss nothing of that fighting race yet it seemed the action passed too swiftly for clear sight of all. Ladd had emptied a magazine and now Blanco Sol quickened and lengthened his running stride.

He ran away from his pursuers. Then it was that the ranger's ruse was divined by the raiders. They hauled sharply up and seemed to be conferring. But that was a fatal mistake. Blanco Sol was seen to break his gait and slow down in several jumps, then square away, and stand stockstill. Ladd fired at the closely grouped raiders. An instant passed. Then Gale heard the *spat* of a bullet out in front, saw a puff of dust, then heard the lead strike the rocks and go whining away. And it was after this that one of the raiders fell prone from his saddle. The steel-jacketed .405 had gone through him on its uninterrupted way to *hum* past Gale's position.

Whereupon the remaining two raiders frantically spurred their horses and fled up the valley. Ladd sent Sol after them. It seemed to Gale, even though he realized his excitement, that Blanco Sol made those horses look slow. The raiders split, one making for the eastern outlet, the other circling back of the mesquites. Ladd kept on after the latter. Then puffs of white smoke and rifle shots faintly *cracking* told of Jim Lash's business in the game. However, he succeeded only in driving the raider back into the valley. But Ladd had turned the other horseman, and now it appeared the two raiders were between Lash above on the stony slope and Ladd below on the level. There was desperate riding on part of the raiders to keep from being hemmed in closer. Only one of them got away and he came riding for life down under the eastern wall. Blanco Sol settled into his graceful beautiful swing. He gained steadily, although he was far from extending himself. By Gale's actual count the raider fired eight times in that race down the valley, and all his bullets went low and wide. He pitched the carbine away and lost all control in headlong flight.

Some few hundred rods to the left of Gale the raider put his horse to the weathered slope. He began to climb. The horse was superb, infinitely more courageous than his rider. Zigzagging, they went up and up, and, when Ladd reached the edge of the slope, they were high along the cracked and guttered rampart. Once, twice Ladd raised the long rifle, but each time he lowered it. Gale divined that the ranger's restraint was not on account of the Mexican, but for that valiant and faithful horse. Up and up he went, and the yellow dust clouds rose and an avalanche rolled, rattling and cracking, down the slope. It was beyond belief that a horse, burdened or unburdened, could find footing and hold it upon that wall of narrow ledges and inverted slanting gullies. But he climbed on, sure-footed as a mountain goat, and, surmounting the last rough stops, he stood a moment silhouetted against the white sky. Then he disappeared. Ladd sat astride Blanco Sol, gazing upward. How the cowboy must have honored that raider's brave steed!

Gale, who had been too dumb to yell the admiration he felt, suddenly leaped up, and his voice came with a rush. "Look out, Laddy!"

A big horse, like a white streak, was bearing down to the right of the ranger. Blanco Diablo! A matchless rider swung with the horse's motion. Gale was stunned. Then he remembered the first raider, the one Lash had shot at and had driven away from the outlet. This fellow had made for the mesquite and had gotten a saddle on Belding's favorite. In the heat of excitement, while Ladd had been intent upon the climbing horse, this last raider had come down with the speed of the wind, straight for the western outlet. Perhaps, very probably, he did not know Gale was there to block it, and certainly he hoped to pass Ladd and Blanco Sol.

A touch of spur made Sol lunge forward to head off the raider. Diablo was in his stride, but the distance and angle favored Sol. The raider had no carbine. He held aloft a gun ready to level it and fire. He sat the saddle as if it were a stationary seat. Gale saw Laddy lean down and drop the .405 in the sand. He would take no chances of wounding Belding's best-loved horse.

Then Gale sat transfixed with suspended breath, watching the horses thundering toward him. Blanco Diablo was speeding, low, fleet as an antelope, fierce and terrible in his devilish action, a horse for war and blood and death. He seemed unbeatable. Yet to see the magnificently running Blanco Sol was but to court a doubt. Gale stood spellbound. He might have shot the raider, but he never thought of such a thing. The distance swiftly lessened. Plain it was the raider could not make the opening ahead of Ladd. He saw it and swerved to the left, emptying his six-shooter as he turned. His dark face gleamed as he flashed by Gale.

Blanco Sol thundered across. Then the race became straightway up the valley. Diablo was cold and Sol was hot: therein lay the only handicap and advantage. It was a fleet, beautiful, magnificent race. Gale thrilled and exulted and yelled as his horse settled into a steadily swifter run and began to gain. The dust rolled in a funnel-shaped cloud from the flying hoofs. The raider wheeled with gun puffing white, and Ladd ducked low over the neck of his horse.

The gap between Diablo and Sol narrowed yard by yard. At first it had been a wide one. The raider beat his mount and spurred, beat and spurred, wheeled around to shoot, then bent forward again. In his circle at the upper end of the valley he turned far short of the jumble of rocks.

All the devil that was in Blanco Diablo had its running on the downward stretch. The strange cruel urge of bit and spur, the crazed rider who stuck like a burr upon him, the shots and smoke added terror to his naturally violent temper. He ran himself off his feet. But he could not elude that relentless horse behind him. The running of Blanco Sol was that of a sure, remorseless, driving power—steadier—stranger—swifter with every long and wonderful stride.

The raider tried to sheer Diablo off closer under the wall, to make the slope where his companion had escaped. But Diablo was uncontrollable. He was running wild, with breaking gait. Closer and closer crept that white, smoothly gliding, beautiful machine of speed.

Then, like one white flash following another, the two horses gleamed down the bank of a wash and disappeared in clouds of dust.

Gale watched with strained and smarting eyes. The thick throb in his ears was pierced by faint sounds of gunshots. Then he waited in almost unendurable suspense.

Suddenly something whiter than the background of dust appeared above the low roll of valley floor. Gale leveled his glass. In the clear circle shone Blanco Sol's noble head with its long black bar from ears to nose. Sol's head was drooping now. Another second showed Ladd still in the saddle. The ranger was leading Blanco Diablo—spent—broken—dragging—riderless.

CHAPTER NINE:
AN INTERRUPTED SIESTA

No man ever had a more eloquent and beautiful pleader for his cause than had Dick Gale in Mercedes Castañeda. He peeped through the green, shining twigs of the paloverde that shaded his door. The hour was high noon and the patio was sultry. The only sounds were the *hum* of bees in the flowers and the low murmur of the Spanish girl's melodious voice. Nell lay in the hammock, her hands behind her head, with rosy cheeks and arch eyes—indeed, she looked rebellious. Certain it was, Dick reflected, that the young lady had fully recovered the willful personality that had lain dormant for a while. Equally certain it seemed that Mercedes's earnestness was apparently having the effect it should have had.

Dick was inclined to be rebellious himself. Belding had kept the rangers in off the line and therefore Dick had been idle most of the time, and, although he tried hard, he had been unable to stay far from Nell's vicinity. He believed she cared for him, but he could not catch her alone long enough to verify his tormenting hope. When alone, she was as illusive as a shadow, as quick as a flash, as mysterious as a Yaqui. When he tried to catch her in the garden or fields, or corner her in the patio, she eluded him, and left behind a memory of dark-blue haunting eyes. It was that look in her eyes that lent him hope. At all other times, when it might have been possible for Dick to speak, Nell clung closely to Mercedes. He had long before enlisted the loyal Mercedes in his cause, but in spite of this Nell had been more than a match for them both.

Gale pondered over an idea he had long revolved in mind and that now suddenly gave place to a decision that made his heart swell and his cheek burn. He peeped again through the green branches to see Nell laughing at the fiery Mercedes.

"*¿Quién sabe?*" he called mockingly, and was delighted with Nell's quick, amazed start.

Then he went in search of Mrs. Belding and found her busy in the kitchen.

The relation between Gale and Mrs. Belding had subtly and incomprehensibly changed. He understood her less than when at first he divined an antagonism in her. If such a thing were possible, she had retained the antagonism while seeming to yield to some influence that must have been fondness for him. Gale was in no wise sure of her affection, and he had long imagined she was afraid of him as of something that he represented. He had gone on, openly and fairly, although discreetly, with his rather one-sided love affair, and, as time passed, he had grown less conscious of what had seemed her unspoken opposition. Gale had come to care greatly for Nell's mother. Not only was she the comfort and strength of her home, but also of the inhabitants of Forlorn River. Indian, Mexican, American were all the same to her in trouble or illness, and then she was nurse, doctor, peacemaker, helper. She was good and noble, and there was not a child or grown-up in Forlorn River who did not love and bless her. But Mrs. Belding did not seem happy. She was brooding, intense, deep, strong, eager for the happiness and welfare of others, and she was dominated by a worship of her daughter that was as strange as it was pathetic. Mrs. Belding seldom smiled, and never laughed. There was always a soft sad hurt look in her eyes. Gale often wondered if there had been other tragedy in her life than the supposed loss of her father in the desert. Perhaps it was the very unsolved nature of that loss that made it haunting.

Mrs. Belding heard Dick's step as he entered the kitchen and, looking up, greeted him.

"Mother," began Dick earnestly. Belding called her that, and so did Ladd and Lash, but it was the first time for Dick. "Mother . . . I want to speak to you."

The only indication Mrs. Belding gave of being startled was in her eyes, which darkened, shadowed with multiplying thought.

"I love Nell," went on Dick simply, "and I want you to let me ask her to be my wife."

Mrs. Belding's face blanched to a deathly white. Gale, thinking with surprise and concern, that she was going to faint, moved quietly toward her, took her arm.

"Forgive me. I was blunt . . . but I thought you knew."

"I've known . . . for a long time," replied Mrs. Belding. Her voice was steady and there was no evidence of agitation except in her pallor. "Then you . . . you haven't spoken to Nell?"

Dick laughed. "I've been trying to get a chance to tell her. I haven't had it yet. But she knows. There are other ways besides speech. And Mercedes has told her. I hope . . . I almost believe Nell cares a little for me."

"I've known that . . . too, for a long time," said Mrs. Belding, low almost as a whisper.

"You know!" cried Dick with a glow and rush of feeling.

"Dick, you must be very blind not to see what has been plain to all of us. I guess . . . it couldn't have been helped. You're a splendid fellow. No wonder she loves you."

"Mother . . . you'll give her to me?"

She drew him to the light and looked with strange, piercing intentness into his face. Gale had never dreamed a woman's eyes could hold such a world of thought and feeling. It seemed all the sweetness of life was there and the pain.

"Do you love her?" she asked.

"With all my heart."

"You want to marry her?"

"Ah, I want to . . . as much as I want to live and work for her."

"*When* would you marry her?"

"Why . . . just as soon as she will do it . . . tomorrow!" Dick gave a wild, exultant little laugh.

"Dick Gale, you want my Nell. You love her just as she is . . . her sweetness . . . her goodness? Just herself, body and soul? There's nothing could change you . . . nothing?"

"Dear Missus Belding, I love Nell for herself. If she loves me, I'll be the happiest of men. There's absolutely nothing that could make any difference in me."

"But your people? Oh, Dick, you come of a proud family. I can tell. I . . . I once knew a young man like you. A few months can't change pride . . . blood. Years can't change them. You've become a ranger. You love the adventure . . . the wild life. That won't last. Perhaps you'll settle down to ranching. I know you love the West. But, Dick, there's your family. . . ."

"If you want to know anything about my family, I'll tell you," interrupted Dick with strong feeling. "I've no secrets about them or myself. My future and happiness are Nell's to make. No one else shall count with me."

"Then, Dick . . . you may have her. God . . . bless . . . you . . . both."

Mrs. Belding's strained face underwent a swift and mobile relaxation, and suddenly she was weeping in strangely mingled happiness and bitterness.

"Why, Mother. . . ." Gale could say no more. He did not comprehend a word seemingly so utterly at variance with Mrs. Belding's habitual temperament. But he put his arm around her. In another moment she had gained command over herself, and, kissing him, she pushed him out of the door.

"There! Go tell her, Dick . . . and have some spunk about it!"

Gale went thoughtfully back to his room. He vowed that he would answer for Nell's happiness, if he had the

wonderful good fortune to win her. Then, remembering
the hope Mrs. Belding had given him, Dick lost his gravity in a flash and something began to dance and sing
within him. He simply could not keep his steps turned
from the patio. Every path led there. His blood was throbbing, his hope mounting, his spirit soaring. He knew he
had never before entered the patio with that inspirited
presence.

"Now for some spunk," he said under his breath.

Plainly he meant his merry whistle and his buoyant
step to interrupt this first languorous stage of the *siesta*
that the girls always took during the hot hours. Nell had
acquired the habit long before Mercedes came to show
how fixed a thing it was in the life of the tropics. But neither girl heard him. Mercedes lay under the paloverde,
her beautiful head dark and still upon a cushion. Nell was
asleep in the hammock. There was an abandonment in
her deep repose, and a faint smile upon her face. Her
sweet red lips, with the soft perfect curve, had always fascinated Dick, and now drew him irresistibly. He had always been consumed with a desire to kiss her and now he
was overwhelmed with his opportunity. It would be a terrible thing to do, but if she did not awaken at once. . . .
No, he would fight the temptation. That would be more
than spunk. It would. . . . Suddenly an ugly green fly
sailed low over Nell, appeared about to alight on her.
Noiselessly Dick stepped close to the hammock, bent over
under the tree, and with a sweep of his hand chased the
intruding fly away. But he found himself powerless to
straighten up. He was close to her—bending over her
face—near the sweet lips. The indolent, dreaming smile
just parted them. Then he was lost. His kiss was quick,
soft, but it was fully upon her mouth.

He had stepped back, erect, when she opened her eyes.
They were sleepy, yet surprised until she saw him. Then
she was wide-awake in a second, bewildered, uncertain.

"Why . . . you here?" she asked slowly.

"Large as life!" replied Dick with unusual gaiety.

"How long have you been here?"

"Just got here this fraction of a second," he replied, lying shamelessly.

It was evident that she did not know whether or not to believe him, and, as she studied him, a slow blush dyed her cheek. "You are absolutely truthful when you say you just stepped there?"

"Why, of course," answered Dick, right glad he did not have to lie about that.

"I thought . . . I was dreaming," she said, and evidently the sound of her voice reassured her.

"Yes, you looked as if you were having pleasant dreams," replied Dick. "So sorry to wake you. I can't see how I came to do it, I was so quiet. Mercedes didn't wake. Well, I'll go and let you have your *siesta*, and dreams." But he made no move to go.

Nell regarded him with curious, speculative eyes.

"Isn't it a lovely day?" queried Dick finally.

"I think it's hot."

"Only ninety in the shade. And you've told me the mercury goes to one hundred and thirty in midsummer. This is just a glorious, golden day."

"Yesterday was fair, but you didn't notice it."

"Oh, yesterday was somewhere back in the past . . . the inconsequential past."

Nell's sleepy blue eyes opened a little wider. She did not know what to make of this changed young man. Dick felt gleeful and tried hard to keep the fact from becoming manifest.

"What's the inconsequential past? You seem remarkably happy today."

"I certainly am happy. *Adiós*. Pleasant dreams."

Dick turned away then, and left the patio by the opening into the yard. Nell was really sleepy, and, when she had fallen asleep again, he would return. He walked around for a while. Belding and the rangers were shoeing a bronco. Yaqui was in the field with the horses. Blanco Sol grazed contentedly, and now and then lifted his head to watch. His long ears went up at sight of his master and he whistled. Presently Dick, as if magnet-drawn, retraced his steps to the patio, and entered noiselessly.

Nell was again deep in her *siesta*. She was inert, relaxed, untroubled by dreams. Her hair was damp on her brow. Dick was not conscious that his motive had been to come back to steal another kiss, but, now that he stood over her, he knew he could not help it. More swiftly, lightly he touched her lips with his and sprang back.

Nell stirred, and gradually awakened. Her eyes opened, humid, shadowy, unconscious. They rested upon Dick for a moment before they became clear and comprehensive. He stood back fully ten feet from her and to all outside appearances regarded her calmly.

"I've interrupted your *siesta* again," he said. "Please forgive me. I'll take myself off."

He wandered away with the sweet touch of Nell's lips clinging to his own. When it became impossible for him to stay away longer, he returned to the patio.

The instant his glance rested upon Nell's face he divined she was feigning sleep. The faint rose flush had paled. The warm, rich, golden tint of her skin had fled. Dick dropped upon his knees and bent over her. Although his blood was churning in his veins, his breast laboring, his mind whirling with the wonder of that moment and its promise, he made himself deliberate. He wanted, more than anything he had ever wanted in his life, to see if she would keep up that pretense of sleep and let him kiss her again. She must have felt his breath, for her hair waved off her brow. Her cheeks were now white. Her breast swelled and sank. He bent down closer— closer. But he must have been maddeningly slow for, as he bent still closer, Nell's eyes opened, and he caught a swift purple blaze as she whirled her head. His kiss only lightly brushed her hair.

Scarlet fired Nell's neck and cheek and brow. "Oh . . . you . . . you wretch! You did . . . you did! I knew it!"

She struggled half up, almost falling, and he reached out to take her, hammock and all, into his arms.

"Of course I did. How could I help it? Nell, I love you! I love you! You looked so sweet that, to save my life, I couldn't help it."

"Let me go!" Nell cried furiously.

Both instinct and remembered advice caused Dick to hold her only the tighter.

"I shall hold you till doomsday."

Nell succeeded in twisting and tangling her head inside the fold of the hammock, and now either the comparative protection afforded by this or the purport of Dick's words materially lessened her struggles.

"Are you a *vaquero* to rope a girl and tie her up?" she asked.

"It's a good way. I never saw a *vaquero* miss a . . . a calf or anything."

"So I'm a calf, am I?"

"Nell, it was your metaphor. And you're a darling. I don't care what I am . . . if you love me."

"But I . . . I don't."

"Nell!"

Slowly he relaxed the tension of his arms and she was free, but the hammock still lay against him and Nell seemed hopelessly tangled in the cords.

"Is that true, Nell? I've been mad enough to dream things. I told your mother I loved you. I asked her to give you to me. She said yes . . . . Do you love me? Will you marry me?"

Evidently she was startled by his reference to her mother and stilled or frightened by some magic in his later words. Her face was practically hidden by her hair and the hammock, but he could see her downcast lashes and cheeks that were now pale as snow. She was breathing rapidly and there was a flutter of white scarf over her bosom. Otherwise, she made no movement and did not seem to be going to speak. There was nothing rebellious about her now.

"Nell, perhaps I was rude. I'm sorry. Your mother advised me to have some spunk and I believe I'd have had a little, anyway. I . . . I think I'll have some more. But, it's a very simple thing for you to keep me away."

Gently he pulled apart the entangling folds of the hammock. Then as gently he slipped his hands under her arms, around her waist, and slowly drew her toward him, Nell did not shrink or pull back. A vivid color flushed out all the white of her face. With both hands she parted her tumbling hair and flung it back. Then she looked at him with her hands outstretching. She was trembling. She was radiant. She had almost recovered the old audacious spirit, as coming swiftly, a purple flash of fire in her eyes, she put her arms around his neck, her lips uplifted.

Mercedes Castañeda lay forgotten beside the lovers, and presently the beautiful head stirred upon the pillow and the dark eyes opened. Her *siesta* had been interrupted. Her eyes opened wide—very wide. Their expression changed wonderfully. Suddenly they shut tightly and the black lashes lay quietly, feigning sleep.

CHAPTER TEN:
ROJAS

No word from George Thorne had come to Forlorn River in weeks. Gale grew concerned over the fact and began to wonder if anything serious could have happened to him. Mercedes showed a slow, wearing strain.

Thorne's commission expired the end of January, and, if he could not get his discharge immediately, he surely could obtain leave of absence. Therefore Gale waited, not without growing anxiety, and did his best to cheer Mercedes. The 1st of February came, bringing news of rebel activities and bandit operations in and around Casita, but not a word from the cavalryman.

Mercedes became silent, mournful. Her eyes were great, black windows of tragedy. Nell devoted herself entirely to the unfortunate girl; Dick exerted himself to persuade her that all would yet come well; in fact, the whole little household could not have been kinder to a sister or a daughter. But their united efforts were unavailing. Mercedes seemed to accept with fatalistic hopelessness a last and crowning misfortune.

A dozen times Gale declared he would ride in to Casita and find out why they did not hear from Thorne; however, older and wiser heads prevailed over his impetuosity. Belding was not sanguine over the safety of the Casita trail. Refugees from there arrived every day in Forlorn River, and, if the tales they told were true, real war would have been preferable to what was going on along the border. Nevertheless, Belding was at length persuaded that someone ought to make the trip to Casita. Accordingly he and Gale, the other two rangers, and Yaqui held a consultation. Not only had the Indian become a faithful servant to Gale but was also of value to Belding. Yaqui had all the craft of his class and superior intelligence, and his knowledge of Mexicans was second only to his hatred of them. The decision arrived at was for Ladd to ride to Casita. That afternoon, late, he started off, intending to travel most of the trail by night.

Early on the morning of the second day following Ladd's departure, Gale, who happened to have acquired a habit of watching the road, saw the ranger riding in with another horseman wearing a blue military cape. Gale leaped up wild with joy and was about to shout the good tidings into the house when he observed that Ladd was supporting his companion in the saddle. Thorne was ill or wounded. Gale ran out through the yard to the gate and met them.

Indeed, it was but a haggard ghost of the cavalryman. Dick involuntarily voiced a greeting that was also questioning, full of distress and fear.

Thorne's answer was a faint smile. He appeared about to drop from the saddle. Gale helped Ladd hold Thorne upon the horse until they reached the house. Belding came out with his wife and Nell. His roaring welcome was checked as he saw the condition of the cavalryman. Thorne reeled into Dick's arms, but he was finally able to stand and walk.

"I'm . . . not hurt. Only weak . . . starved," he said. "Is Mercedes . . . ? Take me to her."

"Wait," whispered the thoughtful Mrs. Belding. "Nell, run in to Mercedes. Tell her Mister Thorne has come . . . that he's ill, but all right, and ready to see her, if she'll try to be calm."

"Nonsense," declared Belding. "She'll be well the minute she sees him."

Thorne was put to bed in Gale's room. He was very weak, yet he would keep Mercedes's hand, and gaze at her with unbelieving eyes. Mercedes's failing hold on hope and strength seemed to have been a fantasy: she was again vivid, magnetic, beautiful, shot through and through with intense and throbbing life. She induced him to take food and drink. Then fighting sleep with what little strength he had left, at last he succumbed.

When Ladd had returned from tending the tired horses, hungry as he acknowledged himself to be, he proposed to light a pipe and tell his story.

"I timed my gettin' into Casita at daylight an' headed straight for the soldier camp. After askin' half a dozen fellows about Thorne, I finally run into an officer who told me Thorne had got leave of absence ten days before. Then I found the fellows he bunked with. Thorne had been shore mysterious an' rode away in the evenin' without tellin' anyone where he was goin'.

"That was enough for me to figger the situation. An' I ain't gainsayin' that I made shore Thorne had been followed an' killed. But I was bent on knowin' for shore. So I left my hoss with the cavalrymen an' walked into town.

"I reckon you'll all be some surprised when you see Casita. It's half burned an' half tore down. An' the rebels are livin' fat. There was rumors of another Federal force on the road from Casa Grande. I seen a good many Americans from interior Mexico an' the stories they told would make your hair stand up. They all packed guns, was fightin' mad at greasers, an' sore at the good old U.S. But shore glad to get over the line! Some were waitin' for trains that don't run regular no more, an' others were reddy to hit the trails north.

"My misgivin's about goin' into the Del Sol saloon were natural, I reckon, but I needn't have bothered to be careful. No one knew me or paid attention to me. Greasers have pore memories. I got hold of a rebel. He had his arm in a sling an' looked sick an' starved. He could talk a little English an' I could talk a little Mex. By spendin' money I got

chummy with him. He wasn't one of Rojas's men. But his
camp was near Rojas's. Then I flashed my roll on him.

"Greasers are traitors at heart, an' I never seen one who
could resist money. This rebel couldn't, anyhow. Shore he
gave up proper. Rojas had a *gringo* prisoner in a 'dobe
shack not two miles outside of Casita. The rebel didn't
know whether the prisoner was a man or woman. But he
said he could find out. He left me, an' after a while came
back. Rojas's prisoner was a cavalryman an' he was bein'
beat an' starved for some reason or other. The rebel
agreed to show me where the 'dobe shack was. We left the
saloon in different directions, an' met out of town where
we climbed a ridge an' located the shack.

"Then I rustled back to the cavalry camp. I found the
officer an' told him where Thorne was. At first he
wouldn't believe me. I had to tell about Mercedes an' Rojas, an' show the reason why the damned bandit was
beatin' an' starvin' Thorne. The officer called in other officers, an' I had to tell my story over again. The colonel had
gone to Nogales an' the camp was in the charge of this officer I met first. He up an' asked me if I'd lead a cavalry
charge to that 'dobe shack where Thorne was captive. I
reckoned I would.

"Shore it dazed me to see the hell a few bugle calls
raised. I have seen some outfits locoed an' more'n one
bunch of cowboys spoilin' for a fight. An' I was one of the
Rough Riders at San Juan Hill. But, say, them cavalrymen
were like a hummin' nest of mad bees. In about ten
shakes of a calf's tail I was on my hoss, leadin' a cavalry
charge.

"Shore it got to me. There was a kind of inspirin' thunder in that troop of hosses. They run so rollin' an' regular.
We had a level stretch an' you can gamble Uncle Sam's
soldiers was goin' some when we crossed the line into
Mexico. It was new to my hoss an' I believe he thought a
herd of stampedin' steers was runnin' him down. He was
tired, too, after travelin' all night. But he kept out in front.

"When I got mebbe a quarter mile or so from the 'dobe

shack, I saw dust an' hosses, an' tents, an' finally greasers. I guessed maybe they wouldn't vamoose, but I never saw such ridin' in my life! We all pulled up at the shack without firin' or hearin' a shot. I was the first down, an', as I made for the door, a greaser opened it, sleepy-like, as if he'd just been roused. I clipped him one on the head with the butt of my gun an' put him out. Then I run in the shack, followed by some of the soldiers.

"Thorne was in there, tied, naked, black an' blue all over, an' thin as a rail. He looked mighty sick. When I cut him loose, he was game to try to walk out, but no go. We lifted him on a hoss an' lost no time gettin' back over the line.

"That happened along in the mornin'. Thorne was given food, drink, clothes. Shore he was a starved man. But he picked up wonderful. An' when I told him Mercedes was about all in, grievin' for him, nothin' could persuade him to rest a day or so. It was all I could do to keep him till dark. An' I wouldn't have been able to do that if I hadn't warned him about Rojas. We must slip away from Casita, leavin' no trail.

"Well, we made as sneaky a start in the dark as I could manage, an' never hit the trail till we was miles away from town. Thorne's nerve held him up for a while. Then all at once he tumbled out of his saddle. Somehow I got him back on. I reckon there's no shape I didn't have him layin' the hoss, but I held him on, an' we got here. An' now some grub an' a bed'll look mighty good to me!"

"Laddy, Rojas was holding Thorne prisoner, trying to make him tell where Mercedes had been hidden?" asked Belding.

"Shore."

"The bandit's crazy over her. That's the Spanish of it," replied Belding, his voice rolling. "Rojas is a peon. He's been a slave to the proud Castilian. He loves Mercedes as he hates her. When I was down in Durango, I saw something of these peons' insane passions. Rojas wants this girl only to have her, then kill her. It's damned strange, boys, and, even with Thorne here, our troubles have just begun."

"Tom, you spoke correct," said Jim Lash in his cool drawl.

"Shore I'm not sayin' what I think," added Ladd, but the look of him was not indication of a tranquil optimism.

For all Dick could ascertain, his friend never stirred an eyelash or a finger for twenty-seven hours. When he did awake, he was pale, weak, but the old Thorne.

"Hello, Dick, I didn't dream it then," he said. "There you are, and my darling with the proud dark eyes . . . she's here!"

"Why, yes, you locoed cavalryman."

"Say, what's happened to you? It can't be just those clothes and a little bronze on your face. Dick, you're older . . . you've changed. You're not so thickly built. By God, if you don't look fine."

"Thanks. I'm sorry I can't return the compliment. You're about the seediest, hungriest-looking fellow I ever saw. Say, old man, you must have had a tough time."

A dark and somber fire burned out the happiness in Thorne's eyes. "Dick, don't make me . . . don't let me think of that fiend, Rojas. I'm here now. I'll be well in a day or two. Then . . . someone is knocking?"

Mercedes came in, radiant and soft-voiced. She fell on her knees beside Thorne's bed and neither of them appeared to see Nell enter with a tray. Then Gale and Nell made a good deal of unnecessary fuss in moving a small table close to the bed. Mercedes had forgotten for the moment that her love had been a starving man. If Thorne remembered it, he did not care. They held hands and looked at each other without speaking.

"Nell, I thought we had it bad," whispered Dick. "But we're not. . . ."

"Hush. It's beautiful," replied Nell softly, and she tried to coax Dick from the room.

Dick, however, thought he ought to remain at least long enough to tell Thorne that a man in his condition could not exist solely on love.

Mercedes sprang up blushing, with a penitent manner and moving white hands eloquent of her contrition.

"Oh, Mercedes . . . don't go!" cried Thorne, as she stepped to the door.

"*Señor* Dick will stay. He is not *mucho malo* for you . . . as I am."

Then she smiled and went out.

"Good Lord," exclaimed Thorne, "how I love her! Dick, isn't she the most beautiful, the loveliest, the finest . . . ?"

"George, I share your enthusiasm," said Dick dryly, "but Mercedes isn't the only girl on earth."

Manifestly this was a startling piece of information and struck Thorne in more than one way.

"George," went on Dick, "did you observe the girl who brought in your breakfast?"

"No. I didn't look at her."

"You long, lean, hungry beggar! That was the young lady who might answer the raving eulogy you just got out of your system. She's engaged to marry me."

Thorne uttered some kind of a sound that his weakened condition would not allow to be a whoop.

"Dick . . . do you mean it?"

"I shore do, as Laddy says."

"I'm glad, Dick, with all my heart. I wondered at the changed look you wear. Why, boy, you've got a different front . . . call the lady in, and you bet I'll look her over."

"Eat your breakfast. There's plenty of time to dazzle you afterward."

Thorne fell to his breakfast and made it vanish with magic speed. Meanwhile Dick told him something of a ranger's life along the border.

"You needn't waste your breath," said Thorne. "I guess I can see Belding and all these rangers have made you the real thing . . . the real Western goods. What I want to know is all about the girl."

"Wait till you see her."

"Fair or dark?"

"Fair."

"Pretty?"

"Well, Laddy swears she's got your girl roped in the corral for looks."

"That's not possible. I'll have to talk to Laddy. But she must be a wonder or Dick Gale would never have fallen for her. Isn't it great, Dick. I'm here. Mercedes is well . . . safe. You've got a girl. Oh . . . but, say, I haven't a dollar to my name. I had a lot of money, Dick, and those robbers stole it, my watch . . . everything. Damn that little black greaser! He got Mercedes's letters. I wish you could have seen him trying to read them. He's simply nutty over her, Dick. I could have borne the loss of money and valuables . . . but those beautiful, wonderful letters . . . they're gone."

"Cheer up. You have the girl. Belding and I will make you a proposition presently. The future smiles, old friend. If this rebel business was only ended."

"Dick, you're going to be my savior twice over. Well, now, listen to me." His gay excitement changed to earnest gravity. "I want to marry Mercedes at once. Is there a *padre* here?"

"Yes. But are you wise in letting any Mexican, even a priest, know Mercedes is hidden in Forlorn River?"

"It couldn't be kept secret much longer."

Gale was compelled to acknowledge the truth of this statement.

"I'll marry her first . . . then I'll face my problem. Fetch the *padre*, Dick. And ask our kind friends to be witnesses at the ceremony."

Much to Gale's surprise neither Belding nor Ladd objected to the idea of bringing a *padre* into the household and thereby making known to at least one Mexican the whereabouts of Mercedes Castañeda. Belding's caution was wearing out in wrath at the persistent, unsettled condition of the border, and Ladd grew only the cooler and more silent as possibilities of trouble multiplied.

Gale fetched the *padre*, a little, weazened, timid man

who was old and without interest or penetration. Apparently he married Mercedes and Thorne as he told his beads or mumbled a prayer. It was Mrs. Belding who kept the occasion from being a merry one, and she insisted on not exciting Thorne. Gale marked her unusual pallor and the singular depth and sweetness of her voice.

"Mother, what's the use of making a funeral out of a marriage?" protested Belding. "A chance for some fun doesn't often come to Forlorn River. You're a fine doctor. Can't you see the girl is what Thorne needed? He'll be well tomorrow, don't mistake me."

"George, when you're all right again, we'll add something to present congratulations," said Gale.

"We shore will," put in Ladd.

So with parting jests and smiles they left the couple to themselves.

Belding enjoyed a laugh at his good wife's expense, for Thorne could not be kept in bed, and all in a day, it seemed, he grew so well and so hungry that his friends were delighted and Mercedes was radiant. In a few days his weakness disappeared and he was going the rounds of the fields and looking over the ground marked out in Gale's plan of water development. Thorne was highly enthusiastic and at once staked out his claim for 160 acres of land adjoining that of Belding and the rangers. These five tracts took in all the ground necessary for their operations, but in case of the success of the irrigation project, the idea was to increase their squatter holdings by purchase of more land down the valley. Numerous families had lately moved to Forlorn River; more were coming all the time, and Belding vowed he could see a vision of the whole of Altar Valley green with farms.

Meanwhile, everybody in Belding's household, except the quiet Ladd and the watchful Yaqui, in the absence of disturbance of any kind along the border, grew freer and more unrestrained, as if anxiety was slowly fading in the peace of the present. Jim Lash made a trip to the Sonoyta

Oasis, and Ladd patrolled fifty miles of the line eastward without incident or sight of raiders. Evidently all the border hawks were in at the picking of Casita.

The February nights were cold with a dry, icy, penetrating coldness that made a warm fire most comfortable. Belding's household usually congregated in the sitting room where burning mesquite logs crackled in the open fireplace. Belding's one passion besides horses was the game of checkers, and he was always wanting to play. On this night he sat playing with Ladd who never won a game and never could give up trying. Mrs. Belding worked with her needle, stopping from time to time to gaze with thoughtful eyes into the fire. Jim Lash smoked his pipe by the hearth and played with the cat on his knee. Thorne and Mercedes were at the table with pencil and paper, and he was trying his best to keep his attention from his wife's beautiful, animated face long enough to read and write a little Spanish. Gale and Nell sat in a corner, watching the bright fire.

There came a low knock on the door. It may have been an ordinary knock, for it did not disturb the women, but to Belding and his rangers it had a subtle meaning.

"Who's that?" asked Belding as he slowly pushed back his chair and looked at Ladd.

"Yaqui," replied the ranger.

"Come in!" called Belding.

The door opened and the short, square, powerfully built Indian entered. He had a magnificent head, strangely staring, somber black eyes, and very darkly bronzed face. He carried a rifle and strode with impressive dignity.

"Yaqui, what do you want?" asked Belding, and repeated his question in Spanish.

"*Señor* Dick," replied the Indian.

Gale jumped up, stifling an exclamation, and he went outdoors with Yaqui. He felt his arm gripped and allowed himself to be led away without asking a question. Yaqui's presence was always one of gloom, and now his stern action boded catastrophe. Once clear of trees he pointed to the level desert across the river, where a row of campfires shone brightly out of the darkness.

"Raiders!" ejaculated Gale.

Then he cautioned Yaqui to keep sharp look-out, and, hurriedly returning to the house, he called the men out and told them there were rebels or raiders camping just across the line.

Ladd did not say a word. Belding, with an oath, slammed down his cigar. "I knew it was too good to last. Dick, you and Jim stay here while Laddy and I look around."

Dick returned to the sitting room. The women were nervous and not to be deceived. So Dick merely said Yaqui had sighted some lights off on the desert and they probably were campfires. Belding did not soon return, and, when he did, he was alone. Saying he wanted to consult with the men, he sent Mrs. Belding and the girls to their rooms. His old gloomy anxiety had returned.

"Laddy's gone over to scout around and try to find out who the outfit belongs to and how many are in it," said Belding.

"I reckon, if they're raiders with bad intentions, we wouldn't see no fires," remarked Jim calmly.

"It'd be useless, I suppose, to send for the cavalry," said Gale. "Whatever's coming off would be over before the soldiers could be notified, let alone reach here."

"Hell, fellows, I don't look for an attack on Forlorn River!" burst out Belding. "I can't believe that possible. These rebel raiders have a little sense. They wouldn't spoil their game by pulling U.S. soldiers across the line from Yuma to El Paso. But, as Jim says, if they wanted to steal a few horses or cattle, they wouldn't build fires. I'm afraid it's. . . ." Belding hesitated and looked with grim concern at the cavalryman.

"What?" queried Thorne.

"I'm afraid it's Rojas."

Thorne turned exceedingly pale but did not lose his

nerve. "I thought of that at once. If true, it'll be terrible for Mercedes and me. But Rojas will never get his hands on my wife. If I can't kill him, I'll kill her. Belding, this is tough on you . . . this risk we put upon your family. I regret. . . ."

"Cut that kind of talk," replied Belding bluntly. "Well, if it is Rojas, he's acting damned strange for a raider. That's what worries me. We can't do anything but wait. With Laddy and Yaqui out there, we won't be surprised. Let's take the best possible view of the situation until we know more. That'll not likely be before tomorrow."

The women of the house might have gotten some sleep that night but it was certain the men did not get any. Morning broke cold and gray, the 19th of February. Breakfast was prepared earlier than usual, and an air of suppressed waiting excitement pervaded the place; otherwise, the ordinary details of the morning's work progressed as on any other day. Ladd came in, hungry and cold, and said the Mexicans were not breaking camp. He reported a good-size force of rebels and was taciturn as to his idea of forthcoming events.

About an hour after sunrise Yaqui ran in with the information that part of the rebels were crossing the river.

"That can't mean a fight yet," declared Belding. "But get in the house, boys, and make ready, anyway. I'll meet them."

"Drive them off the place same as if you had a company of soldiers backin' you," said Ladd. "Don't give them an inch. We're in bad, an' the bigger bluff we put up the more likely our chance."

"Belding, you're an officer of the United States. Mexicans are much impressed by show of authority. I've seen that often in camp," said Thorne.

"Oh, I know the white-livered greasers better than any of you, don't mistake me," replied Belding. He was pale with rage, but kept command over himself.

The rangers, with Yaqui and Thorne, stationed themselves at the several windows of the sitting room. Rifles and smaller arms and boxes of shells littered the tables and window seats. No little force of besiegers could have overcome a resistance such as Belding and his men were capable of making.

"Here they come, boys!" called Gale from his window.

"Rebel raiders I should say, Laddy."

"Shore. An' a fine outfit of buzzards."

"Reckon there's about a dozen in the bunch," observed the calm Lash. "Some horses they're ridin'. Where'n the hell did they get such horses, anyhow?"

"Shore, Jim, they work hard an' buy 'em with real silver *pesos*," replied Ladd sarcastically.

"Do any of you see Rojas?" whispered Thorne.

"Nix, no dandy bandit in that outfit."

"It's too far to see," said Gale.

The horsemen halted at the corrals. They were orderly and showed no evidence of hostility. They were, however, fully armed. Belding stalked out to meet them. It seemed a leader wanted to parley with him, but Belding would hear nothing. He shook his head, waved his arms, stamped to and fro, and his loud angry voice could be heard clear back at the house. Whereupon the detachment of rebels retired to the bank of the river, beyond the white post that marked the boundary line, and there they once more drew rein. Belding remained by the corrals watching them, and manifestly still in threatening mood. Presently a single rider left the troop and trotted his horse back down the road. When he reached the corrals, he was seen to halt and pass something to Belding. Then he galloped away to join his comrades.

Belding looked at whatever it was he held in his hand, shook his burly head, and started swiftly for the house. He came striding into the room, holding a piece of soiled paper.

"Can't read it and don't know as I want to," he said savagely.

"Belding, shore we'd better read it," replied Ladd. "What we want is a line on them greasers. Whether they're Campo's men or Salazar's or just a wanderin' bunch of rebels . . . or Rojas's bandits. ¿*Sabe, señor?*"

Not one of the men was able to translate the garbled scrawl.

"Shore Mercedes can read it," said Ladd.

Thorne opened a door and called her. She came into the room followed by Nell and Mrs. Belding. Evidently all three sensed a critical situation.

"My dear, we want you to read what's written on this paper," said Thorne as he led her to the table. "It was sent in by rebels and . . . and we fear contains bad news for us."

Mercedes gave the writing what seemed a swift glance, then fainted in Thorne's arms. He carried her to a couch and, with Nell and Mrs. Belding, began to work over her.

Belding looked at his rangers. It was characteristic of the man that now when catastrophe appeared inevitable all the gloom and care and angry agitation passed from him.

"Laddy, it's Rojas all right. How many men has he out there?"

"Mebbe twenty. Not more."

"We can lick twice that many greasers."

"Shore."

Jim Lash removed his pipe long enough to speak. "I reckon. But it ain't sense to start a fight when mebbe we can avoid it."

"What's your idea?"

"Let's stave the greaser off till dark. Then Laddy an' me an' Thorne will take Mercedes an' hit the trail for Yuma."

"Camino del Diablo! That awful trail with a woman! Boys, do you forget how many hundreds of men have perished on the Devil's Road?"

"I reckon I ain't forgettin' nothin'," replied Jim. "The water holes are full now. There's grass, an' we can do the job in six days."

"It's three hundred miles to Yuma."

"Belding, Jim's idee hits me pretty reasonable," interposed Lash. "Lord knows, that's about the only chance we've got except fightin'."

"But suppose we do stave Rojas off, and you get safely

away with Mercedes. Isn't Rojas going to find it out quick? Then what'll he try to do to us who're left here?"

"I reckon he'd find out by daylight," replied Jim. "But, Tom, he ain't a-goin' to start a scrap then. He'd want time an' hosses an' men to chase us on the trail. You see, I'm figgerin' all in the crazy greaser's wantin' the girl. I reckon he'll try to clean us up here to get her. But he's too smart to fight you for nothin'. Rojas may be nutty about women, but he's afraid of the U.S. Take my word for it, he'd discover the trail in the mornin' an' light out on it. I reckon with ten hours' start we could travel comfortable."

Belding paced up and down the room. Jim and Ladd whispered together. Gale walked to the window and looked out at the distant group of bandits, and then turned his gaze to rest upon Mercedes. She was conscious now, and her eyes seemed all the larger and blacker for the whiteness of her face. Thorne held her hands and the other women were trying to still her trembling. No one but Gale saw the Yaqui in the background, looking down upon the Spanish girl. All of Yaqui's looks were strange, but this was singularly so. Gale marked it, felt he would never forget. Mercedes's beauty had never before struck him as being so exquisite, so alluring as now when she lay stricken. Gale wondered if the Indian was affected by her loveliness, her helplessness, or her terror. Yaqui had seen Mercedes only a few times and upon each of these he had appeared to be fascinated. Could the strange Indian, because his hate of Mexicans was so great, be gloating over her misery? Something about Yaqui—a noble austerity of countenance—made Gale consider his suspicion unjust.

Presently Belding called his rangers to him, and then Thorne.

"Listen to this," he said earnestly. "I'll go out and have a talk with Rojas. I'll try to reason with him, tell him to think a long time before he sheds blood on Uncle Sam's soil. That he's now after an American's wife! I'll not commit myself, nor will I refuse outright to consider his de-

mands, nor will I show the least fear of him. I'll play for
time. If my bluff goes through, well and good. After dark,
the four of you, Laddy, Jim, Dick, and Thorne will take
Mercedes and my best white horses, and, with Yaqui as
guide, circle around through Altar Valley to the trail, and
head for Yuma. Wait now, Laddy. Let me finish. I want
you to take the white horses for two reasons . . . to save
them and to save you. Savvy? If Rojas should follow on
my horses, he'd be likely to catch you. Also you can pack
a great deal more than on bronc's. Also the big horses can
travel faster and farther on little grass and water. I want
you to take the Indian because in a case of this kind he'll
be a godsend. If you get headed off or lost or have to circle
off the trail, think what it'd mean to have a Yaqui with
you. He knows Sonora, as no greaser knows it. He could
hide you, find water and grass, where you would absolutely believe it impossible. The Indian is loyal. He has
his debt to pay and he'll pay it, don't mistake me. When
you're gone, I'll hide Nell so Rojas won't see her if he
searches the place. Then I think I could sit down and wait
without any particular worry."

The rangers approved of Belding's plan and Thorne
choked in his effort to express his gratitude.

"All right, we'll chance it," concluded Belding. "I'll go
out now and call Rojas and his outfit over. Say, it might be
as well for me to know just what he said in that paper."

Thorne went to the side of his wife.

"Mercedes, we've planned to outwit Rojas. Will you tell
us just what he wrote?"

The girl sat up, her eyes dilating, and, with hands
clasping Thorne's, she said: "Rojas swore . . . by his saints
and his Virgin . . . that if I was not given over . . . to
him . . . in twenty-four hours . . . he would set fire to the
village . . . kill the men . . . carry off the women . . . hang
the children on the cactus thorns."

A moment's silence followed her last halting whisper.

"By his saints an' his Virgin!" echoed Ladd. He

laughed—a cold, cutting, deadly laugh—significant and terrible to hear.

Then the Yaqui uttered a singular cry. Gale had heard it once before and now he remembered it was at the Papago Well.

"Look at the Indian," whispered Belding hoarsely. "Damn if I don't believe he understood every word Mercedes said. And, gentlemen, don't mistake me, if he ever gets near Rojas, there'll be some gory Aztec knife work."

Yaqui had moved close to Mercedes and stood beside her as she leaned against her husband. She seemed impelled to meet the Indian's gaze and evidently it was so powerful or hypnotic that it wrought irresistibly upon her. But she must have seen or divined what was beyond the others, for she offered him her trembling hand. Yaqui took it and laid it against his body in a strange motion and bowed his head. Then he stepped back into the shadow of the room.

Belding went outdoors while the rangers took up their former position at the west window. Each had his own somber thoughts, Gale imagined, and knew his own were dark enough. A slow fire crept along his veins. He saw Belding halt at the corrals and wave his hand. Then the rebels mounted and came briskly up the road, this time to rein in abreast.

Wherever Rojas had kept himself upon the former advance was not clear, but he certainly was prominently in sight now. He made a gaudy, almost a dashing figure. Gale did not recognize the white sombrero, the crimson scarf, the velvet jacket, or any of the features of the dandy's costume, but their general effect, the whole ensemble recalled vividly to mind his first sight of the bandit. Rojas dismounted and seemed to be listening. He betrayed none of the excitement Gale had seen in him that night at the Del Sol. Evidently this composure struck Ladd and Lash as unusual in a Mexican supposed to be laboring under stress of feeling. Belding made gestures, vehemently bobbed his big head, appeared to talk with his body as much as with his tongue. Then Rojas was seen to reply, and after that it was manifest that a conversation ensued that was both painful in subject and difficult of execution. It ended finally in what appeared to be mutual understanding. Rojas mounted and rode away with his men while Belding came tramping back to the house.

As he entered the door, his eyes were shining, his big hands were clenched, and he was breathing audibly.

"You can rope me if I'm not locoed!" he burst out. "I went out to conciliate a red-handed little murderer and damn me if I didn't meet a . . . a . . . well, I've no suitable name handy. I started my bluff and got along pretty well, but I forgot to mention that Mercedes was Thorne's wife. And what do you think? Rojas swore he loved Mercedes . . . swore he'd marry her right here in Forlorn River . . . swore he would give up robbing and killing people, and take her away from Mexico. He has gold . . . jewels. He swore if he didn't get her, nothing mattered. He'd die anyway without her. And here's the strange thing. I believed him. He was cold as ice and all hell a-raging inside. Never saw a greaser like him. Well, I pretended to be greatly impressed. We got to talking friendly, I suppose, though I didn't understand half he said, and I imagine he gathered less what I said. Anyway, without my asking, he said for me to think it over for a day and then we'd talk again."

"Shore we're born lucky!" ejaculated Ladd.

"I reckon Rojas'll be smart enough to string his outfit across the few trails leadin' out of Forlorn River," remarked Jim.

"That needn't worry us. All we want is dark to come," replied Belding. "Yaqui will slip through. If we thank any lucky stars, let it be for the Indian. Now, boys, put on your thinking caps. You'll take eight horses, the pick of my bunch. You must pack all that's needed for a possible long trip. Mind, Yaqui may lead you down into some wild

Sonora valley and give Rojas the slip. You may get to Yuma in six days and maybe in six weeks. Yet you've got to pack light. A small pack in saddles, larger ones on the two free horses. You may have one hell of a fight. Laddy, take the Four-Oh-Five. Dick will pack his Remington. All of you go gunned heavy. But the main thing is a pack that'll be light enough for swift travel, yet one that'll keep you from starving on the desert."

The rest of the day passed swiftly. Dick had scarcely a word with Nell, and all the time as he chose and deliberated and worked over his little pack his heart beat laborsomely, making a pang in his breast.

The sun set, twilight fell, then night closed down, fortunately a night slightly overcast. Gale saw the white horses pass his door like silent ghosts. Even Blanco Diablo made no sound, and that fact was indeed a tribute to the Yaqui. Gale went out to put his saddle on Blanco Sol. The horse rubbed a soft nose against his shoulder. Then Gale returned to the sitting room. There was nothing more to do, but wait and say good bye. Mercedes came in, clad in leather chaps and coat, a slim stripling of a cowboy, her dark eyes flashing. Her beauty could not be hidden, and now hope and courage had fired her blood.

Gale drew Nell off into the shadow and took her into his arms. He had not bade her a good bye since she had become his promised wife, and this departure was infinitely more hazardous than any he had ever before undertaken. He could only hold her close to his breast.

"Dear Dick . . . de-dear Dick, my heart is breaking," faltered Nell as she clung to him. "I'm a selfish . . . little coward. It's so . . . so splendid of you all. I ought to glory in it . . . but I can't. Oh, I love you so, Dick. I never knew it till now. I love you so. I'll be safe and I'll wait . . . and hope and pray for your return. Fight if you must, Dick, fight for that lovely persecuted girl. I'll love you . . . the more. Oh, good bye. Good bye."

Belding was in the room, speaking softly.

"Yaqui says the early hour's best. Trust him, Laddy. Remember what I say . . . the Indian's a godsend."

Then they were all outside in the pale gloom under the trees. Yaqui went up on Blanco Diablo; Mercedes was lifted upon White Woman; Thorne climbed astride Queen; Jim Lash was already upon his horse that was as white as the others but bore no name; Ladd mounted the stallion, El Gran Toro Blanco, and gathered up the long halters of the two pack horses; Gale came last on Blanco Sol.

As he toed the stirrup, hand on mane and pommel, Gale took one more look in at the door. Nell stood in the gleam of light, her hair shining, her face like ashes, her eyes dark, her lips parted, her arms outstretched. That sweet and tragic picture etched its cruel outlines into Gale's heart. He waved his hand, and then fiercely leaped into the saddle. Blanco Sol stepped out.

Before Gale stretched a line of moving horses, white against the dark shadows. He could not see the head of that column; he scarcely heard a soft hoof beat. A single star shone out of a rift in thin clouds. There was no wind. The air was cold. The dark space of desert seemed to yawn. To the left across the river flickered a few campfires. The chill night, silent and mystical, seemed to close in upon Gale, and he faced the wide, glowering, black level with keen eyes and grim intent, and an awakening of that wild rapture that came like a spell to him in the open desert.

CHAPTER ELEVEN:
ACROSS CACTUS AND LAVA

Blanco Sol showed no inclination to bend his head to the alfalfa that softly swished about his legs. Gale felt the horse's sensitive, almost human alertness. Sol knew as well as his master the nature of that flight.

At the far corner of the field Yaqui halted and slowly the line of white horses merged into a compact mass. There was a trail here leading down to the river. The campfires were so close that the bright blazes could be seen in movement, and dark forms crossed in front of them. Yaqui slipped out of his saddle. He ran his hand over Diablo's nose and spoke low, and repeated this action for each of the other horses. Gale had long ceased to question the strange Indian's behavior. There was no explaining or understanding many of his maneuvers. But the results of them were always thought-provoking. Gale had never seen horses stand so silently as in this instance. No stamp, no champ of bit—no toss of head—no shake of saddle or pack—no heave or snort. It seemed they had become inbred with the spirit of the Indian.

Yaqui moved away into the shadows as noiselessly as if he were one of them. The darkness swallowed him. He had taken a direction parallel with the trail. Gale wondered if Yaqui went to try to lead his string of horses by the rebel sentinels. Ladd had his head bent low, his ear toward the trail. Jim's long neck had the arch of a listening deer. Gale listened, too, and, as the slow silent mo-

ments went by, his faculty of hearing grew more acute
from strain. He heard Blanco Sol breathe; he heard the
pound of his own heart; he heard the silken rustle of the
alfalfa; he heard a faint, far-off sound of voice, like a lost
echo. Then his ear seemed to register a movement of air, a
disturbance so soft as to be nameless. Then followed long
silent moments.

Yaqui appeared as he had vanished. He might have
been part of the shadows. But he was there. He started off
down the trail leading Diablo. Again the white line
stretched slowly out. Gale fell in behind. A bench of
ground, covered with sparse greasewood, sloped gently
down to the deep wide arroyo of Forlorn River. Blanco Sol
shied a few feet out of the trail. Peering low with keen
eyes, Gale made out three objects—a white sombrero, a
blanket, and a Mexican lying face down. The Yaqui had
stolen upon this sentinel like a silent wind of death. Just
then a desert coyote wailed and the wild cry fitted the
darkness and the Yaqui's deed.

Once under the dark lee of the riverbank, Yaqui caused
another halt and he disappeared as before. It seemed to
Gale that the Indian started to cross the pale level
sandbed of the river, where stones stood out gray and the
darker line of opposite shore was visible. But he vanished
and it was impossible to tell whether he went one way or
another. Moments passed. The horses held heads up,
looked toward the glimmering campfires, and listened.
Gale thrilled with the meaning of it all—the night—the
silence—the flight—and that wonderful Indian stealing
with the slow inevitableness of doom upon another sentinel. An hour passed and Gale seemed to have become
deadened to all sense of hearing. There were no more
sounds in the world. The desert was as silent as it was
black. Yet—again came that strange change in the intensity of Gale's ear strain, a check, a break, a vibration—and
this time the sound did not go nameless. It might heave
been a moan of wind or wail of far-distant wolf, but Gale
imagined it was the strangling death cry of another guard

or that strange involuntary utterance of the Yaqui. Blanco
Sol trembled in all his great frame, and then Gale was certain the sound was not imagination.

That certainty, once and for all, fixed in Gale's mind the
mood of this flight. The Yaqui dominated the horses, the
rangers, and Thorne and Mercedes were as persons under
a spell. The Indian's strange silence, the feeling of mystery and power he seemed to create, all that was incomprehensible about him were veritable in the light of his
slow, sure, and ruthless action. If he dominated the others, surely he did more for Gale—colored his thoughts—
presaged the wild and terrible future of that flight. If
Rojas embodied all the hatred and passion of the peon-
scourged slave for a thousand years—then Yaqui embodied all the darkness, the cruelty, the white sun-heated
blood, the ferocity, the tragedy of the desert.

Suddenly the Indian stalked, as it were, out of the
gloom. He mounted Diablo and headed down across the
river. Once more the line of moving white shadows
stretched out. The soft sand gave forth no sound at all.
The glimmering campfires sank behind the western bank.
Yaqui led into the willows, and there was faint swishing
of leaves, then into the mesquite, and there was faint
rustling of branches. The glimmering lights appeared
again, and grotesque forms of saguaros loomed darkly.
Gale peered sharply along the trail, and presently, on the
pale sand under a cactus, there lay a blanketed form,
prone, outstretched, a carbine clutched in one hand, a cigarette, still burning, in the other.

The cavalcade of white horses passed within 500 yards
of campfires around which dark forms plainly moved.
Soft pads in sand, faint metallic *tickings* of steel on thorns,
low regular breathing of horses—these were all the
sounds the fugitives made, and they could not have been
heard at one fifth the distance. The lights disappeared
from time to time, grew dimmer, more flickering, and at
last they vanished altogether. Belding's fleet and tireless
steeds were out in front; the desert opened ahead wide,

dark, vast; Rojas and his rebels were believed to be eating, drinking, careless. All was not somber and grim in Gale's heart. He held now an unquenchable faith in the Yaqui. Belding would be listening back there along the river. He would know of the escape. He would tell Nell, and then hide her safely. As Gale had accepted a strange and fatalistic foreshadowing of toil, blood, and agony in this desert journey, so he believed in Mercedes's ultimate freedom and happiness, and his own return to the girl who had grown dearer than life.

A cold gray dawn was fleeing before a rosy sun when Yaqui halted the march at Papago Well. The horses were taken to water, then led down the arroyo into the grass. Here packs were slipped, saddles removed. Mercedes was cold, lame, tired, but happy. It warmed Gale's blood to look at her. The shadow of fear still lay darkly in her eyes, but it was passing. Hope and courage shone there, and affection for her ranger protectors and the Yaqui, and unutterable love for the cavalryman. Jim Lash jocosely remarked how cleverly they had fooled the rebels.

"Shore they'll be comin' along," replied Ladd.

They built a fire, cooked, and ate. The Yaqui spoke only one word: "Sleep." Blankets were spread. Mercedes dropped into a deep slumber, her head on Thorne's saddle. Excitement kept Thorne awake. The two rangers dozed beside the fire. Gale shared the Yaqui's watch. The sun began to climb and the icy edge of dawn to wear away. Rabbits bobbed their cottontails under the mesquites. Gale climbed a rocky wall above the arroyo bank, and there, with command over miles of the back trail, he watched.

It was a sweeping, rolling, wrinkled, and streaked range of desert that he saw, ruddy in the morning sunlight, with the patches of cactus and mesquite roughetched in shimmering green. No Name Mountains split the eastern sky, lowering high, gloomy, grand, with purple veils upon their slopes. They were forty miles away and looked five. Gale thought of the girl who was there under their shadow.

Yaqui kept the horses bunched and he led them from one little park of galleta grass to another. At the end of three hours he took them to water. Upon his return, Gale clambered down from his outlook, the rangers grew active, Mercedes was awakened, and soon the party faced westward with their long shadows moving before them. Yaqui led with Blanco Diablo in a long, easy lope. The arroyo washed itself out into flat desert, and the greens began to shade into gray, and then the gray into red. Only sparse cactus and weathered ledges dotted the great, low roll of a rising escarpment. Yaqui suited the gait of his horse to the lay of the land, and his followers accepted his pace. There were canter and trot, and swift walk and slow climb, and long swing—miles up and down and forward. The sun soared hot. The heated air lifted and incoming currents from the west swept, low and hard, over the barren earth. In the distance, all around the horizon, accumulations of dust seemed like ranging, mushrooming yellow clouds.

Yaqui was the only one of the fugitives who never looked back. Mercedes did it the most. Gale felt what compelled her—could not himself resist it. But it was a vain search. For a thousand puffs of white and yellow dust rose from that backward sweep of desert, and any one of them might have been blown from under horses' hoofs. Gale had a conviction that, when Yaqui gazed back toward the well and the shining plain beyond, there would be reason for it. But when the sun lost its heat and the wind died down, Yaqui took long and careful survey westward from the high points on the trail. Sunset was not far off and there in a bare and spotted valley lay Coyote Tanks, the only water hole between Papago Well and the Sonoyta Oasis. Gale used his glass, told Yaqui there was no smoke, no sign of life; still, the Indian fixed his falcon eyes on distant spots and looked long. It was as if his vision could not detect what reason or cunning or intention, perhaps an instinct, told him was there. Presently, in a sheltered spot, where blown sand had not obliterated marks in the trail, Yaqui found the tracks of horses. The curve of the iron shoes pointed westward. An intersecting trail from the north came in here. Gale thought the tracks either one or two days old. Ladd said they were one day. The Indian shook his head.

No farther advance was undertaken. The Yaqui headed south and traveled slowly, climbing to the brow of a bold bulge of weathered mesa. There he sat his horse and waited. No one questioned him. The rangers got down to stretch their legs, and Mercedes was lifted to a rock where she rested. Thorne had gradually yielded to the desert's influence for silence. He spoke once or twice to Gale, and occasionally whispered to Mercedes. Gale fancied his friend would soon learn that necessary speech in the desert travel meant a few greetings, a few words to make real the fact of human companionship, a few short terse terms for the business of day or night, and perhaps both stern order and soft call to a horse.

The sun went down and the golden, rosy veils turned to blue and shaded darker till twilight was there in the valley. Only the spurs of mountains, spiring the near and far horizon, retained their clear outline. Darkness approached, and the clear parts faded. The horses stamped to be on the move.

"¡Malo!" exclaimed the Yaqui.

He did not point with arm, but his falcon head stretched out, and his piercing eyes gazed at the blurring spot that marked the location of Coyote Tanks.

"Jim, can you see anything?" asked Ladd.

"Nope, but I reckon he can."

Darkness increased momentarily till night shaded the deepest part of the valley.

Then Ladd suddenly straightened up, turned to his horse, and muttered low under his breath.

"I reckoned so," said Lash, and for once his easy, good-natured tone was not in evidence. It was almost harsh.

Gale's eyes, keen as they were, were last of the rangers to see tiny needlepoints of light just faintly perceptible in the blackness.

"Laddy . . . campfires?" he asked quickly.

"Shore's you're born, my boy."

"How many?"

Ladd did not reply, but Yaqui held up his hand, his fingers wide. Five campfires! A strong force of rebels or raiders or some other desert troop was camping at Coyote Tanks.

Yaqui sat his horse for a moment, motionless as stone, his dark face immutable and impassive. Then he stretched wide his right arm in the direction of No Name Mountains, now losing their last faint traces of the afterglow, and he shook his head. He made the same impressive gesture toward the Sonoyta Oasis, with the same somber negation.

Thereupon he turned Diablo's head to the south and started down the slope. His manner had been decisive, even stern. Lash did not question it, nor did Ladd. But both rangers hesitated, showed a strange, almost a sullen reluctance, that Gale had never seen in them before. Raiders were one thing, Rojas was another, Camino del Diablo still another, but that vast and desolate and unwatered waste of cactus and lava, the Sonora Desert, might appall the stoutest heart. Gale felt his own sink—felt himself flinch.

"Oh, where is he going?" cried Mercedes. Her poignant voice seemed to break a spell.

"Shore, lady, Yaqui's goin' home," replied Ladd gently. "An' considerin' our troubles, I reckon we ought to thank God he knows the way."

They mounted and rode down the slope toward the darkening south.

Not until night travel was obstructed by a wall of cactus did the Indian halt to make dry camp. Water and grass for the horses and fire to cook by were not here to be had.

Mercedes bore up surprisingly, but she fell asleep almost the instant her thirst had been allayed. Thorne laid her upon a blanket and covered her. The men ate and drank. Diablo was the only horse that showed impatience, but he was angry, and not in any distress. Blanco Sol licked Gale's hand, and heaved patiently. Many a time had he taken his rest at night without a drink. Yaqui again bade the men sleep. Ladd said he would take the early watch, but from the way the Indian shook his head and squatted against a stone, it appeared, if Ladd remained awake, he would have company. Gale lay down weary of limb and eye. He heard the soft *thump* of hoofs, the sough of wind in the cactus—then no more.

When he awoke, there was bustle and stir about him. Day had not yet dawned and the air was freezing cold. Yaqui had found a scant bundle of greasewood that served for warmth and to cook breakfast. Mercedes was not aroused till the last moment.

Day dawned with the fugitives in the saddle. A picketed wall of cactus hedged them in, yet the Yaqui made a tortuous path that, zigzag as it might, in the main always headed south. It was wonderful how he slipped Diablo through the narrow aisles of thorns, saving the horse and saving himself. The others were torn and clutched and held and stung. The way was a flat sandy pass between low mountain ranges. There were open spots and aisles and squares of sand, and hedging rows of prickly pear and the huge spider-legged ocotillo and hummocky masses of clustered *bisnaga*. The day grew dry and hot. A fragrant wind blew through the pass. Cactus flowers bloomed, red and yellow and magenta. The sweet pale *ajo* lily gleamed in shady corners.

Ten miles of travel covered the length of the pass. It opened widely upon a wonderful scene, an arboreal desert, dominated by its pure light green, yet lined by many merging colors. And it led and ascended to a low, dim, and dark-red zone of lava, spurred, peaked, domed by volcanic cones, a wild and ragged region, illimitable as the horizon.

The Yaqui, if not at fault, was yet uncertain. His falcon eyes searched and roved, and fixed at length toward the southwest in which direction he turned his horse. The great fluted saguaros, fifty, sixty feet high, towered their columned forms, and their every branching limb and curving line added a grace to the desert. It was the low-bushed cactus that made toil and pain of travel. Yet these thorny forms were beautiful.

In the basins between the ridges, to right and left along the floor of low plains, the mirage glistened, narrowed, faded, vanished—lakes and trees and clouds. Inverted mountains hung suspended in the lilac air and faint tracery of white-walled cities.

At noon Yaqui halted the cavalcade. He had selected a field of *bisnaga* cactus for the place of rest. Presently his reason became obvious. With long heavy knife he cut off the tops of these barrel-shaped plants. He scooped out soft pulp, and with stone and hand then began to pound deeper pulp into a juicy mass. When he threw this out, there was a little water left, sweet and cool water, of which man and horse partook with avidity. Thus he made even the desert's fiercest growth minister to their needs.

But he did not halt long. Miles of gray-green spiked walls lay between him and that line of ragged red lava that manifestly he must reach before dark. The travel became faster, straighter, and the glistening thorns seemed fiendishly to clutch and cling to leather and cloth and flesh. The horses reared, snorted, balked, leaped—but they were sent on. Only Blanco Sol, the patient, the plodding, the indomitable, needed no goad or spur. Waves and scarves and wreaths of heat smoked up from the sand. Mercedes reeled in her saddle. Thorne bade her drink, bathed her face, supported her, and then gave way to Ladd who took the girl with him on El Gran Toro Blanco's broad back. Yaqui's unflagging direction, his

iron arm, were bitter and hateful to the proud and
haughty spirit of Blanco Diablo. For once Belding's great
white devil had met his master. He fought rider, bit, bridle, cactus, sand—and yet he went on and on, zigzagging,
turning, winding, crashing through the barbed growths.
The middle of the afternoon saw Thorne bowing over his
pommel, weak, dizzy, and then, wherever possible, Gale's
powerful arm lent him strength to hold his seat.

The giant cactus came to be only so in name. These
saguaros were thinning out, growing stunted, and most
of them were single columns. Gradually other cactus
showed a harder struggle for existence, and the spaces of
sand between were wider. But now the dreaded glistening
frosty cholla began to show, pale and gray and white,
upon the rising slope. Round-topped hills, sunset-colored
above, blue-black below, intervened to hide the distant
spurs and peaks. Mile after mile long tongues of red lava
streamed out between the hills and wound down to stop
abruptly upon the slope.

The fugitives were entering a destroyed and desolate
burned-out world. It rose above them in limitless gradual
ascent and spread wide to east and west. Then the waste
of sand gave place greatly to cinders. The horses sank to
their fetlocks and toiled on. A fine, choking dust blew
back upon the tail of the cavalcade, and men coughed and
horses snorted. The huge round hills rose, smooth, symmetrical, colored as if the setting sun was shining on bare
blue-black surfaces. But the sun was now behind the hills.
In between ran the streams of lava. The horsemen skirted
the edge between slope of hill and perpendicular ragged
wall. This red lava seemed to have flowed and hardened
there only yesterday. It was broken, sharp, dull-rust color,
full of cracks and caves and crevices, and everywhere
upon its jagged surface grew the white-thorned cholla.

Again twilight encompassed the travelers. But there
was still light enough for Gale to see the constricted passage open into wide, deep space where the dull color was
relieved by gray, and gnarled and dwarfed mesquites

grew. Blanco Sol, keenest of scent, whistled his welcome herald of water. The other horses answered, quickened their gait. Gale smelled it, too, sweet, cool, damp on the dry air.

Yaqui turned the corner of a pocket in the lava wall. The file of white horses rounded the corner after him. And Gale, coming last, saw the pale glancing gleam of a pool of water, beautiful in the twilight.

Next day the Yaqui's relentless, driving demand on the horses was no longer in evidence. He lost no time but he did not hasten. The course he led over wound between low cinder dunes that obstructed any considerable view of the surrounding country. These dunes wore out finally, leveled down to black floor as hard as flint with tongues of lava to the left, and to the right the slow descent into the cactus plain. Yaqui was now traveling due west. It was Gale's idea that the Indian was skirting the first sharp-toothed slope of a vast volcanic plateau that formed the western half of the Sonora Desert and extended to the Gulf of California. Travel was slow but not exhausting for rider or beast. A little sand and meager grass gave grayish tinge to the strip of black ground between lava and plain.

That day, as the manner rather than the purpose of the Yaqui changed, so there seemed to be subtle differences in the others of the party. Gale himself lost a certain cold, sickening dread, which had not been for himself, but for Mercedes and Nell, and Thorne and the rangers. Jim might have been patrolling the boundary line for all his good nature. Ladd lost his taciturnity and what had been gloom became a cool, careless air. A mood that was almost defiance began to be manifested in Thorne. It was in Mercedes, however, that Gale marked the most significant change. Her collapse the preceding day might never have been. She was lame and sore; she rode her saddle side-wise and often she had to be rested and helped, but she had found a reserve fund of strength and her mental condition was not the same that it had been. Fear no longer abided with her. Gale reflected on the difference he always sensed in himself after a few days in the desert. Already Mercedes and he, and all of them, had begun to respond to the wild spirit of the desert. Moreover, Yaqui's strange, subtle influence must have been a call to the primitive.

Thirty miles of easy stages brought the fugitives to another water hole, a little round pocket under the heaved-up edge of lava. There was spare, short, bleached grass for the horses, but no wood for a fire. This night there was question and reply, conjecture, doubt, opinion, and conviction expressed by the men of the party. But the Indian, who alone could have told where they were, where they were going, what chance they had to escape, maintained his stoical silence. Gale took the early watch, Ladd the midnight one, and Lash that of the morning.

The day broke rosy, glorious, cold as ice. Action was necessary to make useful benumbed hands and feet. Mercedes was fed while yet wrapped in blankets. Then, while the packs were being put on and horses saddled, she walked up and down, slapping her hands, warming her ears. The rose color of the dawn was in her cheeks and the wonderful clearness of desert light in her eyes. Thorne seldom gazed at anything but her. The rangers watched her. The Yaqui bent his glance upon her only seldom, but when he did look, it seemed his strange, fixed, and inscrutable face was about to break into a smile. Yet that never happened. Gale himself was surprised to find how often his own eyes sought the slender, dark, beautiful Spaniard. Was this because of her beauty, he wondered. He thought not altogether. Mercedes was a woman. She represented something in life that men of all races for thousands of years had loved to see and own, to revere and debase, to fight for and die for.

Yaqui's saving a blanket out of the packs and tearing it in strips to bind the legs of the horses was the most significant action regarding the day's travel. It meant the dreaded cholla and the knife-edged lava. That Yaqui did not mount Diablo was still more significant. Mercedes must ride, but the others had to walk.

The Indian led off into one of the gray notches between the tumbled streams of lava. These streams were about thirty feet high, a rotting mass of splintered lava, rougher than any other kind of roughness in the world. At the apex of the notch where two streams met, a narrow gully wound and ascended. Gale caught sight of the dim pale shadow of a one-time trail. Near at hand it was invisible; he had to look far ahead to catch the faint tracery. Yaqui led Diablo into it, and then began the most laborsome and vexatious and painful of all slow travel.

Once upon top of that lava bed, Gale saw stretching away, breaking into millions of crests and ruts, a vast, red-black field sweeping onward and upward, with ragged low ridges and mounds and spurs leading higher and higher to a great split escarpment wall, above which dim peaks shone hazily blue in the distance.

He looked no more in that direction. To keep his foothold, to save his horse, cost him all energy and attention. The course was marked out for him in the tracks of the other horses. He had only to follow. But nothing could have been more difficult. The disintegrating surface of a lava bed was at once the roughest, the hardest, the meanest, the cruelest, the most deceitful kind of ground to travel. It was rotten, yet had corners as hard and sharp as spikes. It was rough, yet as slippery as ice. If there was a foot of level surface, that space would be one to break through under a horse's hoofs. It was seamed, lined, cracked, ridged, knotted iron. This lava bed resembled a tremendously magnified clinker. It had been a running sea of molten flint, boiling, bubbling, spouting, and it had burst its surface into a million sharp facets as it hardened. The color was dull black, angry red, like no other red, inflaming to the eye. The millions of minute crevices were dominated by deep fissures and holes, ragged and rough beyond all comparison.

The fugitives made slow progress. They picked a cautious, winding way, to and fro in little steps, here and there along the many twists of the trail, up and down the unavoidable depressions, around and around the holes. At noon, so winding back upon itself had been their course, they appeared to have come only a short distance of the lava slope.

If it was rough work for them, it was terrible work for the horses. Blanco Diablo didn't answer here to the power of the Yaqui. He balked, he plunged, he bit and kicked. He had to be pulled and beaten over many places. Mercedes's horse almost threw her, and she was put upon Blanco Sol. The white charger snorted a protest, then, obedient to Gale's stern call, patiently lowered his noble head and pawed the lava for a footing that would hold.

The lava caused Gale toil and worry and pain, but he hated the chollas. As the travel progressed, this species of cactus increased in number of plants and in size. Everywhere the red lava was spotted with little round patches of glistening, frosty white. And under every bunch of cholla along and in the trail were the discarded joints, like little, frosty, pine-cone-covered spines. It was utterly impossible always to be on the look-out for these, and, when Gale stepped on one, often as not the steel-like thorns pierced leather and flesh. Gale came almost to believe what he had heard claimed by desert travelers—that the cholla was alive and leaped at man or beast. Certain it was when Gale passed one, if he did not put all attention to avoiding it, he was hooked through his chaps and held by barbed thorns. The pain was almost unendurable. It was like no other. It burned, stung, beat—almost seemed to freeze. It made useless arm or leg. It made him bite his tongue to keep from crying out. It made the sweat roll off him. It made him sick.

Moreover, bad as the cholla was for man, it was infinitely worse for beast. A jagged stab from this poisoned cactus was the only thing Blanco Sol could not stand. Many times that day, before he carried Mercedes, he had wildly snorted, and then stood trembling while Gale picked broken thorns from the muscular legs. But after Mercedes had been put upon Sol, Gale made sure no cholla touched him.

The afternoon passed like the morning, in ceaseless winding and twisting and climbing along this abandoned trail. Gale saw many water holes, mostly dry, some containing water, all of them catch basins, full only after the rainy season. Little ugly bunched bushes that Gale scarcely recognized as mesquites grew near these holes, also stunted greasewood and prickly pear. There was no grass, and the cholla alone flourished in that hard soil.

Darkness overtook the party, as they unpacked beside a pool of water, deep under an overhanging shelf of lava. It had been a hard day. The horses drank their fill, and then stood patiently, with drooping heads. Appeased hunger and thirst, and a warm fire cheered the weary and footsore fugitives. Yaqui said: "Sleep." And so another night passed.

Upon the following morning, ten miles or more up the slow-ascending lava slope, Gale's attention was called from his somber search for the less rough places in the trail.

"Dick, why does Yaqui look back?" asked Mercedes.

Gale was startled. "Does he?"

"Every little while," replied Mercedes.

Gale was in the rear of all the other horses, so as to take, for Mercedes's sake, the advantage of the broken trail. Yaqui was leading Diablo, winding around a break. His head was bent as he stepped slowly and unevenly upon the lava. Gale turned to look back, the first time in several days. The mighty hollow of the desert below seemed a wide strip of red—a wide strip of green—a wide strip of gray—streaking to purple peaks. It was all too vast, too mighty, too universal for Gale to grasp any little details. He thought, of course, of Rojas in certain pursuit, but it seemed absurd to look for him.

Yaqui led on, and Gale often glanced up from his task to watch the Indian. Presently he saw him stop, turn, and look back. Ladd did likewise, and then Jim and Thorne. Gale found the desire irresistible. Thereafter he often rested Blanco Sol, and looked back the while. He had his field glass, but did not choose to use it.

"Rojas will follow," said Mercedes.

Gale regarded her in amaze. The tone of her voice had been indefinable. If there were fear there, he failed to detect it. She was gazing back down the colored slope and something about her, perhaps the steady falcon gaze of her magnificent eyes, reminded him of Yaqui.

Many times during the ensuing hour the Indian faced about, and always his followers did likewise. It was high noon, with the sun beating hot and the lava radiating heat, when Yaqui halted for a rest. The place selected was a bridge of lava, almost a promontory, considered for its outlook. The horses bunched here and drooped their heads. The rangers were about to slip the packs and remove saddles when Yaqui restrained them.

He fixed a changeless, gleaming gaze down the slow descent, and did not seem to look afar. Suddenly he uttered the strange cry—the one Gale considered involuntary or else significant of some tribal trait or feeling. It was incomprehensible, but no one could have doubted its potency. Yaqui pointed down the lava slope, pointed with finger and arm and neck and head—his whole body was instinct with direction. His whole being seemed to have been animated, and then frozen. His posture could not have been misunderstood, yet his expression had not altered. Gale had never seen the Indian's face change its hard red-bronze calm. It was of the color and the flintiness and the character of the lava at his feet.

"Shore he sees somethin'," said Ladd. "But my eyes are no good."

"I reckon I ain't sure of mine," replied Jim. "I'm bothered by a dim, movin' streak down there."

Thorne gazed eagerly down as he stood beside Mercedes who sat motionlessly, facing the slope. Gale looked and looked till he hurt his eyes. Then he took his glass out of its case on Sol's saddle.

There appeared to be nothing upon the lava but the immeasurable dots of cholla, shining in the sun. Gale swept his glass slowly forward and back. Then into a nearer field of vision crept a long white and black line of horses and men. Without a word he handed the glass to Ladd. The ranger used it, muttering to himself.

"They're in the lava fifteen miles down in an air line," he said presently. "Jim, shore they're twice that an' more accordin' to the trail."

Jim had his look and replied: "I reckon we're a day an' a night in the lead."

"Is it Rojas?" burst out Thorne with protruding jaw.

"Yes, Thorne. It's Rojas and a dozen men or more," replied Gale, and he looked up at Mercedes.

She was transformed. She might have been a medieval princess, embodying all the Spanish power and passion of that time, breathing revenge, hate, unquenchable spirit of fire. If her beauty had been wonderful in her helpless and appealing moments, now, when she looked back, white-faced and flame-eyed, it was transcendent.

Gale drew a long, deep breath. The mood that had presaged pursuit, strife, blood on this somber desert, returned to him tenfold. He saw Thorne's face corded by black veins and his teeth exposed like those of a snarling wolf. These rangers, who had coolly risked death many times, and had dealt it often, were white as no fear or pain could have made them. Then, in the moment, Yaqui raised his hand, not clutched or doubled tightly, but curled rigidly like an eagle's claw, and he shook it in strange, slow action that was menacing and terrible.

It was the woman that called to the depths of these men. And their passion to kill and to save was surpassed only by the strange, fatal, wild hate that was yet love, the unfathomable driving lust of a peon slave. Gale marveled at it, while he felt his whole internal being coldly clamp and tighten, while he turned once more to follow in the tracks of his leaders. The fight predicted by Belding was no great time off. What a fight that must be! Rojas was traveling light, swift; he was gaining. He had bought his men with gold, with extravagant promises, perhaps with offers of the body and blood of an aristocrat hateful to their kind. Lastly there was the wild, desolate environment, a tortured wilderness of jagged lava and poisoned cholla, a lonely, fierce, and repellant world, a red stage most somberly and fittingly colored for a supreme struggle between men.

Yaqui looked back no more. Mercedes looked back no more. But the others looked, and the time came when Gale saw the creeping line of pursuers with naked eyes.

A level line above marked the rim of the plateau. Sand began to show in the little lava pits. On and upward toiled the cavalcade, still very slowly advancing. At last Yaqui reached the rim. He stood with his hand on Blanco Diablo, and both were silhouetted against the sky. That was the outlook for a Yaqui. And his great horse, dazzlingly white as the sunlight, with head wildly and proudly erect, mane and tail flying in the wind, made a magnificent picture. The others toiled on and upward, and at last Gale led Blanco Sol over the rim. Then all looked down the red slope. But shadows were gathering there and no moving line could be seen.

Yaqui mounted and wheeled Diablo away. The others followed suit. Gale saw that the plateau was no more than a vast field of low, ragged circles, levels, mounds, cones, and whorls of lava. The lava was of a darker red than that down on the slope and it was harder than flint. In places fine sand and cinders covered the uneven floor. Strange varieties of cactus vied with the omnipresent cholla. Yaqui, however, found ground that his horse covered at a swift walk.

But there was only an hour, perhaps, of this comparatively easy going. Then the Yaqui led into a zone of craters. The top of the earth seemed to have been blown

out in holes from a few rods in width to large craters,
some shallow, others deep, and all red as fire. Yaqui circled close to abysses that yawned sheer from a level surface, and he appeared always to be turning upon his
course to avoid them.

The plateau had now a considerable dip to the west.
Gale marked the slow heave and ripple of the ocean of
lava to the south where high, rounded peaks marked the
center of this volcanic region. The uneven nature of the
slope westward prevented any extended view, until suddenly the fugitives emerged from a rugged break to arise
upon a sublime and awe-inspiring spectacle.

They were upon a high point of the western slope of the
plateau. It was a slope, but so many leagues long in its descent that only from a great height could any slant have
been perceptible. Yaqui and his white horse stood upon
the brink of a crater miles in circumference, 1,000 feet
deep, with its red walls patched in frost-colored spots by
the silvery chollas. The giant tracery of lava streams
waved down the slope to wear out in undulating sand
dunes. And these bordered a seemingly endless arm of
blue sea. This was the Gulf of California. Beyond the Gulf
rose dim, bold mountains, and above them hung the setting sun, dusky red, flooding all that barren empire with a
sinister light.

It was strange to Gale then, and perhaps to the others,
to see their guide lead Diablo into a smooth and well-
worn trail along the rim of the awful crater. Gale looked
across into that red chasm. It resembled an inferno. The
dark cliffs upon the opposite side were veiled in blue haze
that seemed like smoke. Here Yaqui was at home. He
moved and looked about him as a man coming at last into
his own. Gale saw him stop and gaze out over that red-
ribbed void to the Gulf.

Gale divined that somewhere along this crater of hell
the Yaqui would make his final stand, and one look into
his strange, inscrutable eyes made imagination picture a
fittingly colored doom for the pursuing Rojas.

Chapter Twelve:
The Crater of Hell

The trail led along a gigantic fissure opening in the side of the crater, and then down and down into a red-walled, blue-hazed labyrinth.

Presently Gale, upon turning a sharp corner, was utterly amazed to see that the split in the lava sloped out and widened into an arroyo. It was so green and soft and beautiful in all the angry, contorted, red surrounding that Gale could scarcely credit his sight. Blanco Sol whistled his welcome to its scent of water. Then Gale saw a great hole, a pit in the shiny lava, a dark, cool, shady well. There was evidence of the fact that at flood seasons the water had outlet into the arroyo. The soil of this place appeared to be a fine sand, in which a reddish tinge predominated, and it was abundantly covered with a long grass, still partly green. Mesquites and paloverdes dotted the arroyo and gradually closed in thickets that obstructed the view.

"Shore it all beats me!" exclaimed Ladd. "What a place to hole up in! We could have hid here for a long time. Boys, I saw mountain sheep, the real old genuine Rocky Mountain big horn. What do you think of that?"

"I reckon it's a Yaqui huntin' ground," replied Lash. "That trail we hit must be hundreds of years old. It's worn deep an' smooth in the iron lava."

"Well, all I got to say is Belding was shore right about

the Indian. An' I can see Rojas's finish somewhere up along that awful hell hole."

Camp was made on a level spot. Yaqui took the horses to water, and then turned them loose in the arroyo. It was a tired and somber group that sat down to eat. The strain of suspense equaled the wearing effects of the long ride. Mercedes was calm, but her great dark eyes burned in her white face. Yaqui watched her. The others looked at her with unspoken pride. Presently Thorne wrapped her in blankets, and it seemed she fell asleep at once. Twilight deepened. The campfire blazed brighter. A cool wind played with Mercedes's black hair, waving strands across her brow.

Little of Yaqui's purpose or plan could be elicited from him. But the look of him was enough to satisfy even Thorne. He leaned against a pile of wood he had collected and his gloomy gaze pierced the campfire and at long intervals strayed over the motionless form and white face of the Spanish girl.

The rangers and Thorne, however, talked in low tones. It was absolutely impossible for Rojas and his men to reach the water hole before noon of the next day. And long before that time the fugitives would have decided on a plan of defense. What that defense would be and where it would be made were matters over which the men gravely considered and conjectured. Ladd averred the Yaqui would put them into an impregnable position that at the same time would prove a deathtrap for their pursuers. They exhausted all angles of speculation and then, tired as they were, still kept on talking.

"What stuns me is that Rojas stuck to our trail," said Thorne, his lined and haggard face expressive of dark passion. "He has followed us into this fearful desert. He'll lose men, horses, perhaps his life. He's only a bandit and he stands to win no gold. If he ever gets out of here, it'll be by Herculean labor and by terrible hardship. All for a poor little helpless woman . . . my God, I can't understand it!"

"Shore . . . just a woman," replied Ladd, solemnly nodding his head.

Then there was a long silence during which the men gazed into the fire. Each perhaps had some vague conception of the enormity of Rojas's love or hate—some faint and amazing glimpse of the gulf of human passion. Those were cold, hard, grim faces upon which the light flickered.

"Sleep," said the Yaqui.

Thorne rolled in his blanket, close beside Mercedes. Then one by one the rangers stretched out, feet to the fire. Gale found that he was unable to sleep. His eyes were weary, but would not stay shut; his body ached for rest, yet he could not lie still. The night was so somber, so gloomy, and the lava-encompassed arroyo full of shadows. The dark velvet sky, fretted with white fire, seemed to be close. There was absolute silence, as of death. Nothing moved—nothing outside of Gale's body appeared to live. The Yaqui sat like an image carved out of lava. The others lay prone and quiet. Would another night see any of them lie that way, quiet forever? Gale felt a ripple over him that was at once a shudder and a contraction of muscles. Used as he was to the desert and his oppression, why should he feel tonight as if the weight of its lava and the burden of its mystery were bearing him down? He sat up after a while and again watched the fire. Nell's sweet face floated like a wraith in the pale smoke—glowed and flushed and smiled in the embers. Other faces shone there—his sister's—that of his mother. Gale shook off the tender memories. This desolate wilderness with its forbidding silence and its dark promise of hell on the morrow, this was not the place to unnerve oneself with thoughts of love and home. But the torturing paradox of the thing was that this was just the place and just the night for a man to be haunted.

By and by Gale rose and walked down a shadowy aisle between the mesquites. On his way back the Yaqui joined him. Gale was not surprised. He had become used to the

Indian's strange guardianship. But now, perhaps because of Gale's poignancy of thought, the contending tides of love and regret, the deep, burning premonition of deadly strife, he was moved to keener scrutiny of the Yaqui. That, of course, was futile. The Indian was impenetrable, silent, strange. But maddeningly, inexplicably Gale felt Yaqui's human quality. It was aloof, as was everything about this Indian, but it was there. This savage walked silently beside him, without glance or touch or word. His thought was as inscrutable as if mind had never awakened in his race. Yet Gale sensed something big and splendid and, somehow, he was reminded of the Indian's story. His home had been desolated, his people carried off to slavery, his wife and children separated from him to die. What had life meant to the Yaqui? What had been in his heart? What was now in his mind? Gale could not answer these questions. But the difference between him and Yaqui, which he had vaguely felt as that between savage and civilized man, faded out of his mind forever. Yaqui might have considered he owed Gale a debt, and with a Yaqui's austere and noble fidelity to honor meant to pay it; nevertheless, this was not the thing Gale sensed in the Indian's silent presence. Accepting the desert with its subtle and inconceivable influence, Gale felt the savage and the white man had been bound in a tie that was no less brotherly because it could not be comprehended.

Toward dawn Gale managed to get some sleep. The morning broke with the sun hidden back of the heave of the plateau. The horses trooped up the arroyo and snorted for water. After a hurried breakfast, the packs were hidden in holes in the lava. The saddles were left where they were and the horses allowed to graze and wander at will. Canteens were filled, a small bag of food was packed, blankets made into a bundle. Then Yaqui faced the steep ascent of the lava slope.

The trail he followed led up on the right side of the fissure, opposite to the one he had come down. It was a steep climb, and, encumbered as the men were, they made but slow progress. Mercedes had to be lifted up smooth steps and across crevices. They passed places where the rims of the fissure were but a few yards apart. At length the rims widened out—then the red, smoky crater yawned beneath. Yaqui left the trail and began clambering down over the rough and twisted convolutions of lava that formed the rim. Sometimes he hung sheer over the precipice. It was with extreme difficulty that the party followed him. Mercedes had to be held on narrow foot-wide ledges. The cholla was there to hinder passage. Finally the Indian halted upon a narrow bench of flat, smooth lava, and his followers worked with exceeding care and effort down to his position.

At the back of this bench between bushes of cholla was a niche, a shallow cave with floor lined in what resembled fleece. Ladd said the place was a nest that had been inhabited by mountain sheep for many years. Yaqui spread blankets inside, left a canteen and the sack of food, and with a gesture at once humble, yet that of a chief, he invited Mercedes to enter. A few more gestures and fewer words disclosed his plan. In this inaccessible nook Mercedes was to be hidden. The men were to go around upon the opposite rim and block the trail leading down to the water hole.

Gale marked the nature of this sheep aerie. It was the wildest and the most rugged place he had ever stepped upon. Only a sheep could have climbed up the wall above or along the slanting shelf of lava beyond. Below glistened a whole bank of cholla, frosty in the sunlight, and it overhung an apparently bottomless abyss.

Gale chose the smallest gun in the party and gave it to Mercedes.

"Shore it's best to go the limit on bein' ready," he said simply. "The chances are you'll never need it. But if you do. . . ."

He left off there and his break was significant. Mercedes answered him with a fearless and indomitable flash of eyes. Thorne was the only one who showed any shaken nerve. His leave-taking of his wife was affecting and hurried. Then he and the rangers carefully stepped in the tracks of the Yaqui.

They climbed up to the level of the rim and went along the edge. When they reached the fissure and came upon its narrowest point, Yaqui showed in his actions that he meant to leap it. Ladd restrained the Indian. They then continued along the rim till they reached several bridges of lava that crossed it. The fissure was deep in some parts, choked in others. Evidently the crater had no direct outlet into the arroyo below. Its bottom, however, must have been far beneath the level of the water hole.

After the fissure was crossed, the trail was soon found. Here it ran back from the rim. Yaqui waved his hand to the right where, along the corrugated slope of the crater, there were holes and crevices and coverts for a hundred men. Yaqui strode on up the trail toward a higher point where presently his dark figure stood motionlessly against the sky. The rangers and Thorne selected a deep depression out of which led several ruts deep enough for cover. According to Ladd, it was as good a place as any, perhaps not so hidden as others, but freer from the dreaded chollas. Here the men laid down rifles and guns and, removing their heavy cartridge belts, settled down to wait.

Their location was close to the rim wall and probably 500 yards from the opposite rim, which was now seen to be considerably below them. The glaring red cliff presented a deceitful and baffling appearance. It had a thousand ledges and holes in its surface, and one moment it looked perpendicular and the next a long slant. Thorne pointed out where he thought Mercedes was hidden; Ladd selected another place, and Lash still another. Gale searched for the bank of chollas he had seen under the bunch where Mercedes's retreat lay, and, when he found it, the others disputed his opinion. Then Gale brought his field glass into requisition, proving that he was right. Once located and fixed in sight, the white patch of cholla, the bench, and the sheep aerie stood out from the other features of that rugged wall. But all the men were agreed that Yaqui had hidden Mercedes where only the eyes of a vulture could have descried her.

Jim Lash crawled into a little strip of shade and bided the time tranquilly. Ladd was restless and impatient and watchful, every little while rising to look up the far-reaching slope, and then to the right where Yaqui's dark figure stood out from a high point of the rim. Thorne grew silent, and seemed consumed by a slow, sullen rage. Gale was neither calm nor free of a gnawing suspense or of a waiting wrath. But at best he could put the pending action out of mind.

It came over him all of a sudden that he had not grasped the stupendous nature of this desert setting. There was the measureless red slope, finally ribbing in the white sand dunes to the blue sea. The cold, sparkling light, the white sun, the deep azure of sky, the feeling of boundless expanse all around him—these meant high altitude. Southward the barren red simply merged into distance. The field of craters bulged in huge, dark wheels toward the dominating peaks. When Gale withdrew his gaze from the magnitude of these spaces and bulks, the crater beneath him seemed dwarfed. Yet, while he gazed, it spread and deepened and multiplied its ragged lines. No, he could not grasp the meaning of size or distance here. There was too much to stun the sight. But the mood in which Nature had created this convulsed world of lava was imparted to him.

Meanwhile the hours passed. As the sun climbed, the clear steely lights vanished, the blue hazes deepened, and slowly the glistening surfaces of lava turned redder. Ladd was concerned to discover that Yaqui was missing from his outlook upon the high point. Jim Lash came out of the shady crevice, and stood up to buckle on his cartridge belt. His narrow, gray glance slowly roved from the height of lava down along the slope, paused in doubt, and then swept on to resurvey the whole vast eastern dip of the plateau.

"I reckon my eyes are pore," he said. "Mebbe it's this damn' red glare. Anyway, what's them creepin' spots up there?"

"Shore I seen them. Mountain sheep," replied Ladd.

"Guess again, Laddy. Dick, I reckon you'd better flash the glass up the slope."

Gale adjusted the field glass and began to search the lava, beginning close at hand and working away from him. Presently the glass became stationary.

"I see half a dozen small animals, brown in color. They look like sheep. But I couldn't distinguish mountain sheep from antelope."

"Shore they're big horn," said Ladd.

"I reckon, if you'll pull 'round to the east an' search under that long wall of lava . . . there . . . you'll see what I see," added Jim.

The glass climbed and circled, wavered an instant, then fixed steady as a rock. There was a breathless silence.

"Fourteen horses . . . two packed . . . some mounted . . . others without riders and lame," said Gale slowly.

Yaqui appeared far up the trail, coming swiftly. Presently he saw the rangers and halted to wave his arms and point. Then he vanished as if the lava had opened beneath him.

"Lemme have that glass," suddenly said Jim Lash. "I'm seein' red, I tell you. Well, pore as my eyes are, they had it right. Rojas an' his outfit have left the trail."

"Jim, you ain't meanin' they've taken to that awful slope?" queried Ladd.

"I sure do. There they are . . . still comin', but goin' down, too."

"Mebbe Rojas is crazy, but it begins to look like he. . . ."

"Laddy, I'll be danged if the greaser bunch hasn't vamoosed. Gone, out of sight! Right there, not half a mile away, the whole caboodle . . . gone!"

"Shore they're behind a crust or have gone down into a rut," suggested Ladd. "They're show again in a minute. Look sharp, boys, for I'm figgerin' Rojas'll spread his men."

Minutes passed, but nothing moved upon the slope. Each man crawled up to a vantage point along the crest of rotting lava. The watchers were careful to peer through little notches or from behind a spur, and the constricted nature of their hiding place kept them close together. Ladd's muttering grew into a growl, then lapsed into the silence that marked his companions. From time to time the rangers silently interrogated Gale with a questioning glance. The field glass, however, like the naked sight, could not catch the slightest moving object out there upon the lava. A long hour of slowly mounting suspense wore on.

"Shore it's all goin' to be as queer as the Yaqui," said Ladd.

Indeed, the strange mien, the silent action, the somber character of the Indian had not been without effect upon the minds of the men. Then the weird, desolate, tragic scene added to the vague sense of mystery. And now the disappearance of Rojas's band, the long wait in the silence, the boding certainty of invisible foes crawling, circling closer and closer lent to the situation a final touch that made it unreal.

"I'm reckonin' there's a mind behind them greasers," replied Jim. "Or mebbe we ain't done Rojas credit. If somethin' would only come off!"

That Lash, the coolest, most provokingly nonchalant of men in times of peril, should begin to show a nervous strain was all the more indicative of a subtle, pervading unreality.

"Boys, look sharp!" suddenly called Lash. "Low down to the left . . . mebbe three hundred yards. See, along by them seams of lava . . . behind the chollas. First off, I thought it was a sheep. But it's the Yaqui! Crawlin' swift as a lizard! Can't you see him?"

It was a full moment before Jim's companions could locate the Indian. Flat as a snake, Yaqui wound himself along with incredible rapidity. His advance was all the more remarkable for the fact that he appeared to pass directly under the dreaded chollas. Sometimes he paused to lift his head and look. He was directly in line with a huge whorl of lava that rose higher than at any other point on the slope. This spur was a quarter of a mile from the position of the rangers.

"Shore he's headin' for that high place," said Ladd. "He's goin' slow now. There, he's stopped behind some chollas. He's gettin' up ... no, he's kneelin'. Now what the hell!"

"Laddy, take a peek at the side of that lava ridge!" sharply called Jim. "I guess mebbe somethin' ain't comin' off. See! There's Rojas an' his outfit climbin'. Don't make out no hosses. Dick, use your glass an' tell us what's doin'. I'll watch Yaqui an' tell what his move means."

Clearly and distinctly, almost as if he could have touched them, Gale had Rojas and his followers in sight. They were toiling up the rough lava afoot. They were heavily armed. Spurs, chaps, jackets, scarves were not in evidence. Gale saw the lean, swarthy faces, the black, straggly hair, the ragged, soiled garments that had once been white.

"They're almost up now," Gale was saying. "There. They halt on the top. I see Rojas. He looks wild. And ... there's an Indian guide! The Indian guide points ... this way ... then down. He's showing Rojas the lay of the trail."

"Boys, Yaqui's in range of that bunch," said Jim swiftly. "He's raisin' his rifle slow. Lord! How slow he is! He's covered someone. Which one I can't say. But I think he'll pick Rojas."

"The Yaqui can shoot. He'll pick Rojas," added Gale grimly.

"Rojas ... yes ... yes!" cried Thorne in passion of surprise.

"Not on your life!" Ladd's voice cut in with scorn. "Gentlemen, you can gamble Yaqui'll kill the Papago. That traitor Indian knows these sheep haunts. He's tellin' Rojas. . . ."

A sharp rifle shot rang out.

"Laddy's right!" called Gale. "The Papago's hit . . . his arm falls . . . there, he tumbles!"

More shots rang out. Yaqui was seen standing erect, firing rapidly at the darting Mexicans. For all Gale could make out no second bullet took effect. Rojas and his men vanished behind the bulge of lava. Then Yaqui deliberately backed away from his position. He made no effort to run or hide. Evidently he watched cautiously for signs of pursuers in the ruts and behind the chollas. Presently he turned and came straight toward the position of the rangers, sheered off perhaps 100 paces below it, and disappeared in a crevice. Plainly his intention was to draw pursuers within rifle shot.

"Shore Jim, you had your wish. Somethin' come off," said Ladd. "An' I'm sayin', thank God for the Yaqui! That Papago'd have ruined us. Even so, mebbe he's told Rojas more'n enough to make us sweat blood."

"He had a chance to kill Rojas!" cried out the drawn-faced, passionate Thorne. "He didn't take it . . . he didn't take it!"

Only Ladd appeared to be able to answer the cavalryman's poignant cry.

"Listen, son," he said, and his voice rang, "we all know how you feel. An' if I'd had that one shot, never in the world could I have picked the Papago guide. I'd have had to kill Rojas. That's the white man of it. But Yaqui was right. Only an Indian could have done it. You can gamble the Papago alive meant slim chance for us. Because he'd lead straight to where Mercedes is hidden, an' then we'd have left cover to fight it out. When you come to think of the Yaqui's hate for greasers . . . when you just seen him pass up a shot at one . . . well, I don't know how to say what I mean, but, damn me, my som-brer-ro is off to the Indian!"

"I reckon so, an' I reckon the ball's opened," rejoined Lash, and now that former nervous impatience so unnatural to him was as if it had never been. He was smilingly civil and his voice had almost a caressing note. He tapped the breech of his Winchester with a sinewy brown hand, and in his speech did not appear to be addressing anyone in particular. "Yaqui's opened the ball. Look up your pardners there, gents, an' get ready to dance."

Another wait set in then, and, judging by the more direct rays of the sun and a receding of the little shadows cast by the chollas, Gale was of the opinion that it was a long wait. But it seemed short. The four men were lying under the bank of a half circular hole in the lava. It was notched and cracked, and its rim was fringed by chollas. It sloped down and opened to unobstructed view of the crater. Gale had the upper position, farthest to the right, and therefore was best shielded from possible fire from the higher ridges of the rim, some 300 yards distant. Jim came next, well hidden in a crack. The positions of Thorne and Ladd were most exposed. They kept sharp look-out over the uneven rampart of their hiding place.

The sun passed the zenith, began to slope westward, and to grow hotter as it sloped. The men waited and waited. Gale saw no impatience even in Thorne. The sultry air seemed to be laden with some burden or quality that was at once composed of heat, menace, color, and silence; even the light glancing up from the lava seemed red and the silence had substance. Sometimes Gale felt that it was unbearable. Yet he made no effort to break it.

Suddenly this dead stillness was rent by a shot, clear and stinging, close at hand. It was from a rifle, not a carbine. With startling quickening a cry followed—a cry that pierced Gale—it was so thin, so high-keyed, so different from all other cries. It was the involuntary human shriek at death.

"Yaqui's called out another pardner," said Jim Lash laconically.

Carbines began to *crack*. The reports were quick, light, like sharp *spats* without any ring. Gale peered from behind the edge of his covert. Above the ragged wave of lava floated faint, whitish clouds, all that was visible of smokeless powder. Then Gale made out round spots, dark against the background of red, and in front of them leaped out small tongues of fire. Ladd's .405 began to *spang* with its beautiful sound of power. Thorne was firing somewhat wildly, Gale thought. Then Jim Lash pushed his Winchester over the rim under a cholla, and between shots Gale could hear him singing: "Turn the lady, turn . . . turn the lady, turn. . . . Alarm on left! Swing your pardners! Forward an' back! Turn the lady, turn!"

Gale got into the fight himself, not so sure that he hit any of the round, bobbing objects he aimed at, but growing sure of himself as action liberated something forced and congested within his breast.

Then, over the position of the rangers, came a hail of steel bullets. Those that struck the lava hissed away into the crater. Those that came biting through the chollas made a sound that resembled a sharp ripping of silk. Bits of the cactus stung Gale's face, and he dreaded the flying thorns more than the flying bullets.

"Hold on, boys!" called Ladd as he crouched down to reload his rifle. "Save your shells. The greasers are spreadin' on us, some goin' down below Yaqui, others movin' up for that high ridge. When they get up there, I'm damned if it won't be hot for us. There ain't room for all of us to hide here."

Ladd raised himself to peep over the rim. Shots were now scattering, and all appeared to come from below. Emboldened by this, he rose higher. A shot from in front, a rip of bullet through the cholla, a spat of something hitting Ladd's face, a steel missile hissing onward—these inseparably blended sounds were all registered by Gale's sensitive ear.

With a curse Ladd tumbled down into the hole. His face showed a great, gray blotch and starting blood. Gale had a cold sick assurance of desperate injury to the ranger. He ran to him, calling: "Laddy! Laddy!"

"Shore I ain't plugged. It's a damn cholla burr. The bullet knocked it in my face. Pull it out!"

The oval, long-spiked cone was firmly imbedded in Ladd's cheek. Blood streamed down his face and neck. Carefully, yet with no thought of pain to himself, Gale tried to pull the cactus joint away. It was as firm as if it had been nailed there. That was the damnable feature of the barbed thorns: once set, they held on as that strange plant held to its desert life. Ladd began to writhe, and sweat mingled with the blood on his face. He cursed and raved, and his movements made it almost impossible for Gale to do anything.

"Put your knife blade under an' tear it out!" shouted Ladd hoarsely.

Thus ordered, Gale slapped a long blade in between the imbedded thorns, and with a powerful jerk literally tore the cholla out of Ladd's quivering flesh. Then, where the ranger's face was not red and raw, it certainly was white.

A volley of shots from a different angle preceded the quick *ring* of steel bullets striking the lava all around Gale. His first idea, as he heard the projectiles sing and hum and whine away into the air, was that they were coming from above him. He looked up to see a number of low, white, and dark knobs upon the high point of lava. They had not been there before. Then he saw little, pale, leaping tongues of fire. As he dodged down, he distinctly heard a bullet strike Ladd. At the same instant he seemed to hear Thorne cry out and fall, and Lash's boots scrape rapidly away.

Ladd fell backward, still holding the .405. Gale dragged him into the shelter of his own position and, dreading to look at him, took up the heavy weapon. It was with a kind of savage strength that he gripped the rifle, and it was with a cold and deadly intent that he aimed and fired. The first greaser, huddled low, let his carbine go clattering down, and then crawled behind the rim. The second and third jerked back. The fourth seemed to flop up over the crest of lava. A dark arm reached for him, clutched his leg, tried to drag him up. It was in vain. Wildly grasping at the air, the bandit fell, slid down a steep shelf, rolled over the rim, to go hurtling down out of sight.

Fingering the hot rifle with close-pressed hands, Gale watched the skyline along the high point of lava. It remained unbroken. Then gradually, as Gale cooled, he feared to look back at his companions, and the cold nausea returned to his breast.

"Shore . . . I'm damn' glad . . . them greasers ain't usin' . . . soft-nose bullets," drawled a calm voice.

Swift as lightning Gale whirled. "Laddy! I thought you were done for!" he cried with a break in his voice.

"I ain't a-mindin' the bullet much. But that cholla joint took my nerve, an' you can gamble on it. Dick, this hole's pretty high up, ain't it?"

The ranger's blouse was open at the neck, and on his right shoulder, under the collar bone, was a small hole, just beginning to bleed.

"Sure it's high, Laddy," replied Gale gladly. "Went clear through, clean as a whistle."

He tore a handkerchief into two parts, made wads then, and, pressing them close over the wounds, he bound them there with Ladd's scarf.

"Shore it's funny how a bullet can floor a man an' then not do any damage," said Ladd. "I felt a zip of wind an' somethin' like a pat on my chest. So much for the small calibers with their steel bullets. Supposin' I'd connected with a Four-Oh-Five!"

"Laddy, I . . . I'm afraid Thorne's done for," whispered Gale. "He's lying over there in that crack. I can see part of him. He doesn't move."

"I was wonderin' if I'd have to tell you that. Dick, he went down, hard hit, fallin' you know, limp an' soggy. It was a moral cinch one of us would get it in this fight, but God, I'm sorry Thorne had to be the man."

"Laddy, maybe he's not dead," replied Gale. He called aloud to his friend. There was no answer.

Ladd got up, and, after peering keenly at the height of lava, he strode swiftly across the space. It was only a dozen steps to the crack in the lava where Thorne's boots shone, red with dust. Ladd bent over, went to his knees so that Gale saw only his head. Then he appeared rising with arms around the cavalryman. He dragged him across the hole to the sheltered corner that alone afforded protection. He had scarcely reached it when a carbine *cracked* and a bullet struck the flinty lava to make sparks fly up, to give a hollow *spou* and sing away into the air.

Thorne was either dead or unconscious, and Gale, with a contracting throat and numb heart, decided for the former. Not so Ladd, who probed the bloody gash on Thorne's temple, and then felt his breast.

"He's alive an' not bad hurt. That bullet hit him glancin'. Shore them steel bullets are some lucky for us. Dick, you needn't look so glum. I tell you he ain't bad hurt. I felt his skull with my finger. There's no hole in it. Wash him off an' tie . . . *wow!* . . . did you get the wind of that one? An' mebbe it didn't sing off the lava! Dick, look after Thorne now while I. . . ."

The completion of his speech was the stirring *ring* of the .405, and then he uttered a laugh that was unpleasant.

"Shore, greaser, there's a man's size bullet for you. No slim sharp-point steel-jacket nail! I'm takin' it on me to believe you're appreciatin' of the Four-Oh-Five, seein' as you don't make no fuss."

It was, indeed, a joy to Gale to find that Thorne had not received a wound necessarily fatal, although it was serious enough. Gale bathed and bound it, and lay the cavalryman against the slant of the bank, his head high to lessen the probability of bleeding.

As Gale straightened up, Ladd muttered, low and deep,

and swung the heavy rifle around to the left. Far along
the slope a figure moved. Ladd began to work the lever of
the rifle and to shoot. At every shot the heavy firearm
sprang up and the recoil made Ladd's shoulder give back.
Gale saw the bullets strike the lava behind, beside, before
the fleeing Mexican, sending up dull puffs of dust. On the
sixth shot he plunged down out of sight, either hit or
frightened into seeking cover.

"Dick, mebbe there's one or two left up above, but we
needn't figger much on it," said Ladd, as, loading the rifle, he jerked his fingers quickly from the hot breech. "Listen . . . Jim an' Yaqui are hittin' it up lively down below.
I'll sneak down there. You stay here, an' keep about half
an eye peeled up yonder, an' keep the rest out my way."

Ladd crossed the hole, climbed down into the deep
crack where Thorne had fallen, and then went stooping
along with only his head above the level. Presently he disappeared. Gale, having little to fear from the high ridge,
directed most of his attention toward the point beyond
which Ladd had gone. The firing had become desultory,
and the light carbine shots outnumbered the sharp rifle
shots five to one. Gale made a note of the fact that for
some little time he had not heard the unmistakable report
of Jim Lash's automatic. Then ensued a long interval in
which the desert silence seemed to recover its grip. The
.405 ripped it asunder—*spang—spang—spang*. Gale fancied he heard yells. There were a few pattering shots, still
farther down the trail. Gale had an uneasy feeling that
Rojas and some of his band might go straight to the water
hole. It would be hard to dislodge even a few men from
that retreat.

There ensued a lull in the battle. Gale ventured to stand
high, and, screened behind chollas, he swept the three-
quarter circle of lava with his glass. In the distance he saw
horses, but no riders. Below him, down the slope along
the crater rim and the trail, the lava was bare of all except
tufts of cholla. Gale gathered assurance to his hope. It
looked as if the day was favoring his side. Then Thorne,

coming partly to consciousness, engaged Gale's care. The cavalryman stirred and moaned, called for water, and then for Mercedes. Gale held him back with strong hand, and presently he was once more quiet.

For the first time in hours, it seemed, Gale took note of the physical aspect of his surroundings, to look upon them without keen gaze strained for crouching form, or bobbing head, or spouting carbine. Either Gale's sense of color and proportion had become deranged during the fight, or the encompassing air and the desert had changed. Even the sun had changed. It seemed lowering, oval in shape, magenta in hue, and had a surface that gleamed like oil on water. Its red rays shone through red haze. Distances that had formerly been clearly outlined were now dim, obscured. The yawning chasm was not the same. It circled wider, redder, deeper. It was a weird, ghastly mouth of hell. Gale stood fascinated, unable to tell how much he saw was real, how much the exaggeration of overwrought emotions. There was no beauty here, but an unparalleled grandeur, a sublime scene of devastation and desolateness that might have had its counterpart upon the burned-out moon. The word that had gripped Gale now added to its somber portent an unshakable foreboding of calamity, of catastrophe, of tragic end.

He wrestled with the spell as if it were a physical foe. Reason and intelligence had their voices in his mind, but the moment was not one wherein these things could wholly maintain control. He felt life strong within his breast, yet there, a step away, was death, yawning, glaring, smoky, red as hell. It was a moment—an hour for the savage, born, bred, developed in this scarred and blasted place of jagged depths and red distances and silences never meant to be broken. Since Gale was not a savage, he fought that call of the red gods that sent him back down the long ages toward his primitive day. His mind combated his sense of sight and the hearing that seemed useless, and his mind did not win all the victory. Something fatal was here, hanging in the balance, as the red haze hung along the vast walls of that crater of hell.

Suddenly harsh, prolonged yells brought him leaping erect, with unrealities, with broodings vanishing. Far down the trail, where the crater rims closed in the deep fissure, he saw moving forms. They were three in number. Two of them ran nimbly across the lava bridge. The third staggered far behind. It was Ladd. He appeared hard hit. He dragged at the heavy rifle that he seemed unable to raise. The yells came from him. He was calling the Yaqui.

Gale's heart stood still momentarily. Here then was the catastrophe! He hardly dared sweep his gaze across that fissure. The two fleeing figures halted—turned to fire at Ladd. Gale recognized the foremost one—small, compact, gaudy: Rojas! The bandit's arm was outstretched. Puffs of white smoke rose and shots rapped out. When Ladd went down, Rojas threw his gun and with wild yell bounded over the lava. His companion followed.

A bursting gush of blood, hot as fire, cold as ice, rushed over Gale when he saw Rojas take the trail toward Mercedes's hiding place. The little bandit appeared to have the sure-footedness of a mountain sheep. The Mexican following was not so sure or fast. He turned back. Gale heard the trenchant bark of the .405. Ladd was kneeling. He shot again—again. The retreating bandit seemed to run fully into an invisible obstacle, then fell lax, inert, lifeless. Rojas sped on unmindful of the kicking spurts of dust about him. Yaqui, high above Ladd, was also firing. Then both rifles were emptied. Rojas turned at a high break in the trail. He shook a defiant hand and his exulting yell pealed faintly to Gale's ears. About him there was something desperate, magnificent. Then he clambered down the trail.

Ladd dropped the .405, and rising, gun in hand, he staggered toward the bridge of lava. Before he had crossed it, Yaqui came bounding down the slope and in one splendid leap he cleared the fissure. He ran beyond the trail and disappeared on the lava above. Rojas had not seen this sudden, darting move of the Indian.

Gale felt himself bitterly powerless to aid in that pur-

suit. He could only watch. Presently, when Rojas came out
of the cracks and ruts of lava, there might be a chance of
disabling him by a long shot. His progress was now slow.
But he was making straight for Mercedes's hiding place.
What was it leading him there—an eagle eye, or hate, or
instinct? Why did he go on when there could be no turning back for him on that trail? Ladd was slow, heavy, staggering on the trail, but he was relentless. Only death
could stop the ranger now. Surely Rojas must have known
that when he chose the trail. From time to time Gale
caught glimpses of Yaqui's dark figure stealing along the
higher rim of the crater. He was making for a point above
the bandit.

Moments—endless moments dragged by. The lowering
sun colored only the upper half of the crater walls. Far
down, the depths were murky blue. Again Gale felt the
insupportable silence, and the red haze was a transparent
veil before his eyes. Sinister, evil, brooding, waiting
seemed that yawning abyss. Ladd staggered along the
trail—crawled in places. The Yaqui gained; he might have
had wings; he leaped from jagged crust to jagged crust;
his balance was a wonderful thing.

But to Gale the marvel of that endless period of watching was the purpose of the bandit, Rojas. He had worn no
weapon. Gale's glass made this fact plain. There was
death behind him, death below him, death before him,
and, although he could not have known it, death above
him. He never faltered—never made a misstep upon the
narrow flinty trail. When he reached the lower end of the
level ledge, Gale's poignant doubt became a certainty. Rojas had seen Mercedes. It was incredible, yet Gale believed
it. Then, his heart clipped as in an icy vise, Gale threw
forward the Remington and, sinking on one knee, began
to shoot. He emptied the magazine. Puffs of dust near Rojas did not even make him turn.

As Gale began to reload, he was horror-stricken by a
low cry from Thorne. The cavalryman had recovered consciousness. He was half raised, pointing with shaking

hand at the opposite ledge. His distended eyes were riv-
eted upon Rojas. He was trying to utter speech that
would not come.

Gale wheeled, rigid now, steeling himself to one last
forlorn hope—that Mercedes could defend herself. She
had a gun. He doubted not at all that she would use it. But,
remembering her terror of this peon, he feared for her.

Rojas reached the level of the ledge. He halted. He
crouched. It was the act of a panther. Manifestly he saw
Mercedes within the cave. Then faint shots patted the air,
broke in thick echo. Rojas went down as if struck a heavy
blow. He was hit. But even as Gale yelled in sheer madness, the bandit leaped erect. He seemed too quick, too
supple to be badly wounded. A slight dark figure flashed
out of the cave. Mercedes! She backed against the wall.
Gale saw a puff of white—heard a report. But the bandit
lunged at her. Mercedes ran, not to try to pass him, but
straight for the precipice. Her intention was plain. But
Rojas outstripped her, even as she reached the verge.
Then a piercing scream pealed across the crater—a
scream of despair.

Gale closed his eyes. He could not bear to see the bandit kill her. For what else than lust to kill had drawn this
peon slave?

Thorne echoed Mercedes's scream. Gale looked around
just in time to leap and catch the cavalryman as he staggered, apparently for the steep slope. And then, as Gale
dragged him back, both fell. Gale saved his friend, but he
plunged into a cholla. He drew a hand away with four of
the great glistening cones of thorns. A shock seemed to
deaden all feeling in him. This was the moment to remove
the thorns, before onrushing pain made the thing a fear-
some task. But how? If the cavalryman was not out of his
head, he was surely helpless. Gale could not use his teeth.

"For God's sake, Gale . . . shoot! Shoot! Kill her! Kill
her! Can't . . . you . . . see . . . Rojas . . . ?"

Thorne fainted.

Gale, stunned for the instant, stood with uplifted

hands, and gazed from Thorne across the crater. Rojas had not killed Mercedes. He was overpowering her. His actions seemed slow, wearing, purposeful. Hers were violent. Like a trapped she-wolf she was fighting. She tore, struggled, flung herself.

Rojas's intention was terribly plain.

In agony now, both mental and physical, Gale put the hand down on the lava and, stepping on a cholla burr, tore his hand free. He did it again, and twice more. The bleeding flesh was at last free of the cones of thorns. The strange pain, now coming on, was the opposite of paralysis. Then, quivering as if under burning, piercing, stinging fire, cold and sick and weak, Gale gripped his rifle with that raw and bloody hand and aimed at the struggling forms on the ledge. He pulled trigger—enduring the recoil with the hand poison thorns had pierced to the bone. The bullet struck high. A third—fourth—fifth time the Remington spoke—in vain. The rifle fell from Gale's racked and tortured hand.

How horribly plain that peon fiend's intention! Gale tried to close his eyes, but could not. He prayed wildly for a sudden blindness—to faint as Thorne had fainted. But he was transfixed to the spot with eyes that pierced the red light.

Mercedes was growing weaker, seemed about to collapse.

"Oh, Jim Lash! Where are you?" cried Gale. "Oh, Laddy! Oh, Yaqui!"

Suddenly a dark form slid, like a streak, down the wall behind the ledge where Rojas fought the girl. It sank in a heap, then bounded erect.

"Yaqui!" screamed Gale, and he waved his bleeding hands till the blood bespattered his face. Then he choked. Utterance became impossible.

The Indian bent over Rojas and flung him against the wall. Mercedes, sinking back, lay still. When Rojas got up, the Indian stood between him and escape from the ledge. Rojas backed the other way along the narrowing shelf of lava. His manner was abject, stupefied. Slowly he stepped backward.

It was then that Gale caught the white gleam of a knife in Yaqui's hand. Rojas turned and ran. He rounded a corner of wall where the footing was precarious. Yaqui followed slowly. He made a dark, menacing figure. But he was not in a hurry. When he passed off the ledge, Rojas was edging farther and farther along the wall. He was clinging now to the lava, creeping inch by inch. Perhaps he had thought to work around the buttress or climb over it. Evidently he went as far as possible and there he clung, an unscalable wall above, the abyss beneath.

The approach of the Yaqui had now all the horrible suggestion of doom. If it seemed so to the stricken Gale, what must it have been to Rojas? He appeared to sink against the wall. The Yaqui stole closer and closer. He was the savage now and the moment must have been glory to him. Gale saw him gaze up at the giant circling walls of the crater, then down into the depths. Perhaps that red haze, hanging above him, as the purple haze below, or the deep caverns in the lava, held for Yaqui spirits of the desert, his gods to whom he called. Perhaps he invoked shadows of his loved ones and his race, calling to them in this moment of vengeance.

Gale heard—or imagined he heard—that wild, strange, Yaqui cry.

Then the Indian stepped close to Rojas and, bending low, keeping out of reach, he hacked at a clinging foot with the blade. He disabled it—cut it loose from the wall. Rojas's terrible shrieks made Gale shudder. The ruthless savage stabbed and slashed at Rojas's other foot. Suddenly the bandit lengthened out. He was clinging now by his hands. Yaqui raised the knife and pierced the right one. A kind of wail drifted across the crater to Gale's ears. Rojas sagged a little lower. Then with hellish deliberation Yaqui cut loose the hold of the left hand.

Rojas fell backward and plunged sheer. The bank of white chollas caught him, held him upon their steel spikes. How long did the dazed Gale sit there, watching Rojas, wrestling and writhing in convulsive frenzy? The bandit now seemed mad to win the delayed death. When he broke free, he was a white-patched object no longer human, a ball of cholla burrs, and he slipped off the bank to shoot down, down, down into the purple depths of the crater.

CHAPTER THIRTEEN:
CHANGES AT FORLORN RIVER

The 1st of March saw Federal occupation of the garrison at Casita. After a short, decisive engagement the rebels were dispersed into small bands and driven eastward along the boundary line toward Nogales.

It was the destiny of Forlorn River, however, never to return to the slow, sleepy tenor of its former existence. Belding's predictions came true. That straggling line of home-seekers was but a forerunner of the real invasion of Altar Valley. Refugees from Mexico and from Casita spread the word that water and wood and grass and land were to be had at Forlorn River, and as if by magic the white tents and red adobe houses sprang up to glisten in the sun.

Belding was happier than he had been for a long time. He believed that the evil days of Forlorn River, along with the apathy and lack of enterprise, were in the past. He hired a couple of trustworthy Mexicans to ride the boundary line, and he settled down to think of ranching and irrigation and mining projects. Every morning he expected to receive some word from Sonoyta or Yuma, telling him that Yaqui had guided his party safely across the desert.

Belding was simple-minded, a man more inclined to action than reflection. When the complexities of life hemmed him in, he groped his way out, never quite un-

derstanding. His wife had always been a mystery to him.
Nell was sunshine most of the time, but, like the sun-
dominated desert, she was subject to strange changes,
willful, stormy, sudden. It was enough for Belding now to
sense a lighter happier mood in his wife, and to see Nell
dreamily turn a ring around and around the third finger
of her left hand, and forever seem to be watching the
west. Every day both mother and daughter appeared further removed from the past darkly threatening days.
Belding was hearty in his affections, but undemonstrative,
and, if there was any sentiment in his make-up, it had an
outlet in memory of Blanco Diablo and a longing to see
him. Often Belding stopped his work to gaze out over the
desert toward the west; when he thought of his rangers
and Thorne and Mercedes, he certainly never forgot his
horse. He wondered if Diablo was running, walking,
resting—if Yaqui was finding water and grass.

In March, with the short desert winter over, the days began to get warmer, hot in the noon hours, and seemed to
give promise of the white summer blaze and blasting fur-
nace wind soon to come. No word was received from the
rangers. But this caused Belding no concern, and it seemed
to him that his womenfolk considered no news good news.

Among the many changes coming to pass in Forlorn
River were the installing of postal service and the build-
ing of a mescal drinking house. Belding had long worked
for the Post Office, but he did not like the idea of a saloon
for Forlorn River. Still that was an inevitable evil. The
Mexicans would have mescal. Belding had kept the little
border hamlet free of an establishment for distillation of
the fiery cactus drink. A good many Americans drifted
into Forlorn River, miners, cowboys, prospectors, outlaws, and others of nondescript character, and these men,
of course, made the saloon, which was also an inn, their
headquarters. Belding, with Carter and other old resi-
dents, saw the need of a sheriff for Forlorn River.

One morning early in this spring month, while Belding

was on his way from the house to the corrals, he saw Nell running Blanco José down the road at a gait that amazed him. She did not take the turn of the road to come in by the gate. She put José to a four-foot wire fence, and came clattering into the yard.

"Nell must have another tantrum," said Belding. "She's long past due."

Blanco José, like the other white horses, was big of frame and heavy, and he rolled thunder from under his great hoofs. Nell pulled him, and, as he pounded and slid to a halt in a cloud of dust, she swung lightly down.

It did not take more than half an eye for Belding to see that she was furious.

"Nell, what's come off now?" he asked.

"I'm not going to tell you," she replied, and started away, leading José toward the corral.

Belding leisurely followed. She went into the corral, removed José's bridle, and led him to the watering trough. Belding came up and without saying anything began to unbuckle José's saddle girths. But he ventured a look at Nell. The red had gone from her face and he was surprised to see her eyes brimming with tears. Most assuredly this was not one of Nell's tantrums. While taking off José's saddle and hanging it in the shed, Belding pondered in his slow way. When he came back to the corral, Nell had her face against the bars, and she was crying. He plopped a big arm around her and waited. Although it was not often expressed, there was a strong attachment between them.

"Dad, I don't want you to think me a . . . a baby any more," she said. "I've been insulted."

With a specific fact to make clear thought in Belding's mind he was never slow.

"I knew something unusual had come off. I guess you'd better tell me."

"Dad, I will, if you promise."

"What?"

"Not to mention it to Mother . . . not to pack a gun down there . . . and never, never to tell Dick."

Belding was silent. Seldom did he make promises readily.

"Nell, sure something must have come off, for you to ask all that."

"If you don't promise, I'll never tell, that's all," she declared firmly.

Belding deliberated a little longer. He knew the girl.

"Well, I promise not to tell Mother," he said presently, "and seeing you're here, safe and well, I guess I won't go packing a gun down there . . . wherever it is . . . but I won't promise to keep anything from Dick that perhaps he ought to know."

"Dad, what would Dick do if . . . if he were here and I were to tell him I'd . . . I'd been horribly insulted?"

"I guess that'd depend. Mostly you know Dick does what you want. But you couldn't stop him . . . nobody could . . . if there was reason, a man's reason to get started. Remember what he did to Rojas! Nell, tell me what's happened."

Nell, regaining her composure, wiped her eyes, and smoothed back her hair.

"The other day . . . Wednesday . . . ," she began, "I was coming home, and in front of that mescal drinking place there was a crowd. It was a noisy crowd. I didn't want to walk out into the street or seem afraid. But I had to do both. There were several young men, and, if they weren't drunk, they certainly were rude. I never saw them before, but I think they must belong to the mining company that was run out of Sonora by rebels. Missus Carter was telling me. Anyway, these young fellows were Americans. They stretched themselves across the walk and smiled at me. I had to go out in the road. One of them, the rudest, followed me. He was a big fellow, red-faced, with prominent eyes and a bold look. He came up beside me and spoke to me. I called him a drunken fool and I ran home. And as I ran, I heard his companions jeering.

"Well, today . . . just now . . . when I was riding up the valley road, I came upon the same fellows. They had instruments and were surveying. Remembering Dick and how he always wished for an instrument to help mark out his plan for irrigation, I was certainly surprised to see these strangers surveying . . . and surveying upon Laddy's plot of land. It was a sandy road there and José happened to be walking. So I reined in and asked these engineers what they were doing. The leader, who was that same bold fellow who had followed me, seemed much pleased at being addressed. He was swaggering . . . too friendly . . . not my idea of a gentleman at all. He said he was going to run water all over Altar Valley. Dad, you can bet that made me wild. That was Dick's plan, his discovery, and here were surveyors on Laddy's claim.

"Then I told him that he was working on private land and he'd better get off. He seemed to forget his flirty proclivities in amazement. Then he looked cunning. I read his mind. It was news to him that all the land along the valley had been taken up. He said something about not seeing any squatters on the land, and then he shut up tight on that score. But he began to be flirty again. He got hold of José's bridle, and, before I could catch my breath, he said I was a peach . . . that he wanted to make a date with me . . . that his name was Chase . . . that he owned a gold mine in Mexico. He said a lot more I didn't gather, but when he called me 'Dearie' I . . . well, I lost my temper.

"I jerked on the bridle and told him to let go. He held me and rolled his eyes at me. I daresay he imagined he was a gentleman to be infatuated with. He seemed sure of conquest. One thing was certain . . . he didn't know the least bit about horses. It scared me the way he got in front of José. I thanked my stars I wasn't up on Blanco Diablo. Well, Dad, I'm a little ashamed now, but I was mad. I slashed him across the face with my quirt. José jumped and knocked Mister Chase into the sand. I didn't get the horse under control till I was out of sight of those surveyors, and then I let him run home."

"Nell, I guess you punished the fellow enough. Maybe he's only a conceited softy. But I don't like that sort of thing. It isn't Western. I guess he won't be so smart next time. Any fellow would remember being hit by Blanco José. If you'd been up on Diablo, we'd have to bury Mister Chase."

"Thank goodness I wasn't! I'm sorry now, Dad. Perhaps the fellow was hurt. But what could I do? Let's forget all about it, and I'll be careful where I ride in the future. Dad, what does it mean . . . this surveying around Forlorn River?"

"I don't know, Nell," replied Belding thoughtfully. "It worries me. It looks good for Forlorn River, but bad for Dick's plan to irrigate the valley. Lord, I'd hate to have someone forestall Dick on that."

"No, no, we won't let anybody have Dick's rights," declared Nell.

"Where have I been keeping myself not to know about these surveyors?" muttered Belding. "They must have just come."

"Go see Missus Carter. She told me there were strangers in town, Americans who had mining interests in Sonora and were run out by Orozco. Find out what they're doing, Dad."

Belding discovered that he was, indeed, the last man of consequence in Forlorn River to learn of the arrival of Ben Chase and son, mine owners and operators in Sonora. They, with a force of miners, had been besieged by rebels and finally driven off their property. This property was not destroyed, but held for ransom. And the Chases, pending developments, had packed outfits and struck for the border. Casita had been their objective point, but for some reason Belding did not learn, they had arrived instead at Forlorn River. It had taken Ben Chase just one day to see the possibilities of Altar Valley, and in three days he had men at work.

Belding returned home without going to see the Chases and their operations. He wanted to think over the situation. Next morning he went out to the valley to see for himself. Mexicans were hastily erecting adobe houses upon Ladd's 160 acres, upon Dick Gale's, upon Jim Lash's, and upon Thorne's. There were men staking the valley floor and the riverbed. That was sufficient for Belding. He turned back toward town and headed for the camp of these intruders.

In fact, the surroundings of Forlorn River, except on the river side, reminded Belding of the mushroom growth of a newly discovered mining camp. Tents were everywhere; adobe shacks were in all stages of construction; rough clapboard houses were going up. The latest of this work was new and surprising to Belding, all because he was a busy man with no chance to hear village gossip. When he was directed to the headquarters of the Chase Mining Company, he went thither in slow-growing wrath.

He came to a big tent with a huge canvas fly stretched in front, under which sat several men in their shirtsleeves. They were talking and smoking.

"My name's Belding. I want to see this Mister Chase."

Slow-witted as Belding was and absorbed in his own feelings, he yet saw plainly that his advent was disturbing to these men. They looked alarmed, exchanged glances, and then quickly turned to him. One of them, a tall rugged man, with sharp face and shrewd eyes and white hair, got up and offered his hand.

"I'm Chase, senior," he said. "My son Radford is here somewhere. You're Belding, the line inspector, I take it? I meant to call on you."

He seemed a rough and ready loud-spoken man, withal cordial enough.

"Yes, I'm the inspector," replied Belding, ignoring the proffered hand, "and I'd like to know what in the hell you mean by taking up land claims, staked ground that belongs to my rangers?"

"Land claims?" slowly echoed Chase, studying his man. "We're taking up only unclaimed land."

"That's a lie. You couldn't miss the stakes."

"Well, Mister Belding, as to that, I think my men did run across some staked ground. But we recognize only squatters. If your rangers think they've got property just because they drive a few stakes in the ground, they're much mistaken. A squatter has to build a house and live on his land so long, according to law, before he owns it."

This argument was unanswerable and Belding knew it.

"According to law!" exclaimed Belding. "Then you own up . . . you've jumped our claims."

"Mister Belding, I'm a plain businessman. I come along. I see a good opening. Nobody seems to have tenable grants. I stake out claims, locate squatters, start to build. It seems to me your rangers have overlooked certain necessary precautions. That's unfortunate for them. I'm prepared to hold my claims and to back all the squatters who work for me. If you don't like it, you can carry the matter to Tucson. The law will uphold me."

"The law? Say, on this Southwest border we haven't had any law except a man's word . . . and a gun."

"Then you'll find United States law has come along with Ben Chase," replied the other, snapping his fingers. He was still smooth, outspoken, but a mask had fallen.

"You're not a Westerner?" queried Belding.

"No, I'm from Illinois."

"I thought the West hadn't bred you. I know your kind. You'd last a long time on the Texas border, now, wouldn't you? You're one of the land and water hogs that has come to root in the West. You're like the timber sharks . . . take it all and leave none for those who follow. Mister Chase, the West would fare better and last a damn' sight longer if men like you were driven out."

"You can't drive me out."

"I'm not so sure of that. Wait till my rangers come back. I wouldn't be in your boots, don't mistake me. I don't suppose you could be accused of stealing another man's idea or plan, but sure you're stolen these four claims. Maybe the law might uphold you. But the spirit, not the letter, counts with us border men."

"See here, Belding, I think you're taking the wrong view of the matter. I'm going to develop this valley. You'd do better to get in with me. I've a proposition to make you about that strip of land of yours facing the river."

"You can't make any deals with me. I won't have anything to do with you."

Belding abruptly left the camp and went home. Nell met him, probably intended to question him, but one look into his face confirmed her fears. She silently turned away. Belding realized he was powerless to stop Chase, and he was sick with disappointment for the ruin of Dick's hopes and his own.

CHAPTER FOURTEEN:
A LOST SON

Time passed. The population of Forlorn River grew apace.
Belding, who had once been the head of the community,
found himself a person of little consequence. Even had he
desired it, he would not have had any voice in the selec-
tion of postmaster, sheriff, and a few other town officials.
The Chases divided their labors between Forlorn River
and their Mexican gold mine, which had been restored to
them. The desert trips between these two places were
taken in automobiles. A month's time made the motorcars
almost as familiar a sight in Forlorn River as they had
been in Casita before the revolution.

Belding was not as busy as he had formerly been. As he
lost ambition, he began to find less work to do. His wrath
at the usurping Chases increased as he slowly realized his
powerlessness to cope with such men. They were promoters, men of big interests and wide influence in the Southwest. The more they did for Forlorn River, the less reason
there seemed to be for his own grievance. He had to admit that it was personal—that he and Gale and the
rangers would never have been able to develop the resources of the valley as these men were doing it.

All day long he heard the heavy booming blasts and
the rumble of avalanches up in the gorge. Chase's men
were dynamiting the cliffs in the narrow box cañon. They
were making the dam, just as Gale had planned to make
it. When this work of blasting was over, Belding experi-

enced a relief. He would not now be continuously reminded of his and Gale's loss. Resignation finally came to him. For himself it did not matter. But he could not reconcile himself to misfortune for Gale.

Moreover, Belding had other worry and strain. April arrived with no news of the rangers. From Casita came vague reports of raiders in the Sonoyta country—reports impossible to verify until his Mexican rangers returned. When these men rode in, one of them, Gonzales, an intelligent and reliable half-breed, said he had met prospectors at the oasis. They had just come in on the Camino del Diablo, reported a terrible trip of heat and drought, and not a trace of the Yaqui's party.

"That settles it," declared Belding. "Yaqui never went to Sonoyta. He circled 'round to the Devil's Road, and the rangers, Mercedes, Thorne, the horses, I'm afraid, might have been lost in the desert. It's an old story on the Camino del Diablo."

He had to tell Nell that, and it was an ordeal that left him weak.

Mrs. Belding listened to him and was silent for a long time while she held the stricken Nell to her breast. Then she opposed his conviction with that quiet strength so characteristic of her arguments.

"Well then," decided Belding, "Rojas headed the rangers at Papago Well or at the tanks."

"Tom, when you are down in the mouth, you use poor judgment. You know only by a miracle could Rojas or anybody have headed those white horses. Where's your old stubborn confidence? Yaqui was up on Diablo. Dick was up on Sol. And there were the other horses. They could not have been headed or caught. Miracles don't happen."

"All right, Mother, it's sure good to hear you," said Belding. She always cheered him, and now he grasped at straws. "I'm not myself these days, don't mistake that. Tell us what you think. You always say you feel things when you really don't know them."

"I can say little more than what you said yourself the night Mercedes was taken away. You told Laddy to trust Yaqui, that he was a godsend. He might go south into some wild Sonora valley. He might lead Rojas into a trap. He would find water and grass where no Mexican or American could."

"But, Mother, they're gone seven weeks. Seven weeks! At the most I gave them six weeks. Seven weeks in the desert!"

"How do the Yaquis live?" she asked.

Belding could not reply to that, but hope revived in him. He had faith in his wife, although he could not in the least understand what he imagined was something mystic in her.

"Years ago, when I was searching for my father, I learned many things about this country," said Mrs. Belding. "You can never tell how long a man may live in the desert. The fiercest, most terrible and inaccessible places often have their hidden oases. In his later years my father became a prospector. That was strange to me, for he never cared for gold or money. I learned he was often gone in the desert for weeks . . . once for months. Then the time came when he never came back. That was years before I reached the Southwest border and heard of him. Even then I did not for long give up hope of his coming back. I know now . . . something tells me . . . indeed, it seems his spirit tells me . . . he was lost. But I don't have that feeling for Yaqui and his party. Yaqui has given Rojas the slip or has ambushed him in some trap. Probably that took time and a long journey into Sonora. The Indian is too wise to start back now over dry trails. He'll curb the rangers . . . he'll wait. I seem to know this, dear Nell, so be brave, patient. Dick Gale will come back to you."

"Oh, Mother," cried Nell, "I can't give up hope . . . while I have you."

That talk with the strong mother worked a change in Nell and in Belding. Nell, who had done little but brood and watch the west and take violent rides, seemed to settle into a waiting patience that was sad, yet serene. She helped her mother more than ever; she was a comfort to Belding; she began to take active interest in the affairs of the growing village. Belding, who had been breaking under the strain of worry, recovered himself so that to outward appearances he was his old self. He alone knew, however, that his humor was forced and that the slow-burning wrath he felt for the Chases was flaming into hate.

Belding argued with himself that, if Ben Chase and his son Radford had turned out to be big men in other ways than in the power to carry on great enterprises, he might have become reconciled to them. But the father was greedy, grasping, hard, cold; the son added to those traits an overbearing disposition to rule, and he showed a fondness for drink and cards. These men were developing the valley, to be sure, and a horde of poor Mexicans and many Americans were benefiting from that development; nevertheless, these Chases were operating in a way that proved they cared only for themselves.

Belding shook off a lethargic spell and decided he had better set about several by no means small tasks, if he wanted to get them finished before the hot months. He made a trip to the Sonoyta Oasis, upon which he satisfied himself that matters along the line were favorable, and that there was absolutely no trace of his rangers. Upon completing this trip, he went to Casita with a number of his white thoroughbreds and shipped them to ranchers and horse breeders in Texas. Then, being near the railroad, and having time, he went up to Tucson. There he learned some interesting particulars about the Chases. They had an office in the city—influential friends in the capital. They were powerful men in the rapidly growing finance of the West. They had interested the Southern Pacific Railroad, and in the near future a branch line was to be constructed from San Felipe to Forlorn River. Those details of the Chase development were magnificent when compared to a matter striking close to home for Belding. His responsibility had been subtly attacked. A doubt had been cast upon his capability of executing the duties of immigration inspector to the best advantage to the state. Belding divined this was only an entering wedge. The Chases were bent upon driving him out of Forlorn River, but, perhaps to serve better their own ends, they were proceeding at leisure. Belding returned home consumed by rage. He hid it, however, controlled it, for the first time in his life afraid of himself. He had his wife and Nell to think of, and the old law of the West had gone forever.

"Dad, there's another Rojas around these diggings," was Nell's remark after the greetings were over, and the usual questions and answers passed.

Belding's exclamation was cut short by Nell's laugh. She was serious with a kind of amused contempt.

"Mister Radford Chase!"

"Now, Nell, what the . . . !" roared Belding.

"Hush, Dad! Don't swear," interrupted Nell. "I only wanted to tease you."

"*Humph!* Say, my girl, that name Chase makes me see red. If you want to tease me, hit on some other way. *¿Sabe, señorita?*"

"*Sí, sí,* Dad."

"Nell, you may as well tell him and have it over," said Mrs. Belding quietly.

"You promised me once, Dad, that you'd not go packing a gun off down there, didn't you?"

"Yes, I remember," replied Belding, but he did not answer her smile.

"Will you promise again?" she asked lightly. Here was Nell with arch eyes, yet not the old arch eyes, so full of fun and mischief. Her lips were tremulous; her cheeks seemed less round.

"Yes," rejoined Belding, and he knew why his voice was a little thick.

"Well . . . if you weren't such a good old blind dad you'd have seen long ago the way Radford Chase ran around after me. At first it was only annoying and I did not want to add to your worries. But these two weeks you've been gone, I've been more than annoyed. After that time I struck Mister Chase with my quirt he made all possible efforts to meet me. He did meet me wherever I went. He sent me letters till I got tired sending them back.

"When you left home on your trips, I don't know that he grew bolder, but he had more opportunity. I couldn't stay in the house all the time. There were Mama's errands and sick people and my Sunday school and what-not. Mister Chase waylaid me every time I went out. If he works any more, I don't know when, unless it's when I'm asleep. He followed me until it was less embarrassing for me to let him walk with me and talk his head off. He made love to me. He begged me to marry him. I told him I was already in love and engaged to be married. He said that didn't make any difference. Then I called him a fool.

"Next time he saw me he said he must explain. He meant I was being true to a man who everybody on the border knew had been lost in the desert. That . . . that hurt. Maybe . . . maybe it's true. Sometimes it seems terribly true. Since then, of course, I have stayed in the house to avoid being hurt again.

"But Dad, a little thing like a girl sticking close to her mother and her room doesn't phase Radford Chase. I think he's crazy. Anyway he's a most persistent fool. I want to be charitable, because the man swears he loves me, and maybe he does, but he is making me nervous. I don't sleep. I'm afraid to be in my room at night. I've gone to mother's room. He's always hanging around. Bold! Why, that isn't the thing to call Mister Chase. He's absolutely without a sense of . . . of decency. He bribes our servants. He comes into our patio. Think of that! He makes the most ridiculous excuses. He bothers Mother to death. I feel like a poor little rabbit holed by a hound. And I daren't peep out."

Somehow the thing struck Belding as funny and he laughed. He had not had a laugh for so long that it made him feel good. He stopped only at sight of Nell's surprise and pain. Then he put his arms around her.

"Never mind, dear. I'm an old bear. But it tickled me, I guess. I sure hope Radford Chase *has* got it bad. Nell, it's only the old story. The fellows fall in love with you. It's your good looks, Nell. What a price women like Mercedes and you have to pay for beauty. I'd a . . . a good deal rather be ugly as a mud fence."

"So would I, Dad . . . if . . . if Dick would still love me."

"He wouldn't, you can gamble on that, as Laddy says. Well, the first time I catch this locoed Romeo sneaking around here, I'll . . . I'll. . . ."

"Dad, you promised."

"Confound it, Nell, I promised not to pack a gun. That's all. I'll only shoo this fellow off the place . . . gently, mind you, gently. I'll leave the rest for Dick Gale."

"Oh, Dad!" cried Nell, and she clung to him wistful, frightened, yet something more.

"Don't mistake me, Nell. You have your own way generally. You pull the wool over Mother's eyes and you wind me around your little finger. But you can't do either with Dick Gale. You're tender-hearted, you overlook the doings of this hound Chase. But when Dick comes back, you just make your mind to a little hell in the Chase camp. Oh, he'll find it out. And I sure want to be around when Dick hands Chase the same he handed Rojas."

Belding kept a sharp look-out for young Chase, and then, a few days later, learned that both son and father had gone off on one of their frequent trips to Casa Grande, near where their mines were situated.

April grew apace and soon gave way to May. One morning Belding was called from some garden work by the *whirring* of an automobile, and a hello. He went forward to the front yard and there saw a car he thought resembled one he thought he had seen in Casita. It contained a familiar-looking driver, but the three figures in gray coats and veils were strange to him. By the time he had gotten to the road, he decided two were women and the other a man. At the moment their faces were emerging from dusty veils. Belding saw an elderly, sallow-faced, rather frail-appearing man who was an entire stranger to him, a handsome dark-eyed woman whose hair showed white through her veil, and a superbly built girl whose face made Belding at once think of Dick Gale.

"Is this Mister Tom Belding, Inspector of Immigration?" inquired the gentleman courteously.

"I'm Belding, and I know who you are," replied Belding in hearty amaze as he stretched forth his big hand. "You're Dick Gale's dad, the governor, Dick used to say. I'm sure glad to meet you."

"Thank you. Yes, I'm Dick's governor, and here, Mister Belding . . . Dick's mother . . . and his sister Elsie."

Beaming his pleasure, Belding shook hands with the ladies, both of whom were visibly agitated.

"Mister Belding, I've come West to look up my lost son," said Mr. Gale. "His sister's letters were unanswered. We haven't heard from him in months. Is he still here with you?"

"Well, now . . . sure I'm awful sorry," began Belding, his slow mind at work. "Dick's away just now . . . been away for a considerable spell. I'm expecting him back any day. Won't you come in? You're all dusty and hot and tired. Come in and let Mother and Nell make you comfortable. Of course you'll stay. We've a big house. You must stay till Dick comes back. Maybe that'll be . . . aw, I guess it won't be long. Let me handle the baggage, Mister Gale. Come in. I sure am glad to meet you all."

Eager, excited, delighted, Belding went on talking as he ushered the Gales into the sitting room, presenting them in his hearty way to the astounded Mrs. Belding and Nell. For the space of a few moments his wife and daughter were bewildered. Belding did not recollect any other occasion when a few callers had thrown them off their balance. But of course this was different. He was a little flustered himself, a circumstance that dawned upon him with surprise. When the Gales had been shown to rooms, Mrs. Belding regained the poise momentarily lost, but

Nell came rushing back, wilder than a deer, in a state of excitement even for her.

"Oh, Dick's mother, his sister," whispered Nell.

Belding observed the omission of the father in Nell's exclamation of mingled delight and alarm.

"His mother," went on Nell. "Oh, I knew it. I always guessed it. Dick's people are proud, rich . . . they're somebody. I thought I'd faint when she looked at me. She was just curious . . . curious, but so cold and proud. She was wondering about me. Dick has never written her that he's . . . he's engaged to me. I'm wearing his ring. It was his mother's, he said. I won't . . . I can't take it off, and I'm scared. But the sister, oh, she's lovely and sweet, proud, too. I felt warm all over when she looked at me. I . . . I wanted to kiss her. She looks like Dick when he first came to us. But he's changed. They'll hardly recognize him. To think they've come. And I had to be looking a fright . . . when of all times on earth I'd want to look my best."

Nell, out of breath, ran away, evidently to make herself presentable, according to her idea of the exigency of the case. Belding caught a glimpse of his wife's face as she went out, and it wore a sad, strange, anxious expression. Then Belding sat alone, pondering the dissimilar agitation manifest in his wife and daughter. It was beyond his understanding. Women were creatures of feelings. Belding saw reason to be delighted to entertain Dick's family, and for the time being no disturbing thought entered his mind.

Presently the Gales came back into the sitting room, looking very different without those long, gray, bundling cloaks and veils. Belding saw what he fancied must have been distinction, elegance. Mr. Gale seemed a grave, troubled, kindly person, ill in body and mind. Belding received the same impression of power that Ben Chase had given him, only here it was minus any harshness or hard quality. He gathered that Mr. Gale was a man of authority. Mrs. Gale rather frightened Belding, but he could not have told why. The girl was just like Dick as he used to be.

Their manner of speaking also reminded Belding of
Dick. They talked of the ride from Ash Fork down to the
border, of ugly and torn-up Casita, of the heat and dust
and cactus along the trail. Presently Nell came in, now
cool and sweet in white, with a red rose at her breast.
Belding had never been so proud of her. He saw that she
meant to appear well in the eyes of Dick's people, and began to have a faint perception of what the ordeal was for
her. Belding imagined the sooner the ladies were told that
Dick was to marry Nell the better for all concerned, and
especially for Nell. In the general conversation that ensued he sought for an opening in which to tell this important news, but he was kept so busy answering questions
about his position on the border, the kind of place Forlorn
River was, the reason for so many tents, that he was unable to find opportunity.

"It's interesting . . . very interesting," said Mr. Gale. "At
another time I want to learn all you'll tell me about the West.
It's new to me. I'm surprised . . . amazed, sir, I may say. But,
Mister Belding, what I want to know most is about my son.
I'm broken in health. I've worried myself ill over him. I
don't mind telling you, sir, that we quarreled. I laughed at
his threats. He went away. And I've come to see I did not
know Richard. I was wrong to upbraid him. For a year
we've known nothing of his doings, and now for almost six
months we've not heard from him at all. Frankly, Mister
Belding, I weakened first and I've come to hunt him up. My
fear is that I didn't start soon enough. The boy will have a
great position someday . . . God knows, perhaps soon. I
should not have allowed him to run over this wild country
for so long. But I hoped . . . though I hardly believed . . .
that he might find himself. Now I'm afraid he's. . . ."

Mr. Gale paused, and the white hand he raised expres-
sively shook a little.

Belding was not so thick-witted where men were concerned. He saw how the matter lay between Dick Gale
and his father.

"Well, Mister Gale, sure most young bucks from the East go to the bad out here," he said bluntly.

"I've been told that," replied Mr. Gale, and a shade overspread his worn face.

"They blow their money, then go to punching cows, take to whiskey."

"Yes," rejoined Mr. Gale, feebly nodding.

"Then they get to gambling, lose their jobs," went on Belding.

Mr. Gale lifted haggard eyes.

"Then it's bumming around, regular tramps, and to the bad generally." Belding spread wide his big arms, and, when one of them dropped around Nell, who sat beside him, she squeezed his hand tightly. "Sure, it's the regular thing," he concluded cheerfully.

He rather felt a little glee at Mr. Gale's distress, and Mrs. Gale's crushed I-told-you-so woe in no wise bothered him, but the look in the big dark eyes of Dick's sister was too much for Belding.

He choked off his characteristic oath when excited and blurted out: "Say, but Dick Gale never went to the bad. Listen. . . ."

Belding had scarcely started Dick Gale's story when he perceived that never in his life had he had such an appreciative, absorbed, breathless audience. Presently they were awed, and at the conclusion of that story they sat white-faced, still, amazed beyond speech. Dick Gale's advent in Casita, his rescue of Mercedes, his life as a border ranger certainly lost no picturesque or daring or even noble detail in Belding's telling. He kept back nothing but the present doubt of Dick's safety.

Dick's sister was the first of the three to recover herself.

"Oh, Father, I told you so!" she cried, and there was a glorious light in her eyes. "Deep down in my heart I knew Dick was a man."

Mr. Gale rose unsteadily from his chair. His frailty was now painfully manifest.

"Mister Belding, do you mean my son, Richard Gale, has done all that you told me?" he asked incredulously.

"I sure do," replied Belding with hearty good will.

"Martha, do you hear?" Mr. Gale turned to question his wife. She could not answer. Her face had not yet regained its natural color.

"He faced that bandit and his gang ... alone ... he *fought* them?" demanded Mr. Gale, his voice stronger.

"Dick mopped up the floor with the whole outfit."

"He rescued a Spanish girl ... went into the desert ... without food, weapons, anything, but his hands? Richard Gale, whose hands were always useless?"

Belding nodded with his huge grin bisecting the lower half of his face.

"He's a ranger now ... riding, fighting, sleeping on the sand, preparing his own food?"

"Well, I should smile," rejoined Belding.

"He cares for his horse ... with his own hands?" This query seemed to be the climax of Mr. Gale's strange hunger for truth. He had raised his head a little higher and his eye was brighter.

Mention of a horse fired Belding's blood. "Does Dick Gale *care* for his horse? Say, there are not many men as well loved as that white horse of Dick's. Blanco Sol he is, Mister Gale. That's Mex for White Sun. Wait till you see Blanco Sol. Bar one ... the whitest, biggest, strongest, fastest, grandest horse in the Southwest."

"So he loves a horse! I shall not know my own son. Mister Belding, you say Richard works for you. May I ask at what salary?"

"He gets forty dollars, board, and outfit," replied Belding proudly.

"Forty dollars?" echoed the father. "By the day ... or week?"

"The month, of course," said Belding, somewhat taken back.

"Forty dollars a month for a young man who spent five

hundred in the same time when he was at college! And who ran it into thousands when he got out!"

Mr. Gale laughed for the first time, and it was the laugh of a man who wanted to believe what he heard, yet scarcely dared to do it.

"What does he do with so much money? Money earned by peril, toil, sweat, and blood . . . forty dollars a month!"

"He saves it," replied Belding.

Evidently this was too much for Dick Gale's father and he gazed at his wife in sheer speechless astonishment. Dick's sister clapped her hands as might have a little girl.

Belding concluded this moment to be propitious. "Sure he saves it. Dick's engaged to marry Nell here. My stepdaughter, Nell Burton."

"Oh-h, Dad!" faltered Nell, and she rose, white as her dress.

How strange it was to see Dick's mother and sister rise, also, and turn to Nell with dark, proud, searching eyes! Belding vaguely realized he had made a blunder. Nell's white, appealing face gave him a pang. What had he done? Surely this family of Dick's ought to know his relation to Nell. There was a silence that positively made Belding nervous.

Then Elsie Gale stepped close to Nell.

"Miss Burton, are you really Richard's betrothed?"

Nell's tremulous lips framed an affirmative, but never uttered it. She held out her left hand, showing the ring Dick had given her. Miss Gale's recognition was instant, and her response was warm, sweet, gracious.

"I think I am going to be very, very glad," she said, and kissed Nell.

"Miss Burton, we are learning wonderful things about Richard," added Mr. Gale in an earnest although shaken voice. "If you have had to do with making a man of him . . . and now I begin to see, to believe so . . . may God bless you! Mother, we have not found him yet, but I think we're found his secret. We believed him a lost son. But here is his sweetheart!"

It was only then that the pride and hauteur in Mrs. Gale's face broke into an expression of mingled pain and joy. She opened her arms. Nell, uttering a strange little stifled cry, flew into them.

Belding suddenly discovered an unaccountable blur in his sight. He could not see perfectly, and that was why, when Mrs. Belding entered the sitting room, he was not certain that her face was as sad and white as it seemed.

CHAPTER FIFTEEN:
BOUND IN THE DESERT

Dick Gale sat stunned, gazing down into the purple depths of the crater where Rojas had plunged to his death. The Yaqui stood motionlessly upon the steep red wall of lava from which he had cut the bandit's hold. Mercedes lay quietly where she had fallen. From across the depths there came to Gale's ear the Indian's low, strange, wild cry. Then silence—hollow, breathless, stone silence—enveloped the great abyss and its upheaved lava walls. The sun was setting. Every instant the haze reddened and thickened.

Action on the part of the Yaqui unclamped the spell that held Gale as motionless as his surroundings. The Indian was edging back toward the ledge. He did not move with his former lithe and sure freedom. He crawled, slipped, dragged himself, rested often, and went on again. He had been wounded. When at last he reached the ledge where Mercedes lay, Gale jumped to his feet, strong and thrilling, spurred to meet the responsibility that now rested upon him.

Swiftly he turned to where Thorne lay. The cavalryman was just returning to consciousness. Gale ran for a canteen, bathed his face, made him drink. The look in Thorne's eyes was something hard to bear.

"Thorne. Thorne. It's all right. It's all right!" cried Gale in piercing tones. "Mercedes is safe! Yaqui saved her! Rojas is done for! Yaqui jumped down the wall and drove the bandit off the ledge. Cut him loose from the wall, foot by foot, hand by hand. We've won the fight, Thorne."

For Thorne these were marvelous, strength-giving words. The dark horror left his eyes; they began to dilate, to shine. He stood up, dizzily but unaided, and he gazed across the crater. Yaqui had reached the side of Mercedes, was bending over her. She stirred. Yaqui lifted her to her feet. She appeared weak, unable to stand alone. But she faced across the crater and waved her hand. She was unharmed. Thorne lifted both arms above his head and from his lips issued a cry. It was neither call nor hello or welcome or answer. Like the Yaqui's, it could scarcely be named. But it was deep, husky, prolonged, terribly human in its intensity. It made Gale shudder and made his heart beat like a trip hammer. Mercedes again waved a white hand. The Yaqui waved, too, and Gale saw in the action an urgent signal.

Hastily taking up canteen and rifles, Gale put a supporting arm around Thorne.

"Come, old man. Can you walk? Sure you can walk. Lean on me, and we'll soon get out of this. Don't look across. Look where you step. We've not much time before dark. Oh, Thorne, I'm afraid Jim has cashed in. And the last I saw of Laddy he was bad hurt."

Gale was keyed up to a high pitch of excitement and alertness. He seemed to be able to do many things, although his hand still pained him. But once off the ragged notched lava into the trail he had not such difficulty with Thorne and could keep a keen gaze shifting everywhere for sight of enemies.

"Listen, Thorne. What's that?" asked Gale, halting as they came to a place where the trail led down through rough breaks in the lava. The silence was broken by a strange sound, almost unbelievable considering the time and place. A voice was droning: "Turn the lady, turn. Turn the lady, turn. Alamon left. All swing . . . turn the lady, turn."

"Hello, Jim!" called Gale, dragging Thorne around the

corner of lava. "Where are you? Oh, you son-of-a-gun! I thought you were dead. My God, I'm glad to see you. Jim, are you hurt?"

Jim Lash stood in the trail, leaning over on the butt of his rifle, which evidently he was utilizing as a crutch. He was pale, but smiling. His hands were bloody. A scarf had been bound tightly around his left leg just above the knee. The leg hung limply and the foot dragged.

"I reckon I ain't injured much," replied Jim. "But my leg hurts like hell, if you want to know."

"Laddy . . . where's Laddy?"

"He's just across the crack there. I was trying to get to him. We had it hot an' heavy down here. Laddy was pretty bad shot up before he tried to head Rojas off the trail. Dick, did you see the Yaqui go after Rojas?"

"Did I!" exclaimed Gale grimly.

"The finish was all that saved me from runnin' loco plumb over the rim. You see I was closer'n you to where Mercedes was hid. When Rojas an' his last greaser started across, Laddy went after them, but I couldn't. Laddy did for Rojas's man, then went down himself. But he got up, went on, an' fell again. Laddy kept doin' that till he dropped for good. I reckon our chances are against findin' him alive. I tell you, boys, Rojas was hell-bent. An' Mercedes was game. I saw her shoot him. But mebbe bullets couldn't stop him then. If I didn't sweat blood when Mercedes was fightin' him on the cliff . . . then the finish! Only a Yaqui could have done that. Thorne, you didn't miss it?"

"Yes, I was down and out," replied the cavalryman.

"It's a damn' shame. Greatest stunt I ever seen! Thorne, you're standin' up pretty fair. Dick, is he bad hurt?"

"No, a hard knock on the skull and a scalp wound," replied Dick. "Here, Jim, let me help you over this place."

Step by step Gale got the two injured men down the uneven declivity and then across the narrow lava bridge over the fissure. Here he bade them rest while he went along the trail on that side to search for Laddy. Gale found the ranger stretched out, face downward, a reddened hand clutching a gun. Gale thought he was dead. Upon examination, however, it was found that Ladd still lived. Apparently he had sustained many bullet wounds. Gale lifted him and carried him back to where the others waited.

"He's alive, but that's all," said Dick as he laid the ranger down. "Do what you can. Stop the blood. Laddy's tough as cactus, you know. I'll hurry back for Mercedes and Yaqui."

Gale, like a fleet, sure-footed mountain sheep, ran along the trail. When he came across the Mexican, Rojas's last ally, Gale had evidence of the terrible execution of the .405. He did not pause. On the first part of that descent he made faster time than had Rojas. But he exercised care along the hard, slippery, ragged slope leading to the ledge. Presently he came upon Mercedes and the Yaqui. She ran right into Dick's arms, and there her strength, if not her courage, broke and she grew lax.

"Mercedes, you're safe. Thorne's safe. It's all right now."

"Rojas," she whispered.

"Gone. To the bottom of the crater. A Yaqui's vengeance, Mercedes."

He heard the girl whisper the name of her Virgin. Then he gathered her up in his arms.

"Come, Yaqui."

The Indian grunted. He had one hand pressed closely over a bloody place in his shoulder. Gale looked keenly at him. Yaqui was inscrutable, as of old, yet Gale somehow knew that wound meant little to him. The Indian followed him.

Without pausing, slow in some places, very careful in others, and swift on the smooth part of the trail, Gale carried Mercedes up to the rim and along that to where the others waited. Jim Lash worked awkwardly over Ladd. Thorne was trying to assist. Ladd himself was conscious, but a pallid, apparently a death-stricken man. The greeting between Mercedes and Thorne was calm, strangely so, it seemed to Gale. But he was now calm himself. Ladd smiled at him and evidently would have spoken had the power been his. Yaqui then joined the group, and his piercing eyes roved from one to the other, lingering longest over Ladd.

"Dick, I'm figgerin' hard," said Jim faintly. "In a minute it'll be up to you an' Mercedes. I've about . . . shot my bolt. Reckon you'll do . . . best by bringin' up blankets . . . water . . . salt . . . firewood. Laddy's got . . . one chance . . . in a hundred. Fix him up . . . first. Use hot salt water. If my leg's broke . . . set it best you can. That hole in Yaqui . . . only'll bother him a day. Thorne's bad hurt. Now, rustle . . . Dick, old boy."

Lash's voice died away in a husky whisper and he quietly lay back, stretching out all but the crippled leg. Gale examined it, assured himself the bones had not been broken, and then rose ready to go down the trail.

"Mercedes, hold Thorne's head up, in your lap . . . so. Now I'll go."

At the moment Yaqui appeared to have completed the binding of his wounded shoulder, and he started to follow Gale. He paid no attention to Gale's order for him to stay back. But he was slow, and gradually Gale forged ahead. A lingering brightness of the sunset lighted the trail and the descent to the arroyo was swift and easy. Some of the white horses had come in for water. Blanco Sol spied Gale and whistled and came pounding toward him. It was twilight down in the arroyo. Yaqui appeared and began collecting a bundle of mesquite sticks. Gale hastily put together the things he needed, and, packing them all in a tarpaulin, he turned to retrace his steps up the trail.

Darkness had about set in. The trail was narrow, exceedingly steep, and in some places fronted by precipices. Gale's burden was not very heavy, but its bulk made it unwieldy, and it was always overbalancing him or knocking against the wall side of the trail. Gale found it necessary to wait for Yaqui to take the lead. The Indian's eyes must have seen as well at night as by day. Gale toiled upward, shouldering, lifting, swinging, dragging the big pack, and, although the ascent of the slope was not really long, it seemed endless. At last they reached a level and were soon on the spot with Mercedes and the injured men.

Gale then set to work. Yaqui's part was to keep the fire blazing and the water hot; Mercedes's to help Gale in what way she could. Gale found Ladd had many wounds, yet not one of them was directly in a vital place. Evidently the ranger had almost bled to death. He remained unconscious through Gale's operations. According to Jim Lash, Ladd had one in 100 chances, but Gale considered it one in 1,000. Having done all that was possible for the ranger, Gale slipped blankets under and around him, and then turned his attention to Lash.

Jim came out of his stupor. A mushrooming bullet had torn a great hole in his leg. Gale, upon second examination, could not be sure the bones had been missed, but there was no bad break. The application of hot salt water made Jim groan. When he had been bandaged and laid beside Ladd, Gale went on to the cavalryman. Thorne was very weak and scarcely conscious. A furrow had been plowed through his scalp, deep as the skull. When it had been dressed, Mercedes collapsed. Gale laid her with the three in a row and covered them with blankets and the tarpaulin.

Then Yaqui submitted to examination. A bullet had gone through the Indian's shoulder. To Gale it appeared serious. Yaqui said it was a fleabite. But he allowed Gale to bandage it and obeyed when told to lay quietly in his blanket beside the fire.

Gale attended to his hand as best he could, washing and cleaning the cuts, and then stood guard. He seemed calm and wondered at what he considered a strange absence of poignant feeling. If he had felt weariness, it was now gone. He coaxed the fire with as little wood as would keep it burning; he sat beside it; he walked to and fro close by; sometimes he stood over the five sleepers, wondering if two of them, at least, would ever awaken.

Time had passed swiftly, but as the necessity for immediate action had gone by, the hours gradually assumed something of their normal length. The night wore on. The air grew colder, the stars brighter, the sky bluer, and, if such could be possible, the silence more intense. The fire burned out and for lack of wood could not be rekindled. Gale patrolled his short beat, growing colder and damper as dawn approached. The darkness became so thick that he could not see the pale faces of the sleepers. He dreaded the gray dawn and the light. Slowly the heavy black belt close to the lava changed to a pale gloom, then to gray, and, after that, morning came quickly.

The hour had come for Dick Gale to face his great problem. It was natural that he hung back a little at first, natural that when he went forward to look at the quiet sleepers, he did so with a grim and stern force urging him. At least his hand was better. Yaqui stirred, roused, yawned, got up, and, although he did not smile at Gale, a light shone fleetly across his dark face. He stooped a little at the shoulder and appeared stiff; otherwise, he was as usual. Mercedes lay in deep slumber. Thorne had a high fever and was beginning to show signs of restlessness. Ladd seemed just barely alive. Jim Lash slept as if he was not much the worse for his wound.

Gale rose from his examination with a sharp breaking of his cold mood. While there was life in Thorne and Ladd, there was hope for them. Then he faced his problem and his decision was instant.

He awoke Mercedes. How wondering, wistful, beautiful was that first opening flash of her eyes! Then the dark, troubled thought came. Swiftly she sat up.

"Mercedes . . . come. Are you all right? Laddy is alive. Thorne's not . . . not so bad. But we've got a job on our hands. You must help me."

She bent over Thorne and laid her hands on his hot face.

Then she rose—a woman such as he had imagined she might be in an hour of trial.

Gale took up Ladd as carefully and gently as possible.

"Mercedes, bring what you can carry and follow me," he said. Then, motioning for Yaqui to remain there, he turned down the slope with Ladd in his arms.

Neither pausing nor making a misstep or conscious of great effort, Gale carried the wounded man down into the arroyo. Mercedes kept at his heels, light, supple, lithe as a panther. He left her with Ladd, and went back. When he had started off with Thorne in his arms, he felt the tax on his strength. Surely and swiftly, however, he bore the cavalryman down the trail to lay him beside Ladd. Again he started back, and, when he began to mount the steep lava steps, he was hot, wet, breathing hard. As he reached the scene of that night's camp, a voice greeted him. Jim Lash was sitting up.

"Hello, Dick . . . I woke some late this mornin'. Where's Laddy? Dick, you ain't a-goin' to say . . . ?"

"Laddy's alive . . . that's about all," replied Dick.

"Where's Thorne an' Mercedes? Look here, man, I reckon you ain't packin' this crippled outfit down that awful trail?"

"Had to . . . Jim . . . an hour's sun would kill . . . both Laddy and . . . Thorne. Come on now."

For once Jim Lash's cool, good nature and careless indifference gave precedence to amaze and concern.

"Always knew you was a husky chap. But, Dick, you're no hoss. Get me a crutch an' give me a lift on me side."

"Come on," replied Gale. "I've no time to monkey."

He lifted the ranger, called to Yaqui to follow with some of the camp outfit, and once more essayed the steep descent. Jim Lash was the heaviest man of the three and Gale's strength was put to enormous strain to carry him on that broken trail. Nevertheless, Gale went down, down, swift and sure over the bad places, and he staggered into the arroyo with bursting heart and red-blinded eyes. When he had recovered, he made a last trip up the slope for the camp effects Yaqui had been unable to carry.

Then he drew Jim and Mercedes and Yaqui, too, into an earnest discussion of ways and means whereby to fight for the life of Thorne. Ladd's case Gale now considered hopeless, although he meant to fight for him, too, as long as he breathed.

It seemed to Gale that two days and two nights slipped by as a few hours of labor and watching and nursing. During that time the Indian recovered from his injury and was capable of performing all except heavy tasks. Then Gale succumbed to weariness. Upon getting his much needed rest, he relieved Mercedes of the care and watch over Thorne which, up to that time, she had absolutely refused to relinquish. The cavalryman had high fever and Gale feared he had developed blood poisoning. He required constant attention. His condition slowly grew worse and there came a day Gale thought surely was the end. But that day passed, and the night, and the next day, and Thorne lived on, ghastly, stricken, raving. Mercedes hung over him with jealous, passionate care and did all that could have been humanly done for a man. She grew wan, absorbed, silent. Quite suddenly then, and to Gale's amaze and thanksgiving, there came an abatement of Thorne's fever. With it appeared to go some of the heat and redness of the inflamed wound. Next morning he was conscious, and Gale grasped some of the hope that Mercedes had never abandoned. He forced her to rest while he attended to Thorne. That day he saw that the crisis was past. Recovery for Thorne was now possible and would, perhaps, depend entirely upon the care he received.

Jim Lash's wound healed without any aggravating symptoms. It would be only a matter of time until he had the use of his leg again. All those days, however, there was little apparent change in Ladd's condition, unless it was that he seemed to fade away as he lingered. At first his wounds remained open; they bled a little all the time out-wardly, perhaps internally, also; his blood did not seem to clot, and so the bullet holes did not close. Then Yaqui asked for the care of Ladd. Gale yielded it with opposing thoughts—that Ladd would waste slowly away till life ceased, and that there never was any telling what might lay in the power of this strange Indian. Yaqui absented himself from camp for a while, and, when he returned, he carried the roots and leaves of desert plants unknown to Gale. From these the Indian brewed an ointment. Then he stripped the bandages from Ladd and applied the mix-ture to his wounds. That done, he let him lie with the wounds exposed to the air, at night covering him. Next day he again exposed the wounds to the warm dry air. Slowly they closed and Ladd ceased to bleed externally.

Days passed and grew into what Gale imagined must have been weeks. Yaqui recovered fully. Jim Lash began to move about on a crutch; he shared the Indian's watch over Ladd. Thorne lay a haggard, emaciated ghost of his for-mer rugged self, but with life in the eyes that turned al-ways toward Mercedes. Ladd lingered and lingered. The life seemingly would not leave his bullet-pierced body. He faded, withered, shrunk till he was almost a skeleton. He knew those who worked and watched over him, but he had no power of speech. His eyes and eyelids moved; the rest of him seemed stone. All those days nothing ex-cept water was given him. It was marvelous how tena-ciously, however feebly, he clung to life. Gale imagined it was the Yaqui's spirit that held back death. That tireless, implacable, inscrutable savage was ever at the ranger's side. His great somber eyes burned. At length he went to Gale, and with that strange light flitting across the hard, bronzed face, he said Ladd would live.

The second day after Ladd had been given such thin nourishment as he could swallow, he recovered the use of his tongue.

"Shore . . . this's . . . hell," he whispered.

That was a characteristic speech for the ranger, Gale thought, and, indeed, it made all who heard it smile while their eyes were wet.

From that time forward Ladd gained, but he gained so immeasurably slowly that only the eyes of hope could have seen any improvement. Jim Lash threw away his crutch and Thorne was well, if still somewhat weak, before Ladd could lift his arm or turn his head. A kind of long, immovable gloom passed away like a shadow from his face. His whispers grew stronger. And the day arrived when Gale, who was perhaps the least optimistic, threw doubt to the winds and knew the ranger would get well. For Gale that joyous moment of realization was one in which he seemed to return to a former self, long absent. He experienced an elevation of soul. He was suddenly overwhelmed with gratefulness, humility, awe. A gloomy, black terror had passed by. He wanted to thank the faithful Mercedes, and Thorne for getting well, and the cheerful Lash, and Ladd himself, and that strange and wonderful Yaqui, now beginning to loom so splendidly. He thought of home and Nell. The terrible, encompassing red slopes lost something of their fearful nature, and there was a spirit hovering near.

"Boys, come 'round," said Ladd in his low voice. "An' you Mercedes, an' call the Yaqui."

Ladd lay in the shade of the brush shelter that had been erected. His head was raised slightly on a pillow. There seemed little of him but long lean lines, and, if it had not been for his keen, thoughtful, kindly eyes, his face would have resembled a death mask of a man starved.

"Shore, I want to know what day is it an' what month?" asked Ladd.

Nobody could answer him. The question seemed a surprise to Gale, and evidently was so to the others.

"Look at that cactus," went on Ladd.

Near the wall of lava a stunted saguaro lifted its head.

A few shriveled blossoms that had once been white hung along the fluted column.

"I reckon, accordin' to that giant cactus, it's some-wheres along the end of March," said Jim Lash soberly.

"Shore it's April. Look where the sun is. An' can't you feel it's gettin' hot?"

"Suppose it is April?" queried Lash slowly.

"Well . . . what I'm drivin' at is it's about time you all was hittin' the trail back to Forlorn River, before the water holes dry out."

"Laddy, I reckon we'll start soon as you're able to be put on a horse."

"Shore that'll be too late."

A silence ensued in which those who heard Ladd gazed fixedly at him, and then at each other. Lash uneasily shifted the position of his lame leg, and Gale saw him moisten his lips with his tongue.

"Charlie Ladd . . . I ain't reckonin' you mean we're to ride off an' leave you here?"

"What the hell else is there to do? The hot weather's close. Pretty soon most of the water holes will be dry. You can't travel then. I'm on my back here, an' God only knows when I could be packed out. Not for weeks, mebbe. I'll never be any good again, even if I was to get out alive. You see, shore this sort of case comes 'round sometimes in the desert. It's common enough. I've heard of several cases where men had to go an' leave a feller behind. It's reasonable. If you're fightin' the desert, you can't afford to be sentimental. Now, as I said, I'm all in. So what's the sense of you waitin' here, when it means . . . the old desert story? By goin' now, mebbe you'll get home. If you wait on a chance of takin' me . . . you'll be too late. Pretty soon this lava'll be one roastin' hell. Shore now, boys, you'll see this the right way? Jim, old pard?"

"No, by God! An', Laddy, I cain't figger how you could ever ask me."

"Shore, then, leave me here with Yaqui an' a couple of

the horses. We can eat sheep meat. An' if the water holds out. . . ."

"No!" interrupted Lash violently.

Ladd's eyes sought Gale's face. "Son, you ain't bull-headed like Jim. You'll see the sense of it. There's Nell a-waitin' back at Forlorn River. Think what it means to her. She's a damn' fine girl, Dick, an' what right have you to break her heart for an old worn-out cowpuncher? Think how she's watchin' for you with that sweet face all sad an' troubled, an' her eyes turnin' black. You'll go, son, won't you?"

Dick shook his head.

The ranger turned his gaze upon Thorne, and now the keen, glistening light in his gray eyes had blurred. "Thorne, it's different with you. Jim's a fool an' young Gale has been punctured by cholla thorns. He's got the desert poison in his blood. But you, now . . . you've no call to stick . . . you can find that trail out. It's easy to follow . . . made by so many shod hosses. Take your wife an' go. Shore you'll go, Thorne?"

Deliberately and without an instant's hesitation the cavalryman replied: "No."

Ladd then directed his appeal to Mercedes. His face was now convulsed, and his voice, although it had sunk to a whisper, was clear and beautiful with some rich quality that Gale had never before heard in it.

"Mercedes, you're a woman. You're the woman we fought for. An' some of us are shore goin' to die for you. Don't make it all for nothin'. Let us feel we saved the woman. Shore you can make Thorne go. He'll have to go, if you say. They'll all have to go. Think of the years of love an' happiness in store for you. A week or so now an' it'll be too late. Can you stand for me seein' you . . . let me tell you, Mercedes, when the summer heat hits the lava, we'll all wither an' curl up like shavin's near a fire. A wind of hell will blow up this slope. Look at them mesquites. See the twist . . . the writhe. That's the torture of heat an' thirst. Do you want me or all us men seein' you like that? Mercedes, don't make it all for nothin'. Say you'll persuade Thorne, if not the others."

For all the effect his appeal had to move her, Mercedes might have possessed a heart as hard and fixed as the surrounding lava. "Never!" White-faced, with great black eyes flashing, the Spanish girl spoke the word that bound her, and her companions, in the desert.

The subject was never mentioned again. Gale had an idea that upon reflection he considered it less than a subtle reading or divination of Ladd's mind. To his astonishment Lash came to him with the same strange fancy. After that they made certain there never was a gun within reach of Ladd's clutching, clawlike hands.

Gradually a somber spell lifted from the ranger's mind. When he was entirely free of it, he began to gather strength daily. Then it was as if he had never known patience—he who had shown so well how to wait. He was in a frenzy to get well. His appetite could not be satisfied.

The sun climbed higher, whiter, hotter. At midday a wind from Gulfward roared up the arroyo, and now only the paloverdes and the few saguaros were green and they began to pale. Every day the water in the lava hole sank an inch.

The Yaqui alone spent the waiting time in activity. He made trips up on the lava slope, and each time he returned with guns or boots or sombreros, or something belonging to the bandits that had fallen. He never fetched in a saddle or bridle, and from that the rangers concluded Rojas's horses had long before taken their back trail. What speculation—what consternation those saddled horses would cause if they returned to Forlorn River!

As Ladd improved, there was one story he had to hear every day. It was the one relating to what he had missed— a sight of Rojas pursued and plunged to his doom. The thing had a morbid fascination for the sick ranger. He reveled in it. He tortured Mercedes. His gentleness and consideration, heretofore so marked, were in abeyance to some sinister, ghastly joy. But to humor him Mercedes racked her soul with these sensations she had suffered when Rojas hounded her out on the ledge—when she shot him—when she sprang to throw herself over the precipice—when she fought him—when with half-blinded eyes she looked up to see the merciless Yaqui reaching for the bandit. Ladd fed his cruel longing with Thorne's poignant recollections, with the keen, clear, never-to-be-forgotten shocks to Gale's eye and ear. Jim Lash, for one at least, never tired of telling how he had seen and heard the tragedy, and every time, in the telling, it gathered some more tragic and gruesome detail. Jim believed in satisfying the ranger. Then in the twilight, when the campfire burned, Ladd would try to get the Yaqui to tell his side of the story. But this the Indian would never do more than what was silently expressive in his fathomless eyes and the set passion of his massive face.

Those waiting days grew into weeks. Ladd gained very slowly. Nevertheless, at last he could walk about, and soon he averred that, strapped to a horse, he could last out the return trip to Forlorn River.

There was rejoicing in camp and eager plans were suggested. The Yaqui happened to be absent. When he returned, the rangers told him they were now ready to undertake the journey back across lava and cactus. Yaqui shook his head. They declared again their intention.

"No," replied the Indian, and his deep sonorous voice rolled out upon the quiet of the arroyo. He spoke briefly then. They had waited too long. The smaller water holes back on the trail were dry. The hot summer was upon them. There could be only death waiting down in the burning valley. There was water and grass and wood, and shade from the sun's rays, and sheep to be killed on the peaks. The water would hold unless the season was that dreaded *año seco* of the Mexicans.

"Wait for rain," concluded Yaqui, and now as never before he spoke as one with authority. "If no rain. . . ." Silently he lifted a speaking hand.

CHAPTER SIXTEEN:
MOUNTAIN SHEEP

What Gale might have thought an appalling situation to consider from a safe and comfortable home away from the desert was now for him, shut in by red-ribbed lava walls and great dry wastes, a matter he accepted as inevitable, with the unleashing of a cool, wild spirit. So, he imagined, it was accepted by the others. Not even Mercedes uttered a regret. No word was spoken of home. If there was thought of dear friends, loved ones, it was locked deeply in the mind. In Mercedes there was no change in womanly quality, perhaps because all she had to love was there in the desert with her.

Gale had often pondered over this singular change in character. He had trained himself, in order to fight a paralysis through the desert's influence, to oppose with memory and thought that insidious, primitive retrogression to what was scarcely consciousness at all, merely a savage's instinct of sight and sound. He felt the need now of redoubled effort. For there was a sheer happiness in drifting. Not only was it easy to forget; it was hard to remember. His idea was that a man laboring under a great wrong, a great crime, a great passion might find the lonely desert a fitting place for either remembrance or oblivion, according to the nature of his soul. But an ordinary, healthy, reasonably happy mortal who loved the open with its glare of sun and sweep of wind would have a task to keep from going backward to the unconscious natural man as he was before civilization.

By tacit agreement, Ladd again became the leader of the party. Ladd was a man who would have taken all the responsibility whether or not it was given him. In moments of hazard, of uncertainty, Lash and Gale, even Belding, unconsciously looked to the ranger. He had that kind of power.

The first thing Ladd asked was to have the store of food that remained spread out upon a tarpaulin. Assuredly it was a slender enough supply. The ranger stood for long moments gazing down at it. He was groping among past experiences, calling back from his years of life on range and desert that which might be valuable for the present issue. It was impossible to read the gravity of Ladd's face, for he still looked like a dead man, but the slow shake of his head told Gale much. There was a grain of hope, however, in the significance with which he touched the bags of salt and said: "Shore it was sense packin' all that salt." Then he turned to face his comrades. "That's little grub for six starvin' people corralled in the desert. But the grub end ain't worryin' me. Yaqui can get sheep up on the slopes. Water! That's the beginnin' an' middle an' end of our case."

"Laddy, I reckon the water hole here never goes dry," replied Jim.

"Ask the Indian."

Upon being questioned, Yaqui repeated what he said about the dreaded *año seco* of the Mexicans. In a dry year this water hole failed.

"Dick, take a rope an' see how much water's in the hole."

Gale could not find bottom with a thirty-foot lasso. The water was as cool, clear, and sweet as if it had been kept in a shaded iron receptacle.

Ladd welcomed this information with surprise and gladness.

"Let's see. Last year was shore pretty dry. Mebbe this

summer won't be. Mebbe our wonderful good luck'll hold . . . ask Yaqui if he thinks it'll rain."

Mercedes questioned the Indian.

"He says no man can tell surely. But he thinks the rains will come," she replied.

"Shore it'll rain, you can gamble on that now," continued Ladd. "If there's only grass for the hosses. We can't get out of here without hosses. Dick, take the Indian an' scout down the arroyo. Today I seen the hosses were gettin' fat. Gettin' fat in this desert! But mebbe they've about grazed up all the grass. Go an' see, Dick. An' may you come back with more good news."

Gale, upon the few occasions when he had wandered down the arroyo, had never gone far. The Yaqui said there was grain for the horses, and until now no one had given the question more consideration. Gale found that the arroyo widened as it opened. Near the head, where it was narrow, the grass lined the course of the dry streambed. But farther down this streambed spread out. There was every indication that at flood seasons the water covered the floor of the arroyo. The farther Gale went the thicker and larger grew the gnarled mesquite and paloverdes, the more cactus and greasewood there were, and other desert growths. Patches of gray grass grew everywhere. Gale began to wonder where the horses were. Finally the trees and brush thinned out, and a mile-wide gray plain stretched down to reddish sand dunes. Over to one side were the white horses, and, even as Gale saw them, both Blanco Diablo and Sol lifted heads and with white manes tossing in the wind whistled clarion calls. Here was grass enough for many horses; the arroyo was indeed an oasis.

Ladd and the others were awaiting Gale's report, and they received it with calmness, yet a gladness no less evident because it was restrained. Gale, in his keen observance at the moment, found that he and his comrades turned with glad eyes to the woman of the party.

"*Señor* Laddy, you think . . . you believe . . . we shall. . . ." She faltered, and her voice failed. It was the woman in her, weakening in the light of real hope, of the happiness now possible beyond that desert barrier.

"Mercedes, no white man can tell what'll come to pass out here," said Ladd earnestly. "Shore I have hopes now I never dreamed of. I was pretty near a dead man. The Indian saved me. Queer notions have come into my head about Yaqui. I don't understand them. He seems, when you look at him, only a squalid, sullen, vengeful savage. But Lord, that's far from truth. Mebbe Yaqui's different from most Indians. He *looks* the same, though. Mebbe the trouble is we white folks never knew the Indian. Anyway, Belding had it right. Yaqui's our godsend. Now as to the future, I'd like to know, mebbe as well as you, if we're ever to get home. Only bein' what I am, I say, *quién sabe?* But somethin' tells me Yaqui knows. Ask him, Mercedes. Make him tell. We'll all be the better for knowin'. We'd be stronger for havin' more'n our faith in him. He's a silent Indian, but make him tell."

Mercedes called to Yaqui. At her bidding there was always a suggestion of hurry, which otherwise was never manifest in his actions. She put a hand on his bared muscular arm and began to speak in Spanish. Her voice was low, swift, full of deep emotion, sweet as the sound of a bell. It thrilled Gale, although he understood scarcely a word she said. He did not need translation to know that here spoke the longing of a woman for life, love, home, the heritage of a woman's heart.

Gale doubted his own divining impression. It was that the Yaqui understood this woman's longing. In Gale's sight the Indian's stoicism, his inevitability, the lava-like hardness of his face, although they did not change, seemed to give forth light, gentleness, loyalty. The moment in its power of perception was an extraordinary one for Gale, but, as it did not last, he failed to hold some beautiful, illusive thing.

"*Sí,*" rolled out the Indian's reply, full of power and depth.

Mercedes drew a long breath and her hand sought Thorne's.

"He says yes," she whispered. "He answers he'll save us . . . he'll take us all back . . . he knows!"

The Indian turned away to his tasks, and the silence that held the little group was finally broken by Ladd.

"Shore I said so. Now all we've got to do is use sense. Friends, I'm the commissary department of this outfit, an' what I say goes. You all won't eat except when I tell you. Mebbe it'll not be so hard to keep our health. Starved beggars don't get sick. But there's the heat comin', an' we can all go loco, you know. To pass the time . . . Lord, that's our problem. Now if you all only had a hankerin' for checkers, shore I'll make a board an' make you play. Thorne, you're luckiest. You've got your girl, an' this can be a honeymoon. Now with few tools an' little material see what a grand house you can build for your wife. Dick, you're lucky, too. You like to hunt, an' up there you'll find the finest big horn huntin' in the West. Take Yaqui an' the Four-Oh-Five. We need the meat, but while you're gettin' it have your sport. The same chance will never come again. I wish we all was able to go. But crippled men can't climb the lava. Shore, you'll see some country from the peaks. There's no wilder place on earth, except the poles. An' when you're older, you an' Nell, with a couple of fine boys, think what it'll be to tell them about bein' lost in the lava, an' about huntin' sheep with a Yaqui. Shore I've hit it. You can take yours out in huntin' an' thinkin'. Now, if I had a girl like Nell, I'd never go crazy. That's your game, Dick. Hunt, an' think of Nell, an' how you'll tell those fine boys about it all, an' about the old cowman you knowed, Laddy, who'll by then be long past the divide. Rustle now, son. Get some enthusiasm. For shore, you'll need it for yourself an' us."

Gale climbed the lava slope, away around to the right of the arroyo, along an old trail that Yaqui said the Papagos had made before his own people hunted there. Part way it led through spiked, crested, upheaved lava that otherwise would have been almost impassable even without its silver coating of cholla cactus. There were benches and ledges bare and glistening in the sun. From the crests of these Yaqui's searching falcon gaze roved near and far for signs of sheep, and Gale used his glass on the reaches of lava that slanted steeply upward to the corrugated peaks, and down over endless heave and bulge and red-waved slopes. The heat smoked up from the lava, and this, with the red color and the shiny chollas, gave the impression of a world of smoldering fire.

Farther along the slope Yaqui halted and crawled behind projections to a point commanding a view over an extraordinary section of country. The peaks were off to the left. In the foreground were gullies, ridges, cañons, arroyos, all glistening with chollas and some other and more numerous white bushes, and here and there stood up a green cactus. This region was only a splintered and more devastated part of the volcanic slope, but it was miles in extent. Yaqui peeped over the top of a blunt block of lava and searched a sharp-billowed wilderness. Suddenly he grasped Gale and pointed across a deep wide gully.

With the aid of his glass Gale saw five sheep. They were much larger than he had expected, dull brown in color, and two of them were rams with great curved horns. They were looking in his direction. Remembering what he had heard about the wonderful eyesight of these mountain animals, Gale could only conclude that these had seen the hunters.

Then Yaqui's movements attracted and interested him. The Indian had brought with him a red scarf and a mesquite branch. He tied the scarf to the stick, and propped this up in a crack in the lava. The scarf waved in the wind. That done, the Indian bade Gale watch.

Once again he leveled the glass at the sheep. All five now were motionless, standing like statues, heads pointed across the gully. They were more than a mile distant. When Gale looked without his glass, they merged into the roughness of the lava. He was intensely interested. Did the sheep see the red scarf? It seemed incredible, but nothing else could account for that statuesque alertness.

The sheep held this rigid position for perhaps fifteen minutes. Then the leading ram started to approach. The others followed. He took a few steps, then halted. Always he held his head up, nose pointed.

"By George, they're coming!" exclaimed Gale. "They see that flag. They're hunting us. They're curious. If this desert doesn't beat me."

Evidently the Indian understood, for he grunted.

Gale found difficulty in curbing his impatience. The approach of the sheep was slow. The advances of the leader and the intervals of watching had a singular regularity; he worked like a machine. Gale followed him down the opposite wall, around holes, across gullies, over ridges. Then Gale shifted the glass back to find the others. They were coming, also, with exactly the same pace and pause of their leader. What steppers they were! How surefooted! The leaps they made! It was thrilling to watch them. Gale forgot he had a rifle. The Yaqui pressed a heavy hand low upon his shoulder which action probably meant for him to keep well hidden and to be quiet. Gale suddenly conceived the idea that the sheep might come clear across to investigate the puzzling red thing fluttering in the breeze. Strange indeed would that be for the wildest creatures in the world.

The big ram led on with the same regular persistence, and in half an hour's time he was in the bottom of the great gulf, and soon he was facing up the slope. Gale knew then that the alluring scarf had fascinated him. It was no longer necessary now for Gale to use his glass. There was a short period when the bulge of an intervening crest of lava hid the sheep from view. After that, the two rams and their smaller followers were plainly in sight for perhaps a quarter of an hour. At the end of that time they disappeared behind another ridge. Gale kept watching, sure they would come out farther on. A tense period of waiting passed, then a sudden electrifying presence of Yaqui's hand made Gale tremble with excitement.

Very cautiously he shifted his position. There, not fifty feet distant upon a high mound of lava, stood the leader ram. His size astounded Gale. He seemed all horns. But only for a moment did the impression of horns overbalancing body remain with Gale. The sheep was graceful, sinewy, slender, powerfully built, and in poise magnificent. As Gale watched spellbound, the second ram leaped lightly upon the mound, and presently the three others did likewise.

Then indeed Gale feasted his eyes with a spectacle for a hunter. It came to him suddenly that there had been something he expected to see in the Rocky Mountain big horn, and it was lacking. They were beautiful, as wonderful as even Ladd's encomiums had led him to suppose. He thought perhaps it was the contrast these soft, sleek, short-furred, graceful animals afforded to what he imagined the hard, barren, terrible lava mountains might develop. The splendid leader stepped closer, his round, protruding, amber eyes, which Gale could now plainly see, intent upon that fatal red flag. Like automatons the other four crowded into his tracks. A few little slow steps—then the leader halted.

At this instant Gale's absorbed attention was directed by Yaqui to the rifle, and so to the purpose of the climb. A little cold shock affronted Gale's vivid pleasure. With it dawned a realization of what he had imagined was lacking in these animals. They did not look wild! The so-called wildest of wild creatures appeared as tame—tamer than sheep he had followed on a farm. It would be little less than murder to kill them. Gale regretted the need of slaughter. Nevertheless, he could not resist the desire to show himself and see how tame they really were.

He reached for the .405, and, as he threw a shell into the chamber, the slight metallic *click* made the sheep jump. Then Gale rose quickly to his feet.

The noble ram and his band simply stared at Gale. They

had never seen a man. They showed not the slightest indication of instinctive fear. Curiosity, surprise, even friendliness seemed to mark their attitude of attention. Gale imagined that they were going to step still closer. He did not choose to wait to see if this were true. Certainly it already took something of grimness to raise the heavy .405.

His shot killed the big leader. The others bounded away with remarkable nimbleness. Gale used up the remaining four shells to drop the second ram, and by the time he had reloaded, the others were out of range.

The Yaqui's method of hunting was sure and deadly, and saving of energy, but Gale never would try it again. He chose to stalk the game. This entailed a great expenditure of strength, the eyes and the lungs of a mountaineer, and, as Gale put it to Ladd, the need of seven-league boots. After being hunted a few times and shot at, the sheep became exceedingly difficult to approach. Gale learned to know that their fame as the keenest-eyed of all animals was well founded. If he worked directly toward a flock, crawling over the sharp lava, always a sentinel espied him before he got within range. The only method of attack that he found successful was to locate sheep with his glass, work around to windward of them, and then, getting behind a ridge or buttress, crawl like a lizard to a vantage point. He failed often. The stalk called forth all that was in him of endurance, cunning, speed. As the days grew hotter, he hunted in the early morning hours, and a while before the sun went down. More than one night he lay out on the lava, with the great stars close overhead, and the immense void all beneath him. The pursuit he learned to love. Up on those scarred and blasted slopes, the wild spirit that was in him had free rein. And like a shadow the faithful Yaqui tried ever to keep at his heels.

One morning the rising sun greeted him as he surmounted the higher cone of the volcano. He saw the vastness of the east aglow with a glazed rosy whiteness, like the changing hue of an ember. At this height there was a

sweeping wind, still cool. The western slopes of lava lay
dark, and all that world of sand and gulf and mountain
barrier beyond was shrouded in the mystic cloud of distance. Gale had assimilated much of the loneliness and
the sense of ownership and the love of lofty heights that
might have been attributed to the great condor of the
peak. Like this wide-winged bird, he had an unparalleled
range of vision. The very corners whence came the winds
seemed pierced by Gale's eyes.

Yaqui spied a flock of sheep far under the curved broken rim of the main crater. Then began the stalk. Gale had
taught the Yaqui something—that speed might win as
well as patient cunning. Keeping out of sight, Gale ran
over the spike-crusted lava, leaving the Indian far behind.
His feet were magnets for supporting holds and he passed
over them too fast to fall. The wind, the keen air of the
height, the red of lava, the boundless surrounding blue—
all seemed to have something to do with his wildness.
Then hiding, slipping, creeping, crawling he closed in
upon his quarry until the long rifle grew like stone in his
grip, and the whipping *spang* ripped the silence, and the
strange echo *boomed* deep in the crater and rolled around,
as if in hollow mockery at the hopelessness of escape.

Gale's exultant yell was given as much to free himself of
some bursting joy of action as it was to call the slower
Yaqui. Then he liked the strange echoes. It was a madden-
ing whirl of sound that delved deeper and deeper along
the whorled and caverned walls of the crater. It was as if
these aged walls resented the violating of their silent
sanctity. Gale felt himself a man, a thing alive, something
superior to all this savage dead upflung world of iron, a
master even of all this grandeur and sublimity because he
had a soul.

He waited beside his quarry, and breathed deeply with
labored chest, and swept the long slopes with searching
eyes of habit. When Yaqui came up, they set about the
hardest task of all—to pack the best of that heavy sheep
down miles of steep, ragged cholla-covered lava. But even

in this Gale rejoiced. The heat was nothing; the millions of little pits that could hold and twist a foot were nothing; the blade-edged crusts and the deep fissures and the choked cañons and the tangled dwarfed mesquites—all then were as nothing but obstacles cheerfully to be overcome. Only the cholla hindered Dick Gale.

When his heavy burden pulled him out of sure-footedness and he plunged into a cholla, or when the strange, deceitful, uncanny, almost invisible frosty thorns caught and pierced him, then there was call for all of fortitude and endurance. For this cactus had hellish power to torture a man. Its pain was a stinging, blinding, burning, sickening, poison in the blood. If thorns pierced his legs, he felt the pain all over his body; if his hands rose from a fall full of the barbed joints, he was helpless and quivering till Yaqui tore them out. It was only a dim memory when he had to do this by himself alone.

But this one peril, dreaded more than dizzy height of precipice, or sun blindness on the glistening peak, did not daunt Gale. His teacher was the Yaqui, and always before him was an example that made him despair of a white man's equality. Color, race, blood, breeding—what were these in the wilderness? Verily Dick Gale had come to learn the use of his hands.

So in a descent of hours he toiled down the lava slope, to stalk into the arroyo like a burdened giant, wringing wet, panting, clear-eyed and dark-faced, his ragged clothes and boots white with cholla thorns.

The gaunt Ladd rose from his shaded seat, removed his pipe from smiling lips, and then looked away again.

The torrid summer heat came imperceptibly or it could never have been borne by white men. It changed the lives of the fugitives, making them partly nocturnal in habit. The nights had the balmy coolness of spring and would have been delightful for sleep, but that would have made the red, blazing, roaring days unendurable.

The sun rose in a vast white flame. With it came the blasting, withering wind from the Gulf. A red haze, like that of earlier sunsets, seemed to come sweeping on the wind, and it roared up the arroyo, and went bellowing into the crater, and rushed on as in fury to lash the peaks. During these hot, windy hours the desert-bound party slept in deep recesses in the lava, and, if necessity brought them forth, they could not remain out long. The sand burned through boots and a touch of bare hand on lava raised a blister.

A short while before sundown the Yaqui went forth to build a campfire and soon the others came out, heat-dazed, half-blinded, with parching throats to allay, and hunger that was never satisfied. A little action and a cooling of the air revived them, and, when night set in, they were comfortable around the campfire.

As Ladd had said, one of their greatest problems was the passing of time. The nights were interminably long, but they had to be passed in work or play or dream, anything except sleep. That was Ladd's most inflexible command. He gave no reason. But not improbably the ranger thought that the terrific heat by day spent in slumber lessened wear and strain, if not a real danger of madness.

Accordingly, at first the occupations of this little group were many and various. They worked if they had something to do, or could invent a pretext. They told and retold stories until all were wearisome. They sang songs. Mercedes taught Spanish. They played every game they knew. They invented others that were so trivial children would scarcely have been interested and these they played seriously. In a word, with intelligence and passion, with all that was civilized and human, they fought the ever-impinging loneliness, the savage solitude of their environment. But they had only finite minds. It was not in reason to expect a complete victory against this mighty Nature, this bound horizon of death and desolation and decay. Gradually they fell back upon fewer occupations, and from that to several only, until the time came when the silence was hard to break.

Gale believed himself the keenest of the party, the one

who thought most, and he watched the effect of the desert upon his companions. He imagined that he saw Ladd grow old, sitting around the campfire. Certain it was that the ranger's gray hair had turned white. What had been at times hard and cold and grim about him had strangely vanished in sweet temper and a vacant mindedness that held him longer as the days passed. For hours, it seemed, Ladd would bend over his checkerboard and never make a move. It mattered not now whether or not he had a partner. He was always glad at being spoken to, as if he were called back from some vague region of mind. Jim Lash, the calmest, coolest, most nonchalant, best-humored Westerner Gale had ever met, had by slow degrees lost that cheerful character which would have been of such infinite good to his companions, and always he sat silently brooding. Jim had no ties, few memories, and the desert was claiming him.

Thorne and Mercedes, however, were living wonderful proof that spirit, mind, and heart were free—free to soar in scorn of the colossal barrenness and silence and space of that terrible hedging prison of lava. They were young; they loved; they were together; the oasis was almost a paradise. Gale believed he helped himself by watching them. Imagination had never pictured real happiness to him. Thorne and Mercedes had forgotten the outside world. If they had been existing on the burned-out, desolate moon, they could hardly have been in a harsher, grimmer, lonelier spot than this red-walled arroyo. But it might have been a statelier Eden than that of the primitive day.

Mercedes grew slimmer until she was a slender shadow of her former self. She grew thin, hard, brown as the rangers, lithe and quick as a panther. She seemed to live on water and the air, perhaps, indeed, on love. For of the scant fare—the best of which was continually urged upon her—she partook but little. She reminded Gale of a wild brown creature, free as the wind or the lava slopes. Yet, despite the great change, her beauty remained undiminished. Her eyes, seeming so much larger now in her small face, were great, black, starry gulfs. She was the life of that camp. Her smiles, her rapid speech, her low laughter, her quick movements, her playful moods with the rangers, the dark and passionate glance so often on her lover, the whispers in the dusk as hand in hand they paced the campfire beat—these helped Gale to retain his loosening hold on reality, to fight off a mystic aloofness of thought, to resist the lure of a strange, beckoning life where a man stood free in the golden open, where emotion was not, or trouble, or sickness, or anything but the savage's rest and sleep and action and dream.

Although the Yaqui was as his shadow, Gale reached a point when he seemed to wander alone at twilight, in the night, at dawn. Far down the arroyo, in the deepening red twilight, when the heat rolled away on a slow-dying wind, Blanco Sol raised his splendid head and whistled for his master. Gale reproached himself for neglect of the noble horse. Blanco Sol was always the same. He loved four things—his master—a long drink of cool water—to graze at will—and to run. Time and place, Gale thought, meant little to Sol, if he could have those four things. Gale put his arm over the great arched neck and laid his cheek against the long white mane and then, even as he stood there, forgot the horse. What was that dull, red-tinged, horizon-wide mantle creeping up the slope? Through it the copper sun glowed, paled, died. If he thought about it, he had a feeling that it was the herald of night, and the night must be a vigil, and that made him tremble.

At night he had formed a habit of climbing up the lava slope, as far as the smooth trail extended, and there on a promontory he paced to and fro, and watched the stars, and sat stone still for hours, looking down at the vast void with its moving, changing shadows. From that promontory he gazed up at a velvet-blue sky, deep and dark, bright with millions of cold, distant, blinking stars, and he grasped a little of the meaning of infinitude. He gazed down into the shadows, which, black as they were and impenetrable, yet gave him conception of immeasurable space.

Then the silence! He was dumb; he was awed; he bowed his head; he trembled; he marveled at the desert silence. It was the one thing always present. Even when the wind roared, there seemed to be silence. But at night, in this lava world of ashes and canker, he waited for this terrible strangeness of Nature to come to him with its secret. He seemed at once a little child and a strong man and something very old. What tortured him was the incomprehensibility that the vaster the space, the greater the silence! At one moment Gale felt there was only death here, and that was the secret; at another he heard a slow beat of a mighty heart.

He came at length to realize that the desert was a teacher. He did not know all that he had learned, but he was a different man. And when he decided upon that, he was not thinking of the slow, sure call to the primal instincts of man; he was thinking that the desert, as much as he had experienced and no more, would absolutely overturn the whole scale of a man's values, break old habits, form new ones, remake him. More of desert experience, Gale believed, would be too much for intellect. The desert did not breed civilized man, and that made Gale ponder over a strange thought—after all was the civilized man inferior to the savage?

Yaqui was the answer to that. When Gale acknowledged this, he always remembered his present strange manner of thought. The past, the old order of mind, seemed as remote as this desert world was from the haunts of civilized men. A man must know a savage as Gale knew Yaqui before he could speak authoritatively, and then something stilled his tongue. In the first stage of Gale's observation of Yaqui he had marked tenaciousness of life, stoicism, endurance, strength. Those were the attributes of the desert. But what of that second stage, wherein the Indian had loomed to a colossal figure of strange honor, loyalty, love? Gale doubted his convictions and scorned himself for doubting.

There in the gloom sat the silent, impassive, inscrutable Yaqui. His dark face, his dark eyes were plain in the light of the stars. Always he was near Gale, unobtrusive, shadowy, but there. Why? Gale absolutely could not doubt that the Indian had heart as well as mind. Yaqui had from the very first stood between Gale and accident, toil, peril. It was his own choosing. Gale could not change him or thwart him. He understood the Indian's idea of obligation and a sacred duty. But there was more, and that baffled Gale. In the night hours, alone on the slope, Gale felt in Yaqui, as he felt the mighty throb of that desert pulse, something that drew him irresistibly to the Indian. Sometimes he looked around to find the Indian, to dispel these strange, pressing thoughts of unreality, and it was never in vain.

Thus the nights passed, endlessly long, with Gale fighting for his old order of thought, fighting the fascination of that infinite sky and the gloomy, insulating whirl of the wide shadows, fighting for belief, hope, prayer, fighting against that terrible, ever-recurring idea of being lost, lost, lost in the desert, fighting harder than any other thing that insidious, penetrating, tranquil, unfeeling self that was coming between him and his memory.

He was losing the battle, losing his hold on tangible things, losing his power to stand up under this ponderous, merciless weight of desert space and silence. He acknowledged it in a kind of despair, and the shadows of the night seemed whirling fiends. *Lost! Lost! Lost! What are you waiting for? Pain? Lost! Lost! Lost in the desert!* So they seemed to scream in voiceless mockery.

At the moment he was alone on the promontory. The night was far spent. A ghostly moon haunted the black volcanic spurs. The winds blew silently. Was he alone? No—he did not seem to be alone. The Yaqui was there. Suddenly a strange, cold sensation crept over Gale. It was new. He felt a presence. Turning, he expected to see the Indian, but instead a slight shadow, pale, almost white, stood there, not close or yet distant. It seemed to brighten. Then he saw a woman who resembled a girl he had seemed to know long ago. She was white-faced, golden-haired, and her lips were sweet and her eyes were turning black. Nell! He had forgotten her. Over him flooded a torrent of memory. There was tragic woe in this sweet face. Nell was holding out her arms—she was crying aloud to him across the sand and the cactus and the lava. She was in trouble and he had been forgetting.

That night he climbed the lava to the topmost cone and never slipped on a ragged crust or touched a cholla thorn. A voice had called to him. He saw Nell's eyes in the stars, in the velvet blue of sky, in the blackness of the engulfing shadows. She was with him, a slender shape, a spirit, keeping step with him, and memory was strong, sweet, beating, beautiful. Far down in the west, faintly golden with light of sinking moon, he saw a cloud that resembled her face. A cloud on the desert horizon! He gazed and gazed. Was that a spirit face like the one by his side? No— he did not dream.

In the hot, sultry morning Yaqui appeared at camp, after long hours' absence, and he pointed with long dark arms toward the west. A bank of clouds was rising above the mountain barrier.

"Rain!" he cried, and his sonorous voice rolled down the arroyo.

Those who heard were as shipwrecked mariners at sight of a distant sail.

Dick Gale, silent, grateful to the depths of his soul, stood with arm over Blanco Sol and watched the transforming west, where clouds of wondrous size and hue piled over one another, rustling, darkening, spreading, sweeping upward toward that white and glaring sun. When they reached the zenith and swept around to blot out the blazing orb, the earth took on a dark, lowering aspect. The red of sand and lava changed to steely gray. Vast shadows, like ripples on water, sheeted in from the Gulf with a low, strange moan. Yet like death was the silence. The desert was awaiting a strange and hated visitation—storm! If all the endless, torrid days, the endless mystic nights had seemed unreal to Gale, what then seemed this steep endless spectacle?

"Oh, I felt a drop of rain on my face!" cried Mercedes, and, whispering the name of a saint, she kissed her husband.

The white-haired Ladd, gaunt, old, bent, looked up at the maelstrom of clouds and said softly: "Shore now, we'll get on the hosses . . . an' pack light . . . an' hit the trail . . . an' make night marches."

Then up out of the Gulf of the west swept a bellowing wind and a black pall and terrible flashes of lightning and thunder like the end of the world—fury—blackness—chaos—the desert storm.

CHAPTER SEVENTEEN:
THE WHISTLE OF A HORSE

Belding stood alone in his darkened room. It was quiet there and quiet outside; the sickening midsummer heat, like a hot heavy blanket, lay upon the house. He took up the gun belt from his table and with slow hands buckled it around his waist. He seemed to feel something familiar and comfortable and inspiring in the weight of the big gun against his hip. He faced the door as if to go out, but hesitated, and then began a slow, plodding walk up and down the length of the room. Presently he halted at the table, and with reluctant, slower hands he unbuckled the gun belt and laid it down.

The action did not have an air of finality, and Belding knew it. He had seen border life in Texas in the early days; he had been a sheriff when the law of the West depended on a quickness of wrist; he had seen many a man lay down his gun for good and all. Of late he had done the same thing many times, and this last time it seemed a little harder, a little more indicative of vacillation. There were reasons why Belding's gun held for him a gloomy fascination.

The Chases, these grasping and conscienceless agents of a new force in the development of the West, were bent upon Belding's ruin and, so far as his fortunes at Forlorn River were concerned, had about accomplished it. One by one he lost points for which he contended with them. He carried into the Tucson courts the matter of the staked claims, and mining claims, and water claims, and he lost all. Following that he lost his government position as Inspector of Immigration, and this fact, because of what he considered its injustice, had been a hard blow. He had been made to suffer a humiliation equally as great. It came about that he actually had to pay the Chases for water to irrigate his alfalfa fields. The never-failing spring upon his land answered for the needs of household and horses, but no more.

These matters were unfortunate for Belding, but not by any means wholly accountable for his worry and unhappiness and brooding hate. He believed Dick Gale, and the rest of the party taken into the desert by the Yaqui, had been killed or lost. Two months before a string of Mexican horses, riderless, saddled, starved for grass and wild for water had come in to Forlorn River. They were a part of the horses belonging to Rojas and his band. Their arrival complicated the mystery and strengthened convictions of the loss of both pursuers and pursued. Belding was wont to say that he had worried himself gray over the fate of his rangers.

Belding's unhappiness could hardly be laid to material loss. He had been rich and was now poor, but change of fortune such as that could not have made him unhappy. Something more somber and mysterious and sad than the loss of Dick Gale and their friends had come into the lives of his wife and Nell. He dated the time of this change back to a certain day when Mrs. Belding recognized in the elder Chase an old schoolmate and a rejected suitor. It took time for slow-thinking Belding to discover anything wrong in his household, especially as the fact of the Gales lingering there made Mrs. Belding and Nell, for the most part, hide their real and deeper feelings. Gradually, however, Belding had forced on him the fact of some secret cause for grief, other than Gale's loss. He was sure of it when his wife signified her desire to make a visit to her old house back in Peoria. She did not give many reasons, but she did show him a letter that had found its way from

old friends. This letter contained news that may or may
not have been authentic, but it was enough, Belding
thought, to interest his wife. An old prospector had returned to Peoria and he had told relatives of meeting
Robert Burton at the Sonoyta Oasis fifteen years before,
and that Burton had gone into the desert never to return.
To Belding this was no surprise for he had heard that before his marriage. There appeared to have been no doubts
as to the death of his wife's first husband. The singular
thing was that both Nell's father and grandfather had
been somewhere in the Sonora Desert.

Belding did not oppose his wife's desire to visit her old
home. He thought it would be a wholesome trip for her,
and did all in his power to persuade Nell to accompany
her. But Nell would not go.

It was after Mrs. Belding's departure that Belding discovered in Nell a condition of mind that amazed and distressed him. She had suddenly become strangely
wretched, so that she could not conceal it from even the
Gales who, of all people, Belding imagined, were the ones
to make Nell proud. She would tell him nothing. But after
a while, when he had looked around and through the
thing, he linked this further and more deplorable change
in Nell with Radford Chase. This indefatigable wooer had
not in the least abandoned his suit. Something about the
fellow made Belding grind his teeth. But Nell grew not
only solicitously, but now strangely, entreatingly earnest
in her importunities to Belding not to insult or lay a hand
on Chase. This had bound Belding so far; it had made him
think, and watch. He had never been a man to interfere
with his womenfolk. They could do as they liked and
usually that pleased him. But a slow surprise gathered,
and grew upon him, when he saw that Nell, apparently,
was accepting young Chase's attentions. At least she no
longer hid from him. Belding could not account for this,
because he was sure Nell cordially despised the fellow.
And toward the end he divined, if he did not actually
know, that these Chases possessed some strange driving

power over Nell, and were using it. That stirred a hate in Belding—a hate he had felt at the very first and had manfully striven against, and which now gave him over to dark, brooding thoughts.

Midsummer passed and the storms came late. But when they arrived, they made up for tardiness. Belding did not remember so terrible a storm of wind and rain as that which broke the summer's drought. In a few days, it seemed, Altar Valley was a bright and green expanse where dust clouds did not rise. Forlorn River ran a slow, heavy, turgid torrent. Belding never saw the river in flood that did not give him joy, yet now, desert man as he was, he suffered a regret when he thought of the great Chase reservoir full and overflowing. The dull thunder of the spillway was not pleasant. It was the first time in his life that the sound of falling water jarred upon him.

Belding noticed workmen once more engaged in the fields bounding his land. The Chases had extended a main irrigation ditch down to Belding's farm, skipped the width of his ground, then had gone in down through Altar Valley. They had exerted every influence to obtain right to connect these ditches by digging through his land, but Belding had remained obdurate. He refused to have any dealings with them. It was therefore with some curiosity and suspicion that he saw a gang of Mexicans once more at work upon these ditches.

At daylight next morning a tremendous blast almost threw Belding out of his bed. It cracked the adobe walls of his house and broke windows and sent pans and crockery to the floor with a *crash*. Belding's idea was that the store of dynamite kept by the Chases for blasting had blown up. Hurriedly getting into his clothes, he went to Nell's room to reassure her, and, telling her to have a thought for their guests, he went out to see what had happened.

The villagers were pretty badly frightened. Many of the poorly constructed adobe huts had crumbled almost into dust. A great yellow cloud, like smoke, hung over the river. This appeared to be at the upper end of Belding's plot, and close to the river. When he reached his fence, the smoke and dust were so thick he could scarcely breathe and for a little while he was unable to see what had happened. Presently he made out a huge hole in the sand just about where the irrigation ditch had stopped near his line. For some reason or other not clear to Belding the Mexicans had set off an extraordinarily heavy blast at that point.

Belding pondered. He did not now for a moment consider an accidental discharge of dynamite. But why had this blast been set off? The loose sandy soil had yielded readily to shovel; there were no rocks; as far as construction of a ditch was concerned, such a blast would have done more harm than good.

Slowly, with reluctant feet, Belding walked toward a green hollow, where in a cluster of willows lay the never-failing spring that his horses loved so well, and indeed which he loved no less. He was actually afraid to part the drooping willows to enter the little, cool, shady path that led to the spring. Then, suddenly seized by suspense, he ran the rest of the way.

He was just in time to see the last of the water. It seemed to sink as in quicksand. The shape of the hole had changed. The tremendous force of the blast in the adjoining field had obstructed or diverted the underground stream of water. Belding's never-failing spring had been ruined. What had made this little plot of ground green and sweet and fragrant was now no more. Belding's first feeling was for the pity of it. The pale *ajo* lilies would bloom no more under those willows. The willows themselves would soon wither and die. He thought how many times in the middle of hot summer nights he had come down to the spring to drink. Never again!

Suddenly he thought of Blanco Diablo. How the great white thoroughbred had loved this spring! Belding straightened up and looked with tear-blurred eyes out over the waste of desert to the west. Never a day passed that he had not thought of the splendid horse, but this moment, with its significant memory, was doubly keen, and there came a dull pang in his breast.

"Diablo will never drink here again," muttered Belding.

The loss of Blanco Diablo, although admitted and mourned by Belding, had never seemed quite real until this moment. The pall of dust drifting over him, the din of the falling water up at the dam, diverted Belding's mind to the Chases. All at once he was in the harsh grip of a cold certainty. The blast had been set off intentionally to ruin his spring. What a hellish trick! No Westerner, no Indian or Mexican, no desert man could have been guilty of such a crime. To ruin a beautiful, clear, cool, never-failing stream of water in the desert!

It was then that Belding's worry and indecision and brooding were as if they had never existed. As he strode swiftly back to the house, his head, that for long had been bent thoughtfully and sadly, was held erect. He went directly to his room, and with an air that now was final he buckled on his gun belt. He looked the gun over and tried the action. He squared himself and walked a little more erect. Some long lost individuality had returned to Belding.

"Let's see," he was saying, "I can get Carter to send the horses I've got left back to Waco to my brother. I'll make Nell take what money there is and go hunt up her mother. The Gales are ready to go . . . today if I say the word. Nell can travel with them part way East. That's your game, Tom Belding, don't mistake me."

As he went out, he encountered Mr. Gale coming up the walk. The long sojourn at Forlorn River, despite the fact that it had been one of suspense and a gradual wearing to sad certainty, had been of great benefit to Dick's father. The dry air, the heat, and the quiet had made him, if not entirely a well man, certainly stronger than he had been in many years.

"Belding, what was that terrible roar?" asked Mr. Gale. "We were badly frightened until Miss Nell came to us. We feared it was an earthquake."

"Well, I'll tell you, Mister Gale, we've had some quakes here, but none of them could hold a candle to this jar we just had."

Then Belding explained what had caused the explosion and why it had been set off so close to his property.

"It's an outrage, sir, an unspeakable outrage," declared Mr. Gale hotly. "Such a thing would not be tolerated in the East. Mister Belding, I'm amazed at your attitude in the face of all this trickery."

"You see . . . there was Mother and Nell," began Belding, as if apologizing. He dropped his head a little and made marks in the sand with the toe of his boots. "Mister Gale, I've been sort of half hitched, as Laddy used to say. I'm planning to have a little more elbow room around this ranch. I'm going to send Nell East to her mother. Then I'll . . . see here, Mister Gale, would you mind having Nell with you part way when you go home?"

"We'd all be delighted to have her go all the way, and make us a visit," replied Mr. Gale.

"That's fine. And you'll be going soon? Don't take that as if I wanted to. . . ." Belding paused, for the truth was that he did want to hurry them off.

"We would have been gone before this, but for you," said Mr. Gale. "Long ago we gave up hope of . . . of Richard ever returning. And I believe, now we're sure he was lost, that we'd do well to go home at once. You wished us to remain till the heat was broken . . . till the rains came to make traveling easier for us. Now I see no need of further delay. My stay here has greatly benefited my health. I shall never forget your hospitality. This Western trip would have made me a new man if . . . only . . . Richard. . . ."

"Sure. I understand," said Belding gruffly. "Let's go in and tell the women to pack up."

Nell was busy with the servants preparing breakfast. Belding took her into the sitting room while Mr. Gale called his wife and daughter.

"My girl, I've some news for you," began Belding.

"Mister Gale is leaving today with his family. I'm going to send you with them, part way, anyhow. You're invited to visit them. I think that'd be great for you . . . help you to forget. But the main thing is . . . you're going East to join your mother."

Nell gazed at him, white-faced, without uttering a word.

"You see, Nell, I'm about done in Forlorn River," went on Belding. "That blast this morning sank my spring. There's no water now. It was the last straw. So we'll shake the dust of Forlorn River. I'll come on a little later, that's all."

"Dad, you're packing your gun!" exclaimed Nell, suddenly pointing with a trembling finger. She ran to him, and for the first time in his life Belding put her away from him. His movements had lost the old slow gentleness.

"Why, so I am," replied Belding coolly as his hand moved down to the sheath swinging at his hip. "Nell, I'm that absentminded these days."

"Dad!" she cried.

"That'll do from you," he replied in a voice he had never used to her. "Get breakfast now, then pack to leave Forlorn River."

"Leave Forlorn River," whispered Nell with a thin white hand stealing up to her breast. How changed the girl was! Belding reproached himself for his hardness, but did not speak his thought aloud. Nell was fading here, just as Mercedes had faded before the coming of Thorne.

Nell turned away to the west window and looked out across the desert toward the dim blue peaks in the distance. Belding watched her, likewise the Gales, and no one spoke. There ensued a long silence. Belding felt a lump rise in this throat. Nell laid her arm against the window frame, but gradually it dropped, and she was leaning with her face against the wood. A low sob broke from her. Elsie Gale went to her, embraced her, took the drooping head on her shoulder.

"We've come to be such friends," she said. "I believe it'll be good for you to visit me in the city. Here . . . all day you look out across that awful lonely desert. Come, Nell."

Heavy steps sounded outside on the flagstones, then the door rattled under a strong knock. Belding opened it. The Chases, father and son, stood beyond the threshold.

"Good morning, Belding," said the elder Chase. "We were routed out early by that big blast and came up to see what was wrong. All a blunder. The greaser foreman was drunk yesterday and his ignorant men made a mistake. Sorry if the blast bothered you."

"Chase, I reckon that's the first of your blasts I was ever glad to hear," replied Belding in a way that made Chase look blank.

"So? Well, I'm glad you're glad," he went on, evidently puzzled. "I was a little worried . . . you've always been so touchy . . . we never could get together. I hurried over, fearing you might think the blast . . . you see, Belding. . . ."

"I see this, Ben Chase," interrupted Belding in curt and ringing voice. "The blast *was* a mistake, the biggest you ever made in your life."

"What do you mean?" demanded Chase.

"You'll have to excuse me for a while, unless you're dead set on having it out right now. Mister Gale and his family are leaving, and my daughter is going with them. I'd rather you'd wait a little."

"Nell going away!" exclaimed Radford Chase. He reminded Belding of an overgrown boy in disappointment.

"Yes. But . . . Miss Burton to you, young man."

"Mister Belding, I certainly would prefer a conference with you right now," interposed the elder Chase, cutting short Belding's strange speech. "There are other matters . . . important matters to discuss. They've got to be settled. May we step in, sir?"

"No, you may not," replied Belding bluntly. "I'm sure particular who I invite into my house. But I'll go with you." Belding stepped out and closed the door. "Come away from the house so the women won't hear the . . . the talk."

The elder Chase was purple with rage, yet seemed to be controlling it. The younger man looked black, sullen, impatient. He appeared not to have a thought of Belding. He was absolutely blind to the situation, as considered from Belding's point of view. Ben Chase found his voice about the time Belding halted under the trees out of earshot from the house.

"Sir, you've insulted me . . . my son. How dare you? I want you to understand you're. . . ."

"Chop that kind of talk with me, you son-of-a-bitch!" interrupted Belding. He had always been profane and now he certainly did not choose his language. Chase turned livid, gasped, and seemed about to give way to fury. But something about Belding evidently exerted a powerful quieting influence. "If you talk sense, I'll listen," went on Belding.

Belding was frankly curious. He did not think any argument or inducement offered by Chase could change his mind in past dealings or his purpose of the present. But he believed by listening he might get some light on what had long puzzled him. The masterly effort Chase put forth to conquer aroused passions gave Belding another idea of the character of this promoter.

"I want to make a last effort to propitiate you," began Chase in his quick, smooth voice. That was a singular change to Belding—the dropping instantly into an easy flow of speech. "You've had losses here and naturally you're sore. I don't blame you. But you can't see this thing from my side of the fence. Business is business. In business the best man wins. The law upheld those transactions of mine the honesty of which you questioned. As to mining and water claims, you lost on this technical point . . . that you had nothing to prove you had held them for five years. Five years is the time necessary in law. A dozen men might claim the source of Forlorn River, but if they had no house or papers to prove their squatters rights, any man could go in and fight them for the water. Now I want to run that main ditch along the river through your farm. Can't we make a deal? I'm ready to be liberal . . . to meet you more than halfway. I'll give you an interest in the company. I think I've influence enough up at the capital to have you reinstated as inspector. A little reasonableness on your part will put you right again in Forlorn River, with a chance of growing rich. There's a big future here. My interest, Belding, has become personal. Radford is in love with your stepdaughter. He wants to marry her. I'll admit now, if I had foreseen this situation, I wouldn't have pushed you so hard. But we can square the thing. Now let's get together not only in business, but in a family way. If my son's happiness depends upon having this girl, you may rest assured I'll do all I can to get her for him. I'll absolutely make good all your losses. Now what do you say?"

"No," replied Belding. "Your money can't buy a right of way across my ranch. And Nell doesn't want your son. That settles that."

"But you could persuade her."

"I won't, that's all."

"May I ask why?" Chase's voice was losing its suave quality, but it was even swifter than before.

"Sure. I don't mind your asking," replied Belding in slow deliberation. "I wouldn't do such a low-down trick. Besides, if I would, I'd want it to be a man I was persuading for. I know greasers . . . I know a Yaqui I'd rather give Nell to than your son."

Radford Chase began to roar in inarticulate rage. Belding paid no attention to him; indeed, he never glanced at the young man. The elder Chase checked a violent start. He plucked at the collar of his gray flannel shirt, opened it at the neck.

"My son's offer of marriage is an honor . . . more an honor, sir, than perhaps you are aware of."

Belding made no reply. His steady gaze did not turn from the long lane that led down to the river. He waited coldly, sure of himself.

"Missus Belding's daughter has no right to the name of Burton," snapped Chase. "Did you know that?"

"I did not," replied Belding quietly.

"Well, you know it now," added Chase bitingly.

"Sure you can prove what you say?" queried Belding in the same cool, unemotional tone. It struck him strangely what little knowledge this man had of the West and of Western character.

"Prove it? Why, yes, I think so, enough to make the truth plain to any reasonable man. I come from Peoria, was born and raised there. I went to school with Nell Warren . . . that was your wife's maiden name. She was a beautiful, gay girl. All the fellows were in love with her. I knew Bob Burton well. He was a splendid fellow, but wild. Nobody ever knew for sure, but we all supposed he was engaged to marry Nell. He left Peoria, however, and soon after that the truth about Nell came out. She ran away. It was at least a couple of months before Burton showed up in Peoria. He did not stay long. Then for years nothing was heard of either of them. When word did come, Nell was in Oklahoma . . . Burton was in Denver. There's a chance, of course, that Burton followed Nell and married her. That would account for Nell Warren taking the name of Burton. But it wasn't likely. None of us ever heard of such a thing and wouldn't have believed it if we had. The affair seemed destined to end unfortunately. But Belding, while I'm at it, I want to say that Nell Warren was one of the sweetest, finest, truest girls in the world. If she drifted to the Southwest and kept her past a secret, that was only natural. Certainly it should not be held against her. Why, she was only a child . . . a girl . . . . seventeen . . . eighteen years old. In a moment of amazement . . . when I recognized your wife as an old schoolmate . . . I blurted the thing out to Radford. You see now how little it matters to me when I ask your stepdaughter's hand in marriage for my son."

Belding stood listening. The genuine emotion in Chase's voice was as strange as the ring of truth. Belding knew truth when he heard it. The revelation did not surprise him. Belding did not soften, for he divined that Chase's emotion was due to the probing of an old wound—the recalling of a past both happy and painful. Still human nature was so strange that perhaps kindness and sympathy might yet have a place in this Chase's heart. Belding did not believe so, but he was willing to give Chase the benefit of the doubt.

"So, you told my wife you'd respect her secret . . . keep her dishonor from husband and daughter?" demanded Belding, his dark gaze sweeping back from the lane.

"What? I . . . I," stammered Chase.

"You made your son swear to be a man and die before he'd hint the thing to Nell?" went on Belding, and his voice rang louder.

Ben Chase had no answer. The red left his face, but his son remained standing with a pugnacious expression on his face near the fence.

"I say you never held this secret over the heads of my wife and her daughter!" thundered Belding.

He had his answer in the gray faces, in the lips that fear made mute. Like a flash Belding saw the whole truth of Mrs. Belding's agony, the reason for her departure—he saw what had been driving Nell, and it seemed that all the dogs of hell were loosed within his heart. He struck out blindly, instinctively in his pain, and the blow sent Ben Chase staggering into the fence corner. Then he stretched forth a long arm and whirled Radford Chase back beside his father.

"I see it all now," went on Belding hoarsely. "You found the woman's weakness, her love for the girl. You found the girl's weakness . . . her pride and fear of shame. So you drove the one and hounded the other. God, what a base thing to do! To tell the girl was bad enough, but to *threaten* her with betrayal . . . there's no name for that!"

Belding's voice thickened and he paused, breathing heavily. He stepped back a few paces, and this, an ominous action for an armed man of his kind, instead of adding to the fear of the Chases, seemed to relieve them. If there had been any pity in Belding's heart, he would have felt it then.

"And now, gentlemen," continued Belding, speaking low and with difficulty, "seeing I've turned down your proposition, I suppose you think you've no more call to keep your mouths shut?"

The elder Chase appeared fascinated by something he either saw or felt in Belding, and his gray face grew grayer. He put up a shaking hand. Then Radford Chase, livid and snarling, burst out: "I'll talk till I'm black in the face. You can't stop me!"

"You'll go black in the face, but it won't be from talking," hissed Belding.

His big arm swept down, and, when he threw it up, the gun glittered in his hand. Simultaneously with the latter action pealed out a shrill, penetrating whistle.

The whistle of a horse! It froze Belding's arm aloft. For an instant he could not move even his eyes. The familiarity of that whistle was terrible in its power to rob him of strength. Then he heard the rapid, heavy pound of hoofs—and again the piercing whistle.

"Blanco Diablo!" he cried huskily.

He turned to see a huge white horse come thundering into the yard. A wild, gaunt, terrible horse—indeed the loved Blanco Diablo. A bronzed, long-haired Indian bestrode him. More white horses galloped into the yard, pounded to a halt, whistling home. Belding saw a slim shadow of a girl who seemed all great black eyes.

Under the trees flashed Blanco Sol, a dazzling white, as beautiful as if he had never been lost in the desert. He slid to a halt, then plunged and stamped. His rider leaped, throwing the bridle. Belding saw a powerful, spare, ragged man with dark face and eyes of flame.

Then Nell came running from the house, her golden hair flying, her hands outstretched, her face wonderful.

"Dick! Dick! Oh-h-h, Dick!" she cried. Her voice seemed to quiver in Belding's heart.

Belding's eyes began to blur. He was not sure he saw clearly. Whose face was this now close before him—a long, thin, shrunken face, haggard, tragic in its semblance of torture, almost of death? But the eyes were keen and kind. Belding thought wildly that they proved he was not dreaming.

"I shore am glad to see you all," said a well-remembered voice in slow, cool drawl.

CHAPTER EIGHTEEN:
REALITY AGAINST DREAMS

Ladd, Lash, Thorne, Mercedes, they were all held tightly in Belding's arms. Then he ran to Blanco Diablo. For once the great horse was gentle, quiet, glad. He remembered this kindest of masters and reached for him with warm, wet muzzle.

Dick Gale was standing bowed over Nell's slight form, almost hidden in his arms. Belding hugged them both. He was like a boy. He saw Ben Chase and his son slip away under the trees, but the circumstances meant nothing to him then.

"Dick! Dick!" he roared. "Is it you! Say, who do you think's here . . . here, in Forlorn River?"

Gale gripped Belding with a hand as rough and hard as a file and as strong as a vise. But he did not speak a word. Belding thought Gale's eyes would haunt him forever.

It was then three more persons came upon the scene—Elsie Gale, running swiftly, her father assisting Mrs. Gale, who appeared about to faint.

"Belding! Who on earth's that?" cried Dick hoarsely.

"*Quién sabe*, my son," replied Belding, and now his voice seemed a little shaky. "Nell, come here. Give him a chance." Belding slipped his arm around Nell, and whispered in her ear: "This'll be great!"

Elsie Gale's face was white and agitated, a face expressing extreme joy.

"Oh, Brother! Mama saw you . . . Papa saw you, and

never knew you! But I knew you when you jumped
quick . . . that way . . . off your horse. And now I don't
know you. You wild man! You giant! You splendid barbarian! Mama, Papa, hurry! It *is* Dick! Look at him. Just look
at him! Oh-h, thank God!"

Belding turned away and drew Nell with him. In another second she and Mercedes were clasped in each
other's arms. Then followed a time of joyful greetings all
around.

The Yaqui stood, leaning against a tree, watching the
welcoming home of the lost. No one seemed to think of
him, until Belding, ever mindful of the needs of horses,
put a hand on Blanco Diablo and called to Yaqui to bring
the others. They led the string of whites down to the barn,
freed them of wet and dusty saddles and packs, and
turned them loose in the alfalfa, now breast high. Diablo
found his old spirit; Blanco Sol tossed his head and whistled his satisfaction; White Woman pranced to and fro.
Presently they all settled down to quiet grazing. How
good it was for Belding to see those white shapes against
the rich background of green! His eyes glistened. It was a
sight he had never expected to see again. He lingered
there many moments when he wanted to hurry back to
his rangers.

At last he tore himself away from watching Blanco Diablo and returned to the house. It was only to find that he
might have spared himself the hurry. Jim and Ladd were
lying on the beds that had not held them for so many
months. Their slumber seemed as deep and quiet as
death. Curiously Belding gazed down upon them. They
had removed only boots and chaps. Their clothes were in
tatters. Jim appeared little more than skin and bones, a
long shape, dark and hard as iron. Ladd's appearance
shocked Belding. The ranger looked an old man, blasted,
shriveled, starved. Yet his gaunt face, although terrible in
its record of tortures, had something fine and noble, even
beautiful to Belding, in its strength, its victory.

Thorne and Mercedes had disappeared. The low murmur of voices came from Mrs. Gale's room, and Belding concluded that Dick was still with his family. No doubt he also would soon seek rest and sleep. Belding went through the patio and called in at Nell's door. She was there, sitting by her window. The flush of happiness had not left her face, but she looked stunned, and a shadow of fear lay darkly in her eyes. Belding had intended to talk. He wanted someone to listen to him. The expression in Nell's eyes, however, silenced him. He had forgotten. Nell read his thought in his face, and then she lost all her color and dropped her head. Belding entered, stood beside her with a hand on hers. He tried desperately hard to think of the right thing to say, and realized so long as he tried that he could not speak at all.

"Nell . . . Dick's back safe and sound," he said slowly. "That's the main thing. I wish you could have seen his eyes when he held you in his arms out there. Of course, Dick's coming knocks out your trip East and changes plans generally. We haven't had the happiest time lately. But now it'll all be different. Dick's as true as a Yaqui. He'll go after that Chase fellow, don't mistake me. Then your mother will be home soon. She'll straighten out this . . . this mystery. And, Nell . . . however it turns out . . . I know Dick Gale will feel just the same as I feel. Brace up now, girl."

Belding left the patio and traced thoughtful steps back toward the corrals. He realized the need of his wife. If she had been at home, he would not have come so close to killing two men. Nell would never have fallen so low in spirit. Whatever the real truth of the tragedy of his wife's life, it would not make the slightest difference to him. What hurt him was the pain mother and daughter had suffered, were suffering still. Somehow he must put an end to that pain.

He found the Yaqui curled up in a corner of the barn in as deep a sleep as that of the rangers. Looking down at him, Belding felt again the rush of curious, thrilling eagerness to learn all that had happened since the dark night when Yaqui had led the white horses away into the desert. Belding curbed his impatience and set to work upon tasks he had long neglected. Presently he was interrupted by Mr. Gale, who came out, beside himself with happiness and excitement. He flung a hundred questions at Belding and never gave him time to answer one, even if that had been possible. Finally, when Mr. Gale lost his breath, Belding got a word in. "See here, Mister Gale, you know as much as I know. Dick's back. They're all back . . . a hard lot, starved, burned, torn to pieces, worked out to a limit I never saw in desert travelers, but they're alive . . . alive and well, man. Just wait. Just gamble I won't sleep or eat till I hear that story. But they've got to sleep and eat."

Belding gathered with growing amusement that besides the joy, excitement, anxiety, impatience expressed by Mr. Gale, there was something else that Belding took for pride. It pleased him. Looking back, he remembered some of the things Dick had confessed his father thought of him. Belding's sympathy had always been with the boy. But he had learned to like the old man, to find him kind and wise, and to think that perhaps college and business had not brought out the best in Richard Gale. The West had done that, however, as it had for many a wild youngster, and Belding resolved to have a little fun at the expense of Mr. Gale. So he began by making a few remarks that appeared to rob Dick's father of both speech and breath.

"And don't mistake me," concluded Belding, "just keep out of earshot when Laddy tells us the story of the desert trip, unless you're hankering to have your hair turn pure white and stand curled on end and freeze that way."

About the middle of the forenoon on the following day the rangers hobbled out of the kitchen to the porch.

"I'm a sick man, I tell you," Ladd was complaining, "an' I gotta be fed. Soup! Beef tea! That ain't so much as wind to me. I want about a barrel of bread an' butter an' a whole platter of mashed potatoes with gravy an' green stuff . . . all kinds of green stuff . . . an' a whole big apple pie. Give me everythin' an' anythin' to eat but meat. Shore I never, never want to taste meat again, an' sight of a piece of sheep meat would jest about finish me. Jim, you used to be a human bein' that stood up for Charlie Ladd."

"Laddy, I'm lined up beside you with both guns," replied Jim plaintively. "Hungry? Say, the smell of breakfast in that kitchen made my mouth water so I near choked to death. I reckon we're gettin' most unhuman treatment."

"But I'm a sick man," protested Ladd, "an' I'm a-goin' to fall over in a minute if somebody doesn't feed me. Nell, you used to be fond of me."

"Oh, Laddy, I am yet," replied Nell.

"Shore I don't believe it. Any girl with a tender heart just couldn't let a man starve under her eyes. Look at Dick, there. I'll bet he's had something to eat, mebbe potatoes an' gravy, an' pie an'. . . ."

"Laddy, Dick has had no more than I gave you . . . indeed, not nearly so much."

"Shore he's had a lot of kisses then, for he hasn't hollered oncet about his treatment."

"Perhaps he has," said Nell with a blush, "and, if you think that . . . that would help you to be reasonable, I might . . . I'll. . . ."

"Well, powerful fond as I am of you, just now kisses'll have to run second to bread an' butter."

"Oh, Laddy, what a gallant speech!" Nell laughed. "I'm sorry, but I've Dad's orders."

"Laddy," interrupted Belding, "you've got to be broke in gradually to eating. Now you know that. You'd be the severest kind of a boss if you had some starved beggars on your hands."

"But I'm sick . . . I'm dyin'!" howled Ladd.

"You were never sick in your life, and, if all the bullet holes I see in you couldn't kill you, why, you never will die."

"Can I smoke?" queried Ladd with sudden animation. "My Gawd, I used to smoke. Shore I've forgot. Nell, if you want to be reinstated in my gallery of angels, just find me a pipe an' tobacco."

"I've hung onto my pipe," said Jim thoughtfully. "I reckon I had it empty in my mouth for seven years or so, wasn't it, Laddy? A long time! I can see the red lava an' the red haze, an' the red twilight creepin' up. It was hot an' some lonely. Then the wind, and always that awful silence! An' always Yaqui watchin' the west, an' Laddy with his checkers, an' Mercedes burnin' up, wastin' away to nothin' but eyes! It's all there . . . I'll never get rid. . . ."

"Chop that kind of talk," interrupted Belding bluntly. "Tell us where Yaqui took you . . . what happened to Rojas . . . why you seemed lost for so long."

"I reckon Laddy can tell all that best . . . but when it comes to Rojas's finish, I'll tell what I seen an' so'll Dick an' Thorne. Laddy missed Rojas's finish. Bar none, that was the. . . ."

"I'm a sick man, but I can talk," put in Ladd, "an' shore I don't want the whole story exaggerated none by Jim."

Ladd filled the pipe Nell brought, puffed ecstatically at it, and settled himself upon the bench for a long talk. Nell glanced appealingly at Dick, who tried to slip away. Mercedes did go, and was followed by Thorne. Mr. Gale brought chairs, and in subdued excitement called his wife and daughter. Belding leaned forward, rendered all the more eager by Dick's reluctance to stay, the memory of the quick, tragic change in the expression of Mercedes's beautiful eyes, by the strange, gloomy cast stealing over Ladd's face.

The ranger talked for two hours—talked till his voice weakened to a husky whisper. At the conclusion of his story there was an impressive silence. Then Elsie Gale stood up, and with her hand on Dick's shoulder, her eyes bright and warm as sunlight, she showed the rangers what a woman thought of them and of the Yaqui. Nell clung to Dick, weeping silently. Mrs. Gale was overcome, and Mr. Gale, very white and quiet, helped her up to her room.

"The Indian! The Indian!" burst out Belding, his voice

deep and rolling. "What did I tell you? Didn't I say he'd be a godsend? Remember what I said about Yaqui and some gory Aztec knife work? So he cut Rojas loose from that awful crater wall, foot by foot, hand by hand, slow and terrible? And Rojas didn't hang long by the cholla thorns? Thank the Lord for that! Laddy, no story of Camino del Diablo can hold a candle to yours. The flight and the fight were jobs for men. But living through this long hot summer and coming out ... that's a miracle. Only the Yaqui could have done it. The Yaqui! The Yaqui!"

"Shore. Charlie Ladd looks up at an Indian these days. But, Belding, as for the comin' out, don't forget the hosses. Without grand old Sol an' Diablo, who I don't hate no more, an' the other Blancos, we'd never have got here. Yaqui an' the hosses, that's my story."

Early in the afternoon of the next day Belding encountered Dick at the water barrel.

"Belding, this is river water, and muddy at that," said Dick. "Lord knows I'm not kidding. But I've dreamed some of our cool running spring, and I want a drink from it."

"Never again, son. The spring's gone, faded, sunk, dry as dust."

"Dry!" Gale slowly straightened. "We've had rains. The river's full. The spring ought to be overflowing. What's wrong? Why is it dry?"

"Dick, seeing you're interested, I may as well tell you that a big charge of nitroglycerin choked my spring."

"Nitroglycerin?" echoed Gale. Then he gave a quick start. "My mind's been on home, Nell, my family. But all the same, I felt something was wrong here with the ranch, with you, with Nell. Belding, that ditch there is dry. The roses are dead. The little green in that grass has come with the rains. What's happened? The ranch's run-down. Now I look around, I see a change."

"Some change, yes," replied Belding bitterly. "Listen, son."

Briefly, but not the less forcibly for that, Belding related
his story of the operations of the Chases.

Astonishment appeared to be Gale's first feeling. "Our
water gone, our claims gone, our plans forestalled! Why,
Belding, it's unbelievable. Forlorn River with promoters,
business, railroad, bank, and what-not." Suddenly he became fiery and suspicious. "These Chases . . . did they do
all this on the level?"

"Barefaced robbery! Worse than a greaser hold-up,"
replied Belding grimly.

"You say the law upheld them?"

"Sure. Why, Ben Chase has a pull as strong as Diablo's
on a downgrade. Dick, we're jobbed, outfigured, beat,
tricked, and we can't do a thing."

"Oh, I'm sorry, Belding, most of all for Laddy," said
Gale feelingly. "He's all in. He'll never ride again. He
wanted to settle down here on the farm he thought he
owned, grow grass and raise horses, and take it easy. Oh,
but it's tough. Say, he doesn't know it yet. He was just
telling me he'd like to go out and look the farm over.
Who's going to tell him? What's he going to do when he
finds out about this deal?"

"Son, that's made me think some," replied Belding
with keen eyes fast upon the young man. "And I was
kind of wondering how you'd take it."

"I? Well, I'll call on the Chases. Look here, Belding, I'd
better do some forestalling myself. If Laddy gets started
now, there'll be blood spilled. He's not just right in his
mind yet. He talks in his sleep sometimes about how
Yaqui finished Rojas. If it's left to him . . . he'll kill these
men. But if I take it up. . . ."

"You're talking sense, Dick. Only here, I'm not so sure
of you. And there's more to tell. Son, you've Nell to think
of and your mother."

Belding's ranger gave him a long and searching glance.

"You can be sure of me," he said.

"All right, then . . . listen," began Belding. With deep
voice that had many a break and tremor he told Gale how

Nell had been hounded by Radford Chase, how her mother had been driven by Ben Chase, the whole sad story.

"So that's the trouble. Poor little girl," murmured Gale brokenly. "I felt something was wrong. Nell wasn't natural, like her old self. And when I begged her to marry me soon, while Dad is here, she couldn't talk. She could only cry."

"It *was* hard on Nell," said Belding simply. "But it'll be better now you're back. Dick, I know the girl. She'll refuse to marry you and you'll have a hard job to break her down, as hard as the one you just rode in off of. I think I know you, too, or I wouldn't be saying. . . ."

"Belding, what're you hinting at?" demanded Gale. "Do you dare insinuate that . . . that . . . if the thing were true, it'd make any difference to me?"

"*Aw,* come now, Dick . . . I couldn't mean that. I'm only awkward at saying things. And I'm cut pretty deep."

"For God's sake, you don't believe what Chase said?" queried Gale in passionate haste. "It's a lie. I swear it's a lie. I know it's a lie. And I've got to tell Nell this minute. Come on in with me. I want you, Belding. Oh, why didn't you tell me sooner?"

Belding felt himself dragged by an iron arm into the sitting room, out into the patio, and across that to where Nell sat in her door. At sight of them she gave a little cry, drooped for an instant, then raised a pale, still face, with eyes beginning to darken.

"Dearest, I know now why you are not wearing my mother's ring," said Gale steadily and low-voiced.

"Dick, I am not worthy," she replied, and held out a trembling hand with the ring lying in the palm.

Swift as light Gale caught her hand and slipped the ring back upon the third finger.

"Nell! Look at me. It is your engagement ring. Listen. I don't believe this . . . this thing that's been torturing you. I know it's a lie. She must have suffered once . . . perhaps there was a sad error . . . but the thing you fear is not true. But, hear me, dearest . . . even if it *was* true, it wouldn't make the slightest difference to me. I'd promise you on my honor I'd never think of it again. I'd love you all the more because you'd suffered. I want you all the more to be my wife . . . to let me make you forget . . . to. . . ."

She rose swiftly with the passionate abandon of a woman stirred to her depths and she kissed him.

"Oh, Dick, you're good . . . so good! You'll never know . . . just what those words mean to me. They've saved me . . . I think."

"Then, dearest, it's all right?" Dick questioned eagerly. "You will keep your promise? You will marry me?"

The glow, the light faded out of her face, and now the blue eyes were almost black. She drooped and shook her head.

"Nell!" exclaimed Gale, sharply catching his breath.

"Don't ask me, Dick. I . . . I won't marry you."

"Why?"

"You know. It's true that I . . ."

"It's a lie," interrupted Gale fiercely. "But even if it's true . . . why . . . why won't you marry me? Between you and me love is the thing. Love, and nothing else! Don't you love me any more?"

They had forgotten Belding, who stepped back into the shade.

"I love you with my whole heart and soul. I'd die for you," whispered Nell with clenching hands. "But I won't disgrace you."

"Dear, you have worried over this trouble till you're morbid. It has grown out of all proportion. I tell you that I'll not only be the happiest man on earth, but the luckiest if you marry me."

"Dick, you give not one thought to your family. Would they receive me as your wife?"

"They surely would," replied Gale steadily.

"No! Oh, no!"

"You're wrong, Nell. I'm glad you said that. You give me a chance to prove something. I'll go this minute and tell them all. I'll be back here in less than. . . ."

"Dick, you will not tell her . . . your mother?" cried Nell, with her eyes streaming. "You will not? Oh, I can't bear it! She's so proud! And, Dick, I love her. Don't tell her! Please, please don't. She'll be going soon. She needn't ever know . . . about me. I want her always to think well of me. Dick, I beg you. Oh, the fear of her knowing has been the worst of all! Please don't go."

"Nell, I'm sorry. I hate to hurt you. But you're wrong. You can't see things clearly. This is your happiness I'm fighting for. And it's my life. Wait here, dear. I won't be long.

Gale ran across the patio and disappeared. Nell sank to the doorstep, and, as she met the question in Belding's eyes, she shook her head mournfully. They waited without speaking. It seemed a long while before Gale returned. Belding thrilled at sight of him. There was more boy about him than Belding had ever seen. Dick was coming swiftly, flushed, glowing, eager, erect, almost smiling.

"I told them. I swore it was a lie, but I wanted them to decide as if it were true. I didn't have to waste a minute on Elsie. She loves you, Nell. The governor is crazy about you. I didn't have to waste two minutes on him. Mother used up the time. She wanted to know all there was to tell. She is proud, yes . . . but, Nell, I wish you could have seen how she took the . . . the story about you. Why, she never thought of me at all, until she had cried over you. Nell, she loves you, too. They all love you. Oh, it's so good to tell you. I think Mother realizes the part you have had in the. . . . what shall I call it? . . . the regeneration of Richard Gale. Doesn't that sound fine? Darling, Mother not only consents, she wants you to be my wife. Do you hear that? And listen . . . she had me in a corner and, of course, being my mother, she put on the screws. She made me promise that we'd live in the East half the year. That means Chicago, Cape May, New York . . . you see, I'm not exactly the lost son any more. Why, Nell, dear, you'll have to learn who Dick Gale really is. But I always want to be the ranger you helped me become, and ride Blanco Sol, and see a little of the desert. Don't let the idea of big cities frighten you. We'll always love the open places best. Now, Nell, say you'll forget this trouble. I know it'll come all right. Say you'll marry me soon. Why, dearest, you're crying . . . Nell!"

"My . . . heart . . . is broken," sobbed Nell, "for . . . I . . . I can't marry you."

The boyish brightness faded out of Gale's face. Here, Belding saw, was the stern reality arrayed against his dreams.

"That devil Radford Chase . . . he'll tell my secret," panted Nell. "He swore if you ever came back and married me, he'd follow us all over the world to tell it."

Belding saw Gale grow deathly white and suddenly stand stockstill.

"Chase threatened you, then?" asked Dick, and the forced naturalness of his voice struck Belding.

"Threatened me? He made my life a nightmare," replied Nell in a rush of speech. "At first I wondered how he was worrying Mother sick. But she wouldn't tell me. Then, when she went away, he began to hint things. I hated him all the more. But when he told me . . . I was frightened, shamed. Still I did not weaken. He was pretty decent when he was sober. But when he was half drunk, he was a devil. He laughed at me and my pride. I didn't dare shut the door in his face. After a while he found out that your mother loved me and that I loved her. Then he began to threaten me. If I didn't give in to him, he'd see she learned the truth. That made me weaken. It nearly killed me. I simply could not bear the thought of Missus Gale knowing. But I couldn't marry him. Besides, he got so half the time, when he was drunk, he didn't want to ask me to be his wife. I was about ready to give up and go mad when you . . . you came home."

She ended in a whisper, looking up wistfully and sadly at him. Belding was a raging fire within, cold without. He watched Gale, and believed he could foretell that young man's future conduct. Gale gathered Nell up into his arms and held her to his breast for a long moment.

"Dear Nell, I'm sure the worst of your trouble is over," he said gently. "I *will not* give you up. Now, won't you lie down try to rest and calm yourself? Don't grieve any more. This thing isn't so bad as you make it. Trust me. I'll shut Mister Radford Chase's mouth."

As he released her, she glanced quickly up at him, then lifted appealing hands.

"Dick, you won't hunt for him . . . go after him?"

Gale laughed, and the laugh made Belding jump.

"Dick, I beg of you. Please don't make trouble. The Chases have been hard enough on us. They are rich, powerful. Dick, say you will not make matters worse. Please promise me you'll not go to him."

"You ask me that?" he demanded.

"Yes. Oh, yes!"

"But you know it's useless. What kind of a man do you want me to be?"

"It's only that I'm afraid. Oh, Dick, he'd shoot you in the back."

"No, Nell, a man of his kind wouldn't have nerve enough even for that."

"You'll go?" she cried wildly.

Gale smiled, and the smile made Belding cold.

"Dick, I cannot keep you back?"

"No," he said.

Then the woman in her burst through instinctive fear, and with her eyes blazing black in her white face she lifted parted, quivering lips and kissed him.

Gale left the patio, and Belding followed closely at his heels. They went through the sitting room. Outside upon the porch sat the rangers, Mr. Gale, and Thorne. Dick went into his room without speaking.

"Shore somethin's comin' off," said Ladd sharply, and he sat up with his keen eyes narrowing.

Belding spoke a few words, and, remembering an impression he had wished to make upon Mr. Gale, he made them strong. But now it was with a grim humor that he spoke.

"Better stop that boy," he concluded, looking at Mr. Gale. "He'll do some mischief. He's wilder'n hell."

"Stop him? Why, assuredly," replied Mr. Gale, rising with nervous haste.

Just then Dick came out of his door. Belding eyed him keenly. The only change he could see was that Dick had put on a hat and a pair of heavy gloves.

"Richard, where are you going?" asked his father.

"I'm going over there to see a man."

"No. It is my wish that you remain. I forbid you to go . . . ," said Mr. Gale with a hand on his son's shoulder.

Dick put Mr. Gale aside gently, respectfully, yet forcibly. The old man gasped.

"Dad, I haven't gotten over my bad habit of disobeying you. I'm sorry. Don't interfere with me now. And don't follow me. You might see something unpleasant."

"But, my son, what are you going to do?"

"I'm going to beat a dog."

Mr. Gale looked helplessly from this strangely calm and cold son to the restless Belding. Then Dick strode off the porch.

"Hold on!" Ladd's voice would have stopped almost any man. "Dick, you wasn't a-goin' without me?"

"Yes, I was. But I'm thoughtless just now, Laddy."

"Shore you was. Wait a minute, Dick. I'm a sick man, but at that nobody can pull any stunts 'round here without me."

He hobbled along the porch and went into his room. Jim Lash knocked the ashes out of his pipe, and, humming his dance tune, he followed Ladd. In a moment the rangers appeared, and both were packing guns.

Not a little of Belding's grim excitement came from observation of Mr. Gale. At sight of the rangers with their guns the old man turned white and began to tremble.

"Better stay behind," whispered Belding. "Dick's going to beat that two-legged dog, and the rangers get excited when they're packing guns."

"I will not stay behind," replied Mr. Gale stoutly. "I'll see this affair through. Belding, I've guessed it. Richard is going to fight the Chases, those robbers who have ruined you."

"Well, I can't guarantee any fight on *their* side," returned Belding dryly. "But maybe there'll be greasers with a gun or two."

Belding stalked off to catch up with Dick, and Mr. Gale came trudging behind with Thorne.

"Where will we find these Chases?" asked Dick of Belding.

"They've got a place down the road adjoining the inn. They call it their club. At this hour Radford will be there sure. I don't know about the old man. But his office is now just across the way."

They passed several houses, turned a corner into the main street, and stopped at a wide, low adobe structure. A number of saddled horses stood haltered to posts. Mexicans lolled around the wide doorway.

"There's Ben Chase now over on the corner," said Belding to Dick. "See, the tall man with the white hair and leather band on his hat. He sees us. He knows there's something up. He's got men with him. They'll come over. We're after the young buck, and sure he'll be in here."

They entered. The place was a hall, and needed only a bar to make it a saloon. There were two rickety pool tables. Evidently Chase had fitted up this amusement room for his laborers as well as for the use of his engineers and assistants, for the crowd contained both Mexicans and Americans. A large table near a window was surrounded by a noisy, smoking, drinking circle of card players.

"Point out this Radford Chase to me," said Gale.

"There. The big fellow with the red face. His eyes stick out a little. See. He's dropped his cards and his face isn't red any more."

Dick strode across the room.

Belding grasped Mr. Gale and whispered hoarsely: "Don't miss anything. It'll be great. Watch Dick and watch Laddy! If there's any gun play, dodge behind me."

Belding smiled with a grim pleasure as he saw Mr. Gale's face turn white.

Dick halted beside the table. His heavy boot shot up and with a *crash* the table split, and glasses, cards, chips flew everywhere. As they rattled down and the chairs of the dumbfounded players began to slide, Dick called out: "My name is Gale! I'm looking for Radford Chase."

A tall, heavy-shouldered fellow rose, boldly enough, even swaggeringly, and glowered at Gale.

"I'm Radford Chase," he said. His voice betrayed the boldness of his action.

It was the most savage, brutal, relentless, no-quarter fight that those present had ever witnessed. Radford Chase was the heavier of the two, Dick Gale the faster. It was the massive broadsword against the flexible, relentless rapier. It did not take Gale long to find out he had the fight of his life on his hands. He hit Radford Chase harder than he'd ever hit any man before, but Chase seemed impervious to punishment. Even when Gale knocked him down again and again, Chase came right back, seemingly more powerful than ever.

Gale hit the floor himself, more than once. Behind Chase's fists lay a deadening, brutal power that hurt a man all through when they landed. Yet there was an unquenchable flame in Dick Gale that burned, bright and clear and remorseless, regardless of punishment. They swung punches at long range; they fought in close; they stood toe to toe and swapped blows. They wrestled back and forth, with clawing, ripping fingers. Chase got a handhold on Gale's shirt and with one savage drag ripped it clearly off his back, and the steely muscled torso gleamed, white one moment, the next smeared and spattered with the blood of both men.

There was the sound of a gunshot and a cry of pain, but there was no stopping this thing, no more than the chance of stopping the hurricane, the tornado, the lightning and thunder of a storm-tossed sky. It seemed to Dick Gale that he had been fighting for hours. Breath burned and rasped in his swollen throat, and the salt taste of blood half choked him. Yet his sinewy arms lashed out again and again and the fists at the end of them were like chunks of lead tipping withes of whalebone.

A thunderous blow caught Gale on the side of the head and he went down on the floor again. For a terrible moment he thought he was going to lose the grip on his senses, but that unquenchable flame still burned in him, and he lunged to his feet once more and nailed the charging Chase with two crashing blows, a left and right to the jaw. It seemed that finally Gale had softened his man up, that shock at length was working on the nerve centers of Chase's brain. For, under the impact of those two blows, Chase tottered backward, jaw sagging, eyes rolling.

There was the sound of another gunshot, and again a cry of agony. It wasn't that cry that sent Dick leaping forward, for he never even heard it. Instead, it was an instinctive realization that at last he had really hurt Chase—hurt him badly. So he piled in, galvanized to a new strength and battered his man with relentless, savage blows. Chase could not regain his balance. He kept staggering back and back, his arms flailing wildly, uselessly. Finally he was up against the wall and could retreat no farther. There Dick Gale chopped his man down in one final surge of fighting fury that was as resistless as it was completely remorseless.

Radford Chase's arms began to drop lower and lower, until they dangled uselessly at his sides. He reeled back and forth, back and forth as Gale's punches lashed him from this side and that. Chase's knees began to cave, his head dropped forward, and then he fell, face down and motionless onto the floor.

The fight was over. It had actually been only a few moments. Tables and chairs were tumbled into a heap; one of the pool tables had been shoved aside; a lamp lay shattered with oil running darkly upon the floor. Ladd leaned against a post with a smoking gun in his hand. A Mexican crouched close to the floor, moaning over a broken arm.

In the far corner upheld by comrades another wounded Mexican cried out in pain. These two had attempted to draw weapons upon Gale, and Ladd had crippled them.

On the floor lay Radford Chase, a limp, torn, hulking, bloody figure. He probably wasn't seriously injured, but he was helpless, a miserable beaten wretch, who knew his condition and felt the eyes upon him. He had come to enough to sob and moan and howl. No one offered to help him to his feet.

Backed against the door of the hall stood Ben Chase, for once stripped of all authority and confidence and courage. Gale confronted him, and now Dick's mien was in striking contrast to the coolness with which he had entered the place. Although sweat dripped from his face, it was white as chalk. Like dark flames his eyes seemed to leap and dance and burn. His lean jaw hung down and quivered with passion. He shook a huge gloved fist in Ben Chase's face.

"Your gray hairs save you this time. But keep out of my way! And when that son of yours gets up, tell him every time I meet him I'll add some more to what he got today."

CHAPTER NINETEEN:
THE SECRET OF FORLORN RIVER

In the early morning Gale, seeking solitude where he could brood over his trouble, wandered alone. It was not easy for him to elude the Yaqui, and, just at the moment when he had cast himself down in a secluded shady corner, the Indian appeared, noiseless, shadowy, mysterious as always.

"*Malo,*" he said in his deep voice.

"Yes, Yaqui, it's bad . . . very bad," replied Gale.

The Indian had been told of the losses sustained by Belding and the ranger.

"Go . . . me!" said Yaqui with an impressive gesture toward the lofty, lilac-colored steps of No Name Mountain.

He seemed the same as usual, but a glance on Gale's part, a moment's attention, made him conscious of the old strange force in the Yaqui.

"Why does my brother want me to climb the nameless mountains with him?" asked Gale.

"*Lluvia d'oro,*" replied Yaqui, and he made motions that Gale found difficult of interpretation.

"Shower of Gold," translated Gale. That was the Yaqui's name for Nell. What did he mean by using it in connection with a climb into the mountains? Were his motions intended to convey an idea of a shower of golden blossoms from that rare and beautiful tree, or a golden rain? Gale's listlessness vanished in a flash of thought. The Yaqui meant gold. Gold! He meant he could retrieve the fallen fortunes of the white brother who had saved his life that evil day at the Papago Well. Gale thrilled as he gazed piercingly into the wonderful eyes of this Indian. Would Yaqui never consider his debt paid?

"Go . . . me?" repeated the Indian, pointing with the singular directness that always made this action remarkable in him.

"Yes, Yaqui."

Gale ran to his room, put on hobnailed boots, filled a canteen, and hurried back to the corral. Yaqui awaited him. The Indian carried a coiled lasso and a short stout stick. Without a word he led the way down the lane, turned up the river toward the mountains. None of Belding's household saw their departure.

What had once been only a narrow, mesquite-bordered trail was now a well-trodden road. A deep irrigation ditch, full of flowing muddy water, ran parallel with the road. Gale had been curious about the operation of the Chases, but a bitterness he could not help had kept him from going out to see the work. He was not surprised to find that the engineers who had constructed the ditches and dam had anticipated him in every particular. The dammed-up gulch made a magnificent reservoir, and Gale could not look upon the long, narrow lake without a feeling of gladness. The dreaded *año seco* of the Mexicans might come again and would come, but never to the inhabitants of Forlorn River. That stone-walled, stone-floored gulch would never leak, and already it contained water enough to irrigate the whole of Altar Valley for two dry seasons.

Yaqui led swiftly along the lake to the upper end, where the stream roared down over unscalable walls. This point was the farthest Gale had ever penetrated into the rough foothills, and he had Belding's word for it that no white man had ever climbed No Name Mountains from the west. But a white man was not an Indian. The former might have stolen the range and valley and mountain, even the desert, but his possessions would ever remain mysteries. Gale had scarcely faced the great, gray, ponderous wall of cliff before the old strange interest in the Yaqui seized him again. It recalled the tie that existed between them, a tie almost as close as blood. Then he was eager and curious to see how the Indian would conquer those seemingly insurmountable steps of stone.

Yaqui left the gulch and clambered up over a jumble of weathered slides and traced a slow course along the base of the giant wall. He looked up and seemed to select a point for ascent. It was the last place in that mountainside where Gale would have thought climbing possible. Before him the wall rose, leaning over him, shutting out the light, a dark, mighty mountain mass. Innumerable cracks and crevices and caves roughened the bulging sides of dark rock.

Yaqui tied one end of the lasso to the short, stout stick, and, carefully disentangling the coils, he whirled the stick around and around and threw it almost over the first rim of the shelf, perhaps thirty feet up. The stick did not lodge. Yaqui tried again. This time it caught in a crack. He pulled hard. Then, holding to the lasso, he walked up the steep slant, hand over hand on the rope. When he reached the shelf, he motioned for Gale to follow. Gale found that method of scaling a wall both quick and easy. Yaqui pulled up the lasso, and threw the stick aloft into another crack. He climbed to another shelf, and Gale followed him. The third effort brought them to a more rugged bench 100 feet above the slides. The Yaqui worked around to the left, and turned into a dark fissure. Gale kept close at his heels. They came out presently into lighter space, yet one that restricted any extended view. Broken sections of cliff were on all sides.

Here the ascent became toil. Gale could distance Yaqui going downhill; on the climb, however, he was hard put to keep the Indian in sight. It was not a question of strength or lightness of foot. These Gale had beyond the share of most men. It was a matter of lung power, and the Yaqui's life had been spent scaling the desert heights. Moreover, the climbing was infinitely slow, tedious, dangerous. On

the way up several times Gale imagined he heard a dull
roar of falling water. The sound seemed to be under him,
over him, to this side and to that. When he was certain he
could locate the direction from which it came, then he
heard it no more until he had gone on. Gradually he forgot it in the physical sensations of the climb. He burned
his hands and knees. He grew hot and wet and winded.
His heart thumped so that it hurt and there were instants
when his sight was blurred. When at last he had toiled to
where the Yaqui sat awaiting him upon the rim of the
great wall, it was none too soon.

Gale lay back and rested for a while without note of
anything except the blue sky. Then he sat up. He was
amazed to find that after that wonderful climb he was
only 1,000 feet or so above the valley. Judged by the nature of his effort, he would have said he had climbed a
mile. The village lay beneath him, with its new adobe
structures and tents and buildings in bright contrast with
the older habitations. He saw the green alfalfa fields, and
Belding's white horses, looking very small and motionless. He pleased himself by imagining he could pick out
Blanco Sol. Then his gaze swept on to the river.

Indeed, he realized now why some one had named it
Forlorn River. Even at this season, when it was full of water, it had a forlorn aspect. It was doomed to fail out there
on the desert—doomed never to mingle with the waters
of the Gulf. It wound away down the valley, growing
wider and shallower, encroaching more and more on the
gray flats, until it disappeared on its sad journey toward
Sonoyta. That vast, shimmering, sungoverned waste recognized its life only at this flood season, and was already
with parched tongue and insatiate fire licking and burning up its futile waters.

Yaqui put a hand on Gale's knee. It was a bronzed,
scarred, powerful hand, always eloquent of meaning. The
Indian was listening. His bent head, his strange, dilating
eyes, his rigid form, and that close-pressing hand, how

these brought back to Gale the terrible lonely night hours
on the lava!

"What do you hear, Yaqui?" asked Gale. He laughed a
little at the mood that had come over him. But the sound of
his voice did not break the spell. He did not want to speak
again. He yielded to Yaqui's subtle, nameless influence.
He listened himself, heard nothing but the scream of an
eagle. Often he wondered if the Indian could hear things
that made no sound. Yaqui was beyond understanding.

Whatever the Indian had listened to or for, presently he
satisfied himself, and, with a grunt that might mean anything, he rose and turned away from the rim. Gale followed, rested now and eager to go on. He saw that the
great cliff they had climbed was only a stairway up to the
huge, looming, dark bulk of the plateau above.

Suddenly he again heard the roar of falling water. It
seemed to have cleared itself of muffled vibrations. Yaqui
mounted a little ridge and halted. The next instant Gale
stood above a bottomless cleft into which a white stream
leaped. His astounded gaze swept backward along this
narrow, swift stream to its end in a dark, round, boiling
pool. It was huge spring, a bubbling well, the outcropping
of an underground river coming down from the vast
plateau above. Yaqui had brought Gale to the source of
Forlorn River.

Flashing thoughts in Gale's mind were no swifter than
the thrills that ran over him. He would stake out a claim
here and never be cheated out of it. Ditches on the
benches and troughs on the steep walls would carry water
down to the valley. Ben Chase had built a great dam that
would be useless if Gale chose to turn Forlorn River from
its natural course. The fountainhead of that mysterious
desert river belonged to him.

His eagerness, his mounting passion were checked by
Yaqui's unusual actions. The Indian showed wonder, hesitation, even reluctance. His strange eyes surveyed this
boiling well as if they could not believe the sight they saw.

Gale divined instantly that Yaqui had never before seen the source of Forlorn River. If he had ever ascended to this plateau, probably it had been to some other part, for the water was new to him. He stood gazing aloft at peaks, at lower ramparts of the mountain, and at nearer landmarks of prominence. Yaqui seemed puzzled. He was not sure of his location.

Then he strode past the swirling pool of dark water and began to ascend a little slope that led up to a shelving cliff. Another object halted the Indian. It was a pile of stones, weathered, crumbled, fallen into ruin, but still retaining shape enough to prove it had been built there by the hands of men. Around and around this the Yaqui stalked, and his curiosity attested a further uncertainty. It was as if he had come upon something surprising. Gale wondered about the pile of stones. Had it once been a prospector's claim?

"*Ugh!*" grunted the Indian, and, although his exclamation expressed no satisfaction, it surely put an end to doubt. He pointed up to the roof of the sloping yellow shelf of stone. Faintly outlined there in red were the imprints of many human hands with fingers spread wide. Gale had often seen such paintings on the walls of the desert caverns. Manifestly these told Yaqui he had come to the spot for which he had aimed.

Then his actions became swift—and Yaqui seldom moved swiftly. The fact impressed Gale. The Indian searched the level floor from the shelf. He gathered up handfuls of small black stones, and he thrust them at Gale. Their weight made Gale start, and then he trembled. The Indian's next move was to pick up a piece of weathered rock and throw it against the wall. It broke. He snatched up parts, and showed the broken edges to Gale. They contained yellow streaks, dull glints, faint tracings of green. It was gold.

Gale found his legs shaking under him, and he sat down, trying to take all the bits of stone into his lap. His fingers were all thumbs as with knife blade he dug into the black pieces of rock. He found gold. Then he stared down the slope, down into the valley with its river winding forlornly away into the desert. But he did not see any of that. Here was reality as sweet, as wonderful, as saving as a dream come true. Yaqui had led him to a ledge of gold. Gale had learned enough about mineral to know that this was a rich strike. All in a second he was speechless with the joy of it. But his mind whirled in thought about this strange and noble Indian, who seemed never to be able to pay a debt. Belding and the poverty that had come to him. Nell, who had wept over the loss of a spring. Laddy, who never could ride again. Jim Lash, who swore he would always look after his friend. Thorne and Mercedes. All these people, who had been good to him and who he loved, were poor. But now they would be rich. They would one and all be his partners. He had discovered the source of Forlorn River, and was rich in water. Yaqui had made him rich in gold. Gale wanted to rush down the slope, down into the valley, and tell his wonderful news.

Suddenly his eyes cleared and he saw the pile of stones. His blood turned to ice, then to fire. That was the mark of a prospector's claim. But it was old, very old. The ledge had never been worked. The slope was wild. There was not another single indication that a prospector had ever been there. Where, then, was he who had first staked this claim? Gale wondered with growing hope, with the fire easing, with the cold passing.

The Yaqui uttered the low, strange, involuntary cry so rare with him, a cry somehow always associated with death. Gale shuddered.

The Indian was digging in the sand and dust under the shelving wall. He threw out an object that rang against the stone. It was a belt buckle. He threw out old, shrunken, withered boots. He came upon other things, and then he ceased to dig.

The grave of desert prospectors! Gale had seen more than one. Ladd had told him many a story of such gruesome finds. It was grim, hard fact.

Then the keen-eyed Yaqui reached up to a little projecting shelf of rock and took from it a small object. He showed no curiosity and gave the thing to Gale.

How strangely Gale felt when he received into his hands a flat oblong box. Was it only the influence of the Yaqui, or was there a nameless and unseen presence beside that grave? Gale could not be sure. But he knew he had gone back to the old desert mood. He knew something hung in the balance. No accident, no luck, no debt-paying Indian could account wholly for that moment. Gale knew he held in his hands more than gold.

The box was of tin and not at all rusty. Gale pried open the reluctant lid. A faint, old, musty odor penetrated his nostrils. Inside the box lay a packet wrapped in what once might have been oilskin. He took it out and removed this covering. A folded paper remained in his hands.

It was growing yellow with age. But he descried a dim tracery of words. A crabbed scrawl, written in blood, hard to read! He held it more to the light, and slowly he deciphered its contents.

We, Robert Burton and Jonas Warren, give half of this gold claim to the man who finds it and half to Nell Burton, daughter and granddaughter.

Gasping, with a bursting heart, overwhelmed by an unutterable joy of divination, Gale fumbled with the paper until he got it open. It was a certificate twenty-one years old, and recorded the marriage of Robert Burton and Nellie Warren.

CHAPTER TWENTY:
LLUVIA D'ORO

A summer day dawned on Forlorn River, a beautiful, still, hot, golden day with huge sail clouds of white motionless over No Name peaks and the purple of clear air in the distance along the desert horizon.

Mrs. Belding returned that day to find her daughter happy and the past buried forever in two lonely graves. The haunting shadow left her eyes. Gale believed he would never forget the sweetness, the wonder, the passion of her embrace when she called him her boy and gave him her blessing.

The little wrinkled *padre* who married Gale and Nell performed the ceremony as he told his beads, without interest or penetration, and went his way, leaving happiness behind.

"Shore I *was* a sick man," Ladd said, "an' damn' near a dead one, but I'm a-goin' to get well. Mebbe I'll be able to ride again someday. Nell, I lay it to you. An' I'm a-goin' to kiss you an' wish you all the joy there is in this world. An', Dick, as Yaqui says, she's shore your shower of gold."

He spoke of Gale's finding love—spoke of it with the deep and wistful feeling of the lonely ranger who had always yearned for love and had never known it. Belding, once more practical, and important as never before with mining projects and water claims to manage, spoke of Gale's great good fortune in the finding of gold—he called it desert gold.

"Ah, yes, desert gold!" exclaimed Dick's father softly,

with eyes of pride. Perhaps he was glad Dick had found the rich claim; surely he was happy that Dick had won the girl he loved. But it seemed to Dick himself that his father meant something very different from love and fortune in his allusion to desert gold.

That beautiful happy day, like life or love itself, could not be wholly perfect. Yaqui came to Dick to say good bye. Dick was startled, grieved, and in his impulsiveness forgot for a moment the nature of the Indian. Yaqui was not to be changed.

Belding tried to overload him with gifts. The Indian packed a bag of food, a blanket, a gun, a knife, a canteen, and no more. The whole household went out with him to the corrals and fields from which Belding bade him choose a horse—any horse, even the loved Blanco Diablo. Gale's heart was in his throat for fear the Indian might choose Blanco Sol, and Dick hated himself for a selfishness he could not help. But without a word he would have parted with the treasured Sol.

Yaqui whistled the horses up—for the last time. Did he care for them? It would have been hard to say. He never looked at the fierce and haughty Diablo, or at Blanco Sol as he raised his noble head and rang his piercing blast. The Indian did not choose one of Belding's whites. He caught a lean and wiry bronco, strapped a blanket on him, and fastened on the pack.

Then he turned to these friends, the same emotionless, inscrutable, dark, and silent Indian that he had always been. This parting was nothing to him. He had stayed to pay a debt, and now he was going home.

He shook hands with the men, swept a dark, fleeting glance over Nell, and rested his strange eyes upon Mercedes's beautiful and agitated face. It must have been a moment of intense feeling for the Spanish girl. She owed it to him that she had life and love and happiness. She held out those speaking, slender hands. But Yaqui did not touch them. Turning away, he mounted the bronco and rode down the trail toward the river.

"He's going home," said Belding.

"Home," whispered Ladd, and Dick knew the ranger had felt the resurging tide of memory. Home—across the cactus and lava, through solemn lonely days, the silent, lonely nights, into the vast and red-hazed world of desolation.

"Thorne, Mercedes, Nell, let's climb the foothill yonder and watch him out of sight," said Dick.

They climbed while the others returned to the house. When they reached the summit of the hill, Yaqui was riding up the far bank of the river.

"He will turn to look . . . to wave good bye?" asked Nell.

"Dear, he is an Indian," replied Gale.

From that height they watched him ride through the mesquites, up over the riverbank to enter the cactus. His mount showed darkly against the green and white, and for a long time he was plainly in sight. The sun hung redly in a golden sky. The last the watchers saw of Yaqui was when he rode across a ridge and stood, silhouetted against the gold of desert sky—a wild, lonely, beautiful picture. Then he was gone.

Strangely it came to Gale that he was glad. Yaqui had returned to his own—the great spaces, the desolation, the solitude—to the trails he had trodden when a child, trails haunted now by ghosts of his people, and ever by his gods. Gale realized that in the Yaqui he had known the spirit of the desert, that this spirit had claimed all which was wild and primitive to him.

Tears glistened in Mercedes's magnificent black eyes, and Thorne kissed them away—kissed the fire back to them and the flame to her cheeks.

That action recalled Gale's earlier mood, the joy of the present, and he turned to Nell's sweet face. The desert was there, wonderful, constructive, ennobling, beautiful, terrible, but it was not for him as it was for the Indian. In the light of Nell's tremulous returning smile that strange, deep, clutching shadow faded, lost its hold forever, and he leaned close to her, whispering: "*Lluvia d'oro* . . . shower of gold."

ABOUT THE AUTHOR

Zane Grey® was born Pearl Zane Gray at Zanesville, Ohio in 1872. He graduated from the University of Pennsylvania in 1896 with a degree in dentistry. He practiced in New York City while striving to make a living by writing. He married Lina Elise Roth in 1905 and with her financial assistance he published his first novel himself, *Betty Zane* (1903). Closing his dental office, the Greys moved into a cottage on the Delaware River, near Lackawaxen, Pennsylvania. Grey took his first trip to Arizona in 1907 and, following his return, wrote *The Heritage of the Desert* (1910). The profound effect that the desert had had on him was so vibrantly captured that it still comes alive for a reader. Grey couldn't have been more fortunate in his choice of a mate. Trained in English at Hunter College, Lina Grey proofread every manuscript Grey wrote, polished his prose, and later she managed their financial affairs. Grey's early novels were serialized in pulp magazines, but by 1918 he had graduated to the slick magazine market. Motion picture rights brought in a fortune and, with 109 films based on his work, Grey set a record yet to be equaled by any other author. Zane Grey was not a realistic writer, but rather one who charted the interiors of the soul through encounters with the wilderness. He provided characters no less memorable than one finds in Balzac, Dickens, or Thomas Mann, and they have a vital story to tell. "There was so much unexpressed feeling that could not be entirely portrayed," Loren Grey, Grey's younger son and a noted psychologist, once recalled, "that, in later years, he would weep when re-reading one of his own books." Perhaps, too, closer to the mark, Zane Grey may have wept at how his attempts at being truthful to his muse had so often been essentially altered by his editors, so that no one might ever be able to read his stories as he had intended them. It may be said of Zane Grey that, more than mere adventure tales, he fashioned psycho-dramas about the odyssey of the human soul. If his stories seem not always to be of the stuff of the mundane world, without what his stories do touch, the human world has little meaning—which may go a long way to explain the hold he has had on an enraptured reading public ever since his first Western novel in 1910.

NIGHT HAWK

STEPHEN OVERHOLSER

He came to the ranch with a mile-wide chip on his shoulder and no experience whatsoever. But it was either work on the Circle L or rot in jail, and he figured even the toughest labor was better than a life behind bars. He's got a lot to learn though, and he'd better learn it fast because he's about to face one of the toughest cattle drives in the country. They've got an ornery herd, not much water and danger everywhere they look. The greenhorn the cowboys call Night Hawk may not know much, but he does know this: The smallest mistake could cost him his life.

ISBN 10: 0-8439-5840-5
ISBN 13: 978-0-8439-5840-9

To order a book or to request a catalog call:
1-800-481-9191
This book is also available at your local bookstore, or you can check out our Web site **www.dorchesterpub.com** where you can look up your favorite authors, read excerpts, or glance at our discussion forum to see what people have to say about your favorite books.

MEDICINE ROAD

WILL HENRY

Mountain man Jim Bridger is counting on Jesse Callahan. He knows that Callahan is the best man to lead the wagon train that's delivering guns and ammunition to Bridger's trading post at Green River. But Brigham Young has sworn to wipe out Bridger's posts, and he's hired Arapahoe warrior Watonga to capture those weapons at any cost. Bridger, Young and Watonga all have big plans for those guns, but it's all going to come down to just how tough Callahan can be. He's going to have to be tougher than leather if he hopes to make it to the post...alive.

ISBN 10: 0-8439-5814-6
ISBN 13: 978-0-8439-5814-0

MAX BRAND®

TWISTED BARS

He was known as The Duster. Five times he'd been tried for robbery and murder, and five times acquitted. He'd met the most famous of gunmen and beaten them all. Before he gives it all up, he's got one battle left to fight. The Duster needs a proper burial for his dead partner, but the blustery Rev. Kenneth Lamont refuses to let a criminal rest in his cemetery. The Duster knows if he can't get what he wants one way, there's always another. And this is a plan the reverend won't like. Not one bit...

ISBN 10: 0-8439-5871-5
ISBN 13: 978-0-8439-5871-3

HEADING WEST
Western Stories
NOEL M. LOOMIS

Noel M. Loomis creates characters so real it's hard to believe they're fiction, and these nine stories vividly demonstrate his brilliant storytelling talent. Within this volume, you'll meet Big Blue Buckley, who proves it takes a "Tough *Hombre*" to build a railroad in the 1880s and "The St. Louis Salesman" who struggles with the harsh terrain of the Texas prairie. Most poignant of all is the dying Comanche warrior passing on the ways of his people in "Grandfather Out of the Past," a tale that won Loomis the prestigious Spur Award. Each story sweeps you back in time to the Old West as it really was.

ISBN 10: 0-8439-5897-9
ISBN 13: 978-0-8439-5897-3

BLOOD TRAIL
TO KANSAS

ROBERT J. RANDISI

Ted Shea thinks he is a goner for sure. All the years he's worked to build his Montana spread and fine herd of prime beef means nothing if he can't sell them. And with a vicious rustler and his gang of cutthroats scaring all the hands, no one is willing to take to the trail. Until Dan Parmalee drifts into town. A gunman and gambler with a taste for long odds, he isn't about to let a little hot lead part him from some cold cash. But it doesn't take Dan long to realize this isn't just any run. This is a...*Blood Trail to Kansas*.

ISBN 10: 0-8439-5799-9
ISBN 13: 978-0-8439-5799-0

THE LAST WAY STATION
KENT CONWELL

As soon as Jack Slade and his partner, Three Fingers Bent, arrive in the small Texas town of New Gideon, they know no one wants them there. There's been some rustling in the area, and folks aren't taking too kindly to strangers. But things don't get any better when Slade and Bent move on. The two don't get far before a posse from New Gideon rides up, accuses Bent of murder, and takes him back to face a judge. Slade knows he won't have much time before his partner hangs on a trumped-up charge, and there's only one way he can save his friend—he'll have to find the real killer himself!

ISBN 10: 0-8439-5928-2
ISBN 13: 978-0-8439-5928-4

RIDERS OF PARADISE

ROBERT J. HORTON

Clint and Dick French may be identical twins, but Clint's wild ways contrast sharply with his brother's more sophisticated tastes. But then Dick decides to share his brother's responsibilities at the family ranch—and ends up sharing his enemies as well. When notorious troublemaker Blunt Rodgers mistakes Dick for Clint, the tenderfoot looks to be doomed. Three shots are fired, Blunt ends up dead, and the sheriff doesn't need evidence to peg Clint the killer. And once word gets back to the infamous outlaw Blunt rode with, a whole gang of hardcases will be gunning for *both* brothers.

ISBN 10: 0-8439-5895-2
ISBN 13: 978-0-8439-5895-9